Goldfinch in the Thistle

Khristy Reibel

Open Books

To my mother, who helped me with the ending, and
To my niece, who tirelessly read and encouraged me to keep going

DECEMBER 1542

Prologue

Maggie

THE MOMENT THE LIGHT filtered across the heather, the thistle blossom opened from its thorny leaves and drew the goldfinch to it. He was the thistle—a symbol of Scotland, the king—and she was his goldfinch, flitting around him, savoring his nectar, risking injury to drink among his thorny leaves. Every scar and cut he gave her was worth the nectar, the life-giving essence that invigorated her. But the light had gone out, the thistle was closed and dead.

She clasped her cloak at her throat, holding the wool tight as the December wind whipped around her. The guards at the tawny twin-towered gatehouse of Falkland Palace snapped to attention, but did nothing to stop her. She lifted her chin in acknowledgement as she passed through the gate keep, across an unfinished corridor, and entered the courtyard. The king's suite was on the right side, adjacent to the keep, and she looked up at the Corinthian columns that framed the rectangular windows and carved medallions of Roman emperors, all evidence of the French masons. She remembered the king's pride when he commissioned them, proud that he was bringing French sophistication to Scotland.

At the far end of the courtyard were the king's chambers. She climbed the spiral staircase, thinking of the times they embraced there, unable to wait until they got back to his chambers, not noticing the beautiful Flemish tapestries along the west wall of the hallway to the king's chambers. As she opened the oak carved door to the king's guard hall, no warmth escaped, not when the men saw her face. A fire blazed in the whitewashed fireplace, throwing shadows onto the oak paneling. The upper part of the walls were covered in murals depicting Jason and the Golden Fleece from Greek mythology, painted by the best Flemish painters, which represented the Order of the Golden Fleece heraldic honor bestowed on him by the Holy Roman Emperor Charles V, but also symbolizing Scotland's importance in the continental politics.

"I will see him," she said, trying to stop her chest from heaving. Standing in front of her were the most powerful men in Scotland—the chancellor, secretary, head of the Scottish church. They could make it so she could never see him again. The men's faces froze, conversation cut off. The secretary, Thomas Erskine, her own cousin, pulled himself up, but the red flush across his face belied his cowardice. *Good,* she thought. She knew enough to take him down. Cardinal Beaton, in his red robes, stepped forward, glaring. Her father, grizzled and white, with a beard almost to his waist, made a slight movement with his hand, a cutting motion that stopped Beaton in his tracks. She narrowed her eyes at the cardinal as she strode past them. Beaton and Thomas had not been able to keep her away from the king while he was alive. No one was going to stop her from seeing him one last time now that he was dead. She pushed the heavy oak door of the king's chamber open.

The room was surprisingly bright, curtains drawn back from the lead windows, the weak sun shining on the palace before disappearing behind the distant hills. Her legs stiffened as she moved toward the poster bed. The bed curtains were not open. She grasped the vermeil damask curtains. *Vermeil....* She had learned French with the king, for him, to help him with his diplomatic meetings with the king of France. She knew where it would lead, but yet.... Yet she would not deny him. And now she had command of that very useful language, especially since he was the father of her son. Her son would need allies in France. Although she appreciated the power the language would give her and her son, she would never again enjoy the rhythm of the language, the sensual shapes his mouth made when he practiced phrases and speeches, his throat vibrating as he pronounced the uvular R's, the sound reverberating in her belly.

She pulled back the curtain, and there he was. The light fell on his face, his stark white skin contrasting with the brown freckles across his crooked, aquiline nose. She ran her hand over his auburn hair, part of his Tudor inheritance. If she closed her eyes and felt the course hair springing under her hand, he still seemed alive. Maybe his eyes would open and she could fall into the mahogany pools. But he was gone. Fear seized her heart. She couldn't remember a time when he was *not* in her life, running around Stirling Castle, his mother, the Queen Mother, and her father, Lord Erskine, Keeper of the Castle, scolding them. He for not acting like a king, and she for not acting as a Scottish lady.

"You rogue," she leaned over, lips close to his pale ear. "You win. I'm done playing the game." Her voice remained level, but the tears threatened to fall. She shook her head, straightening up and smoothing her dress. He had won indeed. The game, the dance that began long ago. When she was still innocent and believed the good in people, before the world and he had broken her heart. His mouth yawned open. She cupped his chin and closed it, but the lips had lost their edge, the firm set once he decided on something. She couldn't blame him for hurting her. When he came back, he was already broken, betrayed by the people who should have protected him the most. And he almost let her in, almost. She never stopped trying.

She let go of the curtains and they fell around him again. She glanced around the room, at the tapestries lining the oak paneled walls, those strong walls—as strong as the walls around his heart. How much longer did she have? When would the men in the ante-chamber burst in and remove her? She always had to leave him, admonished by her father, him, his mother, his advisors. But she never left his heart. Even before Solway Moss, the battle against his uncle, the defeat which killed him. Even before then, she told him not to go, begged him. His uncle, the King of England, was too powerful. Henry, that spoiled, egoic brat who nothing was ever good enough for.... She warned James. But he was too much of a Stewart to back down against an English threat, and too much of a Tudor to admit when he was over his head.

Her entire life was entwined with his, he had depended on her for balance, he was the love of her life. How could she go on now that he was gone?

June 1528

Chapter 1

MAGGIE

"THE KING IS HERE!"

Maggie heard the voice cut through the dream-fog. She opened her eyes and looked up from her pallet at the side of the Queen Mother's bed. He father hovered over her, the chamber illuminated by the single candle. The oak timbers on the ceiling buckled under the flickering light, tapestries lining the wall seemed alive. Maggie's father was the keeper of Stirling Castle, had been for years, ever since Maggie could remember. It was the only home she knew.

Maggie rubbed her eyes and stretched her arms over her head, noticing the darkness edging around the single candle. Her father yanked the wooden shutters open, the moon light joining the candle to chase away the darkness. It had to be well past midnight, the half-moon high in the sky.

"The King is here!" her father said again, sharper. "Get up! We must prepare for him! Wake the Queen Mother!"

He pulled a cream-colored kirtle from the walnut armoire and threw it at Maggie, who caught it as she swung her legs over the straw mattress and slid the garment over her head. It was fine wool with laces in the back, which her father tightened. Maggie's heart clutched at her throat as she slipped on velvet flat slippers. The King! She hadn't seen him in, two, almost three years. Had it been that long? She was a girl when the Earl of Angus, the king's stepfather, had taken possession of him. *Kidnapped*, is what the Queen Mother said. The Queen Mother, Margaret Tudor, had married Archibald Douglas, the Earl of Angus, when the king was just two years old.

The king's father, James IV, had been killed at the Battle of Flodden in 1513, along with many of the most powerful nobles in Scotland. The Douglases were the second strongest family in Scotland, after the king's family, the Stewarts. By marrying a Douglas, the Queen Mother gave them the opportunity to become more powerful than the young king. None of the other Scottish nobles trusted Angus, who allied himself with England, so they persuaded the three estates, the three ruling classes of Scotland, to relinquish the Queen Mother's regency, beginning a power struggle over the king's physical body. Whoever controlled the king controlled all of Scotland. Had Angus ever loved the Queen Mother or had he used her to gain more power? Maggie believed the latter, especially when Angus took custody of James V, the King of Scots when he was thirteen.

When her father was satisfied that Maggie would not fall back asleep, he left the chamber. Maggie rubbed the kinks out of her back, looking at the darkness through the leaded windows, which were framed by a green and white painted arch. She padded over to the queen's bed, and pulled back the indigo velvet curtains that surrounded the bed, hung from a circular frame mounted to the ceiling. The Queen Mother's face pressed into the blue satin sheets. Maggie shook the sleeping woman, whose eyes snapped open, rimmed in wrinkled skin.

"Your Grace," Maggie said. "My father said the king has escaped Angus and is here!"

The Queen Mother leapt out of bed, knocking Maggie back. Her hair waved back from her face, brown laced with gray.

"My son is here?" she said. "Help me be presentable!"

Maggie walked over to the armoire, and opened the doors. She looked over the Queen Mother's gowns and chose a yellow kirtle and royal blue over-gown. She helped the Queen Mother slip the kirtle over her head, and then Maggie tightened the laces in back. Next, she held the blue over-gown and the Queen Mother ducked her head into the dress. Maggie smoothed it down in the back for the Queen Mother, who walked out of the room. Maggie followed into the Queen's inner chamber, smoothing the back of the dress.

"Tell me what happened, John," the Queen Mother said as they entered the room, twisting her hair into a bun. The room was too dark to admire the coffered oak ceiling or the red floral tapestries covering the walls, since the fire was not lit.

Her father handed a pair of velvet slippers to the Queen Mother. "He dressed as a groom and stole away on his horse. He rode from Falkland and just arrived."

"I should have listened when people told me he was a feckless fool," she murmured as she followed Maggie's father out of the room and down the hallway to the king's chambers. Maggie had to almost run to keep up with them. "Then they thought they could appease him by giving him possession of *my* son. I knew that *feartie* would never give him up. And his cousin, Earl of Lennox—murdered after he surrendered. And yet *I'm* the English sympathist." Maggie was glad to be behind her father and the Queen Mother so they did not see her grin at the queen calling her ex-husband a *feartie*, a coward in Scots.

Her father just nodded, the Queen Mother often complained about her ex-husband Angus. Maggie had heard this story many times as the Queen Mother's maid-in-waiting. The power struggle over the king in his minority had been the background of her childhood. Neither the Scottish nobles nor church prelates trusted the Queen Mother, always thinking of her as an English woman since her brother, Henry VIII, was the king of England. They were afraid she would turn Scotland into an English vassal state. So they ripped her young son from her arms. At least that was her story.

Maggie trailed after her father and the Queen Mother down the dark hallway between the queen and king's chambers. The limestone walls were cold, lacking tapestries to keep the heat in during the night. She passed through the oak carved door into the king's outer chamber. Servants scurried to light a fire to warm the unused room. She knew the details of the room without needing to look at it—the four-armed candelabra in the center, throwing dim light onto the crimson tapestries behind the red velvet awning over the armed throne. Pacing in front of that throne was the king. Her breath caught, cut off. He was dressed in commoner's clothes, loose fitting twill breeches over the hose tucked into his riding boots, cream rough linen shirt open at the top with a russet jerkin over it. His auburn hair was damp from the exertion of riding hard from Falkland Castle to Stirling, thirty-five miles. Maggie heart hammered, ears tingled. She reached up to smooth the front of her hair, surprised at the betrayal of her body.

"James!" the Queen Mother exclaimed and threw her arms around him. He embraced her briefly and untangled himself. "How in the world were you able to get away?" she asked, recovering from his slight.

"With no help from you, Mother," he said, glancing sideways at her. Maggie shivered from the chilly tone. James had changed during his imprisonment. She remembered him as running around with her brother, playing with wooden swords, trying to rescue her, the princess captured by the evil dragon. But Maggie never wanted to be the rescued princess, she preferred to carry her own sword and fight alongside of them. She remembered when she struck the king in the back with a wooden sword, knocking him down. He must have been nine, and she almost seven. He lay motionless on the ground. She approached him on light feet, her heart in her chest. Even in play, he wore a velvet doublet, rumpled from the rough housing. She reached out to shake him, but as she touched his doublet, he flipped over. Before she could react, he threw her onto her back and sat atop of her.

"See, a princess cannot fight," he said. She struggled to breathe under his weight. "You will always need to be saved by me."

Before Maggie could form a response, his nursemaid was on them, pulling James up to examine his royal body. They rushed James off, and Maggie was forgotten, but the seeds of attachment to him had been planted.

"Surely you can't blame me for his action," the Queen Mother's words snapped Maggie back to the present. The Queen Mother pulled herself up to her full height in an attempt to remind James that she was still royal. "We made numerous attempts to free you from that devil."

"Yes, but none of them worked," he paused. "And no one else married him."

Maggie sucked in her breath. No one talked to the Queen Mother that way. But James was the king, and still angry at his mother's actions. Maggie smirked. Even though the Queen Mother had taken her in as a maid-in-waiting to protect her from being sent to her husband too soon, it was still amusing to see this titan of a woman put into her place.

"My lord," Maggie's father stepped in. "How did you free yourself?"

"Angus and his brother were gone from the castle. I told his cousin that I was planning to go hunting early in the morning and took my supper early. The household went to bed and the watch was set shortly after. My groom John readied my horse. He also brought a set of groom's clothes so I could slip out. I stole away once the household slept. I don't know if he has realized I've escaped yet," his face was drawn, but his eyes danced.

"Well, I am happy to see you, and so will many people," the Queen Mother said and took his arm, trying to lead him to the throne. But he shook her off again, turning towards Maggie's father.

"John, I thank you for keeping my castle instead of surrendering to Angus. Your loyalty never wavered," the king said and clapped Maggie's father's outstretched hand and pulled him in for an embrace. He was referring to when Angus sieged Stirling after an unsuccessful attempt to rescue James two years earlier.

"Never, my lord. You trusted me to keep the castle, and I ken that you needed this castle to resume full control of our country," Maggie's father released James. He had been like a son to her father, her brother and James tutored together at Stirling when they were younger. James clutched his forearm.

"It is so great to be back at Stirling! We will have much to do tomorrow, John!"

"As you wish, your Highness," her father bowed, bending at the waist and revealing Maggie. James's deep brown eyes connected with hers and her stomach flipped. A flash of recognition crossed his face.

"Magpie?" he said. Maggie felt the heat rise, warming her ears and neck. She curtsied to cover her embarrassment. Of course he remembered the awful nickname he and her brother called her. She felt flush creep into her cheeks. "Is that you?" he stepped around her father as she rose to face him. She swallowed, steadied her pounding heart and prepared her barbed retort.

"Oh, you remember Maggie, Sir Erskine's daughter," the Queen Mother interjected. "She has been contracted to Robert Douglas of Loch Leven."

"Don't mention that name, Mother!" he glanced at her, his eyes narrowing. "Loch Leven—that is where your husband Angus went to attend to some family business!"

"He is not my husband, I am not married to him anymore," the Queen Mother smiled, a honey-sweet smile that did not cover her annoyance.

"But you *were*. Besides, I prefer not to be reminded of my captivity!" He spun on his heel and left Maggie stunned. Even dressed as a commoner, Maggie felt the authority in his stare, the intensity of someone who knew how to wield power. She shivered as his heat swung away from her.

"Your Grace, let me show you to your chambers," her father stepped in to veer the discussion. Always the diplomat. "I'm sure you are exhausted from your long ride and would like to sleep. We will prepare the household to receive you properly when you awaken."

James rubbed a hand across his forehead and nodded, "You are right again, John. Let's go and rest so we can begin to take back our country tomorrow." He clasped Maggie's father on the shoulder and they walked out.

In the morning, the Queen Mother was giddy, like a young girl in love. Maggie and the queen's senior ladies-in-waiting, Elizabeth Elphinstone and Agnes Musgrave, helped the Queen Mother into the layers of English style royal dress—a stiff corset, a Spanish farthingale, which was a linen petticoat with a wooden hoop, cream brocade kirtle, a mulberry velvet overgown, cut away to show the patterned kirtle at the front of the skirt. Elizabeth pinned the partlet across the stays of the kirtle, while Agnes took the gable hood from Maggie and placed it on the Queen Mother's head. Maggie backed up, allowing these two women, who had come to Scotland with the Queen Mother twenty-five years ago, to prepare her.

"You may wear my navy velvet gown," the Queen Mother patted Maggie on the back. "I want everything to be perfect to receive the king. Fix your hair and come to the Great Hall." She left the room, sucking the air out with her. Elizabeth held the bottom of the Queen Mother's long overgown, so it didn't drag in the dirt. Maggie smoothed her loose honey curls and pulled her white linen cap over her hair. It was hard to believe that at thirteen, she could now wear a coif, as her linen cap was called. In the excitement of last night, she had almost forgotten that she had been contracted in marriage a year ago. Only because of the Queen Mother's intervention had she been able to remain at Stirling and not moved into her husband's household. She was relieved, not ready emotionally to be a wife, even if the law said she was.

She scowled and shook the thought from her head. She headed to the Queen Mother's armoire and pulled the navy velvet gown out. Even though she was only thirteen, she was as tall as the Queen Mother. It laced up the front so she didn't have to worry about being too tight. She wished she could loosen her kirtle; her father had over tightened her in his excitement. Nothing to be done about it now. Like many things in her life, Maggie had to cope with the difficulties thrown at her. She was adept at turning bad situations into something beneficial to her, no matter what it was. She pinned a matching partlet over the laces, straightened her shoulders, excited to see the king again.

Maggie crossed the inner courtyard and climbed the curved stairs to the Great Hall. Inside, the Queen Mother was lining up everyone in the household, according to rank—her ranking, not their actual noble ranking. Maggie giggled. The Queen Mother didn't care about rank and rules. She married the Earl of Angus secretly when her husband's will forbid it. The Scottish parliament was powerless to stop her impetuousness. This arranging of the household would be no different.

"Maggie, over here. Behind your father," Queen Mother maneuvered her into position. Maggie resisted, wanting to stand next to her father so she could get a good look at the king in the light of day. To see if the bubbling erupted in her stomach again. "No, no," the Queen Mother shoved her. "You must stand behind your father. No, to the left side of him." Finally, she had positioned Maggie in the desired position. "Now, don't move!"

Maggie smiled, but when the Queen Mother turned to the next person, her eyes rolled up into her head. She looked around the room. The ceiling was an intricate web of cross beams and buttresses, sun gleaming through the diamond patterned lead windows. Maggie's eyes came to rest on her contracted husband, Robert Douglas, who stood further back in the procession line. He worked as the royal butcher, but that's not why she was contracted to him. No, he was a Douglas, and that name alone carried heft. Her father saw a chance to strengthen his position and join the Erskine family into the powerful Douglas family. Maggie had not been consulted in the contract. It was not her place. The marriage was a business arrangement, she knew that. The bans had been nailed to the church door, and when no objections were made, she and Robert performed the hand-fasting ceremony and exchanged rings at the same church door a little less than a year ago. She had been prepared for being a wife, knew the expectations in the bedroom, but the Queen Mother had intervened from her being sent straight to Loch Leven, her husband's estate. Maggie was so grateful too, because as she looked at her husband out of the corner of her eye, she was unmoved. He was ordinary looking, average height and built, had the down-turned Douglas eyes, like a sheep dog. He wore a dark beard covering the bottom of his face. Maggie knew it was the fashion, but it made him look untrustworthy.

She shifted her weight back and forth. The velvet dress was warm. She felt the heat building around her legs and the warm air escaped from underneath the heavy fabric when she shifted.

"Maggie, stand still," her father commanded in his low voice that only she could hear. She stood stock-still. His black eyes bore into her and she felt naked under his intense stare. His gray beard was long, reaching past the third button on his doublet. While her husband's beard made him look untrustworthy, her father's made him look learned, patient, and resolute. When he spoke, it was quiet in tone, but weighty. No one questioned her father. None of the household, not Maggie. Even the Queen Mother considered his advice. And she was worse at listening than Maggie.

Time crawled. No one seemed to be breathing, although the hall soon became hot and stuffy. Maggie regretted putting on the velvet gown. She glanced sideways at the Queen Mother, who was wearing a similar velvet gown. She wore a gabled headdress, lined with rubies and diamonds. Her face was pinched. She wanted to look regal, remind her son of who she was and show him how well she had taken care of his kingdom. Maggie smirked, remembering the venom with which he spoke to his mother. Forgiveness would not come easy for her.

"Where is he?" she paced. "It's after noon. Am I to keep the household from eating because my son has lost his manners?" She was talking to no one in particular, and no one dared answer her. Her shoes tapped as she moved across the slate stones. The rhythmic clacking lulled Maggie into dozing, the midnight activities interrupting her sleep. She longed to be back in her soft bed. A sharp pain in her side snapped her back to attention. Her eyes opened to find her father's eyes narrowing in disapproval. She pinched herself to wake up, hoping to deflect her father's intensity. She never wanted to disappoint her father, who she was closer to than her mother, who lived at the family castle with her younger siblings. Her own mother became a mother at fifteen, only two years older than Maggie was! She shuddered and glanced at the Queen Mother, her salvation. It was only because the Queen Mother said Maggie reminded her of herself when she was young, that she was not already at Loch Leven, her husband's castle, raising a family of her own. The Queen Mother was paranoid of early child bearing since her grandmother, Margaret Beaufort, had been damaged by having a baby too young.

Maggie felt him before she saw him. He pulled the air from the room before he entered it. His auburn hair was smoothed back off his high forehead, highlighting the deep-set mahogany eyes and crooked nose. He was dressed as a king should be, his brocade doublet slashed to show his purple silk undershirt, the royal color. He wore an ermine lined cape, clasped with a thick, ornate gold band decorated with thistles. He caught her eye and his lips raised. She felt the flush rising and looked down, wishing she could control her emotions, but the blush always gave her away.

She felt the weight of attention directed at her. She looked up and met her husband's eyes. He gave a curt nod, the corners of his moustache curving up. Her initial reaction was to shudder, but she tamped that down and tried to remain impassive. Instead, she focused on the King's back, broad shoulders stretching the fine velvet, down to his tapered waist. He was a man, not the gangly boy she remembered. Was he the same person? Did he still like to spar, and would he still spar with her? She didn't even know if that was allowed. She was a noble, but she was also married. Maggie sighed, frustrated that everything in her life was determined by men who took little time to get to know who she really was. She was sure the king would be the same. His voice broke her reverie.

"Your loyalty to me and the country will be recognized," he said, standing on the dais at the front of the Great Hall. "We knew this day would come, the day we would escape the fiend Angus's hand and take the rightful, God-given position as the head of Scotland." His voice had deepened, lost its boyish timber. She wondered if her father had helped him prepare his speech.

As the king was addressing the household, a guard approached Maggie's father and whispered in his ear. Her father shot up as if prodded.

"Your Highness," he said, "please excuse my interruption, but it appears that the Earl of Angus has become aware of your escape. He approaches the castle now with his men."

James's face snarled. "He comes here?" he thundered. "Raise the herald and trumpet! Send out a messenger and tell him that if he comes within six miles of me, I'll have him drawn and quartered for treason!"

Her father nodded and stepped out of the room with the guard. Maggie swung back to the king, to see what he would do next. Would he fire the cannons at them? Angus deserved it after everything he put the king through.

"Let's disperse. I...." the king paused. "I'm sorry it was not the homecoming we had hoped for. But the Douglases will pay for the mistreatment and abuse of your king!" He turned on his heel and the room became lifeless without his force. Maggie released her breath, unaware that she had been holding it.

Chapter 2

JAMES

LATER THAT DAY, AFTER Angus had been chased away, James sat at a table in his inner chamber, writing notices to all of his nobles to meet him at Stirling—Huntly, Argyll, Athole, Monteith, Rothes, Maxwell, Livingston, Ruthven, Drummond, and to his closest bishops—Archbishop James Beaton and Bishop Gavin Dunbar, his former tutor. He needed to convince the three estates—the clergy, nobility and town burgers—how dangerous Angus was to Scotland. Thank God he hadn't brought artillery to Stirling! James wanted him tried for treason and executed, but he needed the estate's approval. His hatred burned, overshadowing everything else. Nothing but Angus's neck in a noose would avenge his abuse of power!

When he had turned twelve years old, Parliament terminated his minority, and he was elevated to full sovereign powers. His mother and Angus, who were estranged, fought over control of him. In 1525, when James was thirteen, the Parliament coerced his mother to reconcile with Angus, and he was appointed to the council to govern over James, to rotate with the Earls of Arran, Lennox, and Argyll. Angus took up the responsibility first, and James moved into Edinburgh Castle, which was perched on the top of a basalt crag, towering over the town. In November, James was supposed to be handed over to Lennox's custody, but Angus refused.

"You are holding me against my will," James said, but Angus and his brother George only laughed, the youth's words having no teeth.

"Trust me," Angus thumped James on the back. "We take far better care of you than your mother." His lip curled into a snarl as he pronounced the last word. George held the quill out to James, and he took the quill out of reflex rather than desire.

"Now, write to your mother," George loomed over him, watching to ensure James wrote what was dictated to him. "Tell her that she need not be solicitous to you, that you are content living with your stepfather and wish to remain here." James broke the quill from pressing too hard in anger. He was trapped, too weak to free himself, not clever enough at thirteen to outsmart these grown men. But he had grown up and freed himself, and now the Douglases would pay for their usurpation of power.

Besides dealing with Angus, there were pressing state matters that needed his attention, which Angus had ignored when he appointed himself to the position of Chancellor—borders to secure and England to deal with. His uncle, Henry VIII, King of England, was eager to get Scotland under his thumb. James was leery of Henry. His uncle's country was far more powerful than Scotland, and James couldn't afford the full strength of the English army barreling down on him before he dealt with Angus.

There was so much he didn't know, couldn't know while he was under the control of Angus. Lennox, his cousin, had tried to free him from Angus, but he had been executed—unchivalrously and unceremoniously. And then in the ultimate humiliation, he made James pass judgment on those nobles who fought with Lennox on the king's behalf—Archbishop Beaton, Argyll, even his half-brother Moray. James couldn't even reward his nobles for their fealty towards him.

Who could he trust? Angus had stirred up trouble on the Borders, had failed to provide support against thieves and English raiders. His uncle was looking for retribution for English losses. James dipped his quill in the inkwell to write to his uncle. Without Angus censoring his letters anymore, he could write freely. But what to say to earn his uncle's respect without groveling or demeaning himself? He rubbed his forehead and became aware that someone had entered the room. He looked up and Maggie was standing in the doorway of his study, shifting her feet, almost upsetting the tray of wine she held.

"Come in, Magpie," he smiled. She was a child when he last saw her, her limbs pleated at awkward angles. Not anymore. She walked, hips undulating like a cat, chest heaving—she was no longer a child. Her hazel eyes shifted between him and the space between them. She pursed her coral lips, pearly teeth clamping down. The edges of her flaxen hair curled out from her bonnet.

"I brought you some wine," she said, placing the tray on his desk. She squinted, deciding what to do next. James had seen this same look on her face when he was first invested with the symbols of his sovereignty, which signaled the end of his minority. He had been thirteen when Angus kidnapped him, and Maggie ten or eleven. The ceremony had been here at Stirling, where the regents placed the crown on his head and handed him the scepter and sword of the state. In the inner chamber, James had been very nervous.

"Don't worry, we will be there for you," Maggie said.

"But children aren't allowed in the chamber for the ceremony," James said, brow furrowed.

"I said we will be there!" Maggie said, thrusting her chin at James and squinting her eyes as she decided just how she would be there. As the Earl of Arran handed the scepter to him, James saw a flash of blond hair from beneath the draped table. Maggie peered up from under the table at him, a goofy grin on her face. James stifled a smile, since it was not appropriate at the solemn ceremony. But she saw the smile anyway. That was before Angus had shown him what betrayal was.

He motioned for her to sit. She smoothed her skirt as she sat on a velvet scissor chair and placed her hands on her lap, then thought better of it and sat on her hands. James chuckled. He was confident in his looks and knew the effect he had on women, but to see his playmate, who had flowered into a woman in his absence, roused by his sexuality—it made him want to awaken the woman in her. Even though she was married, James knew from her actions that she had not experienced physically what he had taken pleasure in. Maggie's innocence and skepticism amused him. The simplicity of her walk, unaware of the friction it caused in James. This was not the girl he left, the one who he had played jokes on. Children's games, which he could no longer enjoy, not since his inculcation into the adult world by his stepfather.

"Why do you still call me Magpie?" she said, meeting his eyes and not looking away, challenging him. Her voice was deeper than he remembered, and the flirtatious tone rang in James's ears.

"You don't like it?" he leaned back, enjoying the fight from her. No, she would not just give in because he was the king. Her mouth turned down in irritation, which amused him even more.

"You know I don't. I didn't like it when you and my brother called me it years ago. It hasn't changed. It's a stupid bird who steals jewelry." She shifted in her seat, but didn't drop her gaze, a green dare.

"The magpie is actually very smart. They mimic human voices and get people in trouble, just like you liked to do," he said, trying to suppress a smile and failing. Her mouth screwed into a grimace, a pink sensuous pout. "You did hate it. I think that's why I like it," he continued, unable to take his gaze off her mouth.

"Of course it is. No one can call me that name. Except you. I guess… since you're the king," she tossed her head, but could not contain the mirth in her eyes.

Now he laughed out loud. He held onto the desk to keep from falling out of his chair. Maggie smirked and crossed her arms, self-satisfied.

"Well, I think I will keep calling you that. Since I am the king," he said once the laughter died out. Maggie rolled her eyes and stifled a smile, a rosy blush creeping across her cheeks. Yes, she had become a woman during his captivity, but she didn't realize her attraction or power. He was drawn to her. And wanted to help her discover that potency.

"How long will you be at Stirling?" she asked, breaking the tension that had built in the silence as James studied her. He wanted to get to know the person she had become while he was gone, to learn what she liked and didn't like, what she thought behind those enigmatic eyes. But instead he shrugged.

"I don't know, a week? A month? I need to go to Edinburgh and meet before Parliament and ward Angus before he escapes to my uncle's country and I won't be able to prosecute him."

"Do you think your own uncle would protect him, knowing that he kidnapped you?" Her green eyes narrowed, revealing an inherent distrust of people. Which was exactly how James felt about people, after his stepfather betrayed his trust.

"You work for my mother and you haven't figured out my uncle by now?" he asked in a tone that was harsher than he intended. Her eyes darted down in embarrassment, but she quickly recovered.

"Your mother often talks about how she can't trust him, but I thought it was just older sister complaining. I complain about my brother all the time," she said, tossing her chin up. Fire mixed in her eyes, turning them a golden color.

"I don't know about your brother, but my uncle is treacherous," he said, knowing he should focus on his country, but also wanting banter with this creature on the cusp of becoming a woman. He watched her mouth and almost missed the eyebrow that she raised as a challenge for a retort.

"What else did you learn from my mother? How to marry badly?" he tried to make a joke, but Maggie's face clouded over as soon as he mentioned marriage. Her eyes shut off all the emotions that were on the surface a moment ago—pushed back into the recesses of her mind. James hoped he could reach her again.

"I *had* to get married," she said, looking over James's shoulder, out at the June sunshine and green courtyard. "Unfortunately, we aren't all the King of Scots who can pick a spouse."

James leaned back in the chair, surprised by her confession. "You didn't want to marry a Douglas?"

"Marry a Douglas? No," she shook her head. "That was my father. He arranged everything. My job is just to show up and look pretty." She paused and caught James staring at her. His libido punched him in the stomach, under the solar plexus, choking off his breathing.

"Well, you look pretty today, so I can only imagine how you look when you dress yourself up," he said, trying to keep his voice steady. Maggie flushed all the way to her ears, which only increased James's attraction to her.

"You already knew all of that," she said, meeting his eyes again. "So why even ask me?"

"To see where your loyalties lie," he said, pushing the rising heat back.

"They are with you, until you prove you aren't worthy of loyalty," she said, settling into the banter. The heat threatened to overwhelm James.

"You know that what you said could be seen at treasonous," he replied, trying hard to sound angry, but she heard the laughter in his voice.

"You have matters that are far more important than a little girl like me," she said, looking at him under her thick eyelashes.

"That is right. I have *much* more important matters—like capturing Angus, securing the borders, fulfilling the Auld Alliance. There is so much to do," he said to impress her, but again, the laughter edged around her eyes.

"You love it," she said, seeing his thoughts that he couldn't express himself. "You can't wait to start. I bet you won't even stay here two days," she said and disappointment crept over the last words.

"Will you be sad to see me leave?" he leaned in, wanting to feel the mounting tension again. Now it was her turn to shrug.

"I barely know you anymore. Why would I be sad?" She held his gaze, daring him. To do what, he wasn't sure, but he knew what he would like to do. He smiled. During his imprisonment at Edinburgh Castle, he had experienced many women. He knew how to hook one and how to keep her on the line. For all of Maggie's acting, he knew he had her. She stood up.

"I'll let you get back to ruling the country," she said and turned to leave.

"You'll be at the feast?" he called as she walked away. She paused. "What feast?"

"The feast my mother is planning."

"You tell me. You're the king," she said over her shoulder. He could see the golden down on her cheek and wanted to stroke it.

"Then I'll see you at the feast," he said and she walked out of the door. Even though he couldn't see her face, he knew she was smiling.

Chapter 3

THE QUEEN MOTHER

MARGARET WAS SIFTING THROUGH papers of her own. She needed to make sure her brother was not going to go behind her back again and support Angus as he had done in 1524. He was the petulant younger brother who was now a spoiled brat of a king. But she needed to be diplomatic. She wanted to bring the two countries closer, not cause discord. In 1503, her father had arranged for her to marry James IV, King of Scotland in order to bring England and Scotland to an eternal peace. She may have only been a girl when she came to Scotland, but she was determined to leave her mark on the country—and her husband.

James, her new husband, had ridden out to meet her, too impatient to wait in Edinburgh. His horse was draped in a cloth of gold, but he wore a more subtle crimson doublet, and instead of his hawking lure, his lute was slung over his back. He looked regal, even in his casual clothing, but he also wore a long beard. She dropped into a deep curtsy, but James lifted her up and kissed her in front of her entourage. Margaret blushed under the heat of his kiss. He courted her with lute performances and hunting expeditions. She shaved his beard, and he turned her into a queen.

"Right high excellent and mighty prince and our dearest, most beloved brother," she wrote, "The king, my son, has escaped his wretched stepfather." She paused, tickling her chin with the quill. Then she crossed out "wretched," not wanting to anger her brother. "I hope that your grace will think of your nephew and not harbor the earl of Angus, who may beseech you for asylum." Better to be direct, she thought, than to placate his ego. She would have her secretary rewrite it and then she could sign and seal it.

She finished the draft and turned to something more exciting—a celebratory feast! It needs to show all of Scotland that the king is in charge of his own person, and not under the control of Angus. How could she have married Ard, the Earl of Angus? Of course, she knew in part it was to gain favor with his powerful family to protect the crown for his son, but she had also been a sucker for his puppy eyes. She had married him at Kinnoull Church in Perth in secret, with none of the pomp and pageantry of her first marriage. How could she have known that he would use her and her money? He knew all the right words to bamboozle Margaret and make her believe he was in love.

But now she had a new husband, the new Lord Methven, Henry Stewart, whom her brother playfully referred to as Muffin. Her toes curled when she thought of how young and malleable he was. Five years her junior, he was beholden to her for his position, which Margaret believed would keep him loyal. Because of her insistence, her son had created him Lord Methven, a title he would have not inherited as the second son. Muffin would sit beside her with her son to show a united royal family, even if James had been reluctant to accept him.

"Maggie!" she called for her favorite maid-in-waiting. Her father, Lord Erskine, had contracted her at twelve. Twelve! Far too young for the girl to be a wife. Margaret understood the contract, but still she had taken the young Maggie into her employment to save Maggie from becoming a mother too soon. Her grandmother, Margaret Beaufort, was a descendant of the great English king, Edward III. King Henry VI had contracted her to Edmund Tudor when she was nine, a move that she considered divine intervention. She had her only son, Margaret's father, when she was thirteen. Unable to conceive again, her grandmother believed her female organs had been damaged because she became a mother too young. She swore that her granddaughters would not suffer the same fate. Named after her grandmother, Margaret had been married at thirteen but didn't have her first child until seventeen. Her first husband, King James IV, after having several illegitimate children, was anxious for a legitimate heir. She abhorred each of her eight pregnancies and was ill after every birth—a fate she wanted to keep Maggie from as long as she could.

"Yes Queen Mother," the girl curtsied as she entered the Queen Mother's inner chamber, golden hair bobbing. Maggie was an intelligent, lively child, unafraid to speak her mind.

"We need to prepare a feast for the king's return," she said as Maggie rose. The girl skipped over to her, her eyes crinkling.

"Will there be dancing?" she asked. "I want to dance all night."

Margaret rapped her hand with her quill. "Don't get dreamy now. We have lots to plan," she tried to sound stern, but Maggie grinned at her. The Queen Mother handed her the quill. "Take down this list and deliver it to the kitchen. Maybe you can see your husband."

Maggie's face fell, brows furrowed. Her shoulders slumped as she poised the quill, ready to write.

"We will need hens—fifteen of them, cooked in broth. And we should have goose, yes, and pike from the River Forth. Oh and plum tarts—the plums should be ripe in the orchard. Tell the head cook to prepare cheese—we should still have some Wensleydale that my brother sent from England. Maybe with poached fruit, ask if the cherries are in. And plenty of honeyed almonds—James loves those," she rattled off the menu. Maggie scribbled, a half beat behind. She was used to the Queen Mother's rapid-fire diction. As a noble daughter of the keeper of Stirling, Margaret had seen that Maggie got an adequate education. A real education, not just learning the feminine arts, but also languages and rhetoric. The girl picked up the skills like a cat lapping milk.

"What if he doesn't like them anymore?" Maggie said, quill paused. Margaret narrowed her eyes. Yes, her education had made her bold.

"You think I don't know my own son?" she said, drawing herself up, sitting taller. Maggie shrank a little but still muttered, "He has been gone almost three years."

"A mother knows her son. You'll find out soon enough," she said, knowing it was something Maggie was not looking forward to. She had told the horrors of childbirth to Maggie to scare her into not trying too early. Maggie remained quiet, sulking.

"Let's talk about the music and dancing," she said. Maggie smiled and the awkward air dissipated.

"I'll have the first dance with the king of course," she said. What style was appropriate for a mother to dance with her grown son? "The Pavane, definitely the regal and stately Pavane."

Margaret remembered her brother's queen, Catherine of Aragon, teaching them the Spanish dance.

"Will I dance with my husband, Queen Mother?" Maggie asked. The hesitation in her voice was naked and desperate.

"Well, it is a good way to get to know him. I think you should. It will be expected that you dance with him," she said, caressing her words to remove the harshness. Maggie nodded and bit the inside of her cheek.

"It is going to be fine. You have plenty of time to get to know him before I will let you leave with him. You know I will protect you, right?" She kneaded Maggie's shoulders. The girl's eyes were apprehensive, but she relaxed under Margaret's hand.

"I was thirteen when I came here. A girl like you. And I came to love and respect my husband. It will be this way for you too," she smiled at Maggie, remembering the young girl she had been when she arrived in Scotland, chestnut hair flowing as she rode into Edinburgh on the black horse that her father had given her. How she knew nothing of politics and courtly intrigue. She learned quickly, and Maggie was smart enough to do the same.

"Go! Take the list to the kitchen and say hello to Robert," she shooed Maggie out of the room. She wished her own daughter, also named Margaret, was with her, that she was advising her on her marriage. But her daughter had been taken to Tantallon by Angus, and he was doing his best to turn her own daughter against her. *One day*, she told herself. One day she would bring her daughter back to Stirling and she would have her son and her daughter together. But now, she needed to focus on James and provide him the best environment to lead Scotland.

Chapter 4

Thomas Erskine of Brechin

When the messenger arrived in Brechin, Thomas Erskine could not believe it, the king had actually done it! He had gotten away from Angus and requested Thomas's presence at Stirling to organize the government and charge Angus with treason. Thomas was a cousin of Lord Erskine and had grown up occasionally being invited to Stirling. Like many of the nobles his age, his father had died at the Battle of Flodden, just like the king's father had. King James IV ordered an attack on England to support the Auld Alliance—the alliance between Scotland and France formed in 1295 to protect both countries against England—when Henry VIII invaded France from the English territory of Calais on the continent. The English army decimated the ill-prepared Scots, leaving many noble sons orphans. Thomas had been in Italy attending university when the English slaughtered his grandfather, father, uncle, and older brother.

His cousin, Lord Erskine, had used his influence to have Thomas appointed James's secretary under Angus's stewardship when he returned to Scotland from his university studies, and he had been a part of Lennox's attempt to free the king from Angus's control. The Earl of Lennox had lost his father at Flodden too, and Thomas was eager to join with him to free James. They should have won. The Queen Mother had seen them off from Stirling, his cousin Lord Erskine had lent Thomas the Erskine armor. When the army arrived at Linlithgow Bridge with ten thousand soldiers, they discovered that Angus had persuaded James Hamilton, the 1st Earl of Arran, to fight with him. Arran, being an excellent commander, had placed his men and artillery on Pace Hill, which overlooked Linlithgow and the River Avon.

"Damned him to hell!" Lennox had cursed, surprising Thomas. Lennox was even-tempered, but even he had his breaking point. And he was beyond frustrated with Angus and his manipulation of the king for his own benefit. "His loyalties should have held, even if he didn't agree with the queen's third marriage!" Lennox tugged at his beard, eyes absorbing all the details of the field between him and Arran's men.

Arran had been a favorite of the Queen Mother, having helped to broker the marriage between her and King James IV. It was at her urging that he had been created Earl of Arran. During the disastrous Battle of Flodden, Arran had been commander of the naval fleet and engaged the English navy at Ulster, the stronghold of their navy. After defeating their forces, Arran sailed north fast—but not fast enough. He was too late to help the king at the battle of Flodden, and the guilt over not getting there quick enough drove him to a fierce protectiveness over young James.

Only a year earlier, Arran had sided with the Queen Mother against Angus. But someone had gotten him to betray the Queen Mother through his ethics. And Thomas knew it had been Angus— and Arran's own greedy bastard son Finnart. They used Arran's sense of morality about marriage to turn him against the woman who had always supported him.

Lennox focused on the best course of action. He pointed to the river, "We will cross upstream by the nunnery before reinforcements can arrive from Edinburgh."

Thomas looked toward the river raging and the steep, muddy banks. By going the opposite direction, they could surprise Arran and Angus. This could work. They moved as quickly as ten thousand men could move, dividing into two battalions with archers and arquebusiers forming a screen in front of the pikesmen. Arran saw the movement and blocked the advance, bringing his men to the south side of the ridge. Thomas and the other soldiers slogged through the marshy ground, horses and men up to their knees in muddy water. They charged uphill, swords and maces flashing, sliding and slipping against the incline. Arran sent his men rushing down the hill and the two armies fought face-to-face. It nearly worked, until reinforcements arrived. Thomas spotted the royal banner and James, riding at the rear, head down, slumped in his saddle. They couldn't fight on two fronts, and Lennox surrendered under a white flag, only to be executed later.

But now, it looks like James had freed himself. Two years of aborted plans to rescue him from Angus, and he hadn't needed any of it. Thomas was anxious to help James get revenge and gain favor again. Even though his Erskine cousin was a powerful noble, Thomas had been too insignificant to curry the same favor. In fact, his own fortune and land had diminished under the regency of Angus. Now it was time to take it all back and reestablish his relationship with James.

Thomas went to his room and flung open his wardrobe to pack clothes for his trip to Stirling. His wife followed him into the room.

"What is the news?" she asked, her clear brown eyes shaded by black lashes.

"The king is free," he said, trying to keep the excitement out of his voice. "He's summoned me to Stirling."

His wife sucked in her breath. "Is that safe?" she asked, placing a hand on his arm. Her pessimism bordered on paranoia. He shook her off.

"It doesn't matter. I have to go to the king. I can't ignore his summoning." *Nor would I want to,* he thought. He had married his wife in order to strengthen his own position. She was from the Scrymgeour clan, who had fought with Robert Bruce in the Scottish War of Independence. Like himself, she was left an orphan after the Battle of Flodden. Their mothers, with the help of his cousin Lord Erskine, brokered the marriage. Thomas had not met Elizabeth until after the contract had been decided. She had a quiet beauty, pale coloring, and an obedient disposition. Many would find her to be the perfect Scottish wife. But to Thomas, something was missing. The cries of their baby son, less than a month old, invaded the stony silence.

"I have to get the baby," she ducked her head and left the room. Thomas exhaled. He hadn't realized he had been holding his breath. The pressures—marriage, child, family, tradition—left him paralyzed, trapped in a world that left him no space to truly be who he really was. Too often, he suppressed his feelings and desires in order to conform to the expectations placed on him as the oldest son of a martyred father.

But this was his chance to escape, to be around James and the excitement that entailed. He hadn't been able to act as his secretary, even though he was appointed four years ago, because Angus kept him out. Angus had decided just by looking at him that Thomas was not worthy, didn't deserve his time with the king. And what Angus decided, Thomas was powerless to overturn, wasn't even given the opportunity to prove him wrong. Not that he would have been able to if he wanted to. Thomas was all of the things Angus feared. But none of that mattered now because James was making the decisions again. He hoped he could get back into James's graces and be by his side again as they were when they were kids at Stirling.

Chapter 5

MAGGIE

STIRLING CASTLE WAS A flurry of excitement—the night of the feast had finally arrived. The best tapestries had been taken out of storage and beaten, dust flying; the gold and silver cups, bowls, and platters had all been buffed to a glittering shine; the kitchen a hive of activity, which had kept Maggie's husband occupied. All day, horses arrived, carrying nobles from all over Scotland to celebrate the king's escape from Angus and return as the rightful ruler of the country. She was in the Queen Mother's bedchamber, helping her get dressed with Elizabeth and Agnes, the other ladies-in-waiting. Maggie opened the armoire and pulled out a crimson kirtle. As she walked back to the Queen Mother, she kept pulling at the top of her dress, which revealed much of her bosom. The Queen Mother slapped her hands away.

"Stop fidgeting!" She pulled the gown down and into place. Maggie felt naked, the brocade gown pushing up her breasts, which created two white mounds. Pearls lined the top of the dark fabric.

"Help me with my kirtle," the Queen Mother lifted her arms overhead. Maggie handed the dress to Agnes, who placed it over the Queen Mother's head and pulled it over her conical farthingale. The dress had a matching low square neckline. She lifted her breast from underneath. "Tighten the stays!"

Maggie put her knee into the Queen Mother's back and pulled. "Tighter!" the Queen Mother hissed and held onto the bed post. Maggie pulled with all of her might. Finally, the Queen Mother nodded and Maggie tied her off. Next, her crimson sleeves were pinned onto her chemise. Elizabeth held the overgown, a yellow brocade with Tudor roses and strawberry vines, and slid it over the Queen Mother's shoulders. Agnes pinned the matching brocade partlet over the front of the kirtle. Maggie held the gabled headdress and placed it on the Queen Mother's head. The gable covered her ears and ended at her chin, which was beginning to sag. She studied herself in the mirror, pushing up her chin with her hand. "I look ancient," she said. Maggie and the ladies protested, but not too strenuously.

"The small-pox stole my youth," the Queen Mother sighed. Then she pulled herself up.

"No matter. Tonight is about my son," she said, shaking her head to clear her thoughts. "Let's get Maggie's headdress on." Agnes placed another gabled headdress on Maggie's head. The elaborate gable was too long, ending below her narrow chin. The great wings muffled all sounds. Maggie pinned the left lappet to the crown of the headdress.

The Queen Mother studied her. "You need a necklace," she said and went over to her jewelry box on the side table, pulling out a double strand of Scottish pearls, holding a garnet broach. It was Maggie's favorite necklace.

"Oh Queen Mother!" she clawed at her veil to pull it up. The Queen Mother placed it around her neck and secured the clasp. She placed her hands on Maggie's shoulders and steered her to the mirror.

"Just as beautiful as a Scottish princess," she said in a far away tone. Maggie knew the Queen Mother was thinking of her own daughter, but Maggie didn't mind being treated like a princess. She turned, watching the light refract off the crimson stone. It made her eyes look more green than brown.

"Time to head down!" the Queen Mother said. Maggie lifted the train of the Queen Mother's dress and followed her across the courtyard. She focused on keeping the Queen Mother's train out of the mud, so she couldn't admire the yellow ochre lime-washed walls of the Great Hall, with its crenellated parapet and crow-step roof. They climbed the wooden staircase to enter the cavernous room, which had been set up for a state dinner. Maggie's eyes drifted up to the hammer beam ceiling—a jigsaw of timbers and trusses, which created patterns of angles and squares the length of the hall, oak beams contrasting with the light walls. The servants had hung the tapestries over the cold stone walls, which enclosed the heat around the oak tables lit by iron candelabra. Flames blazed in the five fireplaces to add warmth to the cool June air. The Queen Mother met Lord Methven, her husband and took his arm.

"You may go to your husband now, Maggie," she said over her shoulder, already forgetting Maggie under her husband's gaze. The Queen Mother lit up, brighter than the feeble candlelight. All was forgotten in the presence of her young husband. He ignored Maggie. The two of them moved behind the screen at the far end of the hall to prepare for the royal entrance. Maggie turned to look at the four diamond paned windows with the coat of arms of Scottish heroes inset, below which sat a long oak table held up by four squared legs on the raised dais. In the center of the windows hung a crimson velvet banner, embroidered with the Scots coat of arms—a red lion on a yellow banner, flanked by rearing unicorns. Golden tassels hung from the bottom of the tapestry. She wished she could sit at the head table, but she was not royal. Sighing, she turned to find her designated spot at one of the wooden tables that lined either side of the hall, perpendicular to the dais. She was surprised at the number of nobles who had come for the feast, some riding most of the day to get here. Her husband waited for her at the far end of the hall, standing in front of the paneled screens passage under the musician's gallery. He had been busy preparing the meats for the feast, as the master butcher. His brown hair was slicked back off his face and his beard brushed.

"Hello, my lady," he said as he approached her. There was no fire lit within her at the sight of him, no quickening pulse, no excitement. She curtsied, rather than look in his dull eyes, and then yanked at the top of her dress. He offered his arm to her, and she imagined she still smelled blood on his skin. She shook off the thought and laced her arm though his and allowed herself to be led to her place. Always the ornament.

"I expect things are well with the Queen Mother," he attempted conversation. She nodded. What else could she say that wasn't rude? Of course she was well, her son had escaped and come home. She'd been waiting for this for three years. Her tongue twisted with a sharp retort. Better to just look pretty.

"I got a report from my grandfather at Loch Leven. Repairs are almost finished to the main keep of the castle. You will love it there. I swear the water is the bluest in all of Scotland," he patted her hand. She smiled her widest smile, the one she flashed when she hid her true feelings. She looked away from him and focused on the table setting. Over white linens, the table was laid with the finest bowls and pewter goblets. Honeyed almonds adorned every table, all in silver bowls decorated with strawberry vines, the symbol of Scotland.

They walked the remainder of the hall in silence, with Robert greeting other household members with a nod. The night hadn't even started and Maggie was already exhausted of trying to be someone she was not. She was guided to her seat next to her father's place, who had not yet entered the hall. As one of the important members of the household, he would enter later. She slung her legs over the bench and sat down hard. Robert looked at her, and Maggie struggled to put her mask back on.

"I hope everything is to the king's liking," he said, twisting the bottom of his doublet.

"Who even knows what he likes anymore? Everyone is acting as if he hasn't been gone for almost three years. Heaven knows I'm a different person than I was three years ago," she said, unable to hold in her frustration. She bit her lip to avoid saying more. Robert's eyes widened and he glanced side to side to see if anyone heard his wife acting unladylike. Maggie felt her ears flush and knew her face was red.

"You are a very different person than three years ago. You didn't know me then," he said, a little too loudly, to cover for Maggie's bad behavior. She resented him for it, clutching her hands in her lap and focusing on her crossed fingers.

Finally, her father and the other high-ranking nobles entered and took their place. Lord Methven, the queen's husband, entered alone, walking the length of the hall to a loud consort of trumpets, flutes, and tabors, played by the musicians in the gallery above the far end of the hall, the music echoing through the cavernous room. His doublet was brocade navy, and his white shirt had slashes that revealed a blue silk shirt. When he took his position on the dais, it signaled the musicians to begin the royal procession march. Everyone stood for the entrance of the king.

Maggie saw the Queen Mother, her arm laced through James's, her brocade dress shimmering in the candle light. Her turned-back sleeves revealed deep crimson stripes, which matched James's doublet. His sleeves were slashed, the purple silk showing under the crimson. His doublet was emblazoned with garnets and amethysts, which twinkled as he stepped. He wore a purple hat tilted to the left over his auburn hair, which curled over his ears. The hat also had garnets and gold patterned around it. His eyes met Maggie's, the dark cherry brown glistening in satisfaction that he was in charge of his own person, not his stepfather. Her breath caught, choked off by his brilliance. He smirked as he walked past, his eyes never leaving her face. The heat flashed upward from the base of her stomach, quivering like hundreds of butterflies. She exhaled, and realized that this was missing when she looked at her husband—the excitement, the attraction. Her shoulders wilted as James passed and felt the weight of her husband's intruding presence.

She shook off the feeling as the king took his position in the center of the raised dais. James sat on an ornately carved oak throne with an arched high back, padded with purple velvet. The entire room sat in unison. Maggie looked around the room again, noting the nobles in attendance: Archbishops Beaton and Dunbar, Earl of Arran, Argyll, Eglinton, Glencairn, Monteith, Rothes, Moray. Moray sat on James's left, which surprised Maggie. Moray was James's half-brother, both were sons of the former king, but Moray's mother was one of the king's whores. At least that is what the Queen Mother called her. Moray's mother was Janet Kennedy, descendent from King Robert II of Scotland. She and James IV had an affair and a son two years before he married the Queen Mother, but he continued the affair after his marriage. That was what earned her the epitaph from the Queen Mother.

The cupbearers poured claret wine into the pewter chalices. Only the head table had crystal goblets. Maggie gulped the sweet wine, wiping her chin when she was finished. She glanced sideways to see if her husband or father saw the uncouth gesture. Both were preoccupied with conversations. Suddenly, the king slammed his fist on the table, startling his guests. "Is there no one to challenge me to a flyting?" he shouted, searching the room for someone to engage in a poetry match, a flyting, with him. No one stepped forward. James was quick and vicious with his poetry. Only Sir David Lindsay could keep up with him. He had been James's confidant, tutor, and entertainer before Angus took possession of him. She hadn't seen him since and although she missed his clever poems, he was a bit too sanctimonious for her. Maggie wished she could engage in a flyting, but women were not allowed to compete. James slumped with disappointment. Moray leaned in and said something inaudible, which made the king laugh.

The servers placed the silver platters on the tables, and Maggie inhaled the roasted geese, surrounded by glossy purple plums and green kale. Maggie used her knife to cut some meat off and placed it onto her pewter plate. Her father shot her a warning look, and she reached back out for a plum and kale, even though she hated kale. He nodded, satisfied. Before the next course, a jester tumbled into the center of the room, wearing a red fool's cap, with ass's ears curling forward, golden bells tinkling. The flute player began a lively, quick tune. The jester tried to leap in time to the music, spinning in circles until he was too dizzy and collapsed onto the slate tiles. James laughed and clapped, his face shining. After the jester stumbled out of the hall, the next course was served—pike, roasted with wild rosemary. The servants next brought in the Wensleydale cheese with stewed cherries.

After dinner, tables were pushed against the wall to allow for dancing. As the Queen Mother had said, she danced the first dance with James, a pavane. The tabor began to play and the Queen Mother and her son walked out alone, as she instructed. They sashayed forward as the flute began to play, then stopped and he guided his mother around, circling back on himself. He retreated a few steps while she curtsied, and then he strutted forward and saluted his mother, his legs flexing. Maggie couldn't take her eyes off him. Every move was animalistic, smooth as a stag rolling through his haunches. They entwined their outstretched hands and jumped one, two, three. James found Maggie and held her gaze, jumping side, ball change, side, ball change. Maggie's heart skipped with each footfall. The music built to a crescendo and James and the Queen Mother stepped back from one another, she curtsied, he bowed. The music ended and everyone stood and clapped. Maggie clapped faster to divert her attention from her pounding heart.

The next song started, a galliard, of course. The galliard always accompanied the pavane. James bowed his head to excuse himself from the Queen Mother and she went to her husband's side. He scanned the room for a partner. All the young noble women held their breath. Maggie sighed, knowing that she wouldn't be chosen since she was already married. Her stomach dropped with a weight of disappointment. She tugged at her dress again and looked sideways to see whom James would choose, even though she didn't want to see. He spun on his heel to her side of the room, his eyes on the diamond paned windows above the heads of the ladies. Maggie shifted her weight and scratched her left foot with her right, earning her a glare from her father. She froze as James brought his gaze down to her. His lip curled into the same smirk he gave her when he walked into the hall. He nodded to her. Her heart stopped. She looked to her husband, but his puppy eyes were flat and impassive. She looked to her father, who used his elbow to nudge her forward. James stretched out his hand.

"Lady Douglas, may I have this dance," he said, bowing deeply. Too deeply for a king. Maggie felt he was making fun of her, teasing her as he had done when they were children. The heat rose to her ears again. He looked up from his bow, hand still outstretched.

"Fine," she said through clenched teeth and grabbed his hand. She would show him that she was not a child. He chuckled, but no one heard except her. She did a short curtsey and pulled him into the steps, jump, two, three, four. Jump, two, three, four. They released hands and she pliéd, while he did his sequence of jump steps. She glared at him, but this only made him chuckle more. She twirled to the right, not losing eye contact until she spun to spot his face again. The amusement was replaced with a new look, hungry. She spun and his hunger intensified. Maggie raised her eyebrow as she hopped forward to him for the lavolta. He placed his hands on her waist.

"Why did you pick me?" She said, placing her hands on top of his. He looked down at her chest.

"I wanted to see these duckies for myself," he said. Her eyes widened at his vulgarity. She wanted to run away, but he was lifting her into the air. She clutched his hands and he turned, brushing her against his chest as he brought her down.

"You are vulgar!" She said as she pranced away and into the next step sequence. No one had ever talked to her in this way. She wanted to pull the dress up again, but could not. So she leapt instead— left, right, left. They circled around each other.

"I know," he whispered. "I think you like it." He spun away from her, and she him, his words reverberating in her ears, tingling throughout her body, fluttering against her insides. She shivered, realizing that he was having the same feelings about her. And that she did like it. They leapt toward each other in preparation for another lavolta.

"Well, all you can do is look," she said when he placed his hands on her waist again. His face flinched in surprise. She felt the heat from him as she placed her hand on his shoulder and smirked, self-assured. He lifted her into the air and spun, pressing her against him as he brought her down. Maggie sucked the air in, the sensation of his body against her almost overwhelming her.

"For now," he said and spun away from her. She hopped in a circle, feeling dizzy and thrilled at the same time. She wasn't sure if he was poking fun at her naivety. He leapt toward her again, left, right, left, plié.

"What does *that* mean?" she hissed, trying to keep her face impassive. He grinned.

"You'll see," he grabbed her for the next lavolta. Her skin burned from his touch, the heat radiating through the fabric of her dress. She pressed down on his shoulders as he lifted her, staring into her eyes, the hunger leaping toward her. And she wanted to feel more.

He pressed her to him as he brought her down, his breath ruffling the hair under her gable. Her heart hammered, her breasts heaving—from exertion and emotion.

"I knew you would be a bonnie Scots princess," he said, clutching her before releasing her to end the dance. He bowed, again too deeply for a king. So she curtsied all the way to the floor, sweeping her arm in front of her. He held his bow. She held her curtsey. She knew he was grinning without seeing his face. Silence surrounded them. And then she remembered they were in a crowded hall, with his mother and her father looking on. This was no time for a battle of wills that could embarrass her family. She shot up and stood, stock straight.

"I win," he said right before the band launched into the next song. He turned and looked for the next lady to dance with. Maggie could not control her breathing, fast and shallow. Her head was whirling. The heat left her, trailing him like a comet's tail, leaving her breathless, confused. He didn't look back. His next selection was Elizabeth Shaw, daughter of the Master of the Wine Cellar. She looked up from under her lashes at him with doe-eyes as she followed him to the dance floor, pale hand clutching his. Her dress was not half as beautiful as Maggie's, although Maggie had the advantage of wearing the Queen Mother's gown. She would not be able to afford a gown like this herself. She smoothed the velvet down. James was looking at Elizabeth with the same hunger he looked at her. She was not special. She spun on her heel and into Robert's arms.

"Aye," he said, recovering from her crashing into him, his hands on her arms. "You looked like you still wanted to dance."

She took a deep breath, but it came out ragged. Nodding, she curtsied to Robert to begin the next dance, an Allemande, which was performed in close hold. He placed his arm around her waist; she extended her left arm across his body, right hand on top of his on her hip. They leapt forward, right, left, right.

"You've known the king for a long time," he said after an awkward silence. It wasn't a question, but she nodded. Robert had come to Stirling after their contract. He was five years older than she was.

"Must be nice to see him again," he said as they turned. "He seemed excited to see you." And there it was. The creeping jealousy that older men have for their younger wives.

"He just likes to tease me," she flared her nostrils in annoyance. She was ready for this night to be over. Embarrassed by the king, and feeling something she didn't understand, only to be questioned by her husband was enough for one night. "It's nothing. Look, he's already moved on," she said tilting her head toward the king and Elizabeth. And it was true. He was looking at that girl with the same heat, and she was returning his hunger with an intensity that Maggie did not know how to express. The Queen Mother was right. She was a child. And it irritated her.

"So he has," Robert said, smiling down at her, "so he has." They finished the dance in silence.

Chapter 6

JAMES

JAMES WAS ENJOYING THE softness of Elizabeth, the give of her flesh when he squeezed her wrist or waist.

"How long have you been at Stirling?" he asked her as they hop-stepped in time to the lute.

"My father has been here almost two years. He's your Wine Cellar Master. Your mother hired him while you were..." she trailed off. James knew it was a reflex to avoid offending him.

"Kidnapped?" he suggested, hoping there was lightness in his voice and not anger. She giggled and leaned into his arm. He guessed he was successful. Her dress was a similar cut as Maggie's, square across her breasts, pushing them up into white mounds. They were more ample than Maggie's. Her nose was straight, boxy. He looked over to see Maggie dancing with her husband, her eyebrows knitted together. She was fiery, full of fury and opinions. He needed to focus on getting his country straightened out. He needed simplicity.

"The feast was wonderful," she said, pulling his attention back to her. Blind adoration radiated from her. He would focus on her for tonight.

"Are you going on the hunt tomorrow?" he asked. His mother loved hunting and horseback riding.

"Oh gads no!" she tittered. "I'm no huntress."

"Are you a falconer?" he asked teasing, wanting a snide comment to challenge him. She just giggled and shook her head again. Maggie's husband was looking at her with the same hunger he felt. Jealousy stabbed him, mean monster. He wanted a verbal fight.

"Why aren't you married?" he asked her.

"I haven't been contracted yet. My father is looking though," the hope in her eyes was pathetic, no challenge at all.

"A beautiful woman like you should have no problems," he said and rubbed against her backside, feeling the bounce of her hip. She gave no resistance. He chose to believe that his emotional frustration could be satisfied physically, just as Angus had trained him while he was imprisoned at Edinburgh Castle. He had been introduced to carnal satisfaction at a very early age to distract him from his responsibilities to his country. As a young teen, he had allowed it because it had been exciting. *Force of habit*, he thought as he stroked this girl's body.

The dance ended and he bowed to Elizabeth, boldly kissing her hand and using his tongue. Her eyes widened and she blushed but did not pull her hand away. He looked to make sure Mags had seen, but her back was to him, guided by her husband's hand. A pang knocked him in the gut again. He shook it off and strode over to the head table. He drained the wine from his goblet, impatient for the wine to erase his thoughts.

"Such a fair party," his mother placed a hand on his shoulder. He nodded, trying to smile and failing. "What is wrong, my son?" she placed her other hand on his shoulder. He shook her off.

"I don't know who will be with me," he said, refilling his wine. "Who will come with me to Edinburgh to organize an attack on Angus? Who will fight against him and even kill those who are with him? Will my uncle take him in again?"

"My son, the lords are with you. Look around this room tonight. You have Lord Erskine, Maxwell, Arran, Argyll, Sinclair, even Moray is here," she said, but she couldn't keep the bitterness off the last name. The Earl of Moray was James's half-brother, the son of his father and his favorite mistress, Janet Kennedy. His father was never embarrassed of his bastard children and took good care of them, much to his mother's vexation.

"You are right," he said, ignoring the emotion of his mother. "Even Arran is here, despite fighting against Lennox and my escape."

"Yes, but we both know he was coerced to fight for Angus," she said. "You forget how persuasive he can be, even you loved him for a moment."

"No, Mother," he sneered. "That was only you." He stomped off, realizing he was behaving as an ill-tempered child, but unable to control himself. The insecurity he felt towards his nobles and the desire he felt for Maggie melded into a ball of smelted pain, which made him feel out of control. As the king, he should be respected and in total control. There was nothing he could do about earning the nobles' loyalty tonight, but maybe he could get closer to Maggie. He looked for her—she was not next to her father and her husband was missing too. *He was probably exercising his marital rights with her*, James thought, feeling the anger flare and cover his disappointment. He had not experienced a desire that was not instantly fulfilled, and it left a pit in his stomach, acid creeping up his throat. Angus made sure all of his desires were met; this feeling was disconcerting. Instead of disappointment, he focused on Maggie's insubordination, the disrespect of her monarch. She should not have left without his permission! He would speak to his mother about this—and to Maggie. Her husband, a Douglas, would be punished and dismissed from his household. No one would deny James dismissing a servant.

He spun around and found a suitable substitute—Elizabeth Shaw, the soft and willing woman. Her lips turned up as she met his eye. He would dampen his desire for Maggie with her.

"Come to my room in half an hour," he said, maybe a little too loudly because she blushed to the roots of her dark hair. He turned on his heel and strode out of the hall, leaving many nobles protesting after him, but all he could feel was the building desire clouding his judgment. He needed to physically clear himself and tomorrow he would address all of their concerns and win back their loyalty.

Chapter 7

THE QUEEN MOTHER

MARGARET TUDOR SIGHED AND looked over at her husband, his strawberry blond hair tousled, lips separated in sleep. She had found in him what she had been duped to believe Ard was. Third time was a charm. And her life should have been charmed! She was the second born child of the first Tudor king, Henry VII. Her brief childhood had been indulgent, there was nothing she couldn't have—new dresses, jewels, ponies, anything she desired! Even her first husband, James IV, had indulged her. But now, looking back, she realized it had been placation. Keeping her satisfied and occupied. She was a beautiful thing, chestnut hair, amble figure, large brown doe eyes. And she loved beautiful things, which is why when her first husband, James IV, went into battle against her brother—even when she told him her hideous dream—when he met her brother's wife, Catherine of Aragon on the field at Flodden, when she heard the news of his death, she vowed to herself that she would only choose beautiful things in return. She would not be a pawn; no, she would be the queen that James had molded her to be.

After her husband's death, she needed an ally in Scotland to help her rule the country. The nobles didn't trust her because she was English, accused her of supporting her brother and causing the murder of James. That first year of widowhood, pregnant and scared for her son's future, was lonely and distressing. She lived in fear of the nobles, who supported the return of the Duke of Albany from France to rule Scotland in her son's minority. Albany was next in line to the throne after Margaret's own children, but he had been born and lived his entire life in France. How could he understand Scottish politics? Margaret also feared that he would turn the nobles against her and an alliance with England and turn them towards an alliance with France.

But she remembered the kindness of the old Earl of Angus, who had been too old to fight at Flodden but died of heartbreak a few months later. He supported Margaret and a treaty with her brother to help stabilize the borders where his land lie. His father had also crowed the young James III and protected his sovereign during his minority and Margaret hoped he would do the same for her son. The old earl pushed his grandson on her, and he was so charming—both of them turning toward each other in their grief... but it was all a façade, Ard turned out to be a snake who smelled weakness and struck. His venom was his confidence and charisma, which charmed Margaret completely. She believed every one of his promises, not realizing his silver tongue spoke only lies.

Well, now she was her own queen. No one could take that away from her, even as they took away the regency when she married Ard. She narrowed her eyes. Every thought of him reminded her of his betrayal. Not a single betrayal, no! First stealing her dowry revenues to support his mistress—*his mistress* who he had been engaged to before he married her. In *her* ducal lands. And then he made a deal behind her back with her own brother—oh her brother Harry was not blameless in this either.

She smoothed a hand down her husband Muffin's back, skin as soft as eider down, to remind her that she was no longer that naive woman. She was the vixen now and had her own beautiful thing who would not betray her. He turned over and pulled her to him. She smoothed his unruly hair back and kissed him on his plump lips. He wrapped his arms around her.

"No, no no, my muffin," she whispered, "we need to get up and see what the king needs." But she didn't move. She liked the security of his arms. It was all coming together—everything she had worked for. Her son, her sun—the light of her life was free from his stepfather. James would take over Scotland and give her back control of her lands, which Ard denied her, using *her* money to support his whore and bastard child. She had to beg her brother for money to live on. Now she didn't need to worry about that. She would advise her son with her beautiful husband and finally begin to enjoy the life she had been promised twenty-five years earlier.

She untangled herself from his arms, knowing that she needed to secure his title and lands and not let her son change his mind. Her son was fickle, tempestuous, and proud. She needed to make sure everything went the way she had planned it and guide him to get the country back on track. Scotland had been neglected during the imprisonment of her son, since Ard only concerned himself with lining his own pockets. Even though she knew it would be unpopular, she wanted to finally get her son and brother to meet and sign another perpetual peace, assuring stability to the unstable people of Scotland.

After throwing on an overgown, she went into the inner chamber. Maggie was sleeping, alone of course, on a straw pallet mattress that she had pulled out once she saw the earl would be spending the night. Margaret saw her dance with her husband last night. She noticed the lack of spark in Maggie, the fire that was obvious in the girl's husband. Margaret had forbid the girl from sleeping with her husband, which the girl didn't seem to mind. Her hope was to keep her here another year or two, maybe longer if she couldn't get her own daughter back from England, which was precarious because Angus might keep her there just to punish the mother.

She tossed the curtains open, sunlight flooding the small room. "I need you to help me dress," she said. Maggie rubbed her eyes. The girl could be obstinate. "Let's go, let's go," she yanked the covers back. She could ask Elizabeth or Agnes, but Maggie reminded her of her daughter, so she chose her.

Maggie pulled herself out of bed, still disoriented. The older woman guided her to tighten the stays. "We need to help the king plan his affairs," she said, turning her back and striding into her bed chamber, knowing the girl would follow.

"I need you to draft a letter to the Duke of Norfolk," she handed the quill and paper to Maggie as they reached the desk in the bed chamber. Maggie's handwriting was much neater than hers, rounded and tight. Norfolk was the son of the English duke who thought he could outdo her when she rode to Scotland for the first time. As her entourage neared York, she received a report of the duke waiting with four hundred men, wearing a crimson velvet coat lined with ermine fir and bordered with jewels over a crimson doublet and black velvet boots. Margaret would not be shown up by a mere duke! She ordered the caravan stopped so that she could show the grandeur and power of a Tudor princess, who would be a Scottish queen. Her ladies rushed her into the whirlicote, painted the Tudor colors of white and green. Her Lady of the Wardrobe, Agnes, pulled the velvet curtains and helped her change into her cloth of gold overgown, fastening at her waist a golden girdle-belt studded with sapphires. When she rode through the gates at York to meet the duke, his chest deflated, recognizing he could not compete with a Tudor and a queen. The sun caught the golden fibers of her dress as she stepped to him, enjoying him shrinking back, blinded by her brilliance. Margaret held out her hand, gold rings glinting in the sunlight. He bowed, soiling his velvet coat in the mud as he kissed her hand, an appropriate display of reverence.

"Your Highness," he said once he had risen. "It is a pleasure to accompany you to your new kingdom. As you know, your family's success is my success as I have pledged my life to their service." Margaret tamped her irritation down. Of course he had to remind her of his involvement with her family, ingratiating himself to her father, even after he supported the pretender Richard III against her father at Bosworth.

"We should be in time to receive mass," she said, striding past him, holding her head high. Her ladies rustled behind her to the York Cathedral so she could pray for a safe journey. Norfolk was not someone she trusted, but just as his father had ingratiated himself with her father, his son had done with her brother. The younger duke stroked her brother's ego, and she knew her brother was blind to see through the flattery. But Margaret saw him for who he really was—a pickthank, someone who said whatever the king wanted in order to gain favor. He took advantage of his appointment to Lord Admiral of the English Navy during Flodden to gain wealth for himself, at Margaret's expense! But he could influence her brother in ways that Margaret was not able to, since her own brother saw her as a Scot. She needed Norfolk's confidence and support.

"Tell him that the king has escaped and has taken possession of Stirling," she looked over Maggie's shoulder as she wrote. "He will understand that we are together since I have given him my dowager castle." Maggie's pink tongue stuck out as she scribbled the message.

Her handwriting was beautiful. The Queen Mother smiled, knowing she had chosen wisely to employ the girl in her household.

"List the nobles who are on our side. That will reassure him too," she tapped her lip. "Tell him there will be a change in the council of Scotland."

Before she continued, there was a loud crash from the king's bedchamber. Maggie jumped up and opened the adjoining door to the king's chamber. A girl crept out from James's chambers. Margaret tried to place her—young girl, non-descript hair, long nose, buxom. Her eyes narrowed as she realized this was the young lady that her son had danced with last night. He must have bedded her and left her. *Just like his father*, she scowled. She would need to speak with him about this later. Once he established himself as king. He was allowed his dalliances, of course most Scottish men had affairs. She needed to warn him not to fall in love with a lowly girl when he was destined for a foreign princess to become his queen.

Chapter 8

JAMES

THE SUN HAD JUST broken the horizon when James woke. The woman next to him was still sleeping, hands tucked under her chin, dark hair spread over the pillow. His head was clear, the jealous film through which he had watched Mags dance with her husband had dissipated. He slid out of the bed, pulled on his hose and under-shirt, and grabbed his doublet. He didn't put on his shoes, in fear of making noise and waking her. He had nothing to say to her this morning, all of his charm used up. He should have felt remorse, knowing he had used her sexually, but that didn't cross his mind. He was the king and she had willingly come to his room. He would send his groom to get her out later. Now, he needed to find Lord Er-skine and work on his kingdom. He strode into his inner chamber outside of his bed chamber and dressed, sending a groom in to get rid of the girl. Then he found Lord Erskine.

"Lord Erskine," James said, entering the presence chamber. "Please bring in the earls so we can discuss how to proceed. I want to try Angus for treason."

Erskine bowed, "That is a prudent decision, my lord." He turned to retrieve the earls, who were gathered in the outer chamber wait-ing for the king's presence. Once Arran, Argyll, Moray and the other nobles filed into the inner chamber, he announced that they should proceed to Edinburgh to try Angus for misadministration at least, and treason at most.

Moray, his half-brother, sighed, "He won't go without a fight." Moray, who was also named James, was anti-English and saw Angus

44

as attempting to further English interests in Scotland rather than protecting Scottish interests. James looked up to his brother, who was more level-headed than James himself.

James nodded, "Then there will be a fight. He is a traitor to his king."

"We may lose men if we must extract him from Tantallon," Moray continued. Tantallon was Angus's hereditary castle. It was part of the Douglas land holdings, and was impregnable. Built on a cliff, backed against the North Sea and the Firth of Forth, the castle had been a stronghold during the War of Independence from the English almost two hundred years ago. A red sandstone curtain wall guarded the southwest side of the castle, the only side not protected by water. The wall was fortified with many cannons and artillery.

"Then let's hope he is still in Edinburgh," James replied, the grimace deepening on his face. Losing men was always a possibility in battle, and he was going to war with Angus.

The grooms saddled the horses and James prepared to leave with the men who supported him. The Queen Mother assured the king that she would continue to run Stirling in his best interests.

"As long as those interests are for me and Scotland and not for yourself, Mother, there should be no problems," he said, watching her recoil before composing herself.

"My thoughts are only for your wellbeing, my son," she drew herself up as tall as her short stature would allow.

James smirked and said, "Not when your legs were spread." His mother was stunned, just as he hoped she would be. She would need to earn his trust again, prove her loyalty. Before she could compose a retort, a galloping horse thundered up. Thomas Erskine's face was red with exertion.

"Thomas!" James said and dismounted to embrace him. "Your efforts on my behalf did not go unnoticed."

"Yes, but we could not free you from that devil's grasp," Thomas said, his hands lingering on James's arms. He looked in his eyes with total devotion. James knew he could count on Thomas.

"You will be reinstated as my secretary. There is no one else who I trust to run my affairs," he said and felt his mother blanch again. "Let's get to Edinburgh and have Angus hanged for treason!"

They rode the thirty-six miles hard, hoping to trap Angus in the capital, more men joining to support the king as they rode through the countryside. By the time they passed through the gates of Edinburgh, the party contained three hundred men. They rode down the wide, dirt-packed Cowgate Road, bordered by timbered-fronted buildings hanging over the street. During his father's reign, Cowgate had become a fashionable street for noble and wealthy merchants to live on. They stopped at the house with the hexagonal turret, the house of the archbishop of St. Andrew's, James Beaton, brother of Arran's second wife. James dismounted, throwing his reins and pounded on the heavy oak door. When a servant answered, the flustered boy knelt in front of the king. James demanded to be taken to his master. They followed the servant through the arched doorway and up a wide stone staircase into a bright room lined in oak panels. The shuttered windows were open to the east to let in the sunlight.

"Where is Angus?" James demanded of Beaton when he entered the chambers. James Beaton had been one of the regents during James's turbulent minority. His father trusted Beaton so much that he made him treasurer of Scotland. But James knew his clan loyalties were stronger than his fealty to the king.

"Your Highness, I do not know his exact location, but it is close," he said.

"Call a session of the lords for tomorrow!" he said. Without waiting, he exited the house, mounted his horse, and rode up to Edinburgh castle, perched on jagged rocks above the city. Tomorrow he would charge Angus with treason—present or not.

The next morning, the Lord Council convened in the Great Hall of Edinburgh Castle. James's footsteps echoed on the ochre and grey flagstones as he strode across the vast room. The walls were crimson and matched his doublet. He felt the grandeur of the hall that his father had commissioned, but who died before he could host the council himself. He thrust his chin up as he walked past the lords who were waiting for him at the long oak table. He ran his hand over the smooth wood, revered by his pagan ancestors for its strength and longevity. James hoped to channel the tree's strength as he prepared to exterminate the Douglases. He raised his eyes to the dark ceiling buttressed with overlapping stalwart beams, reminding himself that he was strong too, no longer the child who his step-father abducted. The words of Angus's brother, George Douglas, reverberated in his brain, "We will never let our enemies take you. We will hold your body, even if it is torn to pieces. At least we will still hold a part of it."

He hated them—everyone who was cursed to be born a Douglas. James sat on his throne while he glanced around the room. These men were loyal—today. Would they remain loyal? Would they have the stomach to extinguish the Douglas clan, many of whom had died alongside their own fathers at Flodden? He would soon find out. He tapped his foot as roll was called and muster ordered for troops, impatient to get to Angus and his brother's punishment. Finally, the summons for Angus was read, for him to appear before Parliament and answer to the king and his justice for the treasonable art and part of disobedience and refusing to fulfil the king's command.

"He needs to hang," James banged his fist on the table, upsetting an inkhorn. A servant rushed in to sop up the ink. The summons was not strong enough, didn't convey the humiliation and fear that James endured while held by Angus

"Your Highness," John Ballenden said, clearing his throat. He was the Douglas's attorney. "The earl and his brother would like a pledge of safety."

James scoffed. A pledge of safety—how ironic when they used him as a shield to protect themselves. "I'm sure he has given you an offer to present," the anger clipped his words.

"Yes, sire," Ballenden said. "He would like Maxwell, Argyll, and Hamilton of Finnart to be held hostage by his family until the end of the trial."

"He broke the parliament's order and held me against my will, exposed me to battle and death, which he would have been all too happy to have me killed! And *he* wants a pledge of safety?" he jumped up, pounding the table again.

"No one is denying your suffering, my lord," Moray, his half-brother said in a low voice. James looked around the room. His nobles couldn't hide their shock, eyes panicked even as they held their lips straight. James needed their support, or they could decide to support Angus and overthrow him. He sat back, clutching the carved arms of the chair, his knuckles white.

"The king, my brother, is declining this offer," Moray said, pressing his hand into James's shoulder. He couldn't stop shaking, the audacity of the Douglases. Moray's voice helped to calm him down. "I propose we pass a sentence to seize all of the lands and goods of the earl of Angus, Sir George Douglas, and Archibald Douglas of Kilspindie." Each name was a dagger plunged deeper into James's chest, but Kilspindie's betrayal hurt the worst. Kilspindie had been his friend—once. But he did nothing to assist in his escape, so he would be punished too, because he *should* have helped since they were so close.

"We need to have him warded first. He is clearly not in Edinburgh anymore," Argyll said, his weathered face crinkling under his greying beard. James trusted Argyll, who had not sided with Angus, even though his brother married a Douglas sister. His men had scoured the city for any news of his whereabouts. Their ride from Stirling had given Angus enough notice to vacate with his supporters.

"Offer a royal reward of one hundred pounds for the capture of Angus," he said.

"I'll draw up a summons," Thomas Erskine, the Secretary of State said. James smiled, knowing that Thomas would be precise in his language. Thomas had studied on the continent and spoke fluent French. Someone with those negotiation skills would be valuable to him. Thomas met his gaze, holding steady, a slight smile playing on his face.

"We also need to secure the support of your uncle, the King of England," Thomas continued. He worked closely with the English ambassador and knew how powerful—and erratic—Henry could be. "He has provided asylum for Angus before. We need to make sure he does not harbor him again."

"Yes," James rubbed his chin. "My mother could help smooth the way along with you, Thomas." Thomas nodded, writing a note, smiling.

"Let's draw a summons and declare him guilty of treason in holding our sovereign lord's person against his will, in exposing his person in battle," Arran said.

James nodded, "Their lands will be divided among Arran, Argyll,

Maxwell, and Hamilton." He noticed Thomas deflate at the proclamation. How insensitive. James would make it up to him later. The summons went out, a letter drafted by Thomas to the English ambassador. Now to capture Angus and hang him before he got out of Scotland.

Chapter 9
THE QUEEN MOTHER

MARGARET READ THE LETTER from her brother, Harry, from which spilled his frustration with his wife, Catherine of Aragon, at not providing him an heir—a *male* heir. Harry was seeking a divorce from the pope. *Well, well,* thought Margaret, *how the mighty have fallen.* She tapped the letter on her chin, unable to keep from smiling. Her brother had opposed her divorce of Angus, and now he was trying to divorce Catherine. Catherine—the beautiful Spanish bride who had first married Margaret's older brother Arthur. Arthur was the first born, favorite son, solid and stable, with a keen sense of humor. It nearly broke her father when Arthur died of the sweating sickness. And so Catherine was betrothed to her younger brother, Harry, rather than send her back to Spain and lose the support of her powerful family and her hefty dowry.

She shook her head, hoping her brother knew what he was doing by divorcing the aunt of Charles V, the King of Spain and the Holy Roman Emperor. Harry had been impetuous and impulsive since they were children. She chuckled, remembering the fit he threw when he realized that she, his sister, would be announced before him and he would have to salute her at state dinners because she was the Queen of Scots, while he was only a prince. But that was before her father died and Harry became king. It was because of her brother that Flodden happened, his paranoia over the Franco-Scots alliance. War between England and France commenced, and he sent his standing army north under command of a pregnant Catherine. So many needless deaths, including Margaret's husband.

Margaret feared retaliation from Catherine's powerful family and was saddened because she truly loved her sister-in-law. It would play out as it would, and she knew her brother would not back down, even if he destroyed her beloved England. Her only hope was that he was so preoccupied with his own concerns that he stayed out of Scotland's business.

Autumn had seen James attempt to capture her former husband, but Angus escaped time and again. Now the rumor was that her own brother was giving him asylum. James was back at Stirling, holding council here. Margaret was happy but wary. In her letter to Harry, she remained neutral, flattering her brother to make him more favorable to a lasting peace between Scotland and England. And part of that peace was handing Angus over so that James could try him and get that part of his life behind him. He seemed as fixated as ever on destroying the Douglases.

She was trying to maintain her household too. James flew into her chambers one morning, while she was dictating to Maggie. His brown eyes flashed, consumed with rage.

"I want them all gone," he said, pointing to Maggie. The poor girl shrank back.

"Whom, my son?" Margaret was calm, trying to diffuse her son's fury. "Surely you couldn't mean the Erskines."

He scoffed, "Don't play coy, Mother. I want the Douglases out of this household. All of them. Replace them with loyalty. I won't stand for the Douglas treachery."

Margaret looked at the girl. Her pale skin took on an oily sheen. The quill frozen, poised above the page, hovering in a void.

"Of course. They will be dismissed at once. I assume you also mean their families?" she asked, feeling the girl's imperceptive wince.

"Yes. Every one of them needs to go," he paused, his eyes falling over Maggie's frozen face. "Not you, Magpie," his voice became more tender. He knew the affection his mother had for her. "But your husband will be dismissed. Angus frequented Loch Leven and Sir Robert did nothing to prevent him."

Margaret tried not to smirk. Maggie's husband couldn't have prevented Ard from going to his family castle. But she understood her son's paranoia. *Maybe he is more like his uncle than I realized,* she thought. She didn't want his anger focused on herself, as he frequently did.

"We will have a special visitor for Martinmas dinner tonight," Margaret said to distract him. He raised his eyebrow, interested. "Sir David Lindsay will be joining us."

"Sir Lindsay?" her son's voice rose. She knew he would be happy. Lindsay was his companion in his childhood, his entertainer, his flyting partner. He taught her son the art of poetry and to play the lute. She was indebted to him for his loyal service to her son. "Well, maybe we will have a flyting tonight after all," he smiled before he turned and left the room.

"Let's finish this letter to my brother, his Highness, before we need to prepare for dinner." Margaret had to find a way to convince her brother that she was on his side, while maintaining her loyalty to Scotland and her son. It was a delicate balance.

Chapter 10

MAGGIE

THE DINNER WAS SET up in the king's outer hall. The king's chambers had sat unused for almost three years while James remained in Angus's control. Maggie admired the stenciled blue border surrounding the room in strawberry vines, remembering the times she hid in the cupboard. The main table was in front of the fireplace, the red lion of Scotland looking down from his spot above the mantel. Even though this meal was more intimate, the invited earls were still placed according to rank. But David had the seat of honor. Maggie was sandwiched between her father and her husband. Somehow, her father had convinced James to allow her husband to stay at Stirling without consulting her. She was only the wife, her opinion didn't matter. And it annoyed her that they went behind her back. She pushed it out of her mind and focused on her view of the king, reveling in the flittering he caused in her stomach. Since the banquet, she had wanted to feel the heat between them again. His eyes sparkled as he and David talked, sending the stirring of wings inside her.

"I'm so glad you're here, David," James said, leaning back in his scissor chair, tossing his arm over the red velvet back.

"Ay, and not a moment too soon, from what I've heard," Lindsay replied, matching the easy posture of the king. Even though he was only thirty-eight, Lindsay wore the longer hair of the older generation. James smiled, but did not respond, deferring to his former governor who had instilled in him a love of music, literature, and of course flyting.

"They got to you with vices, your Highness," Lindsay continued, and James nodded. "Gambling, setting you up to lose! And not continuing with your education. That," he jabbed his finger on the table, "is the biggest crime! A king should have a complete and well-rounded education, but instead they plied you with women!"

"A much more rigorous education than you would have provided!" James laughed. Maggie stuffed a poached pear into her mouth to stop herself from giggling along with the king. Maybe she did like his vulgarity. It kicked up the swooping of starlings in her.

"I would have held you up to a royal standard, not encouraged you to be so base. You were a tender and young king," he shook his head. "And taken advantage of by that blackguard for his own benefit."

"Well, don't worry, my old friend," James slapped Lindsay's back. "He will pay and pay handsomely. And you and I must polish my old flyting skills so I can catch more bonnie lasses!"

"You need to find a wife," Lindsay said under his breath. He had lived through James's father's illegitimate children before his marriage to the Queen Mother and didn't want to see the situation repeated by his son.

"I'll let you know when I'm in the market for one so you can negotiate on my behalf!" James laughed and threw back his goblet of wine. He rubbed his hands together. "Now, about that flyting...." He stood up.

"I'll go first, since you are too much of a gentleman to properly flyte the king," James said. A hush fell over the chamber, only the crackle from the fire echoed across the room. He drew himself up and placed his hand over his doublet.

"Sir Lindsay, bribour bard, my flyting will I use to gritly shame you. Evil you are and descended from Beelzebub, but while you may be from low, you are not hung so low, and so must resort to bestial fucking," James smirked, and bowed after uttering the last word. Maggie felt the heat rise, throbbing in her ears.

Her husband placed his hand over hers, "You shouldn't hear this rough poetry."

She recoiled, anger flaring like a badger ready to strike. "If this is who our king is, then I want to know," she turned her back on him, watching James flop back into his chair with a look of triumph. Lindsay stood, wagging his head from side to side.

"My boy, when will you learn? A person such as you is an easy target. Like a boisterous bull, you buck and ride and any old hole will satisfy. A scullery maid taken by force has given the spankie pox to your lower hide. You can never rest from leaping on whores." Lindsay bowed low as he said his final word. The silence reverberated in the hall. No one seemed to breathe. Lindsay had just insinuated that the king had the French disease, syphilis, and everyone awaited his reprimand. The Queen Mother's face was stone, betraying no emotion. James slapped the arms of his chair and burst into laughter.

"Oh, David! You bested me again, just like when I was your pupil. Clearly, I still have a lot to learn from you! I look forward to flyting often." He stood and clasped Lindsay's arm. "And in response to your flyting…. Well, how can I come back from that?" he chuckled, lower this time. "Except to award you an honor for your loyalty and quick wit. Sir David Lindsay, I now pronounce you Snowdon Herald." The collective gasp of air almost extinguished the candles. Snowdon Herald, as part of the Lyon Court, was responsible for all the grant of arms and records of genealogies. He was also be responsible for protecting the rights of the people and the crown, as well as representing the crown on diplomatic missions. A high honor indeed!

"Your Highness, I am deeply honored and for once speechless!" Lindsay bowed, knee touching the floor, arm folded across the breast. James raised him up.

"It is a much deserved office for a morally incorruptible man," James held his shoulders. He turned and lifted his chalice. "And a toast to the new Snowdon Herald!"

"Slange var!" roared from every person in the chamber. It echoed in Maggie's head as she swallowed the wine, watching James over the top of the goblet. His face beamed, like a satisfied cat sìth, the mythical black cat that haunted the Highlands, and Maggie wanted to be a cat with him—chase after rabbits, romp in the forest, play pranks on the people. Her head was buzzing, the wine affected her motor skills and the whirling threw her off balance. James looked at her and his eyes changed, darkened with a new emotion, which Maggie did not recognize. But her husband did. He stiffened next to her, coiling to protect his property. Maggie shrank away from Robert, resentful that she was his wife—anybody's wife! She knew as a woman, she was her father's responsibility to use to strengthen her family and then she was her husband's obligation and her duty was to produce an heir and serve Robert. She forced her face to remain neutral.

After the final course was cleared, James motioned for his lute, which a servant rushed over to him. He tuned the strings, and then plucked the slow, clear melody of "The Ballad of Greysteil." His face relaxed into an amused smirk as he pressed his left fingers onto the neck strings. The song told of the love a knight had for a maiden and how he won her love. Maggie wondered if he was thinking of Elizabeth Shaw, if he loved her like Sir Eger loved Winglayne. Maggie wanted romantic love that Loosepain had for Sir Eger, the desire to be a wife, not the obligation. Robert placed his hand over hers, another reminder that she was not in control of her life, she would never be free to show her true desire. She was a business contract, and now belonged to the man who claimed her with his rough palm. Her first instinct was to pull back, but she was expected to endure the physical touch of a husband. Maggie was glad he was not pressuring her to do more—yet. Desire, mixed with body heat, crawled up her wrist from him. It washed over her, the rich meat turning in her stomach. Maggie turned away from Robert and was surprised to find James staring at her. He sang, his voice thin and tight, and she saw the same desire in his eyes that she felt from her husband. But James's desire kicked up the fluttering inside of her, the flitcherin of a butterfly among the thistles.

"She was clad in scarlet red, and all of fresh gold shone her head," he sang, voice low, heavy with longing, "A fairer creature never seen; Me thinks her coming did me good."

His lips curled into a smile as he repeated the last line, eyes never leaving Maggie's face. She felt her husband's hand tighten, a reflex when one feels their property slipping away. But she remained still, her body tense with desire for this man, the king, who was not her husband, but whose eyes were naked before her, open in their vulnerability. Maggie felt herself lean towards James and caught herself. A jealous husband was a dangerous husband, and she did not want to give Robert a reason to be jealous, no reason to force the execution of her marriage contract. James finished the final chord and broke his gaze away. David clapped and Maggie joined in, almost upsetting her goblet as she wrenched her hand from under her husband's. Robert caught the goblet without taking his glance off her. The clapping echoed in her chest, banging against her ribs. She needed to calm down. James bowed, signaling the end of supper.

Maggie rushed over to the Queen Mother to avoid an awkward parting from her husband. The Queen Mother held onto her husband's arm, the infatuation seeping from her eyes. Maggie followed behind their entwined arms when she felt a hand on her arm. It was the king.

"Meet me at the stables after my mother and her husband fall asleep," he whispered.

"How am I going to do that?" she asked.

"Find a way," he said, slipping away before she could ask more.

She tossed and turned on her straw pallet outside the sleeping chamber as she listened to the Queen Mother having sex. She knew from the crescendo of her moans that it was almost finished and then she could slip away to see what the king wanted. Once the silence perfused the room, she crept out, tossing on one of the Queen Mother's velvet, fur-lined cloaks that she had filched from the armoire to keep her warm, and also to impress the king. What could he want with her, a maid-in-waiting? Her nerves kicked her forward, propelling her towards something she wasn't sure of, but wanted to experience all the same. She crossed the inner close and rounded the chapel to head for the stables, exhaling white clouds of breath.

James was holding two horses at the entrance to the barn. He was dressed as he was the night of his escape—as a yeoman, not the king. The collar of his coarse spun shirt curved up his neck, making his hair look brown, not russet. His eyes scanned her as she walked up.

"I knew you'd find a way," he smirked. She tried to look annoyed, but he stepped close to her and she felt the heat radiate from him. "You can't wear this cape." He grabbed the velvet cloak. She pulled back.

"Why not? It's warm," she hoped he couldn't hear her heart thudding and betraying her—his energy vibrating along her arms.

"It is a noble's cape. We need to blend in where we are going," he said, easing it from her shoulders. She shivered in her kirtle with a thin smock over it. The cloak was the lone luxury item she thought to grab from the Queen Mother's wardrobe.

"Where are we going?" she asked, teeth chattering.

He chuckled, "Oh Magpie, have you even ever left Stirling?" he said and walked into the stable. She made a face at his back and then regretted it. She blew on her hands, wondering how she could act more mature. He returned with a simple wool cloak and fastened it at her neck with a metal pin, covering her shoulders. His breath rustled the hairs on her neck.

"I've left Stirling," she said and yanked away from him. The fluttering inside of her generated its own heat. He nodded. Irritation flared at his presumption of knowing her.

"Anyway, you don't know what I've been doing," she said. His eyes darkened, jaw clenched. Immediately she regretted referencing his captivity. She began to apologize, but he cut her off.

"You're right," he snapped. "I was forced to be away from everything that was familiar and good. The Douglases saw to that. But they also taught me stories about my father. And this was one of his rituals. I thought maybe you would like to have a little adventure."

"What ritual?" she asked the simple question rather than the uncomfortable ones about what the Douglases took from him.

"We're going out riding, as commoners!" he threw the reins of the smaller horse to her. She fumbled them in her surprise, and they fell on the ground. "My father used to do this. Sir Lindsay told me that my father would disguise himself as a commoner and ride out to see the condition of his people. He said it gave my father the true feelings of his people and not just what the nobles wanted to hear. I want to hear what the commoners think about me."

"But no one is up and out right now," Maggie said, picking up the reins.

"We will use this as practice for when the people are out," he laughed and swung up onto his horse. She looked back at the royal palace, thinking of the warmth from the fire and the hot stones the Queen Mother had placed under her straw mattress. "Do you want to have an adventure with me?" he asked.

Maggie saw an openness in his face that was not present in the castle. His eyes were clear, the shield lowered that blocked his true feelings. She wanted very much to have an adventure with James, and she saw that he was unguarded. She nodded and mounted her pony. Her seat slipped and she clutched the wooden pommel to keep from falling. She clucked her horse to catch up to James.

He led them through the back entrance and down the steep road leading off the cliff top that Stirling sat on. Her breath came in fast white spurts as she struggled to keep up with James and not fall off her horse. The night was dark, clouds blocking the moon and stars, muffling all noise. The road leveled off as they moved through the quiet village and toward the River Forth. He slowed his horse and Maggie rode alongside him.

"I think the people will be with me," he said, but doubt crept between the words.

"Of course they will. You are their king," she said, sounding too simple and naïve. "All of the important earls came to Stirling to show their support."

"Yes, but I don't know who I can trust. Who is there for me and not for what they can gain for themselves. That's the problem with the Scottish nobles. They look out for themselves. And no one really looks after the common people. If they love and support me, I can turn this country into the northern jewel that my father intended. I can finish his work that he wasn't able to complete before my uncle ordered his death." Pain surrounded him in the silence. Maggie wanted to reach out and comfort him.

"You can trust me," she said. He lifted his dark eyes, but not his emotional shield. "I know it isn't much and I'm only a girl, but I will help you make our country great like your father envisioned."

His shoulders relaxed as he exhaled. "Let's walk the horses along the river," he pulled up his horse and dismounted. Maggie swung her leg over and slid down the mare's side. Her foot caught the edge of a rock and she stumbled. James caught her arm as she knocked into his chest.

"I've got you Magpie," he said, his breath on her forehead. She tried to pull away, embarrassed and awkward. "I think you are much more than just a girl. I remember how your brother and I would tease you. But you got us back. Remember when you thought that I had spilled ink on your verses that you wrote? And you got me back by ripping up my Latin exercises?" he laughed, chest vibrating against hers. She leaned into him, pulled into his mirth.

"Yes, and Master Dunbar was so mad at me. He told my father to punish me, but my father didn't," she giggled, giddy from his heat.

"No, he never would punish you. You have always been his favorite," he brushed his hand over her coif, fire in his eyes. The movement sent waves through her body.

"No, *you* are his favorite. My brother knows he loves you more than him," she smiled.

"He is like a father to me, since I never had a chance to know my father," he said. His hand cupped her face, lifting her chin so he could see into her eyes. The fluttering threatened to explode out of her stomach, her legs turning to jelly. "You're so young," he said as his eyes moved over her face.

"I'm not *that* young," she bristled, annoyed that he was dismissing the most adult feelings she'd ever had. "I'm almost fourteen, just two years younger than you."

"Have you ever even kissed anyone?" he pulled her face towards his. She held her breath. "Have you kissed your husband?" He spoke softly, but she heard the jealousy.

"No," she tried to jerk away. "It's just a contracted marriage." She wanted to tell him that it meant nothing to her, that she was chained in a loveless marriage, when she wanted to feel the passion of love.

He wrapped his free arm around her back, preventing her from turning away. "The Douglases made sure I had lots of women."

"Why are you telling me this?" she grasped his wrist and tried to wrest her face out of his grip. Now that monster jealousy gripped her, replacing the butterflies she had felt before.

"I want to make sure you understand who I am. Even though I didn't know him, I'm just like my father," his mouth sagged. "I want you to know everything—even the disgusting and mean. I want to know if you'll still support me." He let go of her face, but she didn't move. Her heart hammered against her chest.

"James," she let his Christian name roll off her tongue, vibrate her throat. She paused to see if he would get angry, if she were being disrespectful. He looked defenseless, vulnerable in a way she never thought a king could be. "I might not be as experienced as you are, but I am strong. You won't scare me away."

She placed her hand on his smooth face, pale hand against a

flurry of freckles. He leaned into her hand.

"But I like it better when you aren't being vulgar and arrogant," she said. He laughed and tightened his hold on her waist.

"I think I can make you like it when I'm vulgar and arrogant too," his voice was husky with emotion. She rolled her eyes, unwilling to show him that she agreed.

"And you're back to that," her voice was light, playful.

"Just let me teach you," he whispered, leaning closer. Maggie tilted her head and felt his breath on her lips. She reached up, crushing her mouth on his. His kiss was powerful, potent. Her legs buckled as the feeling moved from her lips, down her stomach and into the base of her abdomen. He held her up, using his tongue to open her mouth, sending more waves through her body. Her own tongue entwined with his, seeking to be closer, wanting the waves to crash over her.

Finally, he pulled back. "Mags, I will have you. I don't care that you are married. It doesn't matter. I'm the king."

"I know, and you take everything you want," she joked, but his face remained serious.

"Yes, but I won't take you… not until you are ready," he said. Maggie didn't understand what he meant. She understood the mechanics of sex, she heard his own mother every time her husband visited her.

"You *think* you're ready," he said, "But not yet. Not tonight." Her heart fell. The adrenaline was still surging through her body. If his kiss made her feel waves of ecstasy, what would his body feel like moving over hers? The strength of her disappointment surprised her.

"We've got all the time in the world," he said as he kissed her again, tongue flicking against her teeth, the waves crashing again. She pulled back this time.

"What if I don't want you then? What if I get bored?" she tried to act indifferent, but he saw right through her.

"Then you'll go to your husband and I'll find someone who is willing. God knows there are enough of them," his comment stung, the accuracy and coldness striking her from both sides. Her face fell. Silence settled in the space between them. There was no heat between her and her husband, no waves, no vibrating. Only with James.

"But they aren't me," she broke the silence. He grinned, teeth glowing in the dim night.

"Look who's being arrogant now," he pinched her behind. She jumped in shock, yelping, which made him laugh harder.

"We deserve each other. And you won't get bored of me. I promise," he said.

"Then you will never get rid of me. That I promise," she said, smiling at her own brazenness. He brought this out in her, allowed her to express what she really felt instead of keeping her own mask on which she had to wear while in the castle. She wanted to always feel this way—no mask hiding who she truly was.

Chapter 11
The Queen Mother

MARGARET WAS PREPARING THE castle for Christmas, ordering Maggie to tack the holly to the mantel in the king's outer chamber, "I think it needs to go higher in the middle."

Maggie set her lip, annoyed at the minute details Margaret insisted upon. Well, she would have to suffer for it because this was her son's first Christmas at Stirling since his escape. There was much to celebrate! Her former husband had surrendered his castle, Tantallon, after Martinmas and a five year peace had been signed by her brother and her son. Harry, her brother, was so caught up in ending his marriage and marrying a new whore that he couldn't be bothered to turn Angus over to Scottish authorities. The only blemish on the perfect Christmas gift.

She picked up another holly branch. "Here, add this to the empty spot on the left."

Maggie looked at the branch and the overflowing mantel, the green branches contrasting with the great Scottish coat of arms painted above. The red lion jumped off the wall, framed by two crisp white unicorns, the mythical animal of Scotland. She saw no place to put more holly.

"Fine, fine, let's cover the window sill," Margaret said, irritation edging into her voice. *Why did this child question everything?* But still, her spirit did comfort her and made her hope that her own daughter was being indulged and taken care of. Although if Harry *was* able to procure a divorce decree from the pope, what would happen to her daughter then?

"And where is the Yule log? It needs to be ready for the feast," she said, spinning on her heel, almost running into a young girl who curtsied deeply. Margaret looked her up and down, trying to place her. *She must be one of the palace servants*, she thought.

"I'm sorry for the intrusion, Queen Mother," she spoke from her curtsey. "But I need to speak with you regarding an urgent matter that involves the king."

Her son? Margaret's heart jumped, apprehension crowding out her Christmas spirit.

"What of him?" She said, smoothing the front of her dress. The girl fidgeted, looking at Maggie.

"I'd rather speak in private," she said, so Margaret motioned for Maggie to leave the room, which she did with haste.

"Yes? What matter must you discuss?"

"I tried to speak with his highness directly, but I could never get an audience with him," the girl wrung her hands. How old was she? Sixteen? Fifteen? Her face was so familiar but her identity would not come to Margaret.

"And why should you have an audience with my son the king?" she snapped, irritated that this girl thought she was important enough for the king's audience.

"I'm going to have his baby," the girl burst out, covering her face in her hands.

So. Margaret's eyes narrowed as she remembered his father's children before they were married. After her triumphant arrival in Scotland, the impromptu first meeting, him riding out in an informal jacket, his lute slung over his back, the way he raised her up from her curtsy and kissed her, she felt a rising excitement to be a queen and a wife. She remembered her wedding day, the white damask gown embroidered in gold and edged with crimson velvet that she couldn't stop rubbing, the trumpet sleeves pinned back to reveal the white silk lining, the train carried by Norfolk's wife. On her head was a gold crown, edged in pearls and gemstones, over a silk coif, her hair unbound, flowing over her shoulders and down her back. Her husband, even though he was sixteen years older than her, looked stunning in his doublet of crimson satin, slashed to reveal white silk undershirt, layered over scarlet hose and a regal robe of white damask embroidered in gold.

After the wedding festivities of food, dance, and jousting tournaments, celebrating not only a marriage, but a union of two kingdoms which promised enduring peace, he brought her to Stirling, her wedding present, the fortress on the granite hill. And that was where a horrifying discovery was made. Housed in this castle, *her* castle, James introduced her to his five children that he fathered before their marriage. Three girls and two boys. They all lived at the castle, reminders of his sexual indiscretions. And he was not ashamed of these bastard children. No! He was openly affectionate and proud of his issue. Her father had never been unfaithful to her mother, and if he were, those bastards would never be treated as natural sons or daughters. Margaret realized that morals were much looser in the Scots highlands. And even though she was thirteen and not ready to have children of her own, Margaret had realized that she needed to produce a male heir before one of these children would challenge for the crown. Now the cycle was continuing with her son.

Margaret remembered her face. This was the girl slinking out of her son's chamber after his welcome banquet. She was a minor noble's daughter, nowhere near good enough for her son. Her dress was pushed out in front, raising her hemline, revealing her shoes. Having been pregnant eight times herself, Margaret guessed she was around six months pregnant.

"You'll give birth in March or April," she said; it was not a question. The girl uncovered her face.

"What will happen now?" she asked Margaret.

"I will do what my husband's caretakers did for his illegitimate children," she breathed deeply. "You will receive the best care while you are carrying royal blood. Once the baby is born, he will live here at Stirling just as the king's illegitimate siblings did."

"But what about me?"

Margaret looked at the girl. She remembered how bitter she had been about the woman that her husband had loved—and still loved—whose evidence ran around the castle, Janet Kennedy. How she had to share space at thirteen with a woman who shared her husband's bed more often than she did, who was his confidant in a way she could not be since she was still a child. She shuddered as she remembered how quickly she had to grow up. This girl was older than she had been when she first came to Scotland, but Margaret at least had been a queen.

"A husband will be found for you, someone suitable for the mother of the king's child," she paused. The girl was looking at her with curious horror. "Don't worry. You will be taken care of."

Margaret went to walk away, but one more thing had to be made clear. "And in case you had the idea, you will never marry my son," she said over her shoulder. "His wife will be a princess from a great kingdom, not an easy Scottish mare who opens her legs to gain a higher position." She strode out of the hall, not needing to see the surprised alarm on the girl's face. Maggie was waiting outside the chamber.

"Find your father and tell him I have a great matter to discuss with him in the king's presence chamber," she said to Maggie. "It appears that I am going to be a grandmother."

1530

Chapter 12

James

JAMES BECAME A FATHER less than a year ago to a healthy son also named James, who was housed at Stirling. He was building on his father's legacy. The birth of his son proved that he was virile, no matter the downturned mouth it gave his mother. An Irish nurse moved into Stirling to assure that his son had the best nutrition available to make him grow strong. He wanted to father more children than his father had, to prove he was just as good of a king and potent ruler.

But while he continued to have sex with Scottish ladies, he abstained from taking Maggie. Magpie, the moniker that ignited the fire inside of her, turning her hazel eyes a delicious green, was growing into a beautiful woman. It was a dangerous game, he knew. She was now almost sixteen and would soon go to her husband's house at Loch Leven. His mother couldn't protect her much longer. And the longer he put off his conquest of her sexually, the closer he got to her emotionally. Only with her could he voice his concerns over the Scottish nobles, his frustration with Angus and his uncle for refusing to give him over. She had all of the ammunition to crush him. And yet he ran to her again and again when he needed to be reminded of a time before his innocence had been ripped away by his stepfather—and by her inability to act, his own mother.

His dark eyes clouded, the shadow draping his face. Angus. That man destroyed his childhood and now James was going to destroy him and his family. The anger burnt off the Scottish winter that surrounded him. The focus of his rage became the Scottish borders.

Angus and his supporters were stirring up trouble, allowing reivers to raid and pillage all along the English border, causing instability in the region. James knew this was his moment to show his uncle and Angus that he would not stand for insurrection in *his* kingdom. He needed to quash this unrest immediately. Maybe once he showed his uncle that he could control his kingdom, Henry would return Angus and James could have his revenge. But his uncle was also problematic. He was consumed with getting a divorce from his long-time queen because she could not give him a male heir. James's mother said it was because he found a new whore. James didn't understand the English way. His uncle should just produce an heir with this other woman. That was the Scottish way, the way his father had done. The English were too proper, but devious at the same time. How could he know exactly what his uncle was thinking when it was filtered through the diplomatic hands of his chancellor Cardinal Wolsey, who equivocated to place himself and his uncle in the best light?

And so he called his advisors together at Stirling to discuss the plan to bring the borders under control. He lost two of his most trusted and experienced nobles last year—both the old Earl of Arran and Argyll had passed away. James worried that the earl of Eglinton would be next. Eglinton fought with his father at battle of Sauchieburn, which meant he had to be at least seventy years old. Despite his hunched back and grizzled hands, his eyes burned with the same hatred for the Douglases, who burnt his castle down on their way out of Scotland.

"The Armstrongs are availing themselves to extort moneys from our people on the borders and destroying the property of those who don't pay. You all know the Douglases are encouraging these attacks and providing arms to the rebels," James said. His assembly of "secret" counselors nodded. The Armstrongs were the leading clan along the Scottish-English border, and their blatant extortions were causing problems on the English side of the border, angering his uncle. And he knew Angus was behind it all, providing the Armstrongs with supplies and money.

"Of course the Earl of Anguish is behind all of this!" James Hamilton of Finnart said, pounding his stout fist on the table. James tried to suppress a smile. Finnart was his third cousin, the

69

illegitimate son of the deceased 1st Earl of Arran. Before he died, his father had legitimized him and appointed him the guardian of his younger brother, the 2nd Earl of Arran. A common fixture at Stirling and Linlithgow during his kidnapping, he was a source of entertainment for James. Even though he was fourteen years older than James, Finnart was his peer, a quick wit and a rouge. He loved to carouse for women and hunt—both past times he taught to James. With four illegitimate children of his own, he made sure James was well acquainted with women and enjoyed them as much as Finnart did. He didn't have much political experience, but James included him for comments like this. James also trusted his opinion on anything French because he had spent time at the French court.

"It's more than just Angus," his brother, Earl of Moray, said, trying to keep Finnart from influencing his brother. Moray was well aware that alienating the nobles at the borders would push them toward supporting the English.

"But you have been in the Highlands. What do you know about the southern borders?" Finnart shot back. James quieted him with a hand movement. Finnart and his brother did not trust each other after the murder of Earl of Lennox, during his attempt to rescue James in 1526. His brother would love to see Finnart punished, but James wasn't so sure of his part in the murder. He refused to believe that his friend would support his enemy.

"Brother, I am aware that it is more than just the Douglases, however you cannot deny that they are providing weapons and support to the Armstrongs to create unrest," James said. Moray nodded, knowing he needed to keep a cool head rather than act from emotion. James admired that about his brother. "But we also need to recognize that Angus should have been responsible for keeping the peace in the borders, not turning a blind eye to raiders and thieves. And Johnnie Armstrong has repeatedly bragged of black mailing our loyal subjects in the borders for his own gain. He is the one we need to make an example of."

Robert Maxwell, who was from the southern borders, said, "Yes, the borders are a lawless place, but they always have been. Armstrong has gotten haughty and needs to be reprimanded so that order can be restored. But your Highness, we also need to be allowed to run the borders in a way to keep peace between England as well."

James nodded, his uncle would be angry if they entered into English lands to maintain order. Care needed to be taken.

"What about a hunting trip to the borders?" Thomas Erskine said, looking up from his stack of papers. James could always count on Thomas to come up with a clear plan.

"Yes! A hunting trip! We all could use a good hunting trip to the country, and we can lure Armstrong there under that guise," he sat back into his chair with satisfaction.

"A solid plan, my lord," Maxwell said, frowning. Part of his wealth was gained by raiding and thieving against the English at the borders, and he had provided support to the Armstrongs when he was feuding with the Johnson clan. Maxwell had shown no disloyalty to the crown in preference for his clan loyalties, but James couldn't count on his support to fight against the English with the Johnsons. He dismissed all but Thomas. The men filed out of the inner chamber.

"I'll see you at the hunt—for women and stags!" Finnart called over his shoulder. James shook his head, always the joker. Once everyone had departed and the door latched, he turned to Thomas.

"We can't take Maxwell with us. He's too close to the reivers himself," James tapped his lip. "We will have to think of a pretense for him to remain."

"Let's keep him in Edinburgh to work on the Justice council," Thomas said, jotting down notes, his brown hair curling over one eye.

"Great idea Thomas! That is why I'm glad you're my secretary," James picked at a splinter under the arm of his chair. Thomas was Maggie's cousin, although they weren't that close. He wanted to pry into Maggie's family life, but he knew that wasn't decorous. But Thomas was so loyal, James wished he were closer to Maggie's family and could give him information about her.

"I'll take Moray with me since he has no affiliation with the borders," he changed the subject, hoping to throw Thomas off. James couldn't reveal his vulnerability—conditioned to hide his true feelings so Angus couldn't exploit them.

"Of course," Thomas was writing again. "I'd like to attend as well."

"Oh no, Thomas! I need you in Edinburgh with Maxwell. You're the only one I trust to keep him here so he doesn't warn his supporters at the borders," James said. Thomas's face fell in disappointment. James wondered why. Thomas was not a hunter, he was bookish.

"Why would you want to go on a hunt?" he asked. Thomas shrugged, apparently keeping secrets of his own. James let it drop and focused on preparing for his border trip.

———————

Two months later, Scotland broke free of the grip of winter and the buttercups blanketed the field below Stirling in yellow. Since yellow was one of the Stewart colors, James took that as a good omen for the party to depart for the borders to punish the Armstrong clan. Maggie had stood at his mother's side, but he couldn't look at her. They had argued the night before.

"Send your brother," she demanded, gripping his arm. "You don't need to go there yourself."

He shook off her arm. "Of course I do," he said, snarling at her. "I'm the king. *I* enforce order in *my* kingdom. No one but me."

Her nose flared in anger. "Why are you so stubborn? Don't you think this could be a trap? That your uncle is going to have men waiting to kidnap you and take you to England, like he tried to do to your father?"

He balked at the mention of his father. Fear seized him, making him angry. Why did she have to voice his worst fear? He towered over her and said, "I'm the King of Scots. He doesn't have power in *this* country."

"Fine," she said through clenched teeth. "Go ahead and risk everything you love for your stupid ego." She turned on her heel, her hood slapping his chest. He seized both of her arms. She cried out in pain, but he did not loosen his hold.

"Don't you ever turn away from me," he hissed as he forced her to turn around and face him.

"You're the one turning away from me, running to your death," she said, anger firing golden in her eyes. "You make me crazy when you act just like your uncle—an arrogant king."

The anguish in her words caused him to drop her arms. He believed the hatred in her eyes, that it was for him.

"Then you should be glad that I'm going," he said and he left the room before she could fling a smart retort and hurt him more. She would see. He would come back and make her beg for his affection again.

The ride to the borders was rough, adrenaline urging him to ride hard. In his mind was the fear that it was a trap, that Maggie was right. She knew things about him that he couldn't even identify in himself. He regretted arguing with her, knowing he was wrong for putting up his wall with her. Sometimes he didn't know when to be James and stop being the king.

Chapter 13

THE QUEEN MOTHER

MARGARET READ THE LETTERS again. One from her son, one from her brother. She was caught between two worlds—the England of her childhood, which would always have her heart, and Scotland the fickle subject over whom she was queen. Her son's letter told of the capture of a reiver leader, Johnnie Armstrong. Margaret's heart dropped as she remembered the English ambassador goading James by saying James could not continue as sovereign king while the Armstrongs burnt churches and property on the western border. She sighed as she read about her son inviting Armstrong on a hunting expedition, only to have him arrested and executed by hanging. The Armstrong clan had turned Johnnie into a martyr. But in his letter, her son said it was going to define his kingship and restore order to the borders. He said the common people were now safe from raiders and thieves and loved him for it. Margaret hoped so.

She flipped her brother's letter open to read again. The pope had refused to grant him a divorce from Catherine. She was claiming to be a virgin when she married Henry. Margaret chuckled. This may have been the one time in his life that her brother couldn't convince someone to yield to his desires. Catherine was holding to her story that her marriage to Arthur had not been consummated, and no one had definitive evidence to prove otherwise, even though Margaret believed they had. After all of the problems her brother had given Margaret when she wanted a divorce from Angus, it was just retribution for Harry to be denied by the pope. Especially when he had told a French ambassador that it was impossible for anyone to lead a more shameful life than Margaret.

The good news was that after months of seclusion in Northern England, Harry had summoned her daughter to London. Angus had taken her daughter Margaret to England with him when he fled, just to spite the Queen Mother. Her notoriously extravagant brother had made sure her daughter was received well, purchasing her gowns in tawny velvet, black damask, and black silk lined with velvet, in addition to kirtles, stomachers, and collars—far more than he had ever given to Margaret when she was in need after Catherine killed Margaret's husband. She tamped down the jealous flare and tried to be happy for her daughter. Thankfully, her daughter was staying with Margaret's sister Mary at Suffolk Place, and not in Harry's house, where there were two camps, Catherine's and Anne Boleyn's. Anne was the niece of the Duke of Norfolk, the man who had led the English Navy against Margaret's husband at Flodden. This affirmed her belief that he was self-serving, pushing his own niece onto her brother in order to gain even more power for himself.

Margaret knew her sister's feelings for Harry's first wife and was sure that Mary was grooming Margaret's daughter to think as she did. Mary had met Anne Boleyn when she had married the old King of France, Louis XII in 1514. Anne had been a maid of honor to François's wife, Claude, where she was said to be charming and gracious. Margaret had to shake her head when she heard that Mary had married her true love, Charles Brandon, after Louis XII had died. Harry was so angry that she married without his permission—and to his best friend! They both were banned from court, but Harry could not stay mad at them for long. Margaret was sure that Mary was glad not to be in the middle of the drama at Hampton Court, since she made no secret of her dislike of Anne, especially when Harry gave a banquet and made Mary sit beneath her. The quill almost ripped through the paper when Mary wrote to Margaret about the incident.

She remembered before her daughter's birth, fleeing from Scotland under the cover of night to escape from the Duke of Albany, who was proclaimed regent after her marriage to Angus. Ard, who was there to comfort her after her husband James's death, who held her in his strong arms as she cried herself to sleep. Her grief clouded her judgment and she married him, despite the mandate that said she could be regent only if she didn't remarry. Harry had begged her to come to England with Ard, her baby son, and the young king. He promised that he would protect them all from the Scottish nobles, but Margaret knew if she fled, she would cost her son all claims to the Scottish throne. She couldn't do that to her son, the rightful king.

So she stayed in her adopted homeland and was humiliated into handing over her own son. She had retreated to Stirling, the impenetrable gift from her husband. Ard pleaded with her to leave through an underground tunnel.

"My family always says it is better to hear a lark in the open country than a mouse cheep in the fortress," he said, but she would not subject her son, the King of Scots, to that humiliation.

As more troops amassed at the gate of Stirling, she knew she would have to turn her sons over. She dressed James up in royal robes of purple and placed a heavy golden crown on his little head to remind these men of exactly whom they were taking possession. She put on a crimson velvet gown and her golden necklace with the garnet pendant, which was a gift from her late husband. The dress had a high waist and emphasized her pregnant stomach. They wouldn't dare hurt a pregnant queen, even if she was pregnant with Ard's baby. She approached the lower portcullis, James clutching her hand but not crying.

"Open the gate and relinquish his Grace," Albany said in French as he approached the gate alone. He wore the flat brimmed hat that was in fashion in France and had a short beard—a definite sign that he was not a native Scot. She shook her head, clutching James's hand, knowing she would have to turn her son over to her enemy, but also wanting to surrender her son on her terms. His eyes clouded with weariness. *Good*, Margaret thought. Scotland would wear him down as it was trying to do to her.

"You need to promise me that I will see my sons again," she pulled herself up. He nodded. "And I want Lord Erskine to be named his governor," she continued. Albany agreed to all of her demands and she gave James the key to open the portcullis. She was led to Edinburgh, trusting the word of Albany, who was more French than Scots. The first of many Scottish betrayals.

And so she fled when she was eight months pregnant, heavy and clumsy, summoning all of her strength to ride to the border and be reunited with her husband. She didn't know all of the sorrow she would suffer because of that decision. Ard left her in England and went back to make a deal with Albany. He abandoned her and took up with the woman to whom he had been engaged before he married Margaret, Jane Stewart, and stole the rents from her dowager properties. She wouldn't discover that until later.

When she finally did get back to Scotland, her younger son was dead, her older son barely recognized her, and her husband was living on her rents and in her castle with his whore lover and their bastard. She had more of a reason to divorce him that Harry had to divorce Catherine, yet her own brother fought her over it, cutting off her money and inheritance. She realized too late that she had only been a pawn in the Douglas's struggle for power over the Stewarts.

Maggie sat in the window seat, lip pursed as she worked on her embroidery. How much longer could Margaret keep her? She was almost sixteen. Her husband had been patient, but soon she would need to go to Loch Leven. Margaret's own first husband had been patient with her, subsidized by his own mistresses, but she had been pregnant by the time she was Maggie's age. Selfishly, she wanted to keep the girl to remind her of the daughter who was now a ward of her baby sister, a sister whose company she had enjoyed during her exile in England.

"Maggie, are you eager to go to your husband?" she asked. The girl's head snapped up in horror. Margaret chuckled. "You're going to have to go at some time, you are aware of that."

Maggie swallowed hard, "I.... I know, Queen Mother. It's just that.... I really enjoy being with you." There was something hovering in her voice. What was the girl hiding?

"Of course, but you are now of age to become a wife in more ways than just a piece of paper," she said, wondering if the fear was over stories she had heard about the marital night activities. No, the girl had heard her making love and had to understand that it could be enjoyable. Maggie nodded, dropping her head over her embroidery again.

"Are you afraid of sex?" Margaret pressed. She wanted to understand the reason for the girl's hesitation. Maggie shook her head. "Are you afraid of getting pregnant?" she tried again, remembering her own fear, both real and imagined regarding childbirth. It was an awful cross for women to bear, and dangerous at all points. But it was necessary to legitimize the female existence.

Maggie sighed, "I guess. I guess I'm afraid of it all, moving away from the only family I've ever known, the people who are comfortable to me."

Margaret patted her hand. "You aren't moving to a new country, like I had to do. Loch Leven is not that far. And you will still be invited to celebrations here at Stirling and elsewhere. Has your husband pressured you to come to him?"

Maggie shook her head. "I told him that he has to wait until you're ready," she said, looking up and smiling. Margaret smiled too. Yes, this child knew how to use what was at hand to manipulate. No one would dare to rush Margaret on a decision. After everything she had been though, she would not ever be rushed to act again. She had lost too much by acting impulsively in her past.

"Such a smart lass," she said. "We need to prepare for summer progress."

Maggie jumped up. "I'm going with you?" she gushed. Margaret nodded. Maggie clapped her hands, reminding Margaret that she was still so young.

"Yes, and we will be leaving to meet the king on his way back from his trip to the borders."

Maggie inhaled and seemed to hold her breath. Margaret was excited to see her son again too, and to entertain her husband and the pope's emissary and show off the Scottish countryside. She could see the girl was excited to experience this trip and see the king too.

Chapter 14

MAGGIE

MAGGIE SAT ON THE domed trunk to get it to shut. As the two sides touched, she slammed down the lock and jumped up. The Queen Mother was determined to make this summer's progress the most elaborate show of splendor, which she knew would get back to her brother in England and the kings on the continent. The caravan would travel from Stirling north to the Earl of Atholl's land in the highlands. She knew this might be her last summer that she would be able to go on progress after the conversation she had with her husband.

"So the Queen Mother is taking you on progress," he said, envy biting in his voice. Maggie nodded, trying not to make eye contact. She busied herself with folding a crimson velvet gown, the Queen Mother's favorite.

"After this trip, I want you at Loch Leven. I've been patient. It's time to fulfill your marital contract." He stepped close to her, hoping to intimidate her. She placed her hands on her hips and met his eyes.

"That is not up to me, it's up to the Queen Mother," she said, trying to control the thumping in her chest. While it was the Queen Mother's call, she also knew that Robert could go to her father and force the execution of the marriage contract. And she was angry that he was using this to bully her. She stepped closer to him, her eyes level to his red beard. She yanked on it to lighten the mood. His hooded eyes widened in surprise. "Soon you will have me all to yourself," she said as beguilingly as she could. She had seen how the Queen Mother manipulated her husband, so Maggie tried a little flirting. He wrapped his arms around her and pressed her against him, which was not the response she was expecting. Something hard and throbbing poked her in the stomach. A wave of apprehension crashed over her. His eyes looked wolfish, focused on its prey. Before she could react, he kissed her hard, bruising her lips. She almost pushed him away as an instinct against an attack, but realized that he was her husband. She relented, allowed the kiss, and forced herself not to cringe. His lips felt cold and clammy, so different from James, whose internal fire burned in his thick lips. He broke away.

"I will allow you to go on progress with the Queen Mother," he said, smoothing down his doublet. "But after this summer..." He trailed off, staring at her heaving chest, misinterpreting her breathing for desire instead of the fear that it was.

The Queen Mother burst into her chambers. She stopped short as she saw Maggie's husband.

"Sir Robert, I didn't know you were so concerned about my summer progress," she said in a flat tone. Robert bowed before her.

"Yes, your Grace," he took her outstretched hand and kissed it. "Is there anything that you need from the royal butcher?" Maggie smirked. One word from the Queen Mother and he was put into his place, the servant.

"I provided Lord Erskine with a list. He may want a word with you," she said, the threat not needed to be spoken. If he made the Queen Mother unhappy, she would dismiss him from Stirling. He caught Maggie's eye before he turned to leave. They were full of desire mixed with frustration. After he left, she turned to Maggie.

"Enjoy this trip, Maggie lass. It will probably be the last one I can take you on."

Maggie felt the tears forming and swallowed them down. She couldn't let the Queen Mother see how upset this made her. No, only James could see how much this last summer progress meant to her.

Maggie rode the Queen Mother's tamest ambler up to the highlands, in the middle of the procession, which included horses, dressed in the king's livery, pulling carts containing the king's royal bed, tapestries, gold plate and cups. The rutted road led them through sheep-shorn meadows, skirting the Ochil Hills. They overnighted at Methven Castle, outside of Perth.

The next morning, the party started on the muddy road, and the flat land became rolling emerald hills, punctuated with lilac from the thistle flowers. At Atholl Castle, the earl met the party and led them northeast and into the Glen Tilt Valley, along the shore of the river. They climbed a small rise and the rustic palace built for James came into view. It was on the south side of the river, woven green birch branches arching between two wooden towers that soared into the air. The roof was green thatch woven to blend in with the countryside. Maggie gasped—it looked like a fairy castle, the true home of cat sith! Maggie hoped that she would have an opportunity to catch the mythical creature with James. Her heart leapt at the chance to apologize to him for her behavior before he left to the boarders.

They dismounted, leaving their horses in the meadow, and crossed the wooden drawbridge that spanned the artificial moat made by diverting the nearby river. Maggie followed at the rear of the Queen Mother's retinue under the woven portcullis, entering the palace, flattening a bed of greenery and flowers, so thick that it looked like a garden. There were white blossoms, purple primrose, yellow buttercup, and pink thrifts dotting the green thrushes. Hanging on the green birch walls were tapestries from Stirling on the north wall and real glass windows built into the young green branches of the south wall. Maggie circled herself in an awed silence.

"Not a bad place for a hunting trip," James said into her ear, vibrating the hairs, sending shivers down her spine. She turned to reply, but the Queen Mother narrowed her eyes, aware of the attraction between them. Maggie hurried over to the trucks to begin unpacking and calm her racing heartbeat. There were four different sets of chambers created, one for the king, one for the Earl of Atholl, one for the pope's ambassador, and one for the Queen Mother.

"Let's have an hour rest and change into our hunting apparel," the king said, moving towards his own room.

"Help me into my hunting dress," the Queen Mother demanded. "You will stay here and prepare my wardrobe. We need to impress the pope's ambassador."

Maggie wondered if this was her punishment for allowing the Queen to see her emotions toward her son. After the birth of James's son, the Queen Mother had the mother married off to a minor courtier and moved far from the castle. Only a princess from a powerful country would be good enough for her son. Maggie would need to be more guarded with her emotions for the king.

James walked out to go hunt with his mother and the ambassador without even a glance in her direction. Maggie felt the sting of rejection. She had worried the whole time he was in the borders that it was a trap. She had been wrong, and she wanted to apologize for making him worry because of her fears. She needed to make him understand how much he meant to her, and how little time she had before she was sent to her husband, an eventuality that they both had been avoiding.

After the departure of the hunting party, she laid out the Queen Mother's dresses and brushed the dust from them. Then she busied herself with laying out the golden plates and goblets, the fine glass bowls with thistle and strawberry designs on them. She arranged the cushions on the floor around the low table so they could enjoy dinner Roman style. After the room had been prepared, she went around to the river to wash up. The highland water was so cold, it took her breath away, but she was determined to look beautiful for James, hoping to catch his attention so she could apologize for being too harsh when he left for the borders. Her hair fanned out around her in the frigid water, surrounding her as she wanted James to do. When she could not tolerate the cold any longer, she laid on the bank, allowing the summer sun to dry her chemise and warm her skin. Then, she plucked some heather, which was growing near the water, and rubbed it into her hair, over her shoulders and breasts. She picked some purple mallow blossoms to weave through the Queen Mother's hair.

The hunting party returned with stags to be dressed and prepared by the staff. Maggie trotted after the Queen Mother to help her get ready. She held out the farthingale and the Queen Mother stepped into it, Maggie securing the ties at the waist.

"I found some heather in the meadow," she said, holding it out as a peace offering to the Queen Mother.

"This will make me irresistible to my husband," she chuckled, rubbing the plant over her breasts as Maggie had done earlier to herself. The Queen Mother held her arms in the air and Maggie slipped a dark blue kirtle over her head, smoothing the skirt over the hooped farthingale. The crimson gown was next. The Queen Mother pulled the square neckline down over her chest, and pushed up her breasts so they threatened to spill over the top. After twisting and securing her hair under the coif, Maggie placed the matching crimson hood over the hair and arranged a few of the mallow blossoms in her hair under the hood. The Queen Mother placed carmine rouge on her lips while Maggie held the lead mirror.

"You should use this too, Maggie," she said through pursed lips, patting the color on her thin lips. "You look a little pallid. You might want to get some sunshine while we are hunting these days."

Maggie turned the mirror to herself as the Queen Mother looked into her jewelry box. Her skin looked porcelain, her hair golden waves down her back, making her hazel eyes look golden brown. Would James still find her attractive?

"Well, don't just stare at yourself," the Queen Mother snapped. "Get dressed!"

Maggie sprang into action, her kirtle already on. She pulled out a green velvet dress, which matched the highland meadow. She tried to keep the square neckline up, but the Queen Mother yanked it down. "This is where it should be," she said. Maggie braided her hair, twisted it under her coif and then placed a golden gable over her plaited hair.

"Let's have a nice dinner," the Queen Mother said, hands on Maggie's shoulders. Butterflies flew up from her navel, causing buzzing throughout. She followed behind the Queen Mother, who took her seat to the left of James; her husband seated on her right. Maggie moved to sit on the other side of Lord Methven, but still able to observe James.

James entered the hall, strumming his lute and singing, "And we'll ay go a-roving, a-roving in the night, For then the maids are loving And the stars are shining bright." He was dressed in sumptuous fabrics, but the colors were subdued. His doublet was light green velvet edged with golden braiding. His silk collar was covered in embroidered strawberry vines. A round cap tilted to the left, his auburn hair waving away from it. His legs were strong and muscular in the dark green hose. He looked at Maggie, desire shining in his clear brown eyes. He had grown an auburn goatee, which only highlighted his full lips. Maggie's whole body erupted into shivers.

She knew she should look away, but she couldn't.

"My son, did you write that yourself?" the Queen Mother asked.

"Ay, Mother, I did, and many more," he said, holding Maggie's gaze. She broke his gaze, shaking in nervous anticipation and glanced to the Queen Mother who was frowning. Maggie picked up the goblet in front of her and took a large drink, the claret wine coating her throat, adding to the fire inside her.

"Let's enjoy the banquet and friendship tonight!" he said, raising his own goblet. He settled in to converse with the pope's ambassador during dinner. Maggie savored the claret, its fruity tang making her lightheaded. The Queen Mother ignored her and turned to the conversation.

After dinner, there was a performance by the Highlanders. The men, wearing yellow wool undershirts and belted plaid over garments, blew the bagpipes and pumped their arms to change the pitch. Maggie loved the haunting sound the bagpipes made, imitating the wind swirling across the highland hills and rustling the grasses. The king stood and approached Maggie. He held out his hand, and she had no option but to stand. The wine slowed her limbs, and she stumbled as she tried to stand, her face pressed against his doublet. He placed his hands under her shoulders and lifted her to standing.

"We will take a walk," James said, leading her to the door. Maggie could feel the disgust from the Queen Mother burning her back. She didn't dare look back, and his mother wouldn't dare stop him. She floated alongside of James, over the drawbridge and out into the meadow.

Once they were away from the green palace, Maggie started to apologize for angering him before he left for the boarders, but the words stuck in her throat. Her pride prevented her from speaking. They walked in silence, his hand on her elbow. They walked around the green palace and towards the river. The gabled hood kept slipping down her forehead. Frustrated she ripped it off her head.

"Leave it," he said, stopping her. "And take off your coif too. You have no husband here." He reached under her chin and pulled the laces. Her throat burned where his hand had brushed it.

"Yes, I have no husband here," she said, desire deepening her voice. He pulled the ribbon from her braid, and she reached up to unwind her hair, giving her head a shake. Her hair tumbled over her shoulders in golden waves. "I'm just a maiden here."

He ran his fingers through the waves, wrapping it around his palms. He held it up to his nose. "Heather," he inhaled. "My favorite highland flower. Where else did you put it?" he ran his hand over her collarbone. "Here?"

Her breath caught, heat moving across her shoulder. She shook her head. His eyes fell on the tops of her breasts. "Here?" he said as he lowered his face to her chest. She inhaled and her chest rose to meet his face. His facial hair was soft against her skin, and then he kissed her, flicking his tongue across the top of her dress. She grabbed the hair at the back of his head to keep from falling.

"Mmmmm, yes here," he said, moving back and forth, smelling and kissing her. "How did you know this was my favorite?"

She didn't, but she said, "I know everything about you."

"Does this mean you aren't mad at me for going to the borders?" he straightened up, brown eyes searching her face like a hunting dog who killed the prey before his master arrived. She could end this discomfort with one denial, but she thought disdain would be more alluring.

"No, I'm still angry that you went," she said. "But it turned out well enough." She flipped her hair over her shoulder, hoping James found it beguiling. Her true emotions shook her, imploring her to make amends for doubting him, to let down her wall and let him see her vulnerability.

"Better than well enough. The people love me and know I will not let the nobles take advantage of them. Just like my father," he said. She let him walk a few steps in front of her so she could calm the quivering, steady her voice so that it wouldn't shake when she did apologize.

"Well," she cleared her throat. "I'm sorry...." She choked the words out, "if I was being bad-tempered." She walked away from him, unable to bear the amusement in his eyes when she was trying to be serious. He confused her—was she just a plaything for him like other women were? And if he was just playing with her, for how long? Maggie's heart squeezed, pain that he might not reciprocate her feelings, that he might find her too childish. Every time he kissed her, her legs buckled, her abdomen exploded into tremors, and she felt a passion that no one else gave her—certainly not her husband. And yet, she knew her time with James was short, that after this trip, she would become a wife in person and in name. Her husband would deflower her maidenhood, but Maggie wanted her virginity to be taken by James. He had already told her that he would have her, but Maggie was afraid to ask when, the fear of rejection even greater than her desire for him. This fear pressed her forward into a thistle patch. The thorns from the purple flowers bit into her flesh.

"Ouch!" she said, the sharp sting traveling up her leg, bringing her back from her emotional agony.

"That's a thistle field, ya gailkit," he laughed. *Gailkit*—Scots for a fool. She rubbed at her leg, her confidence in his feelings for her diminished. Just like the thistle, he stabbed at her heart, making her dizzy with desire and confusion. She both wanted him and wanted to punish him for teasing her. Before she could decide which emotion was stronger, he encircled her waist with his arms, straightening her bent body to him. "Oh Magpie, you are by far the more stubborn one."

"Not me," she said, but leaned back into his arms. "That is you, Sir King." He buried his face in her hair, his breath on the back of her neck.

"But I won't be around forever," she swallowed, allowing the desire to win. She needed James to know that their time together was short. "My husband wants me to come to Loch Leven this autumn." He tensed, arms squeezing her, but he remained silent.

"And after your little display tonight, I'm sure your mother will be happy to be rid of me."

He sighed, releasing her. She saw torment in his face. For her? Because he wouldn't have her as his bauble for much longer?

"I'm just another distraction," Maggie said, snapping the purple flower from a thistle, uncertain of her place with him. "Your mother can't wait to marry you off to some wealthy princess." She couldn't keep the bitterness out of her voice. She knew she was ruining their trip, their last trip together before they both had to face the realities of their stations in life.

"Another distraction," he said, walking away from her. Maggie's legs moved to follow him. She would always follow him. "Not to me,

Mags. Not to me." Maybe Maggie had been wrong about his feel-ings, the emotions behind his eyes were stronger, something Maggie had seen when the Queen Mother looked at her husband Muffin.

They walked in silence, both thinking about how everything would change after this trip. Maggie would go to Loch Leven and be another Scottish noble wife. James would send someone to Eu-rope and broker the best marriage possible for Scotland. It was both of their destinies. She couldn't make it different, no matter how much she wanted it to be.

After rounding a hill, they came to a meadow of heather, the scent filling her nose. The green palace was left behind the hill. They were completely alone.

"I'll find a way to keep you at Stirling," he said, kissing her lips, holding her face in his hands. Her arms went around his waist, and she clung to him to keep from being swept along in the tide of de-sire. Nothing mattered except this moment, the openness in James's eyes, the vulnerability they both were able to experience.

Her head tipped back to find his lips in the mess of hair on his face. It tickled her nose as he moved over her face. "I'm the king," he eased her into the heather. His eyes burned with the same passion that Maggie felt, kicking the flitchering against her stomach.

"You're the king, and you always get what you want." She want-ed to sound playful, but desire thickened her voice, emotion edging out the banter. He kissed her neck.

"And I want you," his breath in her ear shook her entire body. She lifted her arms up in silent agreement as he pulled the dress over her head. Her fingers fumbled to undo the fasteners on his doublet and she pushed it off his shoulders. He kissed her chest as he eased her chemise down and exposed her breasts. She arched in delight as his tongue flicked, sending waves across her abdomen. Her play-mate was introducing her to an adult world of amusement she had only heard through the Queen Mother's door. She wanted to feel more, pulled his undershirt over his head, and ran her hands down his naked chest, freckles splashed across his pale skin. Naked, he was her old playmate, just James, not the king, not the man who held the weight of Scotland on his broad shoulders. They were just two souls, wrapped up in their emotions for each other. Maggie knew he never let anyone else see this side of him. He tried to hide it even from her, pretend it wasn't there, this vulnerability, the rawness. But she knew.

His muscles tensed and flexed as he moved his hands down her hips. She untied his hose, and he yanked them down, entering her at once, thrusting, holding himself in her. Her movements were animalistic, hips grinding against his hips, moving rhythmically as his chest undulated above hers, striving to meld into each other. She couldn't discern their separateness, moving as one complete being, no division—this had to be what God had intended for her, to become one with James, to be his partner and help him to lead Scotland. How could this feeling be wrong? And Maggie's insecurities were thrust out of her as if she never had any doubts about James and his feelings for her. They had loved each other their entire lives, and Maggie knew they would for the rest of it. The intensity of this realization built in her, building as she moved her hips, tighter, stronger until it crashed over her in waves of pleasure. She cried out, unable to stop herself. James made a chuffing noise at the same time, spasms racking his body, as he collapsed on her, laying his head on her chest.

"What was that?" Maggie whispered, bathing in a golden haze, her whole body vibrating, feeling an invisible connection to James more complete than she had ever felt for her own husband. He had total power over her, but she wasn't afraid.

"That," he said, kissing her nose, "is why people have sex."

Maggie wrapped her legs around his back. "Let's do it again," she purred, biting his ear, wanting to maintain the golden connection to him. He laughed, kissing her neck, tongue tracing her jaw.

"Patience, my Magpie," he said. "We have another night of this. I'll hunt deer during the day, and conquer you at night. No one can stop us."

"What if your mother sends me back?" she asked, fearful that the Queen Mother would send her away in anger, and she would not experience this connection again. He rolled over, pulling her onto his chest.

"Let her try to send you away," he said into her hair, smoothing it under his hands, inhaling her.

Chapter 15

JAMES

THE NEXT MORNING, THERE was no sign of Maggie as he prepared for the hunting trip. He hummed as he dressed for the day. What a surprise Maggie had been last night. Her vigor had stripped him of his emotional defenses, allowed him to be vulnerable in a way he had never felt with his other conquests. Maggie was not another physical conquest. No, she knew his innermost feelings and thoughts, holding his heart in her pale hand. The fire raged inside of her, and James wanted to stoke that fire, let it build and consume them together.

"I hope you enjoyed defiling my maid-in-waiting last night," his mother said from behind him. He did not turn around, didn't have the energy to explain himself or his attachment to Maggie. He understood his mother's rage at Maggie, given his father's past and the Scots way of sleeping with the king to improve a family's standing, but James pursued Maggie. He didn't want to hear his mother blaming either of them for what seemed natural and right.

"She's the only one I can trust," was all he replied.

"That is not true. You have many people who you should trust more than some Scottish whore," her nose flared in anger.

"She's not a whore, Mother," James spun around, his anger matching his mother's. How dare *she* of all people criticize his choice in partners? "She didn't marry the first man that flattered her like you did."

"No, she bedded a king in the hopes of becoming what I am—a queen. Do you think she really cares about you? No, she cares about what she can get for herself. All of these Scots are self-serving."

"Be careful Mother. Your son is a Scot," he said, his anger growing. Even though James trusted Maggie, his mother was voicing a concern that hovered in the recesses of his mind. He knew a Scotsman couldn't be trusted—look at Angus, his stepfather who was supposed to guide James, only to use him and kidnap him so that Angus could be in power. And as well as he knew Maggie, that betrayal gnawed at him and told him that she might use him too.

"Half. You are also half Tudor," his mother reminded him. "And so you need to hold yourself to a higher standard. You are the king of a mighty nation who needs a queen from a complimentary kingdom to strengthen what your father was working so hard to do for this country. I didn't sacrifice my life in England to see you married to a common Scot."

"I am the king of a mighty nation regardless of whom I marry," he said. "No one will dictate who I can and can't have a relationship with." Of course he knew his mother was right, he needed a bride who would also bring a strong alliance, but he couldn't bear to voice that, not when Maggie had opened something inside him that he hadn't even realized his captivity with Angus had closed. He wanted to delay thinking about reality for another day, Maggie crowding out everything except the heat of his hands moving over her. The voices of the ambassador and others in their party were nearing.

"And you will not send her away," James hissed as the men came into sight, knowing his mother would not protest in front of their guests. "Gentleman, let's have a successful day of hunting!"

The hunt was exciting as always, James loved riding and turning his best hunting dog, Basche, loose to corner an animal. But Maggie occupied his mind. The feel of the horse moving under him reminded him of her, he thought of things to say to her, to show her. He wanted to smell her heather scented hair and breasts again. He couldn't believe he had waited so long.

After dinner, he asked her once again to accompany him. She jumped up and almost ran to him, gone was the shy girl she had been the night before. He ignored the look from his mother. Once they crossed the moat, he wound his hand in hers. She squeezed back with surprising strength.

"What will we do tonight?" she asked, enthusiasm bubbling from her.

"Do you think there's more?" he asked. "Was last night not enough?"

She pulled her hand away from his. "No, it wasn't. You started this. You can't pretend like you weren't as affected by last night as I was."

She was arrogant and insecure at the same time. He could see through the façade to the person she hid from most people, the insecurities and vulnerabilities. He used the same defense mechanisms to protect him from those who would take advantage of him again. But for tonight, all they had to think about was each other, they could let down those walls and just be. He leaned over and removed her gabled hood and coif, the symbol of her standing in society. Her golden hair tumbled out unbound.

"Oh you didn't even braid it," he laughed, happy that she didn't because it was a sign of trust.

"Of course not," she said, "when you are just going to mess it up. You love the way it feels." The blood pulsed through him, and he struggled to look unaffected. He did not want Maggie to have all of the weapons to hurt him.

"I want to feel you on top tonight," he said, pushing down his feelings. Her smile was broad, pearly teeth flashing.

"That sounds like fun," her eyes deepened into a brown-green. The last remnants of the day hung on the hill tops in pink and purple. But he hardly noticed it because her face was shining. He wasn't expecting that response.

"What have I unleashed?" he tumbled with her into the heather, crushing the flowers and releasing their scent. She laughed as they rolled together. The petals stuck in her hair. He took a strand and twirled it between his fingers.

"James," she said. He loved the way she said his name, the hiss at the end as she drew out. "What is going to happen tomorrow? When we go back to Stirling? Your mother barely spoke two words to me getting ready for dinner."

Her hair looked like spun gold weaving around his hand. He shrugged his shoulders, not trusting himself to speak. He couldn't think about her leaving Stirling, and worse, sleeping with her lawful husband. Bile crept up his throat at the thought.

"I'll figure something out," he said, pressing his mouth on hers.

She pushed him back.

"But what?" she insisted. "My contract has to be fulfilled." He swallowed the sour taste. The picture of her husband, a Douglas, moving over her as he had done last night sickened him. A *Douglas*. He needed to find a way to get her out of the marriage before she was defiled by a Douglas.

"You will never go to a Douglas," hatred colored his words, and he was determined not to put her in the hands of a Douglas, any of them. He would protect her in a way that his mother did not protect him. She sighed and reached for his face, stroking his facial hair.

"You look like a Tudor with this," she said. "Even more handsome than your uncle, who many say is the handsomest king of Europe." She bit his chin. "But they don't know about you."

"But they will. Soon," he said, rolling onto his back and pulling her on top of him. "But let's just enjoy tonight."

She smiled and leaned over to kiss him, enveloping him in a golden cave of hair, the scent of heather making him dizzy. She pulled off her gown and kirtle, leaving her chemise.

"No, take this off too," desire made his voice husky. She lifted the thin garment over her head, and crossed her arms over her breasts.

"I'm so exposed," she giggled, and James saw the blush creep across her cheeks, even in the low light. He peeled her arms away from her breasts, wanting to see her vulnerability.

"You're so pale," he said, tracing his fingers over her chest. "I can't call you Magpie anymore."

Maggie stifled a smile, "No?"

"No," he said, winding a lock of her hair around his finger. "A magpie is dark. You're more of a goldfinch."

"I'll be a goldfinch. Then I can hover around and peck at you," she said, and peppered his face with kisses.

"Now it's your turn," she sat up, tugging at the closures on his doublet. He watched her hands fumble over the toggles, hands trembling in desire. She bit her lip as she worked on the last one. She flung the doublet open and he sat up, catching her in one arm as he wrestled out of the doublet. He released her to take his undershirt off and she began easing his hose down.

"I told you that you would like it when I was vulgar too," James panted, unable to control his breathing, overwhelmed by her nearness. Women did not affect him this way, he affected women. But here was Maggie, awkward in her innocence, making him feel what he never felt in the hands of more experienced women.

"No, not vulgar. But I do like what we did last night. I thought about it all day," she said, taking him into her hand. He groaned as she moved her hand over him. How was she so in tune with his physical needs? But he already knew—it was because she knew him best. He wanted to tell her that he thought about her all day too, but stopped himself. He couldn't be physically and emotionally vulnerable at the same time. It scared him too much. So he tugged at her undergarment, the last piece of clothing she was wearing. She lifted her hips to wiggle out of them. He ran his hands over her hips, smooth and cool like the chalk cliffs in England.

"I don't know what to do," she said, running her hands over his chest. He guided himself into her and she gasped.

"You can do whatever feels good for you," he said, allowing himself to watch her move. She was timid at first, but soon fell into a rhythm, circling her hips, her breasts gliding across his chest. Their breathing united, fast and hard. He kissed her hard, feeling the pulsing blood against his lips. The emotion was so great—he felt his ribs cracking from the enormity of his heart and his feelings for her. He lifted his hips to push even further in her, to become her. She cried out, arching her back. Her body undulated as the contractions came from the base of her abdomen. Her eyes closed, brows drawn together in concentration. The tremor moved from her and into him, his whole body shuddering. He grasped her hips and pushed a final time, releasing himself into her. His heart exploded, splintering his ribs as he felt the final wave of emotion. She collapsed onto him, flattening herself across his chest.

"What sort of revel was that," she murmured. "How do you know exactly what to do?" As she relaxed into him, hair splayed out, something in him shifted, the splinters stuck into his heart, cutting open the scars caused by Angus's betrayal. Suspicion seized him, the intrinsic distrust that he developed while in Angus's hands. Everyone had an ulterior motive. He wanted to ask her how *she* knew exactly what to do. Had she been lying to him about not being with her husband? Was she trying to make a fool of him? He remembered his mother's words about Maggie wanting to better her position. He knew he should push the thought from his mind, just enjoy Maggie and this moment, but skepticism jabbed at him like a hot poker.

"I've had lots of practice," he said. "It seems like you have too." She recoiled as if he had physically hit her. He instantly regretted his words, wished he could pull them back. But they were spoken, and the curtain wall had gone back up. James had to shut Maggie out to preserve himself.

"What are you suggesting?" her voice was stony. He could stop, not say anything to ruin their connection, but paranoia gnawed at him.

"I think you know," he said, remaining immobile, forcing the vulnerability out of his body, becoming stone again, as he had to do when he was disappointed over and over again by his mother, Angus, everyone. She sat up, pulling on her chemise. He wanted to stop her, place his hand on her milky hip, explain his fear. But his hands wouldn't move. *It's better this way*, fear told him. *She will only hurt you in the end.*

"Why are you doing this?" she stood up, yanking her kirtle over her shoulders. Her eyes were rimmed with tears that she held back, face pinched. He could stop all of this with one word, and yet he couldn't say it, couldn't open himself up emotionally to her.

"You think I slept with someone else?" her voice raised into a shrill. He wanted to shake his head, reassure her. "You think I tricked you into thinking I was a virgin? Why? Why would I do that?"

His mother's words came out of his mouth, "To get close to the king. So that you could raise your own position." He stood up, pulling up his hose. His words sealed the entrance to his heart, knowing he had pushed her away, maybe so far away that she would never allow herself to get close to him again. *So be it*, he thought. She already had too much on him, enough to bring him to his emotional knees. She balled her fists and ran at him, striking him in the head, chest, wherever she could hit him. The blows weakened his resolve, each fist tearing a brick from his barricade around his heart. He wanted to throw his arms around her, tell her he was sorry for everything, lie naked with her in the heather and pour out all of his reservations. But he couldn't, and so he grabbed her wrists and twisted. She yelped in pain and he let go. They stood, gasping for air. He wished he could go back and not say anything. He wished that he could allow her in without questioning. But that would open him up to being hurt again. She could incapacitate him with his deepest fears, just like she did before he left for the borders. He couldn't give anyone that much power over himself.

"If you believe that about me, then I should be sent to my husband," she said, wiping tears from her eyes, not allowing them to fall. Both of them had closed themselves off from each other, adversaries in a stalemate, rather than lovers in each other's arms.

"Fine, I can make that happen if that is what you want," he said, knowing that his comment would shut the door between them, but unable to stop himself from saying it.

Chapter 16

Maggie

James had stayed away from Stirling after the hunting trip, which was a second knife wound to Maggie. She had hoped that when they were back at Stirling that they could work out whatever his fears were that caused him to lash out at her. She missed him in every way. She missed his eyes, the goatee, his hands moving over her body. She wasn't with him to better her position. He had to know that.

Not only did she miss James, but she had to deal with the aftermath with the Queen Mother as well.

"This is how you repay my kindness?" her quiet voice covered the rage under the surface.

"I'm sorry, Queen Mother, but—" she started, but the Queen Mother interrupted her.

"I don't want to hear your pathetic excuses," she said. "You were like a daughter to me. I kept you from becoming a mother too soon. Maybe that is what you wanted all along—to be my son's lover and become the queen."

"But that's not it at all," she threw herself down at the Queen Mother's feet. "I do appreciate everything you've done for me and how you kept me from being sent to my husband. I never wanted to be his wife, he's the only friend I have." She stopped herself before she exclaimed that she loved the Queen Mother's son. She hadn't said it out loud to anyone, even though it was her truth.

"After the Michaelmas feast, you will go to Loch Leven," the Queen Mother said.

Maggie swallowed, the reality crushing her. From two nights of pure bliss to being sent to her husband. How could she think about sleeping with her husband after James? She closed her eyes to block it out. A wave of nausea overcame her and she ran for the chamber pot, vomiting nothing but stomach acids. The Queen Mother left the room, and Maggie slumped down on the floor and allowed herself to cry.

She pulled herself together and hurried to the chapel for mass. The chapel was warm, sunlight pouring through the southern windows, illuminating the yellow walls. She took her place next to the Queen Mother and knelt, leaning her forehead on her folded hands. She fought down the nausea that threatened to erupt, and prayed to God that she could see the king and just talk to him. She knew she could make him understand that she didn't care about becoming queen, she just wanted to be near him.

The Queen Mother reached over and patted her hands. Maggie straightened up, composing herself. Her life was not her own, she was reminded again. And it seemed like James was not going to save her from her fate this time.

After mass, they gathered in the Great Hall for the dinner. On the table was the tradition Michaelmas goose and bannock, an unleavened round oatmeal bread. Maggie sat next to her husband, feeling no emotion towards him, no heat, no excitement that James lit in her.

"Are you feeling ill?" he asked. She shook her head, even as she felt the color draining from her face. Her stomach was churning, nerves from leaving for Loch Leven soon, and the thrill of seeing the king again. She just needed to talk to him and then she could accept her fate and go to Loch Leven.

The king entered the hall and everyone stood at attention. He wore a pleated white silk chemise, and a crimson overcoat edged with silver embroidery and trimmed with ermine fur. Over his auburn hair was a flat hat with an upturned brim and ostrich feather. From his silver jeweled collar hung a pendant with amethyst and rubies to represent the thistle and the strawberry. Maggie's heart leapt as he connected with her eyes as he walked to his place on the dais. His face showed a mixture of regret and contrition.

She felt her husband's eyes on her and dared not look at him, unable to calm all of her emotions whipping through her body.

Somehow she held herself together during the dinner.

"Father, I need to speak with the king after dinner," she announced before she lost her nerve. Her father raised an eyebrow, but revealed nothing about his inner thoughts. She knew he had heard about her sexual escapades with him this summer, even though he never said anything to her about it. She didn't know if he was disappointed or not, his attitude towards her neutral. She fought the urge to continue talking and waited for him to speak. Jealousy and bitterness came from her husband's direction, but she couldn't deal with him now. No, she needed to talk to the king first.

"I will see if I can get you an audience," he said, emotions still veiled. She breathed out, shoulders slumping as the nausea came over her again.

"Excuse me," she said as she pushed away from the table. She ran from the hall, into a hallway and threw open a leaded window. The cool wind caressed her face as she leaned out and willed herself not to vomit again. A hand pressed into her back, and she tensed fearing it was her husband, and that she would not be able to pull the mask back on so her husband would not see her true feelings.

"Easy, Mags." It was James. She turned to look at his face, to see his emotions, to see if he still felt for her what she felt for him. And it was all there, longing, regret, desire, concern. He stroked her cheek.

"Are you feeling poorly?" he asked, threading an arm around her waist.

"James," she pushed away, only to bump into the window sash. "Someone will see us."

"I'm the king," he said. "I don't care who sees us."

Maggie relaxed, trapped between him and the cool night air. She shivered. There was so much she wanted to say, but she didn't know where to start. His face was open and vulnerable again, not closed and suspicious like when they last parted.

"Why do you push me away?" she said, nausea climbing again, apprehensive of his answer. He hung his head, his facial hair brushing her breasts, which had grown over the past months.

"I don't know," he murmured. "But I missed you." He kissed her breasts. She inhaled and wound her hands into his hair. "I've missed these."

She slapped at him for being vulgar when she wanted to be serious. He deflected with coarseness when he was uncomfortable. He caught her hands and kissed each palm.

"You look different from this summer. Your skin is glowing," he said, kissing her breasts. "And these are plumper."

"I...." Maggie sighed as he moved to kiss her neck. "I think I might be with child." She held her breath, unsure of his reaction, nausea rising again. Fear gripped her—fear of dying, fear of losing James if he was not excited about being a father again. If this child was not wanted, she would be set aside—by James and her husband, disgraced. He already had one bastard child, did he need another one? He pulled back from her, a wide smile on his face.

"Why are you smiling? This is serious," she tried to escape his arms, annoyed that he thought this was a joke. Her life hung in the balance, what would happen to her? She would surely be sent to Loch Leven and her baby taken from her once it was born. Would she be kept from James? She shook the thought from her head.

"Oh Mags, this is braw!" he picked her up and twirled her around.

"*This* is braw?" she asked as her face screwed into a scowl. "You think this is a good thing?" All she could think of was being trapped at Loch Leven.

"I'm going to have another heir. And it will be a boy," he put her down, but did not release her, the grin erupting from under his beard.

"Not if I can help it! And not if he's anything like you," she protested, but his enthusiasm was easing her fears.

"He will be just like me. He will have red hair, look like a Tudor, but he will be smart like his mother," he placed his hand on her stomach, which was still flat but tight.

"Hmp!" Maggie tried to remain angry but his excitement was infectious.

"We will name him James," he said.

"You already have a son named James," she said, pushing him away, annoyed that he wanted to name her child the same as his child from his other mistress who had been married off and sent away.

"There are never enough Jameses," he said, pulling her towards him again, kissing her lips. She relented and fell into his arms.

"My son," his mother came out of the Great Hall. She pulled up short when she saw his arms around Maggie. "What is the meaning of this? Your guests are waiting. Can't you even control yourself to do your sovereign duties? Must you defile my maid again while you have royal responsibilities?" The Queen Mother flashed the same anger and stubbornness that Maggie saw in James.

"Mother!" he clapped his hands on her shoulders. "You're to be a grandmother again!"

"Another royal bastard. Just what Scotland needs," she scowled. Maggie swallowed hard, remembering the stories of how the king's illegitimate children had been a source of constant embarrassment for the Queen Mother.

"No, Mother," he said, frost covering his words. "Not just another royal bastard. She is carrying a royal son, maybe the future king."

"We will discuss this after dinner," the Queen Mother said as more faces appeared in the Great Hall doorway. "James, let's finish our dinner and entertain our guests. Maggie, you go to my chambers and wait for me."

The Queen Mother grabbed James's arm and steered him back into the Great Hall while Maggie fought down another wave of nausea. She walked back to the Queen Mother's rooms, praying that James would find a solution to keep them together, even though she knew the odds were against her.

Chapter 17
The Queen Mother

"A word with you, Lord Erskine and Sir Robert," Margaret approached the men after the plum pudding was finished. Lord Erskine nodded, and Robert looked confused. *Well, he will be very angry soon,* she thought. But maybe not—these Scots accepted bastard children as badges of honor. Even Lord Erskine had an illegitimate daughter. She would never understand their mentality. Although her own brother acknowledged his illegitimate son, Henry Fitzroy, he at least knew not to bring the boy into the royal chambers and flaunt him in front of his queen. James needed to find a queen quickly, as soon as possible to have a legitimate heir to the Scottish throne. She would speak to him and his secretary, Thomas Erskine, about going to the continent to find a suitable bride and draw up a contract.

The men followed her to the queen's inner chamber. She took a seat in a red velvet scissor chair and motioned for the men to sit. A fire had been lit, illuminating the red tapestries and ornate oak paneled ceiling. Margaret knew the girl would be listening at the door to the bedchamber.

"We have a matter to discuss which affects both of you," Margaret began. Robert sat forward and began to speak, but Lord Erskine stopped him with a motion of his hand. Margaret wondered if he already knew what she was going to say.

Before she could begin, James burst into the room, huffing. "How dare you discuss my child without me, Mother."

Robert and Lord Erskine stood at attention.

"What child?" Robert asked, eyes lowered in suspicion.

"My child," James wheeled around. "With your wife." His posture was aggressive, challenging.

Margaret closed her eyes. This was not how she imagined this conversation going. Her son was too emotionally charged to think clearly. And now he was antagonizing the girl's husband. She had to take control over this situation, so the outcome favored her son and Scotland.

"Yes, Sir Robert," she leaned against the oak table. "It seems that your wife has been dallying with the king while we were on summer progress. I regret to tell you that she is pregnant."

"And why isn't she here?" James said. "You left her out so you wouldn't have to see how much this betrayal hurts her."

"No, my son. I did not want evidence of *her* betrayal of me! I didn't ask her here because her father and husband decide what happens to her," Margaret said through clenched teeth. How dare he make her feel guilty about Maggie's betrayal. He should be able to see that she was using him.

"I'm the king. I decide what happens in my kingdom," James bristled.

Lord Erskine, ever the voice of reason, stepped forward. "Of course, your Grace. Scotland is your kingdom. But Maggie's husband also has a say in what happens with his wife." The words stunned James like the icy waters of the River Forth. "Let us discuss like gentlemen the proper course of action."

James frowned, but took a seat. Margaret took a breath, thinking it might turn out well after all.

"Your Highness Queen Mother," Lord Erskine continued. "Do you have a proposal?"

"Yes, John, I do. Since she is already married, she should go to Loch Leven and have the baby with her husband," Margaret said, feeling her son tense as she spoke.

"No," he said, "Never! She is carrying a royal baby. She will stay here at Stirling."

"So you can continue to have another man's wife?" she shot back.

Lord Erskine held up his hand, as she and her son postured like two fighting cocks. "Let's get Robert's opinion."

It was hard for Margaret to look at Sir Robert. His eyes were mirrors of Ard's eyes, the down-turned hound dog brown eyes that look innocent but masked Ard's cruelty. The hurt washed over her fresh when she looked at Sir Robert.

"I agree with the Queen Mother. Maggie should come to Loch Leven," he said halting, fearful of the king's wrath, but also angry with the king for taking his wife.

James's nostrils flared in anger, "Of course you agree with her, but Maggie is still carrying *my* child." James fought like a bear cornered, lashing out at everyone, even those who were trying to help him.

"Now, your Grace, let's have cooler heads prevail here," Lord Erskine placed a hand on James's shoulder, pulling him back to the reality of the situation. "I also think she should go to Loch Leven to have the baby. We can bring the baby here to Stirling to grow up in the tradition of your father and also with your son, James. You know I would be honored to raise my grandson here with your other child," Lord Erskine said.

James looked from face to face. Margaret was glad they were a united front, she only wished she could have talked to them first without James here and avoided this altogether.

"You know I respect you, John. I think of you as my own father and respect your opinion," James said, softening his posture. Margaret felt both men being drawn to her son's magnetism. "And you all are against me. But I want to see my child grow. And John, I know you want what is best for your daughter. She would have the best doctors here at Stirling and the best care. It would be less stressful since this is the only home she has known. My child deserves the best care that Scotland has to offer, and that is here at Stirling."

There was the Tudor charm. Even Robert, the girl's husband, was being swayed. Margaret was annoyed but still proud that he could use his charm to influence his subjects. It made her confident that he would lead Scotland to what his father intended it to be.

"You are right, your Grace. I do want what is best for my daughter and grandchild. And of course, I will honor whatever you decide for them," Lord Erskine said. "What is your opinion, Robert?"

Robert's red beard shook as he spoke, "I would like my wife at my home, but if the king thinks she would be safer here, then I will honor that."

James looked at Margaret, smug smile on his face. Sir Robert continued, "As long as she is sent to Loch Leven after her confinement."

Margaret knew James was seething, but he said, "Of course. She is your wife. After the birth of my child, she will go to Loch Leven." Margaret knew from the tightness of his lip that he was lying.

"I don't want to see her here at Stirling. She will not be my maid-in-waiting any longer," she said, even though her heart squeezed in pain at the thought of losing the girl who was her replacement daughter. And Margaret *had* treated her like a daughter, overseeing her education, a royal princess's education, which she had taken and used against Margaret. Maggie had taken advantage of her kindness and seduced her son while smiling at Margaret's face. This hurt almost as badly as Ard's betrayal, her kindness and protection repaid with seduction. These Scots couldn't help themselves. They were all *gantin. Horny.* And for that, Maggie would pay.

"Good Mother, we will move her to her own chambers and assign her a lady-in-waiting to care for her and the child. It is settled," James said, standing to signal that the discussion was over. Margaret watched the men leaving, her eyes narrowing. She may have been beaten today, but she would win in the end. Now she needed to focus on James's future and producing a legitimate heir.

Chapter 18

THOMAS ERSKINE

THOMAS ERSKINE RODE THROUGH the arched portcullis and into Stirling's interior. A groom took his horse and he headed towards the palace for his meeting with the king and Queen Mother. It had been an odd request, sent by the Queen Mother, not the king himself. His mind spun as he wondered what it could mean.

The room was bright, even though the day was overcast. September mist hung low in the courtyard. The oak shutters were open, and several candelabras lit. The light flickered off the ornate tapestries and the carved paneled ceiling. The king and his mother sat at a square oak table.

"Thomas!" James came over and clasped his shoulder. His shoulder tingled under the king's hand.

"It is wonderful to see you, your Grace," he said, looking to his mother. "But I'm a little confused about what prompted this meeting." He couldn't stop smiling even in his confusion. James's energy radiated and infected Thomas.

"Thomas," the Queen Mother started. "We need you to go to Europe to procure a marriage contract for James."

Thomas's eyes widened. He knew James would of course marry, but so soon? He was still a young man.

"You're surprised?" she said, her face pinched in anger. "Clearly you haven't heard about the King's sexual roguery."

Thomas didn't understand what the Queen Mother was upset about. James slept with many women, his sexual prowess could not be contained. Sensuality oozed from him. But the Queen Mother continued. James sat back in his chair, stroking his goatee.

"James is going to be a father again," she said. James tried to suppress a smile and failed. He was enjoying his mother's distress. "So, it is time to find a bride for James." She paused and her gaze focused on James. "A *royal* bride."

The smile fell off James's face. His nostrils flared, but he said nothing.

"Of course, Queen Mother," Thomas said, sitting at the table, preparing to write letters to send off. There was King Christian of Denmark, King François of France. And of course he would need to write to the pope as well as he controlled a vast number of lands and had a niece who was coming of age. He was excited to go to the continent again, having studied at the University of Pavia before he was appointed as James's secretary in 1524.

"I think King François will be hesitant to contract his daughter, Madeleine, and his other daughter is too young to be considered," she was passing behind him. James remained silent, his eyes darkening with each word. "It needs to be someone from a family wealthy enough to bring a very large dowry. I'm sure you are aware of how the Earl of Angus depleted the treasury."

"I can request an audience with the pope and Holy Roman Emperor," Thomas stated, his quill gliding over the parchment. "The emperor's daughter is only two, but the pope has a niece, Catherine de Medici, who would bring a considerable dowry."

"Yes, and the King of Denmark has two eligible daughters," Margaret said, looking over his shoulder.

James stood up, knocking over his chair. "I'll only accept a French princess as the Auld Alliance says." James's father had died defending the Auld Alliance against the attack of his uncle, Henry VIII. The alliance between Scotland and France was centuries old, and the Scots even supported Joan of Arc against the English at the Battle of Orleans in 1429. The Queen Mother's irritation flared at the mention of the Auld Alliance—an alliance against her home country of England.

"My son, that is not going to happen," his mother snapped.

"Then I'll marry Maggie," he thrust his chin up. Thomas's head jerked toward the king. His cousin? He knew that she was employed by the Queen Mother as a maid-in-waiting, but he had no idea there was talk of marriage.

"Maggie Erskine?" he asked. James grinned like a satisfied cat.

"She is going to have the king's child," the Queen Mother did not even try to keep the bitterness out of her voice. Thomas raised his eyebrows and James continued grinning.

"I'm a virile, strong king," he shrugged. "What can I say?"

Maggie Erskine, Lord Erskine's daughter. Lord Erskine secured Thomas's employment in the king's court during the regency. He had always seen promise in Thomas when his own father just saw disappointment. Too effeminate, not enough of a Scots man. But Lord Erskine saw his aptitude for administration, his tact in diplomatic matters. And the king did too, keeping him as his secretary. Thomas just wanted to be close to the king, and now Maggie had laid claim to him.

"You're a man whore," his mother retorted. James just laughed. Thomas glanced between the two of them, whose personalities were too similar for there to be concord. "And now, Thomas, you understand the urgency of this marriage."

Thomas nodded, not trusting himself to speak. He was disappointed but he didn't exactly know why. Jealous of Maggie? He had always been jealous of her, that she grew up in the royal palace while he had been shut up in the highlands at Brechin. She was her father's favorite child, remaining at Stirling. And now, it looked like she might become queen.

"But how can you marry Maggie Erskine? Isn't she married already?" Thomas asked.

"Exactly," the Queen Mother said. James waved his hand.

"There can be an annulment. The pope grants them all the time," he said. "Her marriage has never been consummated."

"Are you sure?" his mother said. A dark cloud flashed across his face.

"I'm sure," his voice was confident. "But I would still honor the Auld Alliance and keep Maggie as my mistress like my father did with his." The Queen Mother flinched, her husband's infidelity still stinging after all these years.

Thomas had to play the diplomat between these two stubborn personalities. "Let's start with a letter to France," he said to appease James and pull attention off Maggie.

"I'd prefer if you traveled to France, Thomas. I trust you to be my eyes and ears to speak to King François while I deal with my uncle and the nobles here."

"Speaking of your uncle," the Queen Mother said, softening her tone. "What about Princess Mary?" She hoped to unite the English and Scottish monarchies through a marriage of her brother's daughter to her son. Princess Mary was his sole living child with Queen Catherine.

James scoffed. "Your brother is trying to divorce his queen. If he succeeds, and you know he will, his daughter will be declared a bastard. No thank you."

The Queen Mother bristled but held her retort. Thomas said, "I'll prepare for the journey immediately. I'll start in France and then travel to Rome if your highness deems it necessary."

"That's why you're my secretary, Thomas!" James said, slapping him on the back. Thomas eased a smile onto his face, glad he made the king happy, but disappointed at being sent away from court again. But if he could find a wife for James, then Thomas could come back to Scotland and they would run the country together.

Thomas sailed for the continent, landing in the French port of Le Havre, the fortress city built by King François in 1517. The galley ship glided through the breakwall and into the harbor, past two circular guard towers. On the left side was the stone wharf where many ships of various sizes were docked. A wide flagstone square was a frenzy of activity—burly men unloading crates from ships, containing wool, produce, fabrics, luxury items and necessities. Wood timbered buildings crowded the square and merchants shouted their specials—fresh seafood, fabric, rope and canvas to repair ships. Brokers and merchants were negotiating prices, dressed in better attire than the dockhands, trying to imitate noble clothing like Thomas was wearing. He eased the fur-lined cape off his neck, the September climate warmer in France than Scotland. The French language came flooding back to Thomas, as if he spoke it every day in Scotland.

After departing the ship, he wound his way through the chaotic wharf to a smaller, open boat, traveled down the Seine River to meet with the Duke of Albany in Paris, since James's first choice was to fulfill the Auld Alliance. The duke had grown up in the French court, after his father had been exiled by his brother, James III, and killed in a jousting accident.

"The king is looking to fulfill the Auld Alliance?" Albany said, running a hand over his graying beard. Thomas noticed his weariness.

"My condolences at the death of your wife," Thomas said, even though it was six years too late. Albany had returned to France in 1524 to attend to his ailing wife. He had washed his hands of Scottish politics after the power struggle between Angus and the Queen Mother.

"Thank you," he sighed. "The loss is acute even after so much time. As you know, my niece, Catherine De Medici, is also of age."

"I have orders to first negotiate for Princess Madeline, but perhaps if François declines…" Thomas let the sentence trail off, implying that James would consider the lesser bride. Albany nodded and they set off for the king's palace.

Fontainebleau rose from the landscape with a steep-pitched azure roof. Albany and he entered the oval courtyard through the majestic Porte Dorée entrance, admiring the simplicity of the columns and window adornment. A servant led them up a grand staircase to François's Gallery. Unlike the modesty of the outside, this room was ornate—carved oak door, geometric patterned ceiling. Twenty candle chandeliers hung from the ceiling, highlighting the murals that glorified the king. The paintings were in various states of production, but even the line drawings were raw, emotional. Thomas stopped in front of one dominated by an elephant, draped in a blanket covered with fleur-de-lis, noticing the adolescent cherub boys carved out of white marble perched on top of the gilded frame. Something stirred deep inside him. These sculptures were so real, he could almost feel the feathers of the wings.

François burst into the gallery from his chambers. He wore white hose and tunic, woven with golden threads. His overcoat had golden braids at the shoulders, accentuating his shoulders, which only made his legs look thinner. His cap was brown velvet, brim upturned and edged with white ostrich feathers.

"My Scots brothers!" François bound over on his spindly legs, embraced Thomas and kissed him on each cheek. He clasped Albany's shoulder, smiling. Thomas wondered if the king was remembering that Albany had risked his life for him at Pavia, when François had been taken by the emperor's forces.

"I noticed you admiring my artwork," François said, pride exuded from his voice, his broad shoulders thrown back. Thomas studied his profile, Francis's long nose curving like a beak. He turned to Thomas, focusing his hooded brown eyes on him. "I brought the best Italian painters back with me after my conquest of Milan, even Da Vinci came to experience the superior French culture."

Thomas nodded, he was acquainted with the artist's work but never met the artist himself.

"Brilliant painter. I fell in love with his work, *The Last Supper*, when I saw it in Milan. But he's an even better philosopher," François began walking down the gallery. Thomas had no choice but to follow. "He knew more than any man about architecture, painting and sculpture," François continued. Thomas looked from image to image as they walked the length of the gallery. He was awed at the realism in these portraits, raw emotion coming through the canvas. He couldn't wait to tell James about it.

François led the way through another ornately carved oak door and into a grand salon with a magnificent, gilded chandelier. The walls were covered in tapestries finer than any in Scotland, and behind an oak table with a marble top stood François's new queen, Eleanor of Austria. Her overgown, in the Spanish style to reflect her family's heritage, had voluminous sleeves, which had many slashed panels through which the red silk of her kirtle was pulled. Her embroidered stomacher was higher than the Queen Mother wore in Scotland, but that's not what Thomas noticed. Her chin jutted forward, creating an under bite and the prominent Habsburg chin. It was no wonder the king preferred the bed of his mistress instead of his new queen's bed. She had been a way for François to get close to his enemy, her brother, Charles, the Holy Roman Emperor, who offered his sister as a bride for the French king to seal a peace treaty. He bowed to her out of respect, while stealing a glance at Princess Madeleine, the reason for his visit. The princess was tiny for a ten-year-old, face white and pasty, body thin under her thick gown. She did not look like a match for the vigorous, inexhaustible Scottish king. Thomas feared his heart would not be in negotiation for this child to be the bride of Scotland.

Chapter 19

James

JAMES PREPARED NEW ROOMS for Maggie, adjacent to his with a common oak door, so he could go into her room or she could come to his whenever they desired each other, which was every night he was at Stirling. He had green velvet curtains hung from her bed, and a luxurious tapestry hung from the wall for her to see. The centerpiece of the tapestry was a white unicorn, the tapered horn impossibly long. A maiden who resembled Maggie knelt next to the unicorn, her golden curls embroidered for eternity to admire, but not her eyes. Her lids were lowered. Only James wanted to appreciate the complicated colors of her eyes. Not even the most skilled weaver could capture the color in a tapestry.

"Oh James," Maggie breathed. "This is beautiful! This is a queen's chamber." She spun around, soaking in every detail. She stopped and looked up at him, her brow furrowed. "And I will never be your queen."

"Don't," he said, taking her in his arms. "Didn't I tell you that I would figure out something?"

She leaned into him, her growing belly preventing her from pressing her whole body against his. She brushed her lips against his.

"We both know that you need to marry a French princess," she said. "And I'm going to help you with your French so that you will be able to speak to her."

"I can speak French," he was indignant.

"No, you can *read* French. But you need to practice speaking," she walked into his room through the adjoining door. She came

112

back with a manuscript, *fin amors* poetry. "Let's hear you read a love poem."

She smiled as she held out the book. He grabbed her arm and pulled her to him, "I'd rather do something else."

"Later," she purred into his ear. "First I want you to seduce me in French."

The whisper sent vibrations through his body, but he resisted the urge to throw her on the bed and have her immediately. No, he needed to practice patience. This manuscript was his mother's, which she had brought with her from England. He thumbed through the velum pages and stopped at a ballad.

"Ma dame et mon souverain," his pronunciation was off. His R was too much trill, his vowels too high in his mouth, but he continued. "Qui d'autre puisqu'aucun avec toi ne compare." This one was even worse, too staccato compared to the flowing cadence of French.

"Say it again," Maggie smiled, "But further back in your throat."

"Qui d'autre puisqu'aucun avec toi ne compare," the inside of his throat vibrated. He guided Maggie to the bed, speaking the line into her ear. *Who else, since none with thyself compare.* She sighed and sank back into the bed. He was gentle with her, since her belly was getting larger.

After, they lay with arms and legs entwined. She ran her fingers through his hair, sending shivers down his spine.

"Thomas is on the continent," he said, hoping the desperation was not evident in his voice. "François wouldn't agree to contract his daughter Madeleine, so I might send him to Rome and ask the pope to grant an annulment." He couldn't imagine feeling about some strange European princess what he felt for Mags. When she had told him that she was pregnant, erasing the shame he carried from the hunting palace, where he had been so cruel to her, that was when he realized that he loved her. His mother had angered him by negotiating her future—thinking she could do it behind his back. And Maggie remained constant, yielding to *him*, not her husband, not her father. When she gave herself so willingly to him, that's when James knew he had been immature and foolish to believe his mother, that Maggie was using him to better her own position. He could lower the wall, open the portcullis to his heart and let Maggie in. Sometimes he slammed it shut again, but Maggie was patient and would wedge it open.

James knew that marriages were not love matches, they were contracts to bind countries together, to increase fortunes, but he did love someone. And she was here, in his arms, carrying his child. A child whom he could legitimize by marrying her.

"You know you can't marry me," she said, barely audible. "You need to build Scotland into a northern jewel. I don't have the money to do that."

He pushed himself up on his shoulder. "I'll raise money here," he said. "I'll draft a new tax and raise the money myself." He felt the anger rising. Why couldn't she just agree with him? He was the King of Scots. He would do what he wanted to do, build Scotland with Maggie as his queen. He needed her strength and constancy to deal with the backstabbing nobles of Scotland who placed clan loyalties above fealty to their king. He wanted to tell her all of this, but the words stuck in his throat. With one opposing word from her, he blocked his vulnerability, the portcullis slammed down.

"You need an ally to help protect you from your uncle. An ally who is more powerful than he is," she tried to pull him back, but fear caused him to lash out at her.

"I don't need a marriage to protect me!" He shoved away from her, his ego bruised. "I'll take care of my uncle, and Scotland. I don't need an alliance or a marriage to do that!" He threw on his clothes, he needed to get away, go somewhere where he would not have to defend his feelings. Of course he needed to marry the daughter of an ally to keep his kingdom safe, but just once he wanted her to agree with him. He stomped out of her chambers, thoughts whirling in his head. Why did she do this to him? He knew where he wanted to take Scotland, and he had a plan that included her, but she shot him down every time. It felt like she didn't trust that he could do it, could make her his queen.

Then shame washed over him when he lashed out at her. He *knew* she was telling him the truth, but he also believed he could raise the money, procure a divorce for her and marry her. If she couldn't believe in him, how could he believe in himself? Angus stole his confidence from him, and he sought constant reassurance that he was leading Scotland in the direction to best benefit his people.

Once he had slammed down the wall to his heart, his ego prevented him from going back and apologizing—Maggie could destroy him if he were too vulnerable. So he calmed himself in the way his stepfather had taught him so well—he slept with someone else to prove that Maggie did not have the stranglehold over his heart. Maybe then she would hurt as much as he did when she disagreed with him. He was the thistle, stabbing whoever got too close to him. He didn't want to hurt Maggie, but he wanted her to understand how much pain he was in. Instead of talking with her to make her understand, he lashed out to hurt her by having someone else who wouldn't question him and make him doubt himself. Even though he knew it was wrong, he still went out.

1531

Chapter 20

MAGGIE

THE TREES WERE UNFOLDING their waxy leaves outside her window in the spring sunshine, purple blossoms dotting the garden below, but Maggie could not enjoy it. She was nearing the end of her pregnancy, leaden and rotund. She was stuck in the bed that brought her so much pleasure, so much frustration. James continued his push-pull with her, pushing her away, and then pulling her back in. She was powerless, just like the mill pushed by the water, she kept going around and around. But she would continue as long as he kept pulling her back in. He was her vice, even as she knew he went outside Stirling to find other women. His mother made sure she knew about that to hurt her. But Maggie knew those women were nothing to him, it was only with her that he dropped the heavy shield and let her see his vulnerability, his fears, his joys.

His son was stretching into her rib, pressure and pain building. She pushed his foot back down into her womb that was quickly becoming too small, even though it kept stretching to accommodate him. She was convinced her baby would be a boy. Her intuition, and James, told her that he would be strong and healthy. She hoped for the same herself.

Her room had been prepared in the noble tradition, a false ceiling created with tapestries nailed to the walls to lower the height of the room, tapestries and carpets covering the walls and floors in order to create a safe and cozy place for the birth which mimicked the womb and cut off the dangers of the outside world. When her labor began later that day, she moved to her birthing bed and called for the midwife, who rushed in, closing all the curtains. Her own mother should be there to help Maggie and give her comfort, but in another show of vengeance, the Queen Mother refused to allow her. So Maggie was alone and scared, with no one familiar to guide her through this difficult and dangerous time. She had hoped the Queen Mother would relent, given her own fears surrounding childbirth. But her anger was stubborn.

She felt the contractions coming at closer intervals, and the midwife said it was almost time. Fear gripped her heart, remembering the horror stories of birth that the Queen Mother had told about her own pregnancies and her grandmother's. But she had to believe the pain would be worth it, and they would both survive. The midwife propped her up when the contractions crashed over her, placing an amber amulet of Saint Margaret, the patron saint of pregnant women, under her pillow. The amulet was supposed to protect the mother and child, much as Saint Margaret had been protected when she was eaten by a dragon and spit out because she held a crucifix. But the amulet did nothing to stop the pain, which came in waves and threatened to black her out. She fought back the blackness, breathed into the pain; pushing became an instinct, a response to the pain wracking her body. The midwife positioned herself behind Maggie, holding her up and working in unison through the contractions. After what seemed like hours of labor, the midwife moved to peer between her legs and announced that her baby was crowning. Maggie bit down and pushed with all of her strength, feeling more animal than human. Childbirth reduced her to a primal state. Finally, the shoulders twisted out and then his legs. The midwife tied off the umbilical cord and slapped the baby, a boy, on the back. He began howling. Maggie smiled, exhausted but relieved. She offered silent thanks to the Virgin Mary, glancing at the stucco relief of Mary and the baby Jesus on the side table.

After the baby had been cleansed in salt water and swaddled, and the placenta delivered, the baby was laid in Maggie's arms. His mouth moved, little pink tongue jutting out of his rose petal lips. Maggie began to cry. He was so beautiful. She held him to her breast, wanting him to take her milk, even though he would be provided with the best nursemaid from Ireland. She took off his white linen cap and smoothed the soft red hair on his head, watching his cheeks puff as he took her milk. She had given James another royal son.

The Queen Mother came into the room, holding a porcelain-enameled bowl of caudle, customary first meal of new mothers to restore their strength. Maggie was surprised that the Queen Mother brought it herself. *Maybe she will forgive me*, Maggie thought as she sipped the thick, sweet liquid.

"So he has arrived," the Queen Mother said, her voice losing the anger she projected before the baby was born.

"Yes, Jamie has come into this world," Maggie said, naked pride effusing from her. "Would you like to hold him?" She extended the bundle towards the Queen Mother, who took him, curving her body over his sweet face. The Queen Mother turned away, cooing at the newborn, but not before Maggie saw the look of gratitude. Emotions washed over Maggie—relief, ecstasy, contentment. Her royal son would win over the Queen Mother, and both would be accepted here at Stirling. Maggie knew the Queen Mother's fear of childbirth and now she understood where that fear had originated, the fragility of the tiny baby, but also the fierce protectiveness that she felt for this creature who had just come into the world, who had developed and nurtured inside her. She now understood the Queen Mother's protectiveness over James, trying her best to provide for him, even if those attempts lacked forethought.

"You have given me a grandson," the Queen Mother said, keeping her back to Maggie. "I am happy you made it through childbirth."

Maggie wanted to give gratitude to the woman who saved her from this earlier in her marriage, who kept her at Stirling and made it possible for her to give birth to the king's son. The words stuck in her mouth, pride blocked the tenderness.

"Your son will be pleased," she said instead.

"Yes, he will be," the Queen Mother said, stroking the baby's head. "He is his father's son. My husband was also proud of his *bastards*."

Maggie coiled herself to strike back with venom equal to the Queen Mother's when James burst in. The midwife curtsied, bowing her face to conceal her surprise. Men never entered the birthing room, but who would turn away the king? Maggie reached up to her hair, which was unbound and clinging to her, still damp from the exertion. She didn't want him to see her like this.

"James!" she exclaimed. "What are you doing in here? No man

is supposed to be here until my churching!" She pulled the covers up to cover her nakedness. In her labor, she had shed her chemise, the last semblance of civilization as she descended into an animal state. Men were not allowed in the birthing rooms, so she had not expected him. But she should have known he would not stay away.

James knelt next to the bed, taking her hand. "Are you healthy?" he asked. Auburn stubble covered his face, his hair disheveled, his shirt rumpled. Maggie nodded, touching the hairs on his face. They pricked her hand, reminding her that she had survived childbirth.

"I have given you a son," she said, unable to conceal her pride. James clutched her arms and kissed her forehead. Maggie caught the sheet to keep it from exposing her bosom.

He spun around to his mother, who still cradled the baby to her bosom. "Let me see my son, Mother," he said, reaching for the baby. He nestled the baby in the crook of his elbow, his face beaming. He walked over to the window and pulled the curtains back. Night had fallen, the sky lit by the stars.

"Welcome to the world, James!" he exclaimed. Across the sky shot a white ball of light, a blue tale streaming behind it, dissipating into the night.

"Did you see that?" James spun around. Maggie and the Queen Mother nodded. "He is a charmed baby. His life will be blessed." He came over to Maggie's side again. "Our baby will be protected and revered."

Maggie leaned her head against his as he crawled into the bed with her.

"James! You shouldn't be in the labor bed!" his mother was horrified.

"Mother, please leave us alone," he said and for once, she left without a word. The midwife followed on her heels.

"I knew it would be a boy," James said, stroking his cheek. The baby turned toward his father's finger, and stuck out his pink tongue. James laughed. "He has your personality already!"

Maggie pretended to be angry, but she was bathing in the af- terglow of a successful birth, shining like the blue glow in the sky following after James, her light. And now she had a copy of him, a miniature. She smoothed the downy hair on his head.

"He will be a redhead, just like the Tudors," she said. "You were right. He will look like you, but be smart like me."

The baby began fussing, and Maggie took him into her arms, putting him to her breast. James propped himself up and watched in naked admiration. "You two are perfect together," he said. "But don't weary yourself. He has a nurse maid here who can provide the best nutrition for him."

"I'm his mother," Maggie snapped. "I'm what he needs most right now."

James got out of bed, leaving the room. Maggie feared she had insulted him and he would disappear again as he had done so many times before. From his adjoining room, she heard his lute playing. He entered the room, his eyes shining.

"Let's live like the commoners do," he strummed his lute, sitting on the bed again. Their son relaxed as well, sleeping on her breast. "He took the lassie in his arms, And ga'e her kisses three, And four and twenty hunder merk, To pay the nurse's fee," he sang.

Maggie tried not to smile, but she knew this was his way of apologizing, serenading her and his son. She reached out to him with her free hand, holding his forearm, making a circle from him to her to their son. She drifted into a deep, comforting sleep, unaware that James took their son from her arms.

———

A month later, she neared the end of her confinement and prepared to enter public life again. Today was her churching. She wrapped her still swollen belly in linens. Her abdomen was going down, but the linens helped with the pain. Her breasts had become engorged when her son was taken from her and given to the wet nurse. She bound those as well, reluctantly since she wanted to nurse her son, but the Queen Mother said she couldn't be sent to her husband with sagging breasts. The room felt so lonely without Jamie in it. Maggie would pad to his room at all hours, her breasts leaking, knowing another woman was feeding Jamie. She sighed, knowing it was best for her son, that Irish breast milk was best, but her body didn't understand that. James split his time between Stirling and Edinburgh, meeting with parliament and spending nights with her. She would fall asleep in his bed when he wasn't at Stirling, longing to feel close to him, unsure of her future, but believing him when he said he would think of something to keep them together.

She put on her kirtle with a high collar and a velvet embroidered moss green overgown, a present from James. Green was the color of fertility. As she wound her hair and placed on her coif, the Queen Mother came in.

"I believe it is time for you to return to your husband," she said. "Arrangements have been made for your belongings to be packed and will follow you. You will take my ambler to Loch Leven."

Maggie's eyes widened in surprise. "The king did not say anything about me returning so soon. My son is less than a month old."

"Did you think you would remain here?" the Queen Mother snickered. "You have only stayed on at Stirling because you were carrying royal blood. Now that you have given birth, you have no reason to be here."

"I want to talk to the king," she moved to go to his room.

"You know he is not here. He's in Edinburgh meeting with the three estates," the Queen Mother folded her arms, enjoying Maggie's discomfort.

"I want to take my son with me if I am being banished."

"Don't be so dramatic. You aren't being banished. You are going to your rightful place as the Lady of Loch Leven, wife of Sir Robert Douglas. Did you think having the king's son would change any of that?"

Maggie hung her head. She knew this day would come, but she also believed, hoped naively that James would figure a way for it not to happen.

"Fine," she said, defeated, all of her energy used in healing from childbirth. "I'll go. But just know that everything I have done has been for James's benefit."

"Don't use the Christian name of the king!" the Queen Mother spat at her. "Respect your position. You tried to become the Queen of Scots. And you failed."

"No," Maggie spun around, summoning her strength. "I've always thought about what is best for James. And I will use his Christian name because he has asked me to. He is my best friend, and I only want what is best for him." She felt the tears threatening, and looked at the ceiling to keep them from falling. How could the Queen Mother not understand that everything she did was for James?

The Queen Mother softened. "I too have only wanted what is best for my son. Even though he hasn't always seen it that way. And we both know a queen from a wealthy kingdom is what will keep James and Scotland safe."

"I know, Queen Mother. I know you love him more than anything else in this world," Maggie said, her voice breaking. "I love him too. I love him for giving me a son, for creating a legacy that he so wants. And I love him enough to go to Loch Leven so he will marry a princess because that is what is best for him and for Scotland."

She walked out of the room with nothing but her pride. She knew the Queen Mother had heard what she said—and didn't say—and admired her for it.

The ride to Loch Leven was torturous, even the Queen's smoothest ambler could not comfort Maggie. She felt every step in her healing abdomen. The tears fell, she had no reason to stop them. They fell because she would never see the king again in his intimate chambers, connecting to her room, never circle his wrist and hold their baby. Her family, and her life, would be forever fractured.

Loch Leven's five-story gray stone keep rose from the island in the middle of the lake. A servant took the reins of the ambler as she dismounted and stepped into the boat to be taken across to the castle. She looked back at the rolling hills towards Stirling, towards all that she loved. Tears threatened to fall, but she held them in, not willing to give her husband any ammunition to hurt her. He would have a perfect Scottish wife, unemotional but loyal. And he would never know who she really had been, who she was with the king. The boat pulled alongside the jetty and Maggie disembarked. She walked along the curtain wall, cool gray stones mimicking her own heart, and through a small door next to the keep. Her husband had assembled the household, and anger flared in Maggie when she realized that he had been expecting her.

"Welcome home, my lady," Robert said, holding his hand outstretched. Maggie hesitated. It felt like a trap, was he going to throw her into the circular tower at the far end of the courtyard and never allow her to escape? Would she be allowed back to James's court? Would he even want her?

All eyes were on Maggie. Doubt crept into Robert's eyes, hardening them. She swallowed and took his hand, the obedient wife. This was her life, this was what was expected of her. And she needed to accept it.

Chapter 21

JAMES

THEY HAD SENT HER away, Mags was gone when he came back from Edinburgh. He had gone straight to her rooms, only to find them bare, stripped of tapestries and curtains, and Maggie's light.

His mother was holding an audience with Sir David Lindsay, deciding what to do with his life without him.

"I know you aren't composing a flyting, so you must be conspiring with my mother now, Sir Lindsay," James said, not even trying to keep the anger from surfacing.

"Your Grace," David stood up. "I am conversing with an old friend. And we are both worried about you." James noticed the gray hairs peeking from under his barret.

James glanced at his mother, but her eyes were on the window.

"You sent her away," he said to his mother.

"Yes," her head snapped toward him. "She needed to go to her rightful husband. You claimed her for far too long."

"She had my son, Mother."

"Who is thriving here at Stirling with his wet nurse," she walked around her chair, but not near him. James circled the room, remaining opposite of her. "We need to focus on Scotland's future."

"To find me a proper wife and truly make my son a bastard?" he said. "I'll marry her still if I choose to and then her son will be king."

David stepped in. "Your Highness, emotion is coloring your thinking. This girl is married, and not royal. She is taking you away from what is right for your country."

"Not you too, David," James sank into a chair, hands in his hair, weary from fighting his mother.

"Yes, *Schir*," David knelt in front of him. "The Douglases taught you that this is what a king does, but it is not. You need to be the moral head of the country."

"Why? My father had children and mistresses with real Scottish women," he said. His mother flinched, but quickly recovered.

"Ay, he did. But he married a princess and had legitimate heirs to his throne. He knew he couldn't marry a Scottish woman. His destiny was bigger than that," David stood. He looked at the unicorn tapestry. "Scotland is bigger than common concerns. You need to raise your thinking and not give into your base desires as the Douglases hoped you would. You need to prove Angus wrong."

At the mention of the Douglases, James snapped out of his self-pity. He knew he was the king and needed to take care of his country. He knew Maggie would go to her husband, but he didn't like that his mother had made the decision.

"I will marry a French princess," he said. "When King François is ready. And until then, I will spend my nights with whomever I please." He grit his teeth on the last word.

"But Sir Erskine, your secretary, failed to secure the contract," his mother said. "You need to broaden your search. You didn't even send him to Rome."

"If he went to Rome, it would be to secure an annulment," he snapped. "And I know you wouldn't have wanted that, Mother."

"We will be patient, your Highness," David stepped in again. "But there are finances to think about as well. And a royal bride would help to alleviate that."

James rubbed his beard, still short, but growing. He knew all of what they were saying was true. But he felt like they were backing him into a corner. And like any cornered animal, he would fight.

"I'm the king. I'm the only one who needs to worry about this," he said.

"Your Grace," David tried to sooth him. "We are all with you and want to help you make Scotland prosperous."

"Well then I need to meet with my council to decide the next steps," he moved to leave the room, pausing at the door. "And you two clucking like old hens aren't helping at all."

He pulled the heavy oak door behind him, wanting it to slam, but there was only a dull thud.

Chapter 22

THOMAS

THOMAS TAPPED HIS QUILL against the ink well. His trip had not secured a wife. The king hadn't been upset, too preoccupied with Maggie's pregnancy and birth, but Thomas felt the weight of disappointment from others in Scotland. The Queen Mother for one, whose anger was just as frightening as her son's or her brother's. He also didn't want to be sent away from court again and longed to stay in the country and near James. His small office in Holyrood Castle just outside Edinburgh to the east was lined in oak paneling and covered with earthy colored tapestries. The fireplace was carved with strawberry vines and thistle blooms, jumping as the fire flickered. For the moment, the king's uncle in England, Henry, was preoccupied with putting his wife aside for a new one. Rumors were that the new object of Henry's affections would not have sex with him unless Henry married her. Thomas shuddered. So much effort for a brief carnal moment.

Even his king was not immune to the charms of the female sex. He wanted Thomas to appeal to the pope to annul his cousin's marriage. Luckily, Thomas had talked him out of it, for the moment. But love would make a king do crazy things, so he needed to come up with an alternative plan—and fast.

Finnart came into his office and flicked papers, smiling. Thomas felt the annoyance rising. He did not see the charm of this man. James clearly was infatuated with him, loved having him around, even appointed him Master of the Stables. A position that Finnart abused when the king was not there.

"What are you working on now, dobber? Ya need to get outside, ya look a little peely-wally," Finnart laughed, although his thick eyebrow ridge made it look like he was scowling. He was James's cousin, both of them descending from James II. Finnart was a burly man, with thick calves and broad shoulders, which looked even broader in his padded overcoat. He used his size to intimidate smaller men like Thomas.

"Some of us work for our pay," Thomas said through tight lips. Finnart had never done a day's work, preferring to chase women or animals, and sometimes both at the same time. He was so uncouth that Thomas was sure he chased the animals just to have sex with them.

"Ay, and that's your problem! So serious Thom!" he laughed, flopping into a padded side chair. Finnart was called the king's minion, allowed to sleep in his chambers when they went on a hunt. Thomas sickened at the thought. He turned back to his papers and hoped Finnart would take a hint and leave. Just as Finnart stood up, James burst in.

"Ay!" Finnart slapped the king on the back. "We were just talking about you. And how we need to get old Thom out of the office and out into the wild. Maybe a hunting trip?" His lips barely contained his teeth when he smiled.

"Yes, my friend. We will plan that soon," he said, brushing Finnart off. Thomas stifled a smile. "Right now, I need to discuss business with Erskine."

"Alright. Just don't try to get any Primero tips from Erskine. I still want to beat you," Finnart moved off and James waited until the door clicked behind him until he spoke. Thomas refrained from snorting at Finnart's blatant admission of taking the king's money at cards.

"I need to raise money, Thomas," he said, elbows on the desk. His brown eyes were clouded with worry. "If I were able to raise money here in Scotland, then I wouldn't need a foreign bride."

Thomas held his breath. He knew James still wanted to marry his cousin and legitimize their son. Thomas needed to tread lightly. The king's heart was open, vulnerable, but he also needed to be honest with him.

"The treasury is nearly empty, thanks to Angus," James snarled. Thomas nodded, formulating how he was going to handle this situation. "And we have to punish those who stood with Angus and did nothing to help me. There are so many that need to be brought before the court and tried."

Thomas sat up. He had seen a judicial college when he attended the University of Pavia in Italy. "We could set up a college of justice. And appoint members of the three estates to serve as judges."

"Yes, and then we could try these cases, and raise money from the clergy," James said.

"The pope would agree if you promise to remain loyal to him," Thomas said. "He is worried about your uncle and the divorce he wants. And more and more duchies are accepting Martin Luther's religion—Saxony, Hesse, Prussia, Swabia, Thuringia. He needs your loyalty."

"Then let's appeal to him for an annual tax on the clergy for the College of Justice," James said, excitement bubbling from him. "We can appoint clergy and pay a salary, and most of the money will go into the crown's purse. That will free me to marry whomever I choose."

Thomas's head snapped up. So this was what the king wanted. He didn't care about justice, he wanted money to marry his cousin.

"My lord, that is not a good idea," Thomas said, willing to incur the king's wrath. "The clergy will see through what you are doing and be angry that you are confiscating church moneys just so you can marry..." He stopped himself from saying, *a Scottish whore.*

"I'm the king. They should support me and my decision," his temper flared.

"But you know Archbishop Beaton will not agree. He may talk others into not supporting the tax. And then you will be in the same position financially, but in a worse position with the church. And look at all the trouble that is causing your uncle in England."

"Just draft the proposal for the tax to send to the pope," he said, moving toward the door. "And I'll take care of the clergy."

Thomas stared at the door long after it closed. This was a dangerous plan the king wanted him to propose. All for a woman.

Chapter 23

MAGGIE

MAGGIE SAT AT THE table next to her husband in a high back oak chair. The hall was lit with several candelabras, and the fire blazed from the far end of the hall, the Douglas of Loch Leven red and white arms illuminated over the mantel. She looked at the far wall, the only wall paneled in oak. The walls were covered in fresco murals, not colorful and intricate tapestries as at Stirling. The plates were pewter, not silver, the glasses not finely cut crystal. She was looking at her house and trying to see what James saw. Would the house be too common to him? Would it change how he saw her?

She stole a glance at the king, in the seat of honor. His beard twitched when he spoke, full beard grown in since she had seen him last. Butterflies erupted in her abdomen watching his lips move. Her husband's gaze weighed her down. She met his gaze, with all of its accusations and malice. James's visit had been a surprise to her, but her husband did not believe that.

"You invited him here," he charged.

"I did not," she said, unable to control the excitement at hearing he was coming, and the dread of having him in her husband's home.

"I don't trust you," his eyes narrowed to slits.

"I have been a model wife," she began, but he interrupted.

"Oh yes, a model wife while you were fucking him," he said. She clenched her fists but her face remained calm. No emotion. She wanted him to see no emotions.

"Yes. A model wife after I had his child. You arranged this contract with my *father*, not me," she replied, her voice flat, devoid of the emotions broiling inside of her.

"And I expected a pure wife, not one who had been used," he said.

"You are the one who is benefiting from my affair and my child. Didn't the king grant you more land?" she was finished with this conversation, tired of being punished for her affair by Robert every chance he got. It was exhausting. She turned to leave, but he grabbed her arm.

"You think you are so much better than me, but you aren't. You're just another of the king's whores," his face was an inch from her face.

"I'm here now," she said, teeth clenched.

"You have nowhere else to go," he hissed and flung her arm away from him. She watched him walk away, knowing he was right. She couldn't go back to Stirling, couldn't go to Alloa Tower, her family's ancestral castle. Even though the castle was only eight miles east of Stirling, it had never been Maggie's home as much as Stirling had. Her older sister Katherine had been married off before Maggie was able to establish a relationship with her, so she couldn't go to there either. She had to stay at Loch Leven and accept whatever abuse her husband devised for her. Her life was a prison. Robert would not forgive her, and she still wanted James to find a way for her to become his wife, even though she knew a French wife would be much better for Scotland. She buried her head in her hands. James was coming here, which should be an honor for her husband to entertain the king at his home, but it was going to be torture for her, to see him, watch him and go back to her husband's bed.

And now he was in her dining hall, and her husband's envy was palpable. But for tonight, Maggie didn't care. She caught James's eye. The deep brown reflected her feelings—desire, anticipation, adoration. As long as he still had those feelings, she would continue to hope that he would get her out of this marriage. She wanted to have a private conversation with him, to hear news of Jamie and how he was growing, and to express the feelings they both stifled. But with her husband's watchful eyes on her, that would be impossible.

Finnart, the king's friend, overturned a chalice of wine. Maggie jumped up to avoid any getting on her dress, the green dress the king had given her after she birthed his son. Her lip twitched into a smile. Finnart was a bad influence on the king, took him out carousing for women. But he also encouraged the king to come here to see Maggie and to try to marry her. She appreciated that, even though she heard James had another child on the way from his excursions with Finnart. Her heart squeezed as she thought of him with someone else. Maybe he did what she did.... Imagined it was him while she was with her husband. She closed her eyes and pretended. And her husband believed in the moment that she enjoyed it.

"Finnart, you drunken roaster!" James roared with laughter. Finnart was so drunk that he upset the cup again when he went to pick it up. Maggie grabbed a rag from the servant and rushed over to clean up, kneeling in front of the king. He opened his legs, his cod piece bulging. The naked desire bordered on desperation. She wanted to slide her body up along his and feel him along her. Her face moved to smile, but she pursed her lips.

"The lady of the house should not be cleaning up this jakey's mess," he reached down and took her arm, lifting her from the floor. Robert stared, his puppy-dog eyes wide with jealousy. Maggie knew she would pay for this later, but she couldn't stop the buzzing from climbing up her arm from his hand.

"Looks like the lassie wants to clean up something else," Finnart slapped the king on the back. Maggie snapped to attention, color draining from her face. James grabbed Finnart's doublet.

"Shut your face," he growled. "Don't ever talk about her like that."

No one moved; Maggie froze, limbs leaden with fear. The musicians stopped playing, cut off in the middle of the melody. The candles flickered, throwing menacing shadows. The king held Finnart's shirt, Finnart's face was slack, but his eyes were sober. Her husband froze midstep. He turned to look at Maggie, his eyes hard with malice. Her heart hammered against her chest, not knowing which to fear more—James's anger toward Finnart, or her husband's rage toward her. Even though Maggie had done nothing wrong, rancor seeped from Robert, jealous fangs spitting venom at her. She knew he would punish her for creating this tension in his home. She swung back to James, knowing his rage was equally dangerous. He had the power of life and death in his hands—and by disrespecting Maggie, Finnart had disrespected his king. James flared his nose in anger, which Maggie recognized as his warning sign. She held her breath—caught between her husband and her lover.

Then Finnart laughed. The king released Finnart's doublet in confusion. Finnart laughed and laughed. He pounded on the table, and coughed from laughter. Maggie watched the anger drain from James's eyes, replaced with mirth.

"Oh, your Grace," Finnart said between guffaws. "You are really too much sometimes. The honor you have for your Scottish subjects." The king smiled and shrugged his shoulders, tension broken.

"Please, Sir Robert," he turned to Maggie's husband. "Can we have more wine and finish this bountiful meal?" He turned his back on Maggie and sat down, ignoring her to diffuse the tension. Finnart continued to laugh as her husband motioned for the server to pour the wine. Robert's anger smoldered, dampened by the king's laughter, but Maggie knew he would not forget.

After dinner, the men retired to play cards. Maggie climbed the spiral stairs to her chamber, locking the door behind her. She didn't want her husband to come to her room tonight, not while James was on her mind. The king had let his guard down, and she had too. Her husband had seen her true feelings for the king. Tomorrow she would put her mask back on, but tonight, she just wanted to remember how the king looked at her.

She drifted off to sleep with the king's mahogany eyes on her face, his hands on her hips. A clink against the window jolted her out of sleep. She went to the window and yanked the curtains open. Below, standing in the courtyard was James, grinning like a mischievous boy. The effects of wine caused him to sway. She opened the leaden window, pane creaking.

"Come down!" he whispered. "Let's ride into town together."

"This is an island!" she whispered back. "We can't leave without the servants knowing."

"Then I will have to come up," he said and grabbed the vines growing up the castle wall. The vines groaned and began pulling away from the castle.

"You're going to fall," she said, but the vines held and he reached her windowsill.

"I always get what I want," he said, throwing his leg over. She rolled her eyes at his arrogance, but still glad he was pursuing her.

"I thought you would mature as the king," she said as she backed up to allow him into her chamber. He stood in front of her, drinking her up. He ran his fingers along the collar of her nightdress.

"You bring out the boy in me," he whispered into her ear. She released into his arms, wrapping her arms around his neck, crushing his mouth with hers. He responded with equal hunger, leading her back to the bed.

"God, I missed you," he grunted into her hair, pulling her nightdress up and over her head. She smiled and pulled off his hose, working at the doublet. They quickly came together and collapsed in an ecstatic exhaustion.

"I have a plan," he said, tracing his finger along her hip. She propped herself up on her elbow, wondering what this plan entailed.

"What is your plan?" she nuzzled his neck, so happy to be back in his arms, even if it was just for a night.

"I'm going to bring Jamie here to live," he said. Maggie bounded up.

"Do you mean it? Will your mother allow it? Oh I've missed him so much. Is he well? Has he started sitting up? Crawling?" she said, pulling on his beard. He laughed.

"I haven't seen him much myself," he said. "But if he is here, then I have a reason to be here too. Your husband isn't so stupid to refuse the king's son."

Maggie froze, unsure how her husband would react. "What if he is cruel to Jamie? I wouldn't be able to handle that."

"Oh Mags," he laughed. "No one would dare cross you. I think you spent too much time with my mother."

She turned her head, insulted to be called stubborn and obstinate as his mother, even if it were true.

"I can handle him being unkind to me, but not to my son," she said. Now it was James's turn to sit up.

"He's unkind to you?"

"It's fine," she said, placing her hand on his bearded face. The hair was so soft under her hand. "He's jealous of our relationship."

James laid back down. "He should be. But I've compensated him well." Maggie nodded, not telling him that land and money did nothing to ease her husband's jealousy.

"I'm proposing a tax on the church property," he said, curling her hair around his hand. "To replenish the state coffers."

Maggie murmured and closed her eyes, just wanting to hear his voice echo in his chest and her head.

"So that I can marry you," he said. Maggie's eyes snapped open. He did have a plan!

"So you can marry me?" she asked, unable to keep the anticipation out of her voice. He kissed her forehead.

"Once the churches pay taxes, I'll have more than enough money to marry you and turn Scotland into the northern jewel it should be. And since I am supporting the pope and not embracing my uncle's brand of religion, he will grant me whatever I want. What I want is for him to grant a divorce to you," he said. "What did I tell you? I always get what I want." Maggie knew it was arrogant optimism, but just maybe he could pull it off.

1534

Chapter 24

THE QUEEN MOTHER

MARGARET SIGHED, LOOKING OUT the leaden window, the air damp with Scottish mist. There was so much going on in England, with her daughter, with her brother, that she wanted to be in London. Her younger sister, Mary, had passed away almost a year ago, never fully recovered from the sweating sickness, the same sickness that took their sweet older brother. Margaret wrote to her brother for permission to attend her sister's funeral, but he did not respond.

Instead, she read about Mary's funeral in a letter from her daughter—the procession from her sister's house in Suffolk to Bury St. Edwards where she was lain to rest. The lead coffin, borne on a black velvet carriage, had been drawn by six horses draped in black velvet. The king of France had sent a golden crown and scepter to honor her as the dowager queen of France, her effigy dressed in purple velvet robes of state. At the Requiem mass, Mary's daughters and Margaret's own daughter brought the palls of cloth of gold to the altar. Margaret should have been there, her brother should have allowed her to grieve their sister.

She remembered the last time she had seen her sister, when Margaret fled Scotland. With her baby daughter, she traveled to London and was welcomed at Greenwich Palace, the place of her birth, by her brother, his wife, and Mary, who had been accepted back at court after defying Harry and marrying Charles Brandon in Paris. Margaret couldn't wait to talk to her about it. She looked around for Ard.

"Where is my husband, the Earl of Angus?" she asked, bewildered.

"Done like a Scot," Harry said, shaking his head. "Fled home with his tail between his legs."

Margaret frowned, he was supposed to meet her in London. Before she could think about what this meant, her brother whisked her off to a grand jousting tournament held in her honor. In an octagonal tower built overlooking the tiltyard, she sat between her sister Mary and her sister-in-law Catherine, all three new mothers. In addition to Margaret's daughter, the family had welcomed a daughter born to Catherine and Harry, and a son born to Mary and her husband Charles. The birth of his daughter put Harry in good humor. He provided all of the clothing for the jousters and built the stands. Harry and Charles were both listed to joust. Charles mounted first, clad in blue and black velvet with golden honeysuckle blossoms woven into his saddle blanket and bridle, which shimmered in the May sunshine. He approached the stands and offered lance to Mary, who tied her ribbon to it. The three women burst into giggles. Margaret wished her own husband was there to joust as well, and she felt like the old spinster as her two friends bathed in the glow of their husbands. After Charles unhorsed his opponent, it was Harry's turn. Harry, of course one for pageantry, fought in purple velvet, embroidered with golden Tudor roses. He blew Catherine a kiss before he lowered his visor.

"It vexes me that he endangers his royal person so," she said through tight lips. Mary patted her arm, which reminded Margaret that she was a stranger in her own country, the country she loved so much, the country for which she had sacrificed her own existence in order to bring peace. She was considered too Scottish here, and too English there. She sighed, wishing her husband were there to comfort her.

Harry's opponent, Sir William Kingston, the constable of the Tower of London, was reported to be a good knight. His long arms gave him a slight advantage physically. Harry spurred his horse forward, hugging the wooden tilt barrier. Kingston, however, knowing the superior jousting level of the king, chose to ride wide of the railing. Harry lowered his lance over the barricade and connected with Kingston's chest armor, knocking him off his horse with a clanging thud. But because the hit was not direct, the lance did not shatter, and so Harry was not awarded full points. Harry ripped off his visor, face red from exertion and anger, and yelled into the list at the queued jousters, "I promised never to joust again except against as good a man as myself. My opponents are too lily-livered to joust honorably." Margaret inhaled, losing patience with her brother's childish tantrum. She had hoped he would mature as a king, but he was as selfish as he had been when they were children. His kingdom was rich materially, but Harry's character was still poor.

Being in London, her chambers in Baynard Castle overlooking the Thames, surrounded by the magnificence of the English court, Margaret wished she could stay forever supported by Mary and Catherine. Advent was celebrated as she remembered from her childhood—lighting the wreath candles as they celebrated mass in the chapel, Catherine and Harry being very pious.

Greenwich Palace was full of light and mirth for the Feast of Kings. All three siblings sat in state, on royal dais with their own royal covering. A garden-artificial was rolled in. Inside of the golden gate was green silk arranged to look like grass and silk and gold roses to represent the Tudor siblings and a pomegranate to represent Catherine's Spain. Then twelve men and women performed a ballet in their honor. Margaret felt the connections of her family. She didn't have to deal with the back stabbing Scottish nobles.

But then Albany had to return to France and her brother sent her back north to reconcile with her husband.

She hugged her sister to her, forehead touching hers.

"I want you to have this," she pressed the Book of Hours into Mary's palm.

"No, Margaret," she protested. "Father gave this to you. You need to keep it."

"Mary, if I never make it back to my beloved homeland, I want this book to be here, where my family lies," she said, realizing it was true. Once she left London, she would never see her sister again.

That was before Harry decided to set aside Catherine. Unable to procure a divorce from the pope, he declared himself the Supreme Head of the Church of England in 1532. Margaret had been trying, unsuccessfully, to arrange a meeting between her brother and her son. While her brother was willing, her son was too suspicious.

That her brother was protecting Angus did not help sway her son to trust him. His vendetta against Angus grew the longer Ard was in England. Harry was also not reprimanding the border reivers as he should be on the English side, which was also upsetting James, as he prided himself on protecting his subjects. Margaret would not give up, even when her brother called her the mother of his enemy.

She was saddened that she was unable to join Scotland and England as her father wished when he sent her off to Scotland twenty-one years earlier. She had always been his favorite, the oldest daughter, and with the death of Arthur, his oldest living child. Before he left her, he patted her hand and said, "My dear daughter, you will bring peace between us and our mortal enemy. Your children and my children will keep that peace because of their familiar ties." And Margaret tried, but her son was too much of a Scot to accept what her own father had tried so hard to achieve.

Her brother was not blameless in this. Harry's attention was diverted to his efforts to produce a male heir. He secretly married Anne Boleyn in November, and had a formal wedding in January of 1533. Her sister's letter had told about the wedding, which she did not attend. The bride recommended a new archbishop for Canterbury, who annulled Harry's marriage to Catherine, for which the pope excommunicated Harry. Her own daughter was named first lady of honor to Queen Anne. *Queen Anne*, the name stuck in Margaret's throat. Her brother had put aside a pious, loyal woman because he was *gantin*, as the Scots said. *Horny.*

Her daughter needed her mother to attend to her marriage prospects. At nineteen, she should be arranging for a suitable marriage. She had tried to contract the young girl to the Earl of Lennox's son, but Ard would not hear of it since the earl fought against him to free James in 1526. God knows Ard wasn't thinking about his daughter as he stirred up trouble for James on the Scottish borders.

Chapter 25

JAMES

NOTHING WAS HOW JAMES wanted it to be. As Thomas predicted, the bishops did protest the tax. Archbishop Beaton, still smarting over Dunbar's appointment to chancellor over him, refused to pay. James was livid that one of his subjects should refuse his command.

"I want him tried for treason!" he told Thomas.

"*Schir*," Thomas said, always the diplomat, "withholding taxes isn't a treasonable offense. We can have him warded to send a message."

James sighed and dragged his hand through his hair. "Fine. As long as it is harsh enough that no other prelate will withhold payment."

"I believe the message will be received," Thomas said, exhaling in relief. James noticed that Thomas looked tired, purple rings under his eyes, hair disheveled. He softened.

"When was the last time you took a day off, Thomas?" he asked. Thomas shook his head, light brown curls springing.

"My duty is to you, my lord," he said. He had the same hazel eyes as Maggie. A pang struck him in his chest. He missed her so much, but raising money was slower than he anticipated, especially when the borders were constantly in turmoil. At least his uncle was preoccupied with his new bride.

"Go home, Thomas," James patted his shoulder, his loyal secretary. "Go make a baby, fuck your mistress or whoever gets you off."

Thomas shuddered under his hand. He was wound too tight, James thought. He needed a good fucking.

"Your Highness," Thomas said as James turned to leave the room. "We should discuss a royal marriage. That will fix all of Scotland's money problems."

James came back, sighing, "Alright Thomas. Let's go over the options again." He dropped into a red velvet scissor chair.

"Well, there is still the pope's niece, Catherine de Medici, to consider," Thomas rifled through velum parchments on his desk. "The Duke of Albany is also her uncle and has recommended her."

"Fine. But when you write to the pope, I also need you to request ecclesiastic offices for my sons," he said. Thomas stopped shuffling the papers, surprised. James smiled. "I would be less than human if I didn't take care of my offspring. Yes, I want to take care of my boys and have them trained to become Priors."

Thomas recovered from his shock. "Of course. I will send a letter off at once. And King François offered his cousin, Marie de Bourbon. A sketch was sent." He pushed a sketch across the desk. James studied the drawing. The girl had wide, open eyes, a straight Aquiline nose, and thin lips curled into a half smile. Her face was round and pleasant. But she wasn't Mags.

"I'll think about it," he said, pushing the drawing back, longing to see the fire in Maggie's eyes when she argued with him. He was suffocating under the pressures of his kingdom—money issues, Angus at the borders, coercion to marry a French bride. Only with Maggie could he sort out his feelings, what to do. In front of Thomas and other members of the council, he needed to be the king, the authoritarian. But with Maggie, he could shed the robes of the king and be himself. He needed to see her.

He rode to Loch Leven, surprising the castle. He was shown to the interior chamber, where he paced while he waited. Once he looked into her eyes, he would be reassured that he was taking the right actions, that she still loved him, that her love was constant no matter the time it was taking to free her from her loveless marriage and raise her to be his queen. With her support, he knew he could raise Scotland to a place of prominence, and earn the respect of his uncle and other European kings. He could cast off those doubts that Angus and his brother planted—that he was weak, a poor shadow of his father. He would prove them wrong. If only Angus hadn't drained the treasury, if only he didn't need to raise the money quickly. If only the pope would grant a divorce to Maggie. He paused at the window, looking out at the water, green meadows rolling in the background. He was the island, and everyone was lapping at his shores to advance themselves. Only Maggie thought of what was best for him. He had to find a way to make her his wife. If only...

Hearing the door creak, he turned away from the window as she came in, holding his son's hand. The boy looked just like him, red hair waving in all directions, large brown eyes soaking him in, his head tilted. James wanted to open his arms and have his son run into them. He looked to Maggie for her permission. Maggie stood in an awkward silence, wearing a plain kirtle, stomach huge.

"You're pregnant," he said, unable to keep the emotion out of his voice. Maggie nodded, wrapping her hand around her belly. James stood, unsure what to do next.

"Is it mine?" he asked, hoping it was, that she was carrying another royal child and provide even more reason for him to make her his queen. Her eyes pierced him, jolting his heart. The doubt folded over him like the Scottish fog.

"I don't know," she said. He wanted to go to her, to take her in his arms, but he felt paralyzed. He hoped she would say yes, and he would have another reason for the pope to grant her a divorce. But she hadn't.

"You don't know?" anger crept in his voice. He knew he shouldn't be angry, she was married. Had he expected her to not sleep with her husband? He shook his head, not wanting to think about it.

"No, I don't know," she led their son over to the settee and took a seat. The boy picked up a wooden sap whistle and chewed on it.

"But..." he started but was not able to continue. What could he ask, *did you sleep with your husband?* Of course she had. He knew she had to, whether she wanted to or not.

"James," she exhaled, "I can't lie to you. I don't know. It might be, but it might be his." She buried her face in her hands, shoulders shaking. That shaking broke his bravado, and he rushed to her side, putting his arms around her.

"It doesn't matter," he murmured into her hair. "It doesn't matter."

"But it does," she pushed him back and pointed to their son. "Jamie is your son. He is royal. I want this one to be too. I do." James wiped a tear off her cheek with his thumb. She leaned into his hand.

"This is my life. I am Lady Douglas of Loch Leven. And I have to say this is his child."

Her sadness transferred to him. He felt the tears form.

"It wasn't fast enough," he said. "The tax hasn't raised enough money, Mags. I *want* to marry you, but the treasury is still empty." He hung his head, defeated. She was carrying a child that might be his, *should* be his, but there would always be doubt in his mind, in hers. He couldn't bear the disappointment in her green eyes, washing over him and coating him. All hope was gone.

"No, James," she lifted his face in her hands. "Even if the tax was collected, would it be enough?"

He shrugged, knowing it wouldn't be. The way out of his financial problems was a royal marriage to secure an alliance. But an alliance would not provide him with the emotional security that Maggie gave him.

"You need to marry someone who will bring wealth back into Scotland," she said, her eyes rimmed in red, but not crying, putting on a brave face to protect him. She would always try to protect him, even when he didn't agree with her. He bristled, as he always did, when someone suggested that a marriage alliance was the only way to bring glory to Scotland. No, he wanted to build that glory with Maggie. But that was not possible. His shoulders sagged from the weight of the realization, finally understanding what his mother, his advisors, and Maggie herself had been trying to make him see.

"I want to marry you," he ran his hand over her hair, her golden hair uncovered in her home. Her home, with her husband and their child. The recognition hardened his heart. "But I can't because you're married. And I have to do what is best for Scotland."

She nodded, clenching her jaw and holding back tears. There was nothing else to say. He rode back to Holyrood and told Thomas, "Make arrangements. I'll go to France to meet Marie de Bourbon." Even as he put forth in motion a way to get Scotland out of its financial trouble, he knew part of his life was over forever.

1536

Chapter 26

THOMAS

THE KING WAS ANXIOUS to depart, but Thomas hung back. The July sky was dark—gray, purple, and green swirling clouds which the sea leapt to meet. Even though it was early afternoon, an eerie twilight blanketed the wharf. The sails snapped against the three masts of the *Mary Willoughby*, which bobbed in the turbulent water. The ship had been his uncle's, until the king's men captured it off the coast of Ireland. The ship was fitted with canons to break blockades by the British, to raid English commercial ships. It had been repainted crimson with yellow accents, Scotland's colors, and the royal crest painted on the stern, the twin white unicorns in contrast to the red lion with blue tongue and claws on the yellow coat of arms.

"Nice day for a trip, eh?" Finnart said, slapping Thomas on the back. Thomas flinched but Finnart didn't noticed. He was already at the king's shoulder, leaning into him. "I don't think we will be able to throw bones tonight *Schir*," he said, squinting at the menacing storm. "Guess I'll have to take your money playing cards!"

The king shot a look at Finnart, but he was oblivious. Thomas noted that the king seemed annoyed with Finnart more often. He was losing his place as the favorite. The thought propelled Thomas toward the boat despite his misgivings.

The captain of the ship removed his grey wool cap and bowed before the king. "The weather might not hold, your highness. If need be, to what harbor should we direct our course?" The apprehension over the weather deepened the furrows of his leathered brow. The wind whipped his scarlet and yellow jacket away from his body.

"Any except for England," the king laughed, spirits high. The captain clicked his stiff boots together and turned to prepare for departure.

The boat careened in the harbor, and Thomas's stomach was already flipping. Even with his multiple voyages to the continent, he had never been a sailor, preferring his feet on firm ground. But the king has asked him as the secretary to make this trip to execute a marriage contract with Marie de Bourbon. And he was thrilled to be going with the king.

"Let's go to the great cabin and have a drink to calm our stomachs," James said. The party was small, none of the major earls were invited. James was going to send Finnart and Thomas to secure the marriage contract, but decided last minute that he should also go to see her. They were meeting his half-brother Moray in France.

The great cabin ran the width of the stern, under the Quarter-deck. The white-washed walls reflected the light that shone in from rows of leaden windows above the water's surface. The green waves clawed at the glass. Thomas kept his eyes on a knot in the wood to steady himself.

James had sat at a carved oak desk, "Come on, Thomas. A shot will calm you down." He held out a small pewter cup. Thomas lumbered over to the table on unsteady legs. Finnart chortled when he fell into a chair.

"I still can't believe the pope denied Maggie a divorce," Finnart said as he poured more whisky into the three cups. Thomas threw back the liquor to keep from speaking.

James shook his head, "I'm not going to think about that today. I will contract a royal bride who will bring wealth into Scotland that Maggie couldn't." He stared off a moment before throwing back the shot. Thomas swallowed the guilt that crawled up his throat. James had sent him to Rome earlier that year to procure a divorce.

Upon his arrival in Rome, Thomas was led through a maze of white marble porticos and hallways lined with Swiss guards, the best and most reliable protection in Europe, and was shown into Sala Regia. The current pope had the hall built to hold audience with royal dignitaries and ambassadors. The coffered ceiling arched high above the inlayed marble floor. Sunlight streamed in through large windows, highlighting the gold leaf details. Below the frescoed walls sat the pope in a red velvet throne on the dais. Thomas knelt and kissed the wizened, outstretched hand of Pope Paul III, who had been the head of the Catholic Church for less than two years.

"You know of the break from the church by your highness's uncle, the King of England," the pope stroked his bushy white beard, which contrasted with his red velvet cape and hat.

Thomas nodded, heat building under his doublet, which was much too heavy in the Mediterranean heat. "Yes, your Holiness. It is a pity that some kings feel they are bigger than God's holy leader on Earth." He was rewarded with a snort from the pope. Paul III's family was entwined with the de' Medici and Borgia families, whose corruption of the office was one of the grievances of the Protestants. His sister had been the mistress of Pope Alexander IV. The Italians, in their coarseness, referred to him as Cardinal Cunt before his elevation to pope.

"The criticism of Luther caused the early death of my predecessor," the pope said. Thomas nodded again, holding his tongue. The Protestants had caused many problems for the church. He had heard that Pope Clement VIII had been poisoned by Protestants in 1534, but there was no evidence of that. Thomas wondered if the break from the church by King Henry of England hadn't caused Clement's death.

"Our allies in France are strong, as your king well knows since they are his allies too," the pope said.

"Yes, and our royal king has no intention of following his uncle's wicked path, I assure you," Thomas said, feeling a drop of sweat roll down his spine. He wished for a cool Scottish breeze. This part of negotiations, while important, was not Thomas's strong point. He'd rather get to the reason for his visit. But the game had to be played. And patience was something he had cultivated through his youth in putting his desires aside for the benefit of others.

"Please let him know that we are addressing the corruption within and making reforms to our doctrine and tenets," the pope sat back. Thomas knew the reforms were superficial and didn't address the main problems within the church.

"I most surely will. He is also asking for a divorce for a Scottish noblewoman," Thomas jumped into the crux of the matter, all the while knowing he would betray his king. The pope raised his eyebrow, folding his hands across his chest. "She is a gentlelady, Margaret Douglas, who bore a child by the king."

"She has a child with your king? Was she married at the time?" the pope narrowed his eyes. This was a sin—both to commit adultery and to have a child out of wedlock, even though the pope had his own bastard children. Thomas nodded.

"What is your opinion?" the pope asked. The heat under Thomas's doublet flashed upward. His breath was shallow. He had come here to procure a divorce. James had trusted him to convince the pope to grant a divorce. But…. If he told the truth, he could stop the king from making a mistake. He knew he had the diplomatic skills to sway the pope. All he had to do was use them.

"My opinion is that the lady was married before the king and is leading him into grave temptation and endangering his royal soul," Thomas said. He hoped the pope couldn't see that he was sweating, the back of his undershirt soaked. He sat up tall and forced his eyes to remain steady. His breathing was shallow, so he concentrated on taking deep breaths not to arouse the pope's suspicions. He smoothed his sweaty palms over his hose, knowing that if this got back to James, Thomas would be racked, drawn and quartered, which was the punishment for treason. But even with the threat of death, it was worth it to prevent James from marrying Maggie, the person who had caused him the most harm.

"That is my opinion too," the pope said. "I will not grant a divorce to Lady Douglas."

The pope's decision was final. His word was the judgment of God. Thomas knew he had influenced the outcome, but he told the king he had done everything in his power to change the pope's mind, but it was to no avail. James believed him, sinking into depression.

"Then it was all for nothing," his downturned mouth made his nose look sharper, longer. Thomas wanted to embrace him, tell him it was not for nothing. But he remained standing. The king rubbed his eyes, head low.

"That was my last chance," he said to himself. "That was my last hope to marry her." He seemed to have forgotten Thomas, lost in his grief. The guilt stabbed at Thomas's stomach, but he shoved it down. No, Thomas had done what was necessary. He had to break Maggie's spell over James. Even though Thomas had a deeper reason, one that he could not express, the surface reasons were numerable.

"But, *Schir*, with the tax raised moneys to start a college of justice, you can strengthen Scotland's position with a royal marriage to a French princess," he said.

"But I won't marry a French princess," James snapped, eyes rimmed in red. "François won't allow his daughter to marry. So I have to settle for a bride beneath my station, a lesser French noble."

Thomas could feel his anguish and wanted to comfort the king by telling him that Maggie had also been beneath his station, and at least a French noblewoman would bring a princess dowry from François. But Thomas couldn't say what he truly wanted to say to James, so he remained quiet. James sighed and pushed himself to standing.

"Thomas, make plans to travel to France. Let's see this noble that François offers in place of a real French princess."

And that was how Thomas ended up on the ship, trying not to keel over from nausea—the motion of the boat stirring his guilt, threatening to heave itself out of him. James filled the cups again and all drank the liquor, lost in their own thoughts. To placate Maggie, James had granted Angus's seized castle of Tantallon to their son, Jamie.

Finnart took the denial of Maggie's divorce curiously hard. Why had he wanted James to marry Maggie? Did he hope to advance his own position and his family's? Thomas knew Finnart couldn't be trusted. His loyalty was only to himself and how he could benefit, just like his father. Thomas had to break Finnart's hold over the king.

James looked exhausted, dark circles under his eyes, cheeks gaunt behind his auburn beard. "I'm going to retire. You both should too, if you can rest with this storm," he smiled, but his eyes remained sad. The affable mood on the dock was just an act, Thomas could see now.

"Your highness, you rest. I'll see that we stay on course," Finnart said, helping James to his feet, the liquor affecting both of them as much as the keeling boat. Thomas remained at the table as the two of them stumbled into the bedchamber. A new emotion crept over him, it felt like guilt, some nausea, but it was from a very different place. Finnart came back alone and sat at the table, clutching a goblet of wine so it didn't spill and the boat tilted and keeled with the swells of the sea.

"I'm going to go and see what the captain thinks. The storm seems to be getting worse," he said, striding past Thomas. Thomas remained seated, surrounded with his unsettled emotions. His stomach lurched from the emotions and the sea swells.

Finnart returned a moment later. "The captain said the storm is getting worse the farther we go to sea. We need to make a decision. Should we wake up James?"

The wheels spun in Thomas's head. Maybe this was his chance to ram a wedge between the king and his minion. "No, no, let's go and talk to the captain together," Thomas said. He felt like a newborn colt, gangly on his feet. He stumbled into Finnart, who shoved him back. He glared at Finnart and climbed the stairs to the sterncastle and into the captain's cabin.

The pilot was at the wheel outside of the cabin, fighting against the roiling waves that crashed over the deck. The clouds encroached the sea and Thomas could barely differentiate the two. Rain created a curtain that further confused his eyes. They were sailing blind along the west coast of Scotland, in the narrow North Channel between Scotland and Ireland. Had they entered the Irish Sea? Were they passed the Isle of Mann? Wales could be on their left, but it also could be anywhere in England. Everything was shrouded in gray mist.

"What is the decision?" the captain asked, looking up from his map.

"How bad is the course?" Thomas replied, knowing that without sight, they could crash anywhere and be captured by the English.

"The boat is being blown east and into England's coast. I cannot safely sail us to France, and the king did not want to harbor in England," the captain said.

Thomas turned to Finnart. "You think we should go back to Scotland?" The king was determined to make it to France, to settle on a marriage. Finnart shrugged, noncommittal, which enraged Thomas.

"You are the one he calls his 'minion,'" Thomas said, unable to keep the bitterness out of his voice. "You need to make the decision. I don't want to be responsible for killing the king."

"Do you think we will wreck?" Finnart asked the captain, ignoring Thomas.

Thomas cut him off before he could answer. "You heard what the captain said as well as I did. He does not feel we will make it to France. You're going to put this on the captain? Be a man and make a decision!"

"Ok, fine! Let's go back to Scotland. For the safety of the king," he snarled at Thomas. Thomas spun to face the captain so Finnart would not see his joy.

"You heard him, let's go back to Scotland," Thomas said, satisfied that Finnart had decided to turn them back to Scotland. He turned on his heel to go under and take a nap himself, to stop his spinning stomach. He could not stand on the deck another minute and wonder if they would wreck on English land.

A few hours later, Thomas was shaken awake. Sunlight streamed through the round windows, highlighting the Scottish green hills.

"Are we back in Scotland?" James demanded, shaking Thomas. The ship was not rocking as it had been earlier. Thomas shook the sleep out of his face so he could respond. But James was already stomping up the stairs. Thomas hurried to follow him.

"What is going on?" James thundered at the captain.

"Your Grace, your retinue said to turn back rather than endanger your life," he said, tensing his hands.

"Who? Who said that?" James said. The captain looked at Thomas.

"It was Finnart that made the decision," Thomas said, pinching himself to remain calm.

"Finnart? Why?"

"He thought it would be safer to return rather than continue to France."

James narrowed his eyes, hands on hips, threatening. "He said to turn around? He never wanted me to go to France and find a bride. Has he been against me all along?"

"I don't know, *Schir*. I just know he said to turn back to Scotland," Thomas said, containing his excitement as the king's anger grew.

"He wanted me to marry a Scottish lady so I wouldn't have a foreign ally. Maybe everyone was right about him, maybe he never was there for me," he said, eyes darkening. "Finnart!"

He headed below deck to find Finnart, who was passed out in a hammock. James upset the hammock, dumping Finnart onto the floor.

"Did you turn us back to Scotland?" James asked.

"Aye," Finnart said and looked at Thomas. "We both decided to turn back."

"Not I," Thomas shook his head. "You made the decision." Finnart furled his eyebrows, perplexed.

"No, we decided together."

Thomas shook his head again, setting his lips in a thin line. He would let Finnart implicate himself.

"You never wanted me to marry a noble and make an alliance," James said. "You wanted to isolate me so you and your family could take advantage of me! Is that how you kept your employment when Angus kidnapped me? Is it?" His blood shot eyes bulged in anger.

Finnart's eyes widened. "No! You know I am on your side."

"No, I know you were working for Angus when I was held against my will. You took me out to sleep with women to distract me. It all is making sense now," James said.

"*Schir*! Please," Finnart's eyes darted like a caged animal. "I swear...."

"You swore allegiance to me, but now I see. You have never been on my side. You've only been thinking about how you could advance yourself," James said. The boat docked, and James marched off the boat. Thomas hurried after him, leaving Finnart standing, mouth hanging open.

Chapter 27

JAMES

FOR THE SECOND ATTEMPT at sailing to France, James made sure it was an imposing armada to impress France—and his uncle, should he attempt to thwart the trip. The weather would not cower him, but he wanted a blessing as an extra guarantee. He walked to the shrine of Our Lady of Loretto from Edinburgh to ask God for guidance on his voyage. The hermit monk, dressed in rough woolen robes, met him outside the shrine, a plain gray-bricked building with a domed roof. He bowed, kneeling and grasping James's hand.

"Father," James said, pulling the man to standing. "I come to ask God's blessing for my travels to France to find a queen."

The monk nodded and motioned to come in. James followed the monk to the statue of Our Lady brought back from Italy, draped in gold leaf. James knelt before it and clasped his hands, praying for God and Mary to give him a safe journey, to allow him to marry and bring a queen home for Scotland. And for him to put Maggie not out of his heart, but in a smaller place so that he could have affection for his new wife. He wasn't sure if he would be able to love her like he did Maggie, but at least he wanted to have an amicable marriage. The monk was rumored to be familiar with love potions, but James did not need one. He knew his potential bride would fall for him, and that he would not love anyone other than Maggie.

The *Mary Willoughby* was prepared to make another journey to France, along with five other Scottish ships. All of the nobles who were with him sailed—Arran, Argyll, Rothes, Bishop Beaton, Maggie's father, Lord Erskine, Lord Fleming. James hoped that the invitation of Arran, Finnart's younger, legitimate brother, was a knife in the heart to Finnart, punishment for steering the first voyage back to Scotland. Thomas also remained in Scotland to rule state affairs in James's absence.

Bishop David Beaton would act as his translator, having studied in Paris and been among François's court. Beaton was the youngest of eleven children, so the church was the only viable career open for him; however, he proved to be a quite capable cleric. His uncle, the Archbishop of St. Andrews, had gotten Beaton his start, but Beaton thrived in the structure and intrigue of the church, indissolubly knitted together with the king. And with his knowledge of French court, he would not only translate for James, but help him navigate the complexity of French court life and secure a French marriage.

After ten days at sea, they spotted the harbor city of Dieppe. James held on to the rail of the ship and viewed France for the first time. They sailed along the white chalk cliffs, around a break wall, and the city came into view. Battlements, mounted with cannons, protected the city from an English invasion. When the soldiers, dressed in the red and blue livery of François, saw the red lion of Scotland, they raised their arms and cheered, a welcome that encouraged James. The boat docked, and James bounded off the boat. He was enveloped in the language, which he could not understand at all.

"This is France?" he called over his shoulder to Beaton, who hurried down the gangplank.

"Yes sire," Beaton replied, but James had already taken off down the wharf, noticing the uniformity of dormer windows and elaborate cornices on the buildings that lined the waterfront, far different from the assorted buildings that lined the wharf at Leith. In the distance, James observed a square tower rising above the dark blue roofs of the city. This was a city unlike any in Scotland, the symmetry and power conveyed through architecture was something James had never seen. He committed all the details to memory, so he could recreate this in his own country. He hurried across an arched bridge and through round towers into the gated city.

While James wanted to stay in this port and see everything French, he also was anxious to get to St. Quentin, where the Duke of Vendôme, Marie de Bourdon's father, held court. The disappointment over not being able to marry Maggie weighed him down, and he longed for some levity. Maybe the girl would be so brilliant that she would block Maggie from his mind. He doubted it, but he wanted the girl to like him for being himself, and not just because he was the king.

"Let's switch clothes, like we did when I escaped from Angus," he said to his groom, John Tennent. Thinking of his escape, the adrenaline surged and compelled him to be roguish. "I'll go in disguised as a courtier so that I can get an honest reaction from this lady. The French love their masques."

"I don't think that's wise, your Highness," Rothes said, which only convinced James that this was a good idea. Rothes was a relic from his father's time and out of touch with the vibrant modern courts. After all, his uncle had pulled the same switch on Anne Boleyn when he wanted to impress her, and it worked for him. James was already pulling off his doublet and handing it to John, who was also disrobing. He ignored Bishop Beaton's wagging head, even though Beaton's experience in Paris and France was considerably vaster than James's own knowledge of French customs.

Once James was confident that he looked like a yeoman and not a king, they made their way to Vendôme palace, which lay to the west of Dieppe. The palace was light limestone, which shone almost white in the sunlight. It was U-shaped, with two round towers at either end, topped with a steep pewter tiled turret. It was so light and modern compared to the heavy Scottish palaces. James's party was led through the entry, where he noticed the white marble tiles inlaid with dark blue diamonds. The servant opened the ornately carved oak door and announced the visitors. The Duke of Vendôme was in the center of the hall, wearing a crimson silk doublet and a short black velvet embroidered overcoat. From his neck hung a gold chain with a coral medallion hanging from it. James was too far back in the line to see what was carved on the medallion. Music from the hautboys, tabors, and shawms enveloped James, and he had to restrain his feet from tapping.

John greeted the Duke of Vendôme, wearing the royal crimson doublet and jerkin. John bowed a little too low for a king, his carcanet bouncing off his chest. James held his breath, hoping John hadn't given himself away. The duke's long mustache curled over his short beard, and his hair covered his ears, longer than the Scottish style. He tilted his head and John moved to greet the duchess. James glanced around the hall, noting the differences from his own Scottish palaces. The tapestries on the walls were woven with gold thread and fine silk, more luxurious than James had in his own palace. That would change as soon as he married a French bride. As the Scottish retinue lined up, James took his place near the end of the line. He placed his hands behind his back in what he thought was a yeoman's posture.

Marie wore a rounded hood, lined in pearls, which revealed her tawny hair, parted in the middle and piled under the hood. Her gown was a deep blue velvet, also inset with pearls. She pulled a paper from her purse and studied it, her brow furrowed. Her fawn-colored eyes met James, and his heart sank.

A smirk pulling at the edges of her thin lips, she turned to James, curtsied and said in Scots, "Your Grace, you're standing too far aside when you should be in the front." She took his hand and led him to the front of the hall. Her father chuckled, not fooled by James's disguise either for all that he played along. James felt the heat rise, but threw his shoulders back to cover the embarrassment.

"My lady, you are very wise," he said, bowing almost to the floor. "Please, allow me and my men to retire and properly dress for dinner." He spoke in halting French.

James escaped to his room, which was carpeted in a thick silk, and from the bedposts hung cloth of gold. James rubbed his hands over it, remembering the story of his uncle and King François meeting for the field of the Cloth of Gold when James was still a boy. David Lindsay entertained him by telling him of the extravagant event, taking place on the field outside of Calais, the lone English possession on the continent. The reason for the meeting was to celebrate the betrothal of his uncle's two-year-old daughter, Mary, to the Dauphin Francis, the oldest son of the French king. Both kings were eager to be seen as modern princes and to show Charles V, Holy Roman Emperor, a united alliance of strength. So many tents were installed using cloth of gold, thin gold strands wrapped around silken weft yarns that created a fabric of gold. The whole field seemed to be on fire when the sun shone. David said François's tent was sixty feet high and had to be supported with two ship masts lashed together. Of course, the alliance didn't last as his uncle betrayed François by making an alliance with his enemy, Charles V. James hoped to use that to his advantage to strengthen his own kingdom.

He brought his thoughts back to the matter at hand and called John in to help him dress in his best clothes, the crimson doublet and overcoat with slashes to reveal the purple silk, he wore a crimson hat with the turned up rim. He pinned a golden lion broach to the brim. The crimson deepened the russet color of his hair and eyes. At dinner, he took the seat of honor, between the duke and his daughter. They spoke quickly, but slowed down for him when they saw he was struggling to understand their French. Beaton translated when the vocabulary and pronunciation proved too difficult for James. A pang of longing struck him as he remembered Maggie trying to make him speak French. He felt staccato and clumsy when he spoke, hearing the nasal Scots accent over the round rhythms of their language.

After dinner, the music continued. James held his hand out for Marie to dance a galliard with him. She was taller than Maggie, but her back curved forward, making her appear shorter, almost hunchbacked. Her dress was cut higher than the Scots style, and had enormous, pinned back sleeves, revealing slashed sleeves of her kirtle, and embroidered cuffs. The skirt swished around her legs, not held out by a farthingale, which most ladies wore in Scotland. James stepped right, left, right, and Marie mirrored him. She stepped in for the lavolta. He placed his hands on her hips and froze. There was no fire in her eyes, no witty retort on the tip of her tongue. She was pleasant, but James didn't want pleasant. He wanted the passion he felt with Maggie, the blood pulsing through his groin. She didn't throw her shoulders back with defiance as Maggie did. There was no challenge there.

Despite his disappointment, he remained with Vendôme for eight days, enjoying the jousting and music, but longing for Maggie. When they arrived in Rouen, his brother Moray was waiting.

"Where is your minion?" his brother said, mouth twisting into a smirk. James knew to whom he was referring.

"He was not invited nor will he ever be again. He has offended me so much that he shall never be in my favor again," James said, knowing his brother's distrust of Finnart. James should have believed his brother instead of being swayed by Finnart's charms.

"By God, there was a time when he could never offend you,

even if he shart in your hand!" his brother laughed. James remained glum. His brother slapped him on the back. "Cheer up brother, soon you will meet the king and beg for his daughter. No one can resist your charms in person!"

James smiled, but did not feel reassured. He wished Maggie was there to console him.

Chapter 28

MAGGIE

MAGGIE WATCHED HER CHILDREN playing in the courtyard of Loch Leven, the thin October sun warming her back. The morning mists had lifted, so Maggie was enjoying the last of the sun before the Scottish winter descended upon them. Jamie ran with a wooden sword, chasing his Scottish hound, a gift from his father. The brindled dog weaved back and forth as the five-year old giggled behind him, his copper-colored hair shining in the weak sunlight.

"Mam, watch!" he called out and jumped, thrusting his sword. "I'm the King of Scots! I'll get you, dragon!" He chased after the dog, who complied by running in circles.

"I see you, my son," Maggie couldn't help smiling, imagining that this is what his father looked like when he was five. But her son's life was more constant than his father's has been. At five, James had already been ripped from his mother, whose poor choice to re-marry had caused his precarious childhood. That began the descent into his distrust of everyone, even Maggie. She would protect her son and give him the stable home that James had craved.

Near her feet on a blanket played Euphemia, the daughter she had been pregnant with two years ago and uncertain of the paternity. Euphemia, Effy, had the same downturned eyes of her father, a tell-tale sign of Douglas blood, and flaxen curls. Maggie chose her name, which meant good repute, hoping Robert would accept her. Her worries were unfounded because Robert immediately recognized her as his child, spoiling her. Effy wore a light chemise and overgown, in a similar fashion to Maggie. The girl tottered after her brother.

On Maggie's lap sat another baby girl, Janet, named after the Douglas women. She was four months old; Maggie's water had broken during a stormy afternoon. James had tried to see her after Finnart diverted their trip to France because of the storm, but Maggie had been in her confinement. Her mother told Maggie that he had been adamant, almost breaking through the group of ladies to see her. Maggie wished she could have seen his face when the women refused to let him in, even though he was the king of Scotland. Her heart seized with longing for him.

"My lady, a package from the king," her servant crossed the courtyard, holding a small package wrapped in brown parchment. Maggie thanked him, turning the package over and trying to calm the nerves erupting in her belly. She untied the string around the package and it unfolded, revealing an oval gold pendant. One large cream pearl was suspended from the bottom. In the center was a round lilac stone and four rubies were set into the intricately curved filigree. The pendant was attached to a long golden chain. Maggie yanked the letter open, seeing James's angular handwriting.

My lovit Magpie,

the letter began. Maggie shook her head. Of course he would write that detested name.

Enclosed is a pendant in the Italian style called Arabesque. I can't wait to commission Falkland to be built in this style, it is truly magnificent. The purple is the thistle, and the gold is you, my goldfinch. How I wish I didn't need to be on this expedition to find a queen, but I am learning so many innovations from the French to turn Scotland into the magnificent kingdom of the north. I trust you are healing from your confinement, and I will expect you to be at my homecoming celebration that Sir Lindsay is planning for my return.

Your King, James.

Maggie sighed and clasped the pendant around her neck. She placed it inside her dress, the metal cool against her skin. The letter brought her anguish to the surface yet again. She tried to push her feelings into a small recess of her heart, but it split wide open every time she had contact with him. His letter didn't mention what he thought of Marie de Bourbon or when he would be coming home.

She dressed for dinner, her husband returned from Edinburgh. Her new jewelry rested against the front of her gown. She sat next to Robert, who gave her a perfunctory kiss on her offered cheek.

"We received news from the continent," he said, cutting into his meat. Maggie nodded, fingering the ornate filigree of her gift. She had heard all she needed for the moment. Robert looked at her chest and she froze. His eyes lowered in suspicion.

"The king has rejected Marie de Bourbon for a bride," he continued. Her heart sped, what could this mean? She forced herself to look calm.

"What does this mean, my lord?" a servant asked, saving Maggie from needing to speak. Her heart was in her throat.

"He is traveling to Paris, according to your father," Robert directed the comment to her.

"My father is home?" the surprise was genuine. Her father had departed with the rest of the flotilla in September. She *assumed* he would return with the king.

"The king sent essential men home to conduct business in Scotland while he convinces the French king for the hand of his royal daughter," Robert emphasized *royal*, but Maggie ignored the dig. She had already talked to him about marrying a French princess. Scotland needed the money she would bring and Maggie understood that. It wouldn't change his feelings for her.

After dinner, Maggie retired to her rooms, already planning when she would see James again. She went to close her door and lock her husband out, but he was faster. He inserted his foot, pushing the door open. Maggie stepped back and allowed him to enter, cursing herself for getting lost in her thoughts.

"You didn't seem surprised to hear the king wouldn't marry the Bourbon lady," Robert said, hands on his hips. Maggie steeled herself for the argument.

"No, I wasn't. I got a letter from the king today," she said, removing her coif and unfastening her hair. It tumbled over her shoulders like honey.

"Of course he wrote to you," Robert said, bitterness hardening his voice. Maggie shrugged and untied her overgown. If he was in her room, she would need to sleep with him quickly so he would leave her alone. She was used to this routine. Until she produced a male heir, he would be allowed to her body. But never her emotional self. "You're his Scottish whore. Good enough to fuck, but not good enough to marry."

Maggie held herself erect as the words slapped her across the face. All of her rage exploded. "He would have married me, he *wanted* to marry me," she said in a low voice that belied her rage. "A French princess is what is best for Scotland. But he will always love me. He tried to get a divorce for me so that I would be away from you."

He stepped towards her, grabbed the pendant and yanked it from her neck, golden clasp breaking open. She clutched her chest, but was too late.

"Give that to me," she hissed. "It was a gift from the king to *me*!"

"I know it was from him. You couldn't keep your hands off of it," he yelled. "Now you will never see it or him again!" He stormed out the door, pulling it shut behind him. Maggie heard the key in the lock. She ran for the door, pulling on the handle.

"You can't lock me in here forever!" she screamed. "I have to take care of the children!"

"The nurse will take care of them," he said. "No one needs you anymore."

Maggie listened to the sound of his footsteps growing fainter and fainter. She slumped against the door. She knew better than to throw her relationship with James in her husband's face, but he instigated the argument, needling her. If only he hadn't called her a whore. She had heard the Queen Mother call many low women that. Maggie was not low, she just loved a man who could not be her husband, even though he kept trying.

What would happen once the French princess came to Scotland? Would Maggie still be James's love? Or would she just be another one of his ladies who he had illegitimate children with? Her son was one of six known bastards. Why did Maggie continue to believe that she was special? Maybe her husband was right. Maybe she was just one of his whores.

Chapter 29

THE QUEEN MOTHER

MARGARET WAS ANXIOUS TO hear from her son also. From Stirling, she tried to manage her family, to no avail. The news from England was awful. Tragedy struck twice in January. First Catherine, Harry's loyal queen whom he set aside, died. Then his new queen, Anne, miscarried a baby boy. Harry was disconsolate, although Margaret did think he and his wife brought it on by wearing yellow, the color of joy, the day after Catherine's death. Rumors were that Harry had grown bored of Anne and had his eye on a new lady, Jane Seymour, who was Anne's opposite. Jane had worn a locket given to her by Harry with his miniature in it, which she would open in front of Anne. Margaret felt no sympathy for either woman when she heard that Anne ripped the locket off Jane's neck with such force that she cut her fingers.

What shocked Margaret was that he had the audacity to accuse Anne of incest and adultery and executed her only four months later. A queen was God's representative! The fall he'd suffered when he was unhorsed in a jousting tournament had affected his reasoning. But no one dared to question Harry, for fear of ending up on the block next. She was the only person who could stand up to him and not worry about execution, but Cromwell told her that she was not welcome in England without her son.

But her son was as obstinate as her brother, refusing to meet with him on English soil. He said, "You only want me to meet him so I will forgive Angus and you can return to him!"

That was the furthest thought from Margaret's mind, reconciliation with Angus, even though she suspected her own husband was giving in to the Scottish way of keeping a mistress.

Before she could catch her breath, the young Margaret was in trouble of her own. It seemed she had fallen in love while she was in service to Queen Anne. Thomas Howard was the queen's uncle, the son of the older Duke of Norfolk, from his second marriage. Thomas had been a part of their court since 1533, and even carried a canopy post at Princess Elizabeth's baptism. Her daughter had fallen in love with the charming young man, who was four years her senior. Margaret wondered if this wasn't Anne's plan to ingratiate her family into the royal family. However it happened, her daughter had entered into a betrothal without her mother or her uncle's consent.

Margaret was livid. She had negotiated twice for her to marry a Stewart and consolidate power for her son in Scotland. Of course Ard blocked her every move. And now look what has happened.... The girl had taken it upon herself to secretly become engaged, incurring the wrath of her uncle. The Queen Mother had passed her misfortunes in love onto her daughter.

When Harry heard about the secret betrothal, he imprisoned both lovers in the tower. He became convinced that Lord Howard, English diplomat to Scotland, had told Margaret of the secret engagement and she had encouraged it. His scathing letter called her a traitor to her home country and brother and accused her of trying to reconcile with Angus. Margaret scoffed. She would never return to Ard.

And yet, Harry had ordered his own niece's death. He had become a monster. Nothing was sacred to him anymore except his obsession to procure a male heir. Margaret wrote a groveling letter to him. "Dearest brother," she began, using the most intimate address she could, "We have been informed that your Grace is angered...." Margaret crossed out angered, and wrote, "displeased that our daughter should promise to marry Thomas Howard and that your Grace is resolved to punish her."

The tears prevented Margaret from continuing. Young Margaret was the Queen Mother's only daughter; it hurt her heart to think of her brother, whom she loved and had been close to, would kill her only daughter. She shook the tears free, blotting her cheeks, and continued writing, "Please consider that she is our natural daughter, and we will not believe that you will do such extremity upon your own. I beseech you to have compassion and grant our daughter pardon and send her back to Scotland. If you do, brother, I promise she will never bother you again. Please grant my piteous and most humble request."

She signed her name and closed the letter, unable to read the ingratiating words she was compelled to write to appeal to her brother's enormous ego. She only hoped it would be enough to move him to grant a pardon.

After the letter was taken by her servant, she pushed herself to standing, her hands in the crook of her lower back. She was tired, and feeling all of her forty-six years. Her son's resentment at the Douglases continued to grow, and now James was paranoid that his friend, Finnart, was using him to advance his own standing. Margaret shook her head, remembering Finnart's kindness when Angus was stealing her rents and fornicating with his mistress. James was becoming as irrational as her own brother. And now, he was in France arranging a marriage that would make her brother his enemy forever. She was weary of Scottish politics and intrigue, her heart was broken, body sore. When would she be able to rest?

Chapter 30

THOMAS

THOMAS SAT AT HIS desk in Holyrood. Being one of the essential cogs of the Scottish government, James had sent Thomas back home to run the country while he charmed King François into contracting his frail daughter in marriage. Thomas knew that once the French king met James, he would not say no to him. James was too charming. Thomas sighed, knowing he should either go to his house and see his wife and child, or bring them to Edinburgh. As he was deciding what to do, Finnart burst in.

"You set me up," he said, his eyes displaying his malice. "You made me take all of the blame for turning back to Scotland."

Thomas folded his hands under his chin, but said nothing. He knew Finnart would confront him, had prepared for it.

"And so I was grounded here in Scotland while you went to France with him," he stepped closer and Thomas restrained himself from flinching. "You pushed him to turn down the Vendôme girl, you pushed him to try for Princess Madeleine's hand again."

"I did nothing of the sort," he said. "The king made that decision all on his own." Thomas tried to keep the satisfaction out of his voice, but failed.

"What do you get out of him not marrying Maggie? You spend as much time with him as I do. You know his feelings for her," he stood at Thomas's desk. *No,* Thomas thought, *he never spent as much time with me as he spent with you.* But Thomas could not say that without giving himself away, he would be unable to keep the jealousy out of his voice.

"Lady Douglas was already married," he said instead, tying to deflect Finnart who was more tenacious than James's hunting hounds. "And he needs a French dowry to properly build Scotland into a modern country. You know that."

"The money could have been raised here. *You* know that. And the pope could have granted an annulment. You had the power to make that happen. But, you didn't."

Finnart rounded the desk. Thomas jumped up, his instinct for self-preservation kicking in. Finnart looked feral, desperate to capture his quarry. Thomas grasped for the words to throw Finnart off his scent, his mind spinning. He looked to the left for something to protect himself with.

"It won't work, what you have planned," Finnart leaned into Thomas, who backed up and tumbled into his chair. "I've seen the way you look at him."

Thomas felt his heart constrict as if it forgot how to beat. The blood thundered in his ears as he tried to remain impassive. "What look?" he asked, fearing the answer. Finnart placed his hands on the arms of the chair. Thomas could feel his breath on his face.

"That you want to fuck the king," Finnart whispered, breath ruffling Thomas's hair. Finnart's chest was heaving under his doublet, straining to get Thomas to admit to the aberrant act. But Thomas would not do that, would not give Finnart the weaponry to use against him. The penalties for homosexuality were confiscation of lands and wealth and his body hanged and then burned. No one had been charged in Thomas's memory, but with England's passage of the Buggery laws in 1533, Thomas did not want to bring attention to himself.

"I think you are projecting your feelings onto me," Thomas said. He stood and shoved Finnart out of the way and walked over to the window, unable to look Finnart in the face and betray his true emotions. He watched the autumn rain course down the window, distorting the dead landscape, knowing he should remain quiet, but he felt compelled to add, "After all, you're his *minion*." The final word carried all of the frustration Thomas felt that he could never admit, all of the societal expectations that pinned him to his station.

"Yes, I am. Or rather I was—until you set me up. And you just confirmed why you did it. All of it," Finnart sat in Thomas's chair and crossed his legs, enjoying the discomfort.

"You're the one who was using the king for your own gain. You only wanted him to marry Maggie because then Scotland wouldn't have a strong continental ally and you could insert your family to be the ally."

Finnart placed his hands behind his head. "It is the Scottish way to promote one's family. Look at the Erskine's."

"I am not a part of that branch of the family!" Thomas exploded. "I've earned my position, and I only want what's best for the king and Scotland."

"You want what's best for your prick," Finnart laughed. "And you're jealous because of my relationship with the king."

Thomas turned back to the window, wishing the heavy rain would wash his true feelings away so he didn't have them anymore. He hadn't admitted even to himself, even though he knew, had known for a long time what his true nature was. Finnart sidled up behind him, pressing himself against Thomas, trapping him against the window.

"Do you want to know what it was like?" Finnart whispered in Thomas's ear. The words shuddered through Thomas's body, betraying him before he could stop himself. His hands shook from desire. His body was reacting, after Thomas had kept his desires so carefully under control. Finally, his natural desires would not be contained. He longed to spin around and take Finnart in his arms, a weak substitute for the king, but maybe that would quench Thomas's thirst for him. Finnart reached around and put his hand on Thomas's mouth. His fingers curled inside Thomas's mouth, probing, imploring him to act. But Thomas couldn't react, couldn't give Finnart the evidence to turn the king against him. Thomas bit down on Finnart's fingers.

Finnart jumped back, yowling in pain. Thomas moved away from him, to calm himself, regain his composure. He was disgusted with Finnart for bringing those long hidden feelings to the surface, and sickened by his body's reaction.a

"Fine," Finnart growled. "You and I both know the truth. And if you think I'm out of the king's favor, just know that he has named me Master of Works."

"Yes, but he also took your brother with him to France," Thomas said, meeting Finnart's eyes for the first time. The Earl of Arran was Finnart's half-brother who inherited the earldom when his father died in 1529. The young earl was almost of age; taking him to France was a way to show Finnart had been replaced since he was illegitimate and would never again be close to the king. Until the king had a legitimate heir, the Earl of Arran was next in line for the Scottish throne.

"We shall see who he prefers to spend time with when he comes back from France," Finnart said. He spun around and ambled towards to door, enjoying Thomas's discomfort. He opened the heavy oak door and paused before he left.

"Just so you know, I was minion to the king in name only," he said. "Never physically. Never wanted to be, unlike you."

The door shut behind Finnart, but his final comment echoed in the empty room. Thomas knew he had made a dangerous enemy— one who could have him banished from court, or executed. Thomas wasn't sure which would be worse. If Finnart told the king what happened, soon the whole country would know what Thomas was. He had to make sure that never happened.

Chapter 31

JAMES

HE RODE HARD FROM Paris south when he heard the news. The sky was dark, which made the buff castle look yellow, dark blue turrets blending into the sky. The king of France was in his chambers when James arrived at the Château de la Motte in Lyons. Henri, the king's son, met the Scots in the courtyard, embracing James and holding on.

"Your Grace," Henri said. "My father has taken to his bed. My brother, the dauphin, has died."

The air deflated from James's stance, shoulders slumping. "How?" he asked, clasping Henri's arm. The Dauphin had been François's favorite son, his heir.

"My father thinks it was poisoning," Henri sighed. "But his health had not been good since we came back from captivity in Spain. The dampness of the country settled into his lungs."

The thought of the dauphin's imprisonment causing his death enraged James. That could have happened to James while he was in Angus's care. *And Angus would have allowed it to happen*, he thought, bile crawling up his throat.

"Take me to your father," he said and followed Henri to the king's bedchamber. Henri knocked on the door. They heard the anger in his father's rough answer.

"Father, it is the King of Scots come to give you comfort!" Henri yelled. A moment later, the door flew open and there stood the king. His dark hair was disheveled, and his face was sallow and grey. His eyelids drooped, but his thick lips curled into a smile when he saw James.

"Ah, God took my son but sent the noble prince, the King of Scots, in his place!" François wrapped James in his arms, thumping his back. James heard the sorrow behind the cheery greeting. "Henri! Wait upon the King of Scots as if he were your own brother!"

Henri smiled and nodded in agreement. "Prepare rooms for him and his retinue and let the queen know we will have a royal guest at supper tonight!" François said, shaking Henri's arm. "Please excuse me for this evening while I compose myself. We shall hunt and catch up tomorrow, your Grace."

James clasped his arm and bowed. "It would be my honor, sire."

James and Henri watched the door close, and the seventeen-year-old turned to James and said, "Come, brother. Let me show you to your rooms!"

While James prepared for dinner, the thoughts raced through his mind. How did the death of François's son affect his chances for marrying his daughter? Would the fear of death be too great to overcome? If that happened, could he appeal again to the pope himself for a divorce for Maggie? Would François support that? James would worry about that as it came up, for now, he concentrated on looking his best. He fastened the clasps on his doublet, admiring the slashes, which showed the purple silk chemise underneath. He pulled on his overcoat, lined with spotted ermine fur. He placed his flat hat off centered on his head and smoothed his hair under the upturned brim.

He entered the Great Room for dinner and spotted François's wife, Eleanor of Austria. Her white chemise came all the way to her ears; her overdress was square cut and emerald green, enormous sleeves with paned slashes to show the fine silk beneath. Instead of her hair covered by a coif, it coiled into buns on either side of her head and covered with a golden net, and a flat black hat was perched to the left of center. A ruby pendant hung to the right side of her hair. She had two thick entwined golden chains across her chest. Her eyes were set far into her face, giving her a tired look. James could understand why, if the rumors of her sexual appetite were true. François's own sister said that the new queen was hot in bed and wanted to be taken constantly.

When Eleanor smiled at James, her jaw jutted forward, the unfortunate Hapsburg jaw. A sadness crowded her eyes, and James felt sorry for her. She was a prize bride, the Holy Roman Emperor's sister, married to François to create an alliance, which her brother kept reneging on. And François treated her like a toy he had never really wanted.

"Bonsoir, your Majesty," James took her hand and bowed. The ladies twittered behind her. James noticed they all wore the high-necked kirtles. Maybe it was a Spanish fashion.

"Ah, la Dame Madeleine est arrivée!" the queen said, motioning behind James. As he turned, he noticed a gilded chariot enter the room. Seated on the velvet pillows was a fair girl, chestnut hair contrasted against her skin. Her dark eyes drooped like her father's and she had his hooked nose. She wore a brocade crimson dress, which arched across her flat chest. Her kirtle was also high up on her neck, fastened with a golden braided choker.

She rose from the litter and approached James. Although she was sixteen, she looked like a child. Her cheeks flushed as she curtsied.

"C'est un bonneur de vous rencontrer, Votre Majesté," she said, her voice high and childlike. *It is an honor to meet you, your highness.* He took her outstretched hand. It was so small in his palm.

"Le plaisir est à moi, Princesse," he said and brushed his lips across her hand. He felt the quiver go all the way up her arm. Such a child.

"J'espère que vous me ferez l'honneau de vous asseoìr à côté de moi pendant le dîner?" she smiled. James leaned forward, knowing this would not help him to understand her French, but unable to stop it. James looked for Beaton to translate for him, cursing himself for not listening to Maggie when she said he needed to practice. The sounds that Madeleine was making sounded nothing like the French he spoke, which was heavy with Scots. Beaton rushed over, long cleric robe flailing behind him. Beaton smoothed his thinning hair across his forehead to compose himself.

"I can't understand her French," James barked, harsher than necessary, but frustrated with himself.

Beaton turned and spoke with Madeleine in French. He motioned to James, and she nodded, answering in a lilting language that should have been familiar, but was not.

"The princess would like you to honor her by sitting next to her at dinner," Beaton said, motioning to her and raising his eyebrows.

Beaton had always been in favor of a French alliance and marriage since he had studied here; he appreciated both the French culture and their adherence to Catholicism and wanted James to bring that back to Scotland. James understood Beaton's passion now that he had experienced the modern and sophisticated country.

"You need to sit next to me and translate," he hissed; Beaton nodded in agreement.

James turned to the girl and said, "Ce serait avec plaisir." She looked at Beaton in confusion, who repeated what James had said, in the Parisian accent—*it would be his pleasure.* Madeleine nodded. James heard the difference, his longer vowels, sharper consonants. Her language was liquid, always moving and rolling, where Scots English was sharp cliffs of sound pushed through the nose. He wished he could speak this sensual language, and he thought he was speaking it when he spoke with Maggie, but this language in Madeleine's mouth was far more seductive. He wanted to speak this language to Maggie, up and down her body. He shivered thinking of her movement under the music of his words. He looked at Madeleine and recognized the look in her eyes, the look of a girl entranced by his looks and charm. She may speak the language of seduction, but James lived it, he was a walking seduction and he knew it. Maggie had that look and would force herself to remove it. James chuckled, once again wishing Maggie were in front of him, challenging him and making him work for his affections.

Madeleine was a blank manuscript, unblemished by life. She was a girl. And James didn't want to marry a girl, someone who he would have to teach to love, to rule, to be an equal. He had lived through all of what still lay ahead for Madeleine. He had experienced it with Maggie, Maggie had been there for him, Maggie grew as he grew once he escaped from Angus. Maggie was the only person he could trust; even Finnart, who he believed had loved him, had abandoned him for self-serving reasons. Maggie had been a girl when he had been a boy, and they had grown together. But, he had to remind himself, his father had married a girl and turned her into the Queen of Scots. He could do the same. He would teach Madeleine, with Maggie's help, to be a regal queen. And James would move Maggie back to Stirling to serve as her lady-in-waiting and James could have his queen and his lover together in one castle. And because Madeleine was young, she would accept that this was life. James had found a way to save Scotland financially but allow him to live with the woman in his heart. He probably should have felt guilty for Madeleine, knowing he would never really love her, but after she had an heir, she could find her own love too. James would encourage that. So she could find happiness too.

The next day, he prepared to ride with François to his hunting chalet in the Loire valley. James pulled on his riding boots and his tunic. As he entered the king's chamber, Madeleine was sitting in a chair, tawny hair arranged in low buns on either side of her ears. Her lowered eyelids gave her a dreamy, wistful expression, which suited her for adoring James. Her face lit up as James entered the room.

"Bonjour!" she said, grasping his hands. James looked at François, his nerves jangling, not wanting to insult the French king by holding his daughter's hands. "I wanted to bid my father and my soon-to-be betrothed good-bye," she said in Scots, which surprised James—both at her speaking Scots and at her boldness.

He began to apologize to François; he had not said anything to Madeleine about an engagement last night. He would never be that bold.

"Don't worry," Madeleine interrupted. "My father knows I will marry you. It is in the treaty of Rouen, and it is also in my heart. He can't deny us both." James had to remind himself not to let his mouth drop in surprise. This meek girl had a backbone after all. James smiled at her, nodding, understanding now that her father wasn't going to be convinced by James to allow the marriage, but he would not say no to his daughter.

François had the best hunting horses saddled. The two kings would ride ahead, alone, to discuss state matters. The household would catch up and meet them at Château de Chambord. The sun was directly overhead as they set off.

"You impressed my daughter last night," François said in Latin, not slowing his canter. James gulped his nervousness and kicked his horse to keep up.

"She is very charming," he said, glad he could focus on riding and not the mental aerobatics that these negotiations were going to take. As much as François seemed to have taken to James, he still knew this was a tenuous situation. One insulting word from James, the Auld Alliance—and marriage—would be forever off the table. "And quite persuasive."

"Yes, she is," François said. "And once she sets her mind on something, she rarely can be talked out of it."

James nodded, unsure of the appropriate response. He knew from the look in her eyes that her mind was already set on him. He chose to remain quiet and let François talk this out.

"My mother always knew I would be king, even though we were from a minor line and my chances were slight," François said. "She never doubted me. Once my father died, she married her ambition to make me king. She negotiated my marriage to King Louis's daughter, Claude, Madeleine's mother. My mother had gambled that the king would not have a male heir. She always believed in my destiny, and worked to marry me to the king's oldest daughter, so that I would be named king."

"Sire, your mother sounds like an incredible woman. My mother tried to secure my future as well, but she married a Scottish noble to protect my throne," James responded, "which failed. My stepfather held me against my will for almost three years." Even years after his captivity, James could still feel the fear—no, the terror—that surrounded him while Angus imprisoned him, the uncertainty of his future, isolation from his family. And he would never be able to get that security back, to feel truly safe. As long as Angus and his brother were alive, he would always be looking over his shoulder.

"I've been in captivity too. I was also held by my enemy against my will," said François. "They say it strengthens a man's character." James had heard of François's capture at the Italian town Pavia by the emperor's men. He was taken to Spain and had to raise his own ransom. His release was contingent upon his agreement to marry the emperor's sister Eleanor and put his two sons into captivity in his place. James didn't agree that imprisonment built a man's character. Maybe because James was still a teen when Angus detained him, but he became distrusting and paranoid, although he could not voice those concerns right now to François. He focused on the trail, the trees crowding the rolling path worn down by horses and carts. The landscape was flatter than Scotland, but blanketed in trees, where Scotland's moors, which covered most of the southern country, were covered in grasses and heather.

"I have heard the stories of your carousing for women," François interrupted James's contemplation. "And I am not one to judge that."

James had heard that during Queen Eleanor's reception parade into Paris, François had been standing in the window overlooking the avenue, having his mistress while everyone watched. At least, that was the rumor.

"I must be honest," James gambled that François would want to hear the truth. "I love a Scots woman. A married Scots woman. She has a son by me. I tried to have her marriage annulled, but the pope denied me. She still has my heart, but I will be a decent and kind husband for your daughter. She will be the Queen of Scots, the jewel of the north that it will become under my kingship. She won't want for anything in my country."

"As a father, I am worried that you will hurt my daughter. As a man, I understand that passion is vital for a fulfilling life," he said. "How do I know you will not hurt my daughter with this Scots woman?"

"I will promise to treat her as my queen, and shower her in all the privileges of that office," James said, hoping he wouldn't make him promise to relinquish Maggie. As much as he wanted to fulfill the Auld Alliance and marry a French princess to get his country out of financial trouble, he couldn't promise that he could stay away from Maggie.

"And provide an heir?" François asked.

James smiled. "Of course provide an heir."

They galloped along the wooded road in silence, James enjoying the October warmth and sunshine. Scotland was probably already bathed in fog, mist, and frost.

"You know," François said, breaking the silence. "I almost slept with your aunt, the woman that nature could not make more beautiful, according to Erasmus."

James had never met his aunt Mary, his mother's sister. She had married the old king of France in an effort to join France and England together. If Erasmus, the greatest scholar of their time, claimed there was no one more beautiful, then James believed it.

"But I didn't," he said. "It would have kept me from being king had she become pregnant and birthed a son."

François fascinated James. They talked about women, both of

their escapades, the love of sensual experiences.

"Your uncle, he is a wily one," he changed the subject.

"Yes, I don't trust him myself. He has been harboring the Earl of Angus and encouraging him to cause strife on my borders," James was unable to keep the anger from his voice. François nodded.

"He also made promises to me and then went behind my back with my enemy," François's voice softened. The betrayal made the two kings move toward each other in trust. "After the Field of Cloth of Gold, that snake Wolsey convinced your uncle to side against my claim to become Holy Roman Emperor. They sided with the Spanish and surrounded me with my enemies."

"And my father lost his life fighting to protect France from my uncle. Henry sent his queen to Scotland while he was warring in France. Please remember that," James studied the man's profile. François's nose curled like the beak of an eagle, sharpened by his betrayals. Here was a man who had been betrayed almost as much as James had. And he had overcome to create France as a shining example of Humanism, intellect, and art.

"But, we will trust each other, no?" François smiled. "Let's talk about nicer subjects. I can't wait for you to see my château. I brought Italian architects and artists to build it. Have you seen Italian art and architecture?"

James shook his head, his heart raced at the thought of learning about the beauty that François surrounded himself with. François told him of the art of Leonardo da Vinci, Michelangelo, Titus, the architecture with its classically inspired Roman columns, symmetrical arched facades, and wide domes.

"Do you write? I have tried my hand at poems and ballads," François said.

"Yes, I love to write songs and sing," James said. "And also have flytings."

"Flytings?" the king cocked his head in confusion.

"It's a verbal poetry contest. My teacher, Sir David Lindsay, can best any man!" James said.

"You remind me of myself when I was younger," François smiled. "It's good to be reminded of being young. Let's enjoy youth tonight."

In the days it took to ride from Lyon to Château de Chambord, the men talked about the loss at Flodden, politics of the continent and British Isles, love and marriages. At night, the two men dressed as commoners, an idea which François loved, and marauded through the streets causing mayhem.

Château de Chambord rose from the green countryside. The butter yellow castle had four round towers with steep, indigo slate roofs, but that was where the similarities ended. Wide arches lined the front of the building, and the roofline was a chaotic assortment of domes, minuets, and spires. James had never seen frenzied cornices such as these. The building seemed to rock with life, held in place by the sky.

"It is modeled on the skyline of Constantinople," François explained. James was in awe. Constantinople, the capital of the Eastern Roman Empire, now under the control of the Ottoman Empire. James knew that Francis had made a treaty with the Ottoman Ruler, Suleiman the Magnificent.

"What is Suleiman the Magnificent like?" Sarcasm clung to the epitomic title.

"He is an honorable, cautious man," François replied. "Who he prays to doesn't concern me, it is how he lives."

The men crossed the Loire River on horseback. James dismounted his horse and followed François over a fake moat, an homage to the chivalric era that François believed he truly belonged. The main building had vaulted, ornately carved barrel ceiling. But what caught James's attention was the staircase in the center. The natural light streamed in the four arched doorways, making the tuffeau sandstone soften into a matted cream, which twisted into two separate helix staircases framed with Doric columns.

"So, you like the donjon?" François asked James, motioning him to follow. "This staircase was designed by da Vinci, the greatest artist of all time."

The men ascended the stairs and James was in another vaulted room. He noticed the coffered ceiling, with carvings of salamander, François's sovereign beast, and the letter "F." On opposite sides of the large room were alabaster fireplaces. Intricate tapestries lined the walls and luxurious carpets lay on the floor.

"I am rebuilding this château in the style I found in Milan," François said. James nodded, soaking in all the details. Compared to the lightness of this château, Scotland's castles seemed medieval, not modern. He needed to take this architecture back to his home and prove that he was as great of a king as François.

They rose late in the morning and prepared for the hunt. It took three grooms to hold back at least twenty dogs, russet dogs straining against the leash. François's main huntsman, Perot, coordinated all of the parts—grooms, running footman, the running dogs and baying dogs.

"What sort of dogs are those?' James asked, pointing to three dogs with barrel chests, thick legs, and powerful jaws. His Scottish dogs were slender and sleek. He wondered how these dogs could be fast enough to catch a stag or boar.

"These are my mastiffs," François patted one of the beasts on its head. The copper colored dog lapped at the king's hand, leaving a trail of slobber. "The bravest dogs in all of France."

"So you prefer hunting with dogs to falconry?" James asked. He too preferred to hunt with dogs, but also loved the beauty of falcon hunting. Of course, the highlands were better suited to falconry than the heavily wooded French countryside before him.

"Yes, it is the way a real gentleman hunts," François puffed out his chest, "And it resembles the pageantry and honor of battle."

James nodded, even though he had never been in battle, not like François's campaigns to take Milan. James had overseen the skirmishes along the border, but these were not true battles. For not the first time, envy at François's experiences crept up James. From the architecture and culture to the war experiences, Italy had made François the sort of king that James wanted to be. Here was someone open to inviting new culture into his kingdom in order to make it better. His uncle was his only model for a king, but he was too concerned with producing an heir to bring England into modern times. James wanted to be like François, not his own uncle. He wanted to bring all of what he was experiencing back to his country, to share it with his people, and also to share with Maggie. The buildings, people, and art would intrigue her. But to bring it all back to Scotland would be a failure if he didn't come back with a French princess as his bride.

The Master of the Hunt had already tracked the location of a boar and released the pack of raches, scent hounds, to chase down the beast. They mounted and the handler turned the dogs loose, sending them charging into the dappled woods. James spurred his horse into action, feeling the muscular courser pulling the earth beneath him, shoulders and haunches flexing. He allowed François to lead, even though his horse could have overtaken the king's. The dogs were lost in the underbrush, so the party continued along a well-worn game trail. In the distance, to the south of the trail, the dogs began braying.

"They've got one!" Perot called, motioning them to the left. François charged forward, hacking at branches that blocked the path. James ducked to avoid a large branch hitting him in the head. The barking intensified. On the banks of a bend in a creek, one of the mastiffs had the boar around the neck, avoiding his sharp tusks, while the other dogs stopped barking on command. François dismounted, so James did the same. Perot blew his horn to call others who had spread in different directions. François, too impatient to wait, unsheathed a gilded boar spear. He jabbed the spear in the side of the boar's head, carefully avoiding his prized mastiff's face. The boar collapsed and the dog released the animal.

"Come, James!" the king called. James was already off his horse, behind the king.

"You may deliver the final cut," François stepped back from the boar, which was still shallowly breathing. James used his dagger to slit the boar's throat, blood covering his blade, but it lacked the excitement of the initial wound. He wanted to show François that he was brave and unafraid to approach the wild animal, risk being gored while delivering the most dangerous wound. François cut off the boar's right foot and offered it to James, a great honor. He accepted the foot with all the grace he could summon. François didn't seem to notice his disappointment.

After the hunt, James and François prepared for the feast. James descended the helix staircase and noticed that the empty room with the vaulted ceilings had been transformed into a banquet hall. Beautiful tapestries in jeweled tones lined the walls, depicting the king's victory in Milan. In front were long oak tables and benches.

On the right side of the room was the boar, dressed and centered on the king's table. James was given the seat of honor next to the king. François and James's retinue were split between the two tables, with Beaton sitting to James's right in case he needed help translating. Interspersed among the men were several lovely ladies, dressed in a more modern style that clearly was not influenced by Queen Eleanor. François loved having women at his court, saying, "A court without ladies is a court without a court." Musicians were playing from the far side of the room. Even though it was getting late in the evening, the room was warm, lit with several multi-tiered candelabra. In addition to the boar, bowls of fruits and vegetables lined the table.

"My son," François greeted James, leading him to the center of the table. "This is the Duchess Etampes, Lady Anne d'Heilly."

The lady held out a delicate white hand, but when James took the hand, she gripped with all of her strength. James met her grey eyes and saw the same determination and intelligence that he saw in Maggie. *So this was the mistress*, James thought. Blond curls framed her temples, the rest of her hair was smoothed under a French hood, which sat behind her ears and matched her golden hair with its gilded edging. Her dress was cut across her bosom, gold embroidery edging the top and her sleeves. Her chin was sharp, her lips thin, but James knew that wasn't her hold on François. No, he recognized the fire in her; pain stabbed his heart as he was reminded of Maggie and wished she were there.

"C'est un plaisir de vous rencontrer," James said, releasing his grip, even as she held hers. The thin lips quivered, as she tried not to laugh at his pronunciation.

"Nous aurons besoin de vous trouver une dame qui pourrait vous apprendre à parler français—au lit," she said, taking François's arm, both of them laughing. An embarrassed heat flushed James's face as he looked to Beaton for a translation.

"She said you need to find a lady to teach you French—in bed," Beaton whispered. The duchess's hips undulated and bumped François as they walked to their seat. James smiled; he was going to enjoy France.

He turned to find his cousin, Robert Stewart, who was the uncle of the slain Lennox. Robert had come to France to join *les Gardes*

Ecossaises, the Scottish Guard who had served as the bodyguards to the French kings for centuries. He fought with King Louis XII and François in the Italian Wars and was given the honorary title at Marshall of France. Lennox's sons went to France after the death of their father and were wards of Robert. James studied this man who had spent the majority of his life in France and in service to the French king who he needed to convince to grant a royal marriage. His clothes belonged to a different era, his father's era. His grey hair curled over his ears and his shoulders were stooped, but his eyes were as sharp as a falcon homing in on prey. Yes, James trusted that he might help persuade François to allow Madeleine to marry James.

"Cousin!" James said, embracing this man whom he had heard so much about, but never met. "We are honored that you were able to join us. I have never properly thanked you for fighting against my uncle when he sent his queen to slaughter the Scottish nobility at Flodden."

"It was my honor to defend my French king in partnership with my Scots cousins and king," the old man's voice was as gruff as his grizzled hands.

"Well, we shall have a much belated celebration tonight," James led Robert to the table and they took their places. Once François and his mistress were seated, the servers began to bring out course after course—pheasant in an orange sauce with roasted ox tongue with apricots, rabbit stew with red currant sauce and roasted boar that was gilded, a gooseberry tart with saffron pastry and marzipan salamanders and unicorns—the symbol of François and Scotland.

After dinner, more wine was poured and James was feeling the effects. The wine was heavy, coating his mouth and lips, reminding him of Maggie's lips. The musicians were playing louder and faster, and François' jester, Triboulet, was in rare form. The wine made his back hunch, making him look like an ape. His tri-corn hat was off-kilter, dangerously close to falling off. The king stood to make a toast and Triboulet slapped his butt before the king could speak. The room went silent, music broken off. The king's eyes flashed with rage, and Triboulet knew he had gone too far. He began to backpedal, but the king silenced him.

"Why should I not have you executed for bodily harming your sovereign king?" François narrowed his eyes to contain his rage. No one dared to move, not even James, even though he wanted to lighten the mood, to get back to good feelings.

"I have no reason, my lord," Triboulet knelt, holding his hands over his head, praying for clemency. James's mouth was dry, but he didn't reach for his cup. François looked around the room at the frozen faces. The horror he saw, even in James's face, made him change his mind.

He laughed, but no one joined him. "I'll make a deal with you, Triboulet… if you can come up with an apology that is more insulting than the slap, I will let you live."

Triboulet swayed on his wine-soaked legs, screwed his face in concentration. James caught his brother's eye across the room and saw they both were thinking how very different from Scotland this whole transaction was. More barbaric and yet more sophisticated at the same time. Triboulet pulled his doublet down and shook his head twice.

"My apologies, your Highness," he began. "I didn't recognize you." A nervous twitter escaped from a few of James's men. He shot them a threatening look. James couldn't read François, couldn't tell what he was thinking about Triboulet's apology. How could his servant not recognize the king?

Triboulet continued, "I mistook you for your wife."

François burst out laughing, taking Anne's hand. She also laughed, tears forming in her eyes. For a moment, James almost felt sorry for Eleanor. She was the bride the king had to take but never wanted, the butt of all French jokes, a laughing stock of a queen. And the tension evaporated, forgot in the echoing laughter, and they all continued to drink as if Triboulet had never really been in grave danger.

The next day, the entourage travelled to another palace of François's in the Loire Valley, Château de Blois, to meet the Queen and Princess Madeleine. James peered up at the castle, rows of symmetric arched windows, panes painted crimson in contrast with the gray stones. He pulled his cloak to cover his neck from the drizzle of rain that followed them to the castle. At least when the weather was like this in Scotland, he could count on Maggie's arms to warm him up.

He shook the thought from his mind as he crossed the river to the looming castle; he needed to focus on Madeleine and making her fall in love with him.

At dinner, James found that would not be a difficult task. He entered the magnificent Great Hall, called *Salle des États Généraux*, his breath cut off by its grandeur. The floor was a red, salmon, and slate blue terracotta tiles lain in a diamond pattern, and the giant hall was split into two vaulted chambers, supported by six pointed arches carried by five bright columns that had an exotic feel. James wondered if this was inspired by the palaces in Milan and Venice. The domed ceiling was painted azure and covered in gold leaf fleurs-de-lis. Six circular chandeliers lit the hall. James was positioned between Madeleine and her father, with Beaton not too far away. He stood in front of the enormous fireplace, supported by two Doric columns painted vibrant green with gold spirals. Madeleine was brought in her gilded litter again, her cream satin dress spread out to show the intricate gold embroidery. She did not wear the high kirtle like her stepmother, Queen Eleanor; instead, her dress was cut low and arched across her pale bosom, in Madame d'Heilly's style. The cream fabric looked almost yellow against Madeleine's white skin.

"Bonsoir Princesse," James bowed over her hand, kissing it, allowing his lips to linger. He felt the shiver of desire again from her. She giggled as she pulled her hand away from his, perceiving her stepmother's disapproving glare. James didn't worry about the queen, he knew she had no influence on François.

James turned to watch François stride into the Great Hall. Even though he was in mourning for his son, he looked splendid, wearing a cloth of gold doublet with a wide neck and diamond slashes to reveal the white silk chemise. Over the doublet, he wore a black silk jerkin belted at his waist and flaring over his thighs. His overcoat was black velvet, with voluminous sleeves ending at his elbows to accent his wide shoulders. The sleeves had slashed panes to show the red silk lining. The overcoat had iridescent pearls sewn all over it. On his head was a black velvet barret with an upturned brim adorned with pearls and gemstones. François embraced James, kissing him on each cheek in the French style. James beamed, welcomed as a son. This boded well that François was warming to James, and maybe to the idea of giving Madeleine to him.

"Let's feast!" François slapped James on the back and they both sat. The courses came, some which James had only heard of in Scotland but never tasted—roasted peacock, tail plumage redressed and gilded in gold, pears poached in wine, venison pie with the lightest and butteriest crust James had ever eaten. The wine glasses sparkled in the firelight, the light broken into all of the colors of the rainbow.

"It's Venetian glass," François said when he noticed James admiring them. James wanted to take these back to Scotland with him to show his country the elegance that he would bring.

During the final course, marzipan sculptures of salamander and unicorn delighted Madeleine. James smiled at her child-like innocence and felt compelled to learn more about her.

"Ask her how her trip from Lyon was," James said to Beaton, who relayed the message. The words in her reply all ran together and James could only understand a word or two. Her eyes sparkled, heavy with longing and infatuation.

"She said it was fine, except for the rain," Beaton said. "She asked how your hunt was with her father."

"C'était...." He searched for the word, successful, frustrated at his inability to communication with her. He swung to Beaton. "How do you say successful?" he barked.

"C'était un grand succès," Beaton replied to Madeleine, whose eyes crinkled as she smiled. James didn't know if she was laughing at him or just affected by him. She said something else and James caught the word "marriage." His head snapped toward Beaton, impatient to hear what she had said about marriage.

"She said that she hopes her father agrees to the marriage," Beaton said. James relaxed, his face easing into a wide smile. He would be *un grand succès* in marriage too, despite his ineptitude of the French language.

"Moi aussi, Princesse," he said. *Me too.*

After dinner, Madeleine and her sister prepared a dance. James watched her leap, her feet impossibly small to hold up the rest of her tiny body. Her limbs moved as if she were a puppet, pulled along by her strings. She held James's gaze as she danced.

"I know I'm not supposed to say this, but she is my favorite child," François said to James.

James nodded since he already knew this. "My lord, having made the princess's acquaintance, it is obvious why she is your favorite."

"She's been sickly since she was a babe. Her lungs are weak, just like her mother's were. Your climate in Scotland is not favorable to someone who has lung illness. It is horrible to hear her gasp for breath," the King watched his favorite daughter prance around her sister. She seemed healthy and vigorous, but James knew this was an act for his benefit. Her chest heaved from the exertion of the dance, and the smile, once authentic, had become wooden.

"I can only imagine the helplessness you must feel," James said, unsure how to make the king feel more comfortable about the marriage. He knew everything François said about the Scottish climate was true. The damp air in Scotland weighed down the lungs, making breathing even more difficult. People came south when they had lung ailments, not north. James gulped his wine to cover his frustration and disappointment. He could not change the Scottish clime, and with Francois's loss of his favorite son, there was no way he would send his favorite daughter to her death.

The dance ended and Madeleine returned to James's side. He heard the rattle in her chest when she took a breath, even as adoration shone from her hooded eyes. She was so delicate that James wanted to give her his strength.

"My daughter," François said. "Do you realize that if you marry this man, you will move to Scotland, whose climate is damp and cool?"

"Of course I know this Father!" she said, laughter bubbling from her in a rasping hiss.

"And you know this could result in your death?"

"Father, at least I would be a queen for as long as I lived and this is what I have always wished for," Madeleine said, her eyes glassy with emotion. François studied her face, the love of a father struggling against the wishes of a king. James sucked in his breath, knowing that if François made a decision as a worried father who thought of the well-being of his child, not as a king upholding the treaty to unite two countries together, he would have to marry a lesser French woman, not a princess of royal blood. All of his travel would be for naught; no wealthy dowry to build Scotland. James was wooden in his seat, afraid to move, afraid of François's condemnation of the marriage. He felt his back dampen, fear threatening to drown him.

"Well," the king said, patting his daughter's hand. "I will have to take that under advisement." It was not a refusal, and James could work on Madeline—and she would convince her father.

———————

James traveled with François and the royal entourage to his many château in the Loire Valley. At Château de Loches, a joust tournament had been planned in James's honor. Madeline rode in a gilded carriage behind James and her father, so there wasn't much chance to converse with her. While James's French was getting better, Madeline's Scots was progressing much faster. She spoke Scots in front of her father, whose hooded eyes betrayed no emotion to cue James as to which decision he was leaning.

The square limestone keep dominated the village of Loches, another brilliant show of François's power as a monarch. James was shown to his chamber in the king's apartments to prepare for the joust. He was glad that he had bought new clothing in Paris so that he appeared to be François's equal and worthy of the princess's hand. John helped him into his crimson hose and boots. A new Stechzeug, armor for the joust, had been purchased in Paris. He held his arms out and John tied the breast plate over his purple velvet tunic. The back plate and arm guards were tied on next.

"Don't forget this," John held a golden ring out for James. The ring held a ruby, a stone known to promote health, and on the inside of the band was inscribed "mon coeur est à vous." *My heart is yours.* The symbolism harkened the age of chivalry, which James hoped would impress François as much as Madeline. John tied the ring to a ribbon of entwined purple and red velvet, which James would offer to Madeline as she offered her favor. They went down to the tiltyard, which was a flurry of activity. James was listed on the king's side, who would not joust himself. *Then I will have to joust well to honor him,* James thought. His destrier was clad in the crimson and purple colors of Scotland. John helped James mount and he rode to the stands where Madeline sat on a velvet throne next to her stepmother. She was richly dressed in a low cut cloth of silver dress and a broad smile, color flushing her cheeks.

"My lady," James said in Scots, holding Madeline's gaze. She tittered as he lowered his lance to her with the ribbon tied to the end. "Please accept my favor and grace me with your prayers for a successful joust." She untied the ribbon and saw the ring.

"You have my heart," she translated to the inscription in Scots. "I accept your favor and pray that you will have success today on the tiltyard…. And with my father." Her eyes sparkled, and she ignored the disapproving frown from her stepmother. Madeline placed the ring on her hand and held it to her chest. A wave of optimism buoyed James as he guided his horse to the tilt. He pulled his helmet on and lowered the visor. At the crier's signal, he spurred his horse forward, dirt flying from under the hooves. The horse galloped at full speed and James lowered his lance, aiming at the chest of his opponent. His spear struck in the center, splinting on contact, his opponent thrown off balance and causing his lance to glance off James's shoulder. His opponent fell to the ground, and James was triumphant! He looked over to see Madeline's chest heaving with excitement and François nodding in approval. The wave climbed higher.

———————

At the banquet in the king's chamber at Loches, James sat between François and Madeline, who kept the ring on her middle finger. The room was warm, James back to the fireplace, the wood beam ceiling reflecting the heat.

"Are you still determined to marry the princess?" François asked James. James nodded.

"Aye my good father," he gulped. "Even more determined since becoming better acquainted with her." Madeline lowered her eyes, cheeks flushed a rosy flame.

"She has been in better health lately," the king responded, observing his daughter.

"If my health is improved, it is due to my betrothed," she laughed, reaching over James to touch her father's arm. He hoped the touch would swing François to decide in his favor. François sighed.

"Very well," François sighed and lifted his crystal goblet. "It seems you both are of the same mind against me. I cannot convince you, my sweet, of the dangers should you go to Scotland. It is with a heavy heart that I give my consent," François said. "You may marry my Madeleine." James's head snapped up, he hadn't expected to get the royal princess this quickly, he thought he would have to work harder. Madeleine sat up taller, but otherwise refrained from showing her excitement.

"I can't fight my daughter and my adopted son. But remember your promise that you will treat her as a queen should be treated."

James nodded. Of course he would treat Madeleine like a queen, silently grateful that François hadn't asked James to give up Maggie. In the following weeks, they traveled to Château Amboise and the marriage contract was drawn up—they were officially affianced. And it was done. He would be bringing home a royal princess as Queen of Scots.

1537

Chapter 32

JAMES

IT WAS THE DAY of his wedding—January 1st. *A new year and a new life*, James thought as he pulled on his white hose with gold fringe edging the length of his leg. David Lindsay held out the cloth of gold overcoat edged with pearls that James had made for his wedding. The red satin lining matched the red velvet of his doublet. The buttons on his doublet were gold, inset with iridescent pearls. James glanced in the lead mirror, admiring the cloth of gold coat he had made and then touching the purple bruise under his eye that he had gotten in the melee after the previous day's joust.

"Thank God you're finally getting married," David Lindsay said, brushing off James's shoulder. "Not a moment too soon! Hopefully the queen will be strong enough to give you a son."

James sighed. David was so excited for James to finally marry and provide Scotland a legitimate heir. In the months between his betrothal and today, James had seen just how weak Madeleine was physically. She was intellectually sharp, picking up Scots from James, the two of them reading Boece's *History of Scotland*. Her capacity for language was much better than James, she was already listening and understanding conversations. James tried to speak French for her, but she protested, "No, I need to speak Scots for my people."

But while her mind was sharp, her body was failing. James noticed that at banquets, they could only dance one number before she needed to rest. In his strong arms, she seemed to have hollow bones, which he could feel under her gowns. He was afraid to truly embrace her because he didn't want to hurt her. They had exchanged innocent kisses, but James could feel her desire building. And it scared him. If she died before she gave him an heir, he would be to blame for taking her to Scotland, which could leave him vulnerable to an Anglo-French alliance against him. He shuddered.

But that seemed a remote possibility after his triumphant entrance into Paris. François and his son, Henri, along with clerical dignitaries and members of the French parliament welcomed him to Paris. François had presented him as his natural born son, a dauphin, wearing the crimson fabrics of French royalty. A knock at the door pulled him back to the present. Henri stuck his head in, "Ready, brother?"

James clasped Henri's arm, "Of course, brother!"

Henri whistled, looking at James's eye. "Hell of a wedding present!" he laughed.

James laughed too, "Hopefully it won't scare off my bride!"

"No, brother," Henri said. "Nothing will prevent her from being your wife. No warning from my father nor me. She wants to be your queen."

"Then let's make her my queen," James said, smiling. "The musicians are already playing! Let's join them."

A raised walkway had been built from the palace of the bishop where James had stayed to the west door of Notre Dame. François was waiting at the door to the platform.

"My son, today you become my son in marriage. May it be long and fruitful," he said, linking arms with James. Henri and his brother Charles walked in front of them and then they started down the elevated aisle. The people of Paris had all come out to see the marriage of the King of Scots to the Princess of France. Along the street hung banners and tapestries of the Scottish and French coat of arms, biblical scenes, and heraldic allusions. The cathedral loomed at the end of the platform, ending at the center door, flanked by two identical arched doorways. Above the doorways was a lintel that depicted the resurrection gallery of biblical kings. Above that were two balconies framing the West Rose window with a colonnade above it, ending in two bell towers.

At the door, James turned to watch his bride come down the walkway. The King and Queen of Navarre, who were her uncle and her aunt, and the Queen of France, her stepmom, walked with her.

Madeleine wore a white silk gown embroidered with gold. The arms were slashed and showed the crimson silk kirtle. Her stomacher was lined with pearls, and a bejeweled collar framed her face. Her dark eyes danced as she approached James, but clouded when she saw his black eye.

"What is this?" she asked in accented Scots. He took her hand, shaking off her question. They turned and were married by the Cardinal of Bourbon and then entered the cathedral for mass.

After the mass, the entire party retired to the Palais de la Cite. The *Grand'Salle* had a double nave, each covered with a high arched wooden roof. A row of eight columns in the center of the hall supported the wooden framework of the roof. On each of the pillars, and on columns around the walls, were polychrome statues of the great Kings of France. In the center of the hall was an enormous table made of black marble, quarried in Germany. Rich tapestries covered the walls, gold and silver plates and cups adorned the black marble top table of honor. Everything sparkled under the candlelight. James studied his new bride. Her dark eyes were shining, chin thrust upward, lips stretch in a wide smile. His whole body vibrated as he realized that he had fulfilled the Treaty of Rouen, the Auld Alliance that his father had died for. Now, all he had to do was produce an heir.

After dinner, the first dance was expected to show off the new bride and groom. James took Madeleine's hand, which was shaking, although it wasn't visible to the guests.

"Are you feeling up to this dance?" James asked. Her face glowed as she nodded. The drums started beating, signaling the beginning of a pavane. James bowed as the flute wavered its light notes across the hall. Madeleine curtsied. James chuckled, remembering his first dance with Maggie, how he had bowed too deeply and entered into a battle of wills with her. He would not embarrass his new bride by reenacting that bow. As the violin began, James and Madeleine faced each other, stepping one, two three, one, two, three. Madeleine's chest heaved from the physical exertion. He stepped to her, taking her left hand, and they began to walk—step, élevé, step, élevé. She was laboring to breathe, her chest making a rattling sound as they hopped in a circle. They turned to face each other, still moving— step, élevé, step, élevé.

"Are you sure that you are hale?" James asked, switching hands with her.

"Yes, now stop haivering!" she said, faltering before the last word.

"Haivering, huh? You think I'm talking nonsense?" He was impressed by her use of Scots slang. She beamed, pursing her lips together. He shook his head, amazed again at her ability to become the Queen of Scots. He turned back on himself, step, élevé, step, and brought his bride around with him. Even though the pace was slow, James noticed the sweat darkening the hair at her temples.

The song ended, and James bowed, releasing her hand. As she curtsied, her legs gave out and she stumbled into James. He caught her round the waist and lifted her into his arms.

"As the Queen of Scots, I am your servant," he whispered into her ear, feeling her shiver with desire.

"And are you going to carry me everywhere when I am too weak to walk?" she looked up from under her ebony lashes.

"Whatever you command," he murmured, kissing her ear. He carried her back to the table, placing her in her velvet-upholstered seat. As he took his seat, he noticed François nodding his approval. The galliard began, and James tried to stifle his disappointment at not being able to dance with his new bride. He would have to be patient, a virtue he did not possess. The couples kicked and jumped across the dance floor. At the volta, the memory of Maggie almost knocked him off his chair. It was as if she were in front of him, glittery eyes and biting smile. He grabbed Madeleine's hand to steady himself.

"I'm sorry that I am not as sturdy and strong as the women you are used to," she said. "Do you regret marrying me?"

He stared into her eyes, unencumbered by the suffering that darkened his eyes. "No, I will never regret marrying you and making you the Queen of Scots," he said, and it was the truth. Even though Maggie occupied much of his consciousness, there was room for this sweet girl, who he could mold into the perfect queen, much like his father intended for his mother to become before he died. She squeezed his hand in reassurance.

"Brother, let's dance!" Henri slapped James on the back, propelling him out of his chair, against his mild protestations. While James wanted to stay with Madeleine, his legs twitched under the table in time to the music. Henri introduced him to his cousin, Francis de

Lorraine. James knew the Lorraines were one of the most powerful families in France, and he wondered if they caused François as
much trouble as the Douglases had caused James. He shook the
thought from his mind and listened to see what dance it would be.

"A Saltarello!" James exclaimed, grateful that he has learned
this new Italian dance while he had been in France. The three men
grabbed partners and began chasséing across the floor. James galloped after Henri, pulling his partner with him, feeling his blood
pulsing. He laughed as he turned around with his partner in a circle,
feeling the effects of the wine. He looked over and caught Madeleine's eye. Her mouth was smiling, but there was a tightness of
regret around her eyes. He stopped pulling his partner along, his
enthusiasm deflated. He returned to Madeleine's side after the song
and stayed there for the remainder of the banquet.

"Come!" François stood and addressed James and the whole hall.
"It is time to put these two to bed!" He slapped James on the back.
The bedding ceremony was a tradition of seeing the newlywed cou-
ple off to bed to signify the completion of the marriage.

"Can you walk?" James asked Madeleine.

"I think so. I just need your arm to lean on," she said, lacing
her arm through his. He pressed her arm against him to give
her stability.

The musicians led the procession, tabor and fife sounding. Madeleine took small steps, her lungs wheezing. Her father, stepmother,
and everyone from the Scottish and French courts followed behind,
dancing and singing. James felt Madeleine drooping with each step.

"I can't bear to listen to you labor," he said, putting his arm
around her waist. "Please, allow me to carry you to our bed."

Madeleine nodded and placed her arms around his neck, so light
he barely felt it. He placed his other arm under her legs and lifted
her up. She laid her head on his shoulder.

"I hope you aren't disappointed once we get there," she sighed.
James smiled, he knew she was inexperienced, but he would teach her.

The oak door to their chamber was opened and James laid her on
the bed. He turned to dismiss the entourage.

"Well, my son," François said. "I do not need to stay to know
you will consummate the marriage. Just be gentle. She loves you so
and will do anything to make you happy."

"Of course, Father," James said. François leaned down and embraced his favorite daughter.

"I hope you realize what you have gotten yourself into," he said with mirth. Madeleine laughed, a high, girlish giggle that filled the room.

"Of course, father! We will give you a grandson," she said, tweaking his nose.

He stood, looked at his favorite daughter as if it was the last time and said, "Very well, we will leave you to your marriage duties." Then he shooed everyone out of the room, excited at the possibility of becoming a grandfather. James breathed a sigh of relief. He knew François had stayed in the room when Henri married Catherine de Medici to make sure his son fulfilled his marital duties.

Once the room was empty, James began to shed his clothing. He unbuttoned his doublet and let it drop. He pulled off his hose, exposing his bare skin. Madeleine sucked in her breath at the sight of his legs. She clawed at her dress, pulling the many layers up.

"No, my lovit," he said, using the word he called Maggie, "let me do it." He pulled her to sitting and untied the back of her dress. She wiggled out of the overgown and he pulled it over her head. Her kirtle was next, but he pulled at the pins in her hair.

"Madeleine, Madeleine, let down your hair," he said, unwinding her chestnut hair. It was darker than Maggie's, but softer, like eider down. Guilt ate at him for comparing his new bride to his lover and he tried to push Maggie from his mind. He needed to focus on Madeleine, she deserved his full attention. How would he be able to be a loyal husband in Scotland if he couldn't even keep Maggie out of his bedroom while he was in France?

He buried his face in her hair, kissing it, moving to her ear. She gasped and clutched his undershirt as he ran his tongue along her neck. He eased the shirt over his head and was now naked. Her hands moved over his chest, firm and muscular from his hunting and jousting. Her touch was light, but still sent waves of desire pulsing. He lifted her chemise over her head and she was naked too. Her chest was so pale that he could see the blue veins crisscrossing her breasts. He kissed them, wishing that he could transfer his physical strength to her.

"Will it hurt?" she asked, her hands encircling him. He felt the surge of blood and adrenaline.

"I'll be as gentle as you need me to be," he said, easing himself forward. Her breath caught, a small yelp of pain escaping. James paused, not wanting to hurt her.

"No, keep going," she said through tight teeth. "Teach me what to do."

And so James talked to her in Scots, telling her how to move and where to place her hands, her legs. She was a willing pupil, but the grimace of pain never left her face. When he was finished, relief washed over her face.

"I promise I will get better," she said, resting her head on his chest. He stroked her hair and thought about his future. Madeleine would get better, because she wanted to please him. But would she ever be able to be as physical as he liked his partner to be? Her hips were impossibly narrow. James felt that even if she did get pregnant, she wouldn't survive childbirth. He wanted to protect her, shield her from the difficulties of life, but also knew that he would kill her—either his bedroom activities would kill her or the harsh climate of Scotland would. He wanted to make sure she was carrying an heir when they arrived in Scotland.

James and Madeleine stayed in France, much to François's delight. He staged jousting tournaments on land and sea battles, which James had never seen before. The streets of Paris were blocked off and flooded, war ships facing off against each other, firing cannons. Above these, James saw a dragon flying across the sky, fire spurting from his mouth.

After almost two months of celebrating in France, James received a letter from his uncle Henry. The malice jumped from under his uncle's great seal. He was upset that James had accepted a sword and hat with the title of Defender of the Faith from the pope. That had been his uncle's title before he broke from the church and was excommunicated. He flipped the letter open, ready for the disapproval and vitriol.

Across the top of the page read, "Articles against the passage of the Scottish king through the realm of England." James chuckled.

So his uncle thought he wanted permission to cross England? While he was in France, he had ignored the English ambassadors and their questions. They wanted him to make peace with Angus and accept him back into Scotland, and so James would walk away when they approached him. There were so many issues that his uncle could have with him, but permitting safe passage through England had not even crossed James's mind. He read the article. It said that James would only be allowed passage if he acknowledged that he was a vassal of England. James shook his head. His marriage to Madeleine had guaranteed an alliance with France, which strengthened Scotland. James would never lower himself to say he were a *vassal* of England.

The next point of the decree illustrated how immature his uncle could be. Because James hadn't met his uncle in York, his uncle wasn't letting him into England now. Like a child who is denied his desire, his uncle was denying James. And the jabs kept coming—he pouted that James wouldn't forgive his stepfather, that he didn't inform his uncle of his marriage, that James hadn't supported his uncle by embracing his new religion.

The hatred his uncle poured out in this decree surprised James. He felt he was justified in not trusting his uncle, not accepting his religion, not meeting him in England. He could explain point by point why he was keeping his distance, the memory of his father's death reason enough that James could not trust his uncle. And yet, he had hoped his uncle might understand, might be reasonable, might see it from James's side of the border. His mother was right—her brother was a jackanapes, but a dangerous jackanapes with a powerful army. He knew his uncle would be angry that he married a French princess, that the English enemy was now a Scottish friend. And yet, James had married Madeleine without consulting or advising his uncle, knowing he would incur the wrath. It was a dangerous game, and James couldn't back down, couldn't show weakness. He had to move forward, and bring Scotland with him. A modern kingdom for a modern king. He would show his uncle that he was no one's vassal; he was a modern monarch.

Chapter 33

THE QUEEN MOTHER

MARGARET STOMPED INTO THOMAS Erskine's office in Edinburgh. She smoothed her hair back off her face, disheveled from her ride from Stirling.

"When is my son coming back?" she asked the surprised secretary. She pulled herself up to her full height, which was not tall. But she wanted to appear bigger than her problems—multiple problems, some new, some old. Some old but with a new person. Only her son could help her, but he had prolonged his honeymoon.

Her brother, her younger, bothersome brother, was behaving badly again. He was blaming Margaret for not telling her that her son had married a French princess. She wrote back, "As to the King, my son, not asking your counsel about his marriage; my son at his departure told me he would have your counsel in all that he did, and I am evil content that he has not done so." She did not add that she could not control what her grown sovereign son did.

Her daughter was still imprisoned in the Tower of London. Margaret had been corresponding with her brother's secretary, Cromwell, to secure the young Margaret's release. In his last letter, Cromwell had said that the king might be more lenient soon. The note was confusing at the time, but then Harry announced that his new bride was with child. So if the child was a boy, her daughter might be released. All of her hopes tied to something she had no control over. It was just like her brother to give her hope of a release only to crush it with an impossible condition. Margaret prayed the child would be a boy.

The other problem felt like repetition of the past—a disappointment that she had already lived through with Ard. She wasn't supposed to feel it again with Muffin. No, this husband was supposed to be *her* toy to use, not the other way around. But he was a Scot. She should not have been surprised when she heard the news. He had stolen rents from her lands and had a bastard child with a Scottish wench. Just like Ard.

And so she wanted a divorce, but James only could grant it.

"Hello, Queen Mother," Thomas stood and bowed to her. She curtsied and hurried to hear the answer to her question. "He departed from Le Havre on May 10, so if the weather holds, he should be at Leith in a few days."

"Thank you, Sir Erskine," Margaret said, already leaving the room. Her son would be back in a few days—with his new bride. A *French* bride, which angered her brother because he had wanted her to convince her son to marry English. But a bride held the promise of children soon. Then maybe she would be able to retire in England and live her life out with her daughter and quit the Scottish games.

Four days later, on the banks of Leith, Margaret stood on the crowded wharf, watching the approach of a French convoy of warships surrounding a galley ship, masts at full sail, gliding into the harbor. The sun had set behind them, turning the storm clouds vibrant orange and pink—a glorious omen for her son and his new bride. From the main masts flew the Scottish flag, a white X on a blue background. Along the deck were banners combining the Scottish and French coat of arms. Margaret tried to swallow her heart, which had lodged itself in her throat. The fear she had felt over her son's trip to France was dissipating, but Margaret was irritated that it lingered even as his ship approached the harbor.

The boat docked and Margaret got her first look at the new queen, her daughter-in-law. Madeleine held onto James's arm as they descended the gangplank. She was slight, still had the body of a prepubescent girl. Her crimson stomacher laid against her chest, flat, and the fullness of her skirt swallowed her, making her look like a doll, porcelain skin tinged blue. The girl sank to the ground and said in Scots, "Thanks to God that He safely brought me and my husband to our own country." She clenched two fistfuls of Scottish earth and kissed both of her hands. Margaret smirked. The girl did have a flare for the dramatic. And the nobles in attendance fell in love with her in that moment.

James approached his mother. "Mother," he embraced her, whispering in her ear. "Where is your husband?"

"That is a matter for a different time," Margaret said, choking back her bitterness. "Today, we celebrate our new Queen. She looks weak."

"Yes, Mother, but she is the sweetest queen I could ever ask for," James said. Margaret was surprised at the affection in her son's voice. She had not expected him to fall for his bride—it was an alliance marriage, but this child had won her promiscuous son over.

"Is she with child?" she asked the question that all the people of Scotland would be wondering.

"Perhaps," James winked. "I see no reason why I would not endow my wife with a child."

"Is she strong enough to carry a child?" Margaret narrowed her eyes. If this girl didn't produce an heir, Scotland would be in the same position as England. Worse—because the Earl of Arran, next in line for the throne, had come of age. James needed a legitimate heir.

"Queen Mother," the girl said in Scots. "It is an honor to meet you." She curtsied and her knee touched the ground. Margaret pulled the girl up, light as a bird.

"The honor is mine," Margaret answered in French, although it was rusty since she hadn't used it in a long time.

"Please speaks Scots with me," Madeleine said, her eyes misty. "It is the language of my people."

James placed his arm around his slight bride, looking at her with protectiveness and pride.

"Let's retire for the evening. It has been a long trip. Tomorrow we will enter Edinburgh and show the country her new queen."

Madeleine held her head high, but Margaret saw her hand shaking as she took James's arm, clutching to support herself.

Margaret noticed the ships unloading—chests full of jewels and luxurious fabrics, tapestries, precious stones, an elaborate French bed, tableware. As much as she didn't want it to, jealousy crept up her back, winding around her. She remembered the magnificence with which her father had sent her north—purple velvet and green cloth of gold gowns, farthingales, kirtles, a whirlicote covered with cloth of gold and embroidered with the Tudor arms—four panels, two with three yellow lions on a red background and two with gold fleur-de-lis on a blue background. Her father had given her a book of hours, a prayer book, and wrote inside, "Pray for your loving father, who gave you this book, and I give you all times God's blessing and mine." Even though he had been notorious for being stingy, he had sent her north with a treasure to show the Tudor wealth and strength. Bitterness once again washed over her as she thought of all she lost. She would need to write her brother to send money so she could have a new dress made for the coronation.

"Come, Mother!" James called over his shoulder. She hurried to follow him, when her eyes locked with familiar moss-colored eyes. Maggie! She was not the girl whom Margaret had dismissed from her service. Her face had lost its baby fullness, revealing high cheekbones and deepening her eyes. The intelligence that had always been present had also matured. Margaret noticed that as Maggie looked at James's back, even with his new queen in his arms, her naked desire evident. Her gaze swung from James to Margaret. There was no malice coming from the woman, just indifference. Margaret shuddered. Even to the girl who was once her closest servant, Margaret had become irrelevant. James needed to produce an heir before he took back up with his Scottish whore. She knew he would return to Maggie, just like his father had returned to his mistress even after Margaret had given him a son. She couldn't change a Scotsman, so she needed to concentrate on securing his future, even if he wasn't thinking about it.

———————

Plans were made for summer progress, to show Madeleine her new country and allow her people to see and appreciate her. James had begun work on remodeling Holyrood like the French palaces he had seen, injecting Italian ornamentation. Margaret began to relax, at last her son had married and, given his history, should soon be expecting an heir. She still wanted to push him to grant her a divorce from Muffin, but every time she brought it up, he turned surly and rude. He accused her of wanting to remarry Angus, embarrassing her in front of the French queen. She would bide her time, hoping that after the announcement of a pregnancy, James's mood would mellow and he would be more compassionate toward her situation.

But, as the French king predicted, the harsh Scottish climate proved too much for the delicate health of the princess. Madeleine became weaker and weaker, even though she glowed under James's espousal. He called off her state entry into Edinburgh and coronation. They retired to Holyrood, now Madeleine's castle as part of the marriage contract. James spent most of his time by her side, Margaret noted with mirth, and did not go to Loch Leven. The frail Madeleine grew smaller and more pale. Margaret realized there would be no Scottish heir. In July, Madeleine died in James's arms. The festive mood became sober, and instead of a celebration, a state funeral was planned.

Chapter 34

MAGGIE

MAGGIE'S EYES WERE FOCUSED on one spot in the church at Holyrood, James's bent back. She itched the back of her arms where the black wool irritated her skin. The deceased queen lay at the front of the church, her coffin draped in purple velvet with black fringe. The pall had an embroidered cross in white, along with a golden, twisted letter S for Stewart. Above the coffin was a *castrum dolorus*, a black velvet covered stepped pyramid holding two hundred and ten lit candles. Between the arches, surrounding the knave, hung black velvet and the Scottish and French heraldic banners. Maggie noticed that the women the queen brought with her from France—six ladies-in-waiting—were clad in black velvet gowns with fur-lined sleeves. Maggie felt the power of the French princess and mourned that she had died before her wealth could help Scotland.

While Bishop Cairncross delivered the requiem mass, Maggie studied James. His head was erect, red circles around his dark eyes. His hands were folded in prayer, but Maggie noticed the tension in his white knuckles under his embroidered shirt cuffs. The Queen Mother patted his back, her hand quivering.

Maggie ran her fingers through her son's hair, the same cinnamon color of his father. Jamie looked up at her, his eyes exact copies of his father's. At least she had purchased mourning clothes for her son, so that he looked like a royal son, even if he wasn't legitimate. With the death of the French princess, James was once again without a bride to cement the Scot-Franco alliance. Maggie sighed. All of that travel and political maneuvering just to end up in the same position.

She had watched the girl queen disembark at Leith and had been unimpressed. The young queen had a spark of intelligence, but Maggie noticed the innocence that blocked that intelligence from being realized. But the young queen would learn the ways of the Scots and the innocence would be stamped out. Did the girl know about her husband's children? Did she know her husband's feelings toward Maggie? But before she could figure out what her role would be in the king's life now that he had a proper wife, Madeleine's health deteriorated. Her lungs were not strong enough to withstand the damp Scottish climate, and the king holed himself up with his young bride. Even though Maggie knew this marriage would change their relationship, even though she pushed for him to marry a French princess because that was what Scotland needed, even though she had willingly given him up, jealousy still enveloped her when she saw the tenderness in James's face when he looked at his wife. It was protective, nurturing, almost loving. Maggie had to look away.

The coffin was placed in the crypt and Maggie followed the procession out of the church and to the Great Hall of Holyrood for a banquet. The walls were draped in black, tables covered in black. James approached her. Without thinking, her arms surrounded Jamie.

"Hello, my son," the king said to Jamie. The six-year old bowed, the black feather in his barret quivering. Maggie smiled, proud of her small son's perfect courtly behavior. Her son was being raised to understand a prince's role, even if he was illegitimate.

"We need to speak about the future of my son," James said, "Where is your husband?'

Maggie's mouth fell open in surprise. "You don't know?" she asked, voice rising with incredulity. James shook his head. "Maybe you should ask your secretary," she said.

The three of them walked into the courtyard of palace. James kept reaching for Jamie and patting his shoulder or his head. Maggie knew the death of Madeleine had shaken him, but she hadn't realized how much he had isolated himself in his grief.

"Robert is warded in Edinburgh for treason," she said once they were alone. Jamie ran ahead of them, scattering birds in his wake. "I thought you had him arrested for what he did to me."

James swung his full attention to Maggie. His nose flared, lips tight.

"What did he do to you?" he asked, teeth clenched.

"He locked me in my chamber. He wouldn't let me go to Stirling to celebrate Easter with our son, even though my father invited us there," Maggie said, digging her fingernails into her palms to stop the tears from forming.

"Oh Magpie," James said, his voice lower, catching her arm. "I didn't know, I didn't know."

"When he was arrested right before you came back, I thought...." She paused. Could she really voice her thoughts? She had hoped that James had arrested him because he was coming back from France to marry her, even though she knew that he was bringing back a French bride because that was what Scotland needed. Selfishly, she still wanted him for herself. And looking into his face, she knew he still wanted her too.

"You know you can still tell me anything," he said, brushing the back of his hand along her jaw. Her head tilted toward his hand. It was comforting, safe.

"I know," she said, unable to keep her eyes clear. "It was awful. And then he was gone. I hoped you had ordered his arrest."

James looked past Maggie, to their son who was splashing water out of the fountain. His hair shone like copper as the sun peeked out. Maybe Maggie had overestimated the strength of his feelings.

"I'm so sorry, lovit," he looked back at her, his face dark with remorse. "I had been so busy with the alliance, the marriage, her death. I thought you and Jamie were taken care of."

"Jamie is fine," Maggie's voice softened, knowing James's fierce protection over his son. Regret jabbed her stomach, seeing the alarm on his face. She hadn't wanted to add to it. "We are fine, really. I'm sorry I brought it up. I shouldn't have said anything."

"No, Mags," he caught her hands. "He will never do anything like this to you again. I promise."

Maggie smiled and turned toward Jamie, but allowed her hand to linger in the king's. She wasn't sure what he would do to her husband, but she trusted his word. He had always found a way, and only married the French princess because Maggie had told him to. He was here, back in her sphere. Whatever happened next, Maggie knew she and Jamie would not need to worry.

Chapter 35

THOMAS

IN HIS OFFICE AT Holyrood, Thomas had no time to think about Maggie. While the king had been convincing François to allow him to marry Madeleine, there had been an uprising in Northern England along the Scottish border. The people were unhappy with Henry's dissolution of the Catholic monasteries and the taxes that he authorized during peacetime. Beaton and Dunbar of course wanted to send Scottish support and arms. Thomas knew that with the marriage uncertain, the alliance with France was tenuous and didn't want to interfere with English problems and aggravate Henry, so he deferred decision.

By the time James could have been told of the uprising, Henry had already executed the leaders and James had brought Madeleine back to Scotland only to have her succumb to her illness. He knew the king was in no mood to support upheaval on the borders. Thomas also knew that Angus was in the border town of Berwick and may have had something to do with the uprisings, lending his support to anti-Scottish factions to goad James into attacking. Thomas needed to tactfully tell all of this to James in a way that didn't make James want to retaliate and drag Scotland into a war for which they were not prepared.

Second concern, which was more disconcerting than the first, was if James had been reunited with Finnart. And if Finnart had told Thomas's secret. He had been avoiding Finnart, which hadn't been difficult since Finnart had been named Master of Household for Linlithgow. The palace was under substantial remodeling for the arrival of a new queen.

As Thomas planned his next step to alienate Finnart, James came into his office, his face full of rage and grief. Thomas's stomach lurched, apprehensive. He swallowed as James strode toward him. Thomas was sure that Finnart had told.

"Thomas, is it true that Sir Robert Douglas of Loch Leven has been warded for treason?" James leaned into the desk, hands supporting him. Thomas exhaled, releasing his held tension. This wasn't about England or Finnart, just a matter, which had already been taken care of. Chancellor Dunbar didn't feel the matter required them to disturb the king in his mourning.

"Yes, *Schir*. Lady Glamis was retried for poisoning her husband, but the court added the charges of attempting to poison the king and assisting and communicating with her brothers," he said. Lady Glamis had been tried in 1532 for poisoning her husband Lord Glamis, who had been one of James's first supporters upon his escape from Angus. "She was brought in with her husband, Sir Campbell of Skipness, and Sir Robert Douglas of Loch Leven. Lady Glamis was found guilty and executed. Her husband was not charged, but before he could be set free, he tried to escape and fell to his death."

"And what of Sir Robert Douglas?" James prompted.

"He was also not charged, but remains in custody. Would you like him to be released?"

"Do you think he was communicating with his cousins?" James asked, sitting hard as if his weight was too heavy to support.

"There is no definitive evidence, no letters in his own hand," Thomas said, knowing he should not go further, but relief that his secret had not been told made him bold. "He does have a reason for helping the Douglases," Thomas said in a low voice, not adding that his reason was that the king was sleeping with Robert's wife. That would be a step too far, and Thomas knew that James's anger was a slow burn. But at the same time, he wanted Maggie's husband to be punished and Maggie to fall from the king's favor. Maybe he could convince the king that Maggie was also assisting the Douglases.

"But he has benefited from his position. He will be released," James said. "After I speak with him. I want him to understand exactly why he is not being executed."

Thomas exhaled as the door clasped shut. He hadn't realized he'd been holding his breath, on edge to see if Finnart had told James what he discovered about Thomas. But it seemed Finnart was still out of James's favor. Thomas needed to ensure it stayed that way.

Chapter 36

JAMES

JAMES MADE HIS WAY from Holyrood to the Tolbooth. The building stood in front of St. Giles Cathedral opposite the lawn market on High Street. The guards snapped to attention at his approach and opened the metal-studded door. James climbed a narrow staircase to the prisoner chambers. Sunlight sifted through a barred window on the north side of the room, which was the only light. No fire was lit in the hearth. A man was sitting on the floor, arms crossed over his knees. He scrambled to standing as James ordered the guards to open the door. Robert Douglas was dirty—his hose streaked with mud, his doublet rumpled and soiled. His hair waved in every direction, and his brown eyes drooped with exhaustion, widening when he saw the king. He genuflected as soon as he realized who was visiting him.

"My lord," Robert began, his voice breaking with fear. James remained quiet, allowing Robert to sit in his fear, the uncertainty of the king's visit weighing him down. He knew that two of his kin, Master Forbes and Lady Glamis, were dead. James wanted him to feel the same fear Robert instilled in Maggie when he punished her.

"You know what happened to the others who supported and communicated with Angus," James said after the silence settled. Robert nodded, his head bobbing.

"Everyone who aided Angus will suffer," James continued, his teeth clenched in anger. "Perhaps you're wondering why you are still alive."

"No, I'm well aware of why I am still alive," Robert hoisted his chin in defiance. "You fucked my wife."

James chuckled, "You're quite arrogant for someone who has been arrested for treason."

"Then I have nothing to lose," Robert said. James smiled, but he wanted to rip this man's face off. This *Douglas,* who should be grateful for his life, was mocking the king's mercy.

"You have everything to lose," James said, reining in his anger, turning on the Tudor charm to persuade. "Your lands, your wealth, your children, even your wife."

"You stole my wife before I even had a chance to fulfill the marriage contract," Robert said. "She has never been mine. Wouldn't it be convenient to murder your lover's husband and marry her? Is that what you're planning?"

"No, if you talked to your wife, you would know that it was she who pushed me to marry a French princess. For the good of Scotland."

"She doesn't talk to me about you," he said, running his hand through his hair. James felt sorry for him—almost. He knew that Maggie would never open up to Robert as she did to James. And it was his fault—James had fallen in love with his childhood companion who had become a complex woman while he was in Angus's clutches. And since Maggie had sacrificed her desires for the good of Scotland, he could now use her husband to make sure she was provided for.

"I am pardoning you," James said. "You will be released and returned to Loch Leven." Robert nodded, surprised at his luck, but waiting for what it would cost him. Because it would cost him.

"You will never again lock up your wife and deprive her of seeing my son," James said. "You may deprive your children of their mother, but I will not tolerate it." James wanted him to feel like a parasite, which is what he was, glomming off Jamie's lifestyle, while punishing Maggie. Robert nodded again, his eyes remained downcast.

"My son will be removed from your household," James continued. "And his mother will be allowed to visit and stay with him whenever she desires. If he tells me that he asked for his mother, and she did not visit, I will assume it is because of you. You will be arrested for treason. And this time, there will be no clemency."

James spun on his heel, not wanting to see this man prostrate himself in gratitude. He couldn't stand the affected appreciation from Robert for his mercy. By executing Lady Glamis, the message was sent that anyone communicating with the Douglases would die. Robert wasn't so stupid to think he would be spared twice. So he would not aide Angus, nor would he be cruel to Maggie again. James was satisfied with this visit to the underworld. And he couldn't wait to tell Maggie.

As autumn marched through Scotland, James went to Falkland to hunt and relax. He had tested Maggie's husband by asking her to come to Stirling with Jamie in August. Maggie had come and helped him write a letter to François, the letter he had put off writing because it was too painful—to cause grief to the man James thought of as a father, to recognize Scotland's weak position yet again.

His hand shook as he wrote, "*Sire, there is nothing in this world that could be more unpleasant than this occasion where I have to write to you regarding the death of your daughter, my dear spouse, which happened after a long period of illness. And because of the comfort and trust that I have for you, I would like you to still be my good father like I forever want to be your good and humble son.*" She held him as he cried for another woman, not bitter or jealous. She was his rock, the one who he could always count on. He headed up to Badenoch to hunt with his cousin, George Gordon, Earl of Huntly in some of the best hart country. After hunting, he went to the city of Inverness, capital of the Highlands, and then came back down the east coast to meet Maggie and Jamie at Stirling for Martinmas.

The household gathered in the Great Hall for the Martinmas dinner, a celebration for not only the royal family, but for all of the servants and people who took care of Stirling. Gilded platters held roasted geese covered in herbs and butter surrounded by poached pears. Jamie sat on one side of James, his oldest son on the other side. Also at the table were his sons John and Robert, who were six and four, and his only daughter, Jean, who was two. Seated across from each other were Maggie and his mother, each eating in silence while hurling daggers at each other with their eyes. Maggie sipped her wine, her eyes never leaving the Queen Mother. James signaled for the musicians to play a festive song to drown out the tension.

"My son, how go the marriage negotiations in France?" his mother asked, taking a drink of wine to cover her smile. Maggie frowned, unhappy to discuss another French marriage.

"Beaton is doing his best," James said, although he was apprehensive, since it seemed like the negotiations were taking longer than he expected. He sent Beaton to France to secure another French bride—a fertile woman who could provide an heir. And since he had already married a French princess, the pressure to secure the alliance was lessened. François offered Marie de Lorraine, Duchess of Longueville. James had met the young duchess when he called on Marie de Bourbon, who was the duchess's cousin, and he had danced with her brother and Henri at his wedding. She was a widow from the powerful de Guise family. François had offered the widow to James when he asked his father-in-law for advice. James trusted Beaton would finalize the matter soon, given his diplomatic skills.

"My brother has announced his intention to marry the Duchess of Longueville. With the death of his queen, he is already looking for another one. Of course he is turning this marriage into a competition—who will France choose to ally themselves with by giving the lady's hand..." his mother continued. Henry's wife, Queen Jane, had died from complications of childbirth after giving the king his long-sought-after son in October. He rewarded her by providing an elaborate tomb and a queen's funeral and burial. And now he, too, was looking for another queen.

"I'm going to put Jamie to bed," Maggie said, upending her chair. It clanked against the flagstones, echoing around the vast hall. She rushed out of the hall, jostling a protesting Jamie in front of her.

"Are you happy now, Mother?" James said, standing to follow Maggie. His mother was lashing out because he wouldn't grant her a divorce from her husband, Lord Methven. James had chuckled when he heard the gossip spread by Methven that the Queen Mother wanted to marry the Earl of Arran, thirty years her junior. He dismissed this, but the rumor that his mother wanted to reunite with her former husband, Angus, couldn't be so easily ignored. And so he refused her request to get divorced. She attempted to flee to England, which James took as a sign she wanted to reunite with Angus. She was captured before she got to the border and now was at Stirling under guard.

"She should know that you must remarry to maintain the Auld Alliance. Surely that can't be a surprise," his mother said, her outrage barbed with malice. He knew Maggie was a convenient target to use to punish James for not granting his mother's divorce.

"Of course she does. I wanted a calm Martinmas dinner with my children. You couldn't allow me that? You're so spiteful—all because I won't grant you a divorce from the second man you have chosen to marry," he said, gulping his wine. His servants glanced between themselves. Jean began to cry, wailing moans that drowned out the music.

"My son, I have sacrificed so much for you and your throne. Yes, I would like a divorce, but you've made it abundantly clear that you will not grant it. I've accepted that. But I am still your mother, and I'm not going to censor myself because it might upset one of your bastard's mothers," the Queen Mother crossed her arms. She was just as stubborn as James. He knew he wasn't going to change her now. He rushed up to Jamie's rooms to find Maggie pulling the door to his room shut behind her.

"He is sleeping already?" James said, hoping to soothe Maggie. She shook her head.

"He will be soon. His nurse is with him," she said, smoothing her hair back off her forehead. James caught her hand and kissed it.

"I'm sorry that my mother ruined our dinner," James said. He held Maggie's hand, and she didn't pull away.

"She thinks I'm still a naïve girl that I was when I was her maid-in-waiting," Maggie said, walking and pulling James after her. He followed like an obedient hound lapping at her heels for a scrap of food. Her hair curled from under her coif around the top of her kirtle at the nape of her neck. He placed his hand there, feeling the tension in her muscles, the ligaments taut as lute strings. He wanted to tell her that nothing would change, that she would always be Jamie's mother and therefore a part of his life, that he would always need her calm support. But the words stuck in his throat.

"She thinks I don't know that you will remarry a French bride," she said, her voice taking a hard edge. "I know you will need to remarry a French bride. *I* know."

He placed his hands on her shoulders and squeezed. "Yes, I have to remarry a French noblewoman. But she will never have my heart like you do."

She stopped in front of her chamber door. "Queen Madeleine had your heart," she said, eyes downcast. James could feel the insecurity that his mother's comments had created in Maggie.

"Yes, she did," he said, cupping her chin and raising her face to look at him. Her wide eyes were deep green, color of jealousy. "And if she would have survived, you would have loved her too. I wanted you to be her lady-in-waiting. To teach her how to be a good wife."

Maggie laughed, "You wanted me to teach her to be a good wife? My husband might disagree with you, since I did give myself to you while I was contracted."

"I wanted you as badly as you wanted me. We fell in love. You know I wanted to marry you."

"I do. But it wasn't what Scotland needed. It needed French money. And still does."

"Beaton will secure a French bride. She is a widow, and from the de Guise family," James said, knowing Maggie understood the power of that family. "I will stay here with you at Stirling with my children."

"I will go wherever you want me to go, James," Maggie answered, her eyes brightening.

"Good, I want you to go in your room," he said, pressing himself against her. "And I'm spending the night with you. And we are not going to sleep one bit."

Maggie smiled, teeth flashing. "I'm not tired at all," she said, her eyes penetrating him. James closed the door behind them and they both forgot about England, France, his uncle, a new bride. For the moment, Maggie was everything he needed.

Chapter 37

MARIE DE LORRAINE

IN JOINVILLE CASTLE, HER parent's estate in eastern France, Marie sat in her black mourning clothes, without saying a word, and sized up her opponent, her uncle Jean, the Cardinal de Lorraine. Joinville Castle had been built on a rocky hill above the River Marne with a chapel and cemetery, lovely gardens, vineyards and orchards. At the center was the round Jovin's Tower, which her mother said was built after Caesar conquered Gaul. Marie had learned to be like the castle—silent and imposing. She had learned that if she remained silent, she could influence men more than if she spoke, since she was not as intellectual as the king's sister, Marguerite, nor was she as charming and vivacious as the king's mistress, Duchess de E'tampes. No, her strength lay in silence, allowing her to formulate an effective response. She bore her steel gray eyes into her uncle.

"You are to remarry, niece," her uncle's brown beard twitched as he spoke. Jean was her father's brother. Her father was the second son of Rene de Lorraine. The House of Lorraine was a cadet branch of the royal family in France, one that descended from a younger son of a monarch. The Lorraines could trace their ancestry back to Charlemagne, and controlled vast areas of land in the eastern part of France, bordering on the Holy Roman Empire, ruled by Charles V. For that, the family was seen as more German than French. Marie's father, Claude, would not inherit his father's ducal title and estates, but he was a noble son. He was raised with King François, who was two years older. Claude fought for François in the Italian Wars, and was shot in the thigh by an arquebus. He would have died if his groom hadn't thrown his body over Claude to protect him. François rewarded him by making him Duke of Guise.

"But she is still mourning," her mother, Antoinette de Bourbon said. Marie looked at her mother, a strong and practical woman, who was calm and resourceful. Her mother had a nose like a beak and gray eyes, which made her look austere. Her uncle ran his fingers through his hair, knowing this conversation was not going to be easy. After all, Marie's husband, Louis, the Duke of Longueville, had just died four months earlier. She had been contracted and married to Louis at eighteen, and to her pleasant surprise, she fell in love with him. And then he suddenly died in June while she was pregnant with their second son, whom she cradled in her arms. No, she was not ready to remarry. She had hoped that she would be able to retire to the Longueville estate, raise her sons, and manage their inheritance, much like her grandmother, Philippa de Guelders, her father's mother, had done after her husband's death.

"The king's son-in-law, the King of Scots, is looking for a new bride," her uncle said. "And I suggested Marie."

"But Queen Madeleine has not even been in her grave for three months!" her mother was indignant. Marie had been Madeleine's friend when Marie was a maid-in-waiting in Queen Eleanor's court at age fourteen. Five year her junior, Madeleine had looked up to Marie as a role model and older sister. Madeleine would beg Marie to come to her room and sleep with her. They would pull the thick curtains around the bed and be lost in their own worlds. Marie would invent stories to entertain Madeleine, who giggled at familiar tales where the main character was replaced with an animal, her favorite being a dog. Madeleine would fall asleep on her side, and Marie slept to the wheezing of Madeleine's lungs. Marie knew that Madeleine would not survive in Scotland, but Madeleine was resolute that she would be a queen. Marie felt the pull of grief on her heart—for her sweet friend and for her beloved husband. She couldn't marry, especially not the King of Scots.

"This is a day for rejoicing, I suggested your daughter to be the next Queen of Scots. And the king has agreed," her uncle faced off against her mother, his red robes flashing in the sunlight.

"Scotland killed the king's daughter, and now you offer *my* daughter," her mother placed her hands on Marie's shoulders, strong hands to keep Marie from flying off into her grief. Her husband used to keep Marie grounded in the same way. She would never feel his strong hands knead her shoulders again or hear his quiet voice in her ear.

"Antoinette, you are looking at this all wrong. This is an honor and will bring more prestige to our family," the cardinal said.

"This is indecent!" her mother snapped. Marie knew it was not just that Marie was mourning and it was not appropriate to approach remarriage. It was also that Scotland was so far away. Her mother and she were very close, Marie was her first born and the child most like her. She was also thinking of her father. Marie was his favorite child, which he proclaimed unabashedly.

"And what does my husband, the Duke, think?" her mother asked. Her father remained in Lyon with the king and court, he was too valuable a commander to be allowed to bring this news. François and the Emperor, Charles, were preparing to face off over territory in northwestern Italy again. The king wanted to repossess Milan and territories in the Lowlands and depended on her father to lead the troops.

"Of course your husband is in favor. He will convince you," her uncle placed his red galero hat on his head, signaling the end of the conversation.

After her mother had him shown out, she returned and embraced Marie, rocking her. The silence echoed in the cool room, reflecting Marie's anguish at the thought of remarrying so soon after her own husband's death.

"Marie, Marie," her mother murmured. "What will we do?"

"We will see what father says," she said, clutching her mother to her. "And if he and the king decide, then I will become the Queen of Scots."

"I will do everything in my power to keep you here in France," her mother said. And Marie knew she meant it. But Marie also knew that she was the property of France as a member of the royal family, and that meant she needed to be of service to France, which for a woman meant a political marriage.

A month passed before her father returned to Joinville Castle, a three-month truce signed between François and the emperor. Her uncle had been in the emperor's court in Italy to negotiate a lasting peace. The day was warm, but Marie felt the crisp November chill in her feet, the first place she felt the weather change. She knew the night would get colder, and her bed would be empty. The grief waved over her again.

Her father showed signs of battle stress—crow's feet around his eyes, gray streaking his blond beard. She embraced him, his back a little stooped, but she still had to lift onto her toes. Marie inherited her stature from her father. After he embraced her mother, she got right to the point.

"Husband, tell me that the king isn't seriously thinking of contracting our daughter again? Not while she is in mourning?" her mother said.

"I am afraid he is quite serious," he said, pulling off his overcoat. "And our daughter has not one king pursuing her, but two."

Marie's head snapped up. Two? She knew of the King of Scots. She remembered meeting him when he pulled the crude masquerade on her cousin, Marie de Bourbon. Her cousin, shrewdly, recognized him by his red hair and crooked nose, but he still broke her heart by breaking their marriage contract to marry Princess Madeleine. While Marie would never say it, she felt the King of Scots was uncouth, backward, unrefined.

"Who is the second king?" Marie asked.

"The King of England," her father's piercing eyes bore into her, trying to read his daughter's face. Marie lowered her eyes and focused on her embroidering so her father couldn't see her surprise or her aspiration. Her father-in-law was taken prisoner in 1513 after the French loss at the Battle of Spurs and spoke of Queen Catherine's hospitality when he was ransomed and returned to France.

Her father continued, "Sieur de Castillon had hardly arrived in London when the King pounced on him to arrange a French marriage. He first suggested Marguerite, which angered François!"

Marie and her parents laughed at the audacity of the English king to offer himself to François's youngest, and only living, daughter.

"But once he heard that his nephew was in negotiations for Marie, he said she should be contracted to him because he is a big person and needs a big wife," her father chuckled at the reference to Marie's height.

"I may be a big woman, but I have a little neck," Marie fired back, alluding to a comment Anne Boleyn made to her executioner about the ease of killing her because she had a little neck. Her father stifled his laughter, proud of his daughter's quick wit, but also knowing it was inappropriate.

"But," her mother said with none of the mirth of her father, "England is a stronger country, more prestigious."

"True, but the King of Scots is like a son to our own king," her father conceded.

"Tell King François that I will offer myself to whomever he wishes," Marie said, feeling fatigued. The words had a feeling of finality, a knowing that her life would soon never be the same.

Her father returned to François in Lyon and informed the king that Marie would submit to his decision. Before the king's decision could reach Joinville, tragedy struck for Marie.

On December 7, her baby son, Louis, passed away. Marie heard his little lungs filling up with fluid, incapable to help him as he struggled for air. She returned to Châteaudun, buried her baby son in the family crypt next to her husband, and plunged into fresh grief. The crypt was in the Sainte Chapelle, a beautiful gothic chapel built by Louis's ancestor who fought alongside Joan of Arc. The chapel was narrow with a high vaulted ceiling, stained glass windows along both sides. Marie walked to the crypt, past the fresco of the Last Judgment, dipping her head to avoid the reproach in the Lord's face, as if she could change her future marriage. She lit a candle and then knelt before a statue of the Virgin Mary holding Baby Jesus. The statue's face looked how Marie felt—weary. So many losses. She trusted that God had a plan for her, but her faith was shrouded in pain. *Blessed Mother, give me the strength to continue for my living son,* she prayed and made the sign of the cross. Her burden seemed unendurable—but if the Holy Mother survived the death of her son, Marie knew she would too.

Even though the castle was full of servants, it felt empty without her husband. She walked through the wing her husband's father had built, which faced the chapel and circular keep. Her feet padded on the mottled colored square tile, and she entered her chamber that she shared with Louis. She ran her hand over the velvet curtains surrounding their bed. She opened the walnut chest at the foot of the bed, a wedding gift from her parents. She found his last letter that he had written her, when he was on summer progress with François, while she remained at Châteaudun to deliver their second child. The wax seal was blood red, as intense as her pain. Her breath was ragged as she opened the letter and saw his tall, formal handwritten, as serious on paper as he had been in real life. He had written, "My wife, I kindly warn you that I was so ill the past six days that I could not write. The doctors tell me it is little more than a slight affliction, a case of chicken pox, and that if it is God's mercy, I will be well soon. I'm sure you are doing well and pray God give us a healthy baby." She ran her fingers over the valediction, "Your good husband and friend." Tears swelled, knowing she would never get another letter from him again. She was unwilling to let him go and become a wife to someone else.

She remembered the first time she met Louis, Duke de Longueville. Five years her senior, Marie had watched him play-joust with the dauphin. He was quiet, serious, preferring to allow the other boys to cause mischief while he hung back to avoid punishment. He was a second son, like her father, but his older brother had died in 1524 during the siege of Pavia, the same battle where King François had been taken captive. Their families negotiated the betrothal, which was officially announced on the feast of Pentecost, which celebrated the Holy Spirit entering the twelve apostles, giving them the ability to speak in tongues and spread the message of Christ. The king approved and provided an extra dowry of forty thousand livres. Marie found comfort and safety in her husband's dark, almond shaped eyes. They both were quiet in public, preferring to converse in the privacy of their shared chamber. Marie had seen a marriage based on mutual respect and a partnership between her parents. Her husband, like her own father, was required to defend King François's territories. And like her mother, Marie decided not to follow her husband, but to remain at their estate and prove she was a capable manager of their land ownings. But that meant that she was not there to hold her husband as he died.

She opened the door to the terrace that overlooked the steep drop to the Loire River. The December air cut off her breath, but it reminded her that she was alive. Alive and available for a new husband. She gripped the stone rail to keep herself upright, the weight of her grief threatening to catapult her over the edge. The winter air revitalized her, filled her up with indifference so she could continue, could push this grief away. Then she would accept her fate and agree to marry whomever François chose. Her gaze swept over the countryside, remembering the common people whom she had helped through sickness, crop failure, children dying. She had to grieve the loss of them as well.

At the end of January, she had a surprise visitor from the English court. She met Peter Mewtes, an agent sent by Sir Cromwell, Henry's secretary and chief minister. He was a typical English courtier, with light brown hair and wide eyes, wearing a padded overcoat lined in satin. She sat behind the carved desk that had been her husband's. The walnut paneled room was cozy with the fire blazing. She channeled her husband's quiet strength as she began her own negotiations.

"Madame la Duchesse," he began, removing his overcoat, "thank you for meeting me in your time of grief."

Marie just nodded, a tight smile on her face, forcing herself to accept the empty consolations. This man had no idea what she was feeling and no comment from her was going to make him understand.

"The King of England also sends his condolences," he continued. Marie inhaled in silence, waiting for him to get to the reason why he was there. "And he would like to ask for your hand in marriage. He would like you to be his queen."

Marie sat back in the chair, elbows on the curved arms, fingers under her chin. "As you know, the decision is not mine."

Mewtes leaned against the desk, his excitement evident. "Are you not yet contracted to the King of the Scots?"

Marie shook her head. She hadn't heard anything from François or her father, both being consumed with the negotiations for peace with the emperor. And she had been occupied with her son dying.

"Do you not want to marry the Scottish king?" he probed. Marie shrugged, not giving him any information. She felt his frustration rise.

"I will marry whomever my king decides for me to marry," she replied.

"My king will give you everything you desire. Just tell me what you want from him and he guarantees to meet all of your demands," his naked desperation amused Marie, and she had to suppress her smile.

"My father assured my king that the Scottish match met his approval, but I have not given *my* consent," she said, lowering her eyes in a way that men found demure. "But I am ready to obey my king in everything, and as I have not personally promised to marry the King of Scots, my king might grant me to your king—if you can persuade him." She hoped that by playing this diplomat and convincing him that Henry might have a chance, she could prolong the negotiations and remain with her only living son. Mewtes sat back and rubbed his long beard, satisfied that Marie's comment meant she was interested in Henry. She hoped the equivocation worked to her benefit.

Later in January, a letter was delivered by a Scottish messenger. Marie broke the Scottish seal and saw James's scrawling script. "Madame," the letter began. The French was very stiff and formal. "I am only twenty-seven years old and life already weighs as heavily upon me as my crown does. Fatherless since childhood, I have been the prisoner of my ambitious nobles. The powerful house of Douglas kept me in servitude for a long time and I hate their name. There is no safety for my person from my uncle to the south, and I await your support and counsel to overthrow these Douglases and build Scotland into the great country it should be." Marie didn't trust Henry either, as a statesman or as a husband. Even though the climate had killed her friend, James's directness swayed her. After reading the letter, she decided she would marry him and help him modernize Scotland. He gave her a sense of purpose, which she had lost in her grief. She remembered his face at his wedding to Madeleine, the loving and tender way he gazed at her sweet friend. Although she knew the rumors of his volatile personality, his philandering, that gaze held promise of a private inner man who could be compatible with Marie's inner self.

1538

Chapter 38

THOMAS

IN FEBRUARY, JAMES GOT impatient that Beaton wasn't pushing François in the negotiations, so he sent Thomas to France to close the deal. He travelled by land through England with a letter of safe passage from the Queen Mother and sailed from Dover, landing in Calais and then traveling by horseback to Lyon in the south of France, where the king was holding court. Even though the weather was warming as he traveled south, he arrived in Lyon during a cold spell. Spurts of white clouds appeared when he exhaled, but despite the cold, the city was thrumming. The cobblestone streets were crowded with merchants and pink stone buildings rising five and six stories. The city had a decisively Italian feel, being on the main route between Milan and Paris. He heard a mix of languages as he passed the market and merchant area where the new bourgeois built sumptuous residences that imitated the royal palaces with their loggias, arched doorways, and ornate columns. He passed into the Saint-Jean section, which contained the Saint-Jean Cathedral—Cardinal Lorraine's diocese in whose palace François was staying. The cathedral backed up to the River Saône and sat on a wide flagstone plaza. The cathedral mirrored Notre Dame in Paris—it also had three arched doorways, a large rosetta stained glass window framed by two bell towers. The cardinal's residence resembled the Italian architecture on the outside, but inside were all the furnishings, tapestries, and luxuries from François's palaces.

"What are you doing here?" Beaton pulled Thomas aside before he was able to get an audience with François. Thomas didn't trust

Beaton—he was a younger son of an ambitious family. His uncle was the Archbishop of St. Andrews and had gotten Beaton his first position after he graduated from the University of Paris.

"James sent me to finish the marriage contract since you appear to be busy," Thomas said, knowing the comment would nettle Beaton. François had made Beaton the Bishop of Mirepoix in Languedoc, and Beaton had been ordained by the pope. Thomas knew that hadn't delayed the marriage negotiations, but he said it to nettle Beaton.

"I have been busy," he said, indignant. "The king has been working on a peace treaty with the Emperor, as our Highness must be aware." He bristled from the criticism, just as Thomas knew he would.

"Well, I am here to help you pressure him," Thomas said, walking away from Beaton and into the Great Hall for supper. Beaton grabbed his arm and held him back.

"Before you go in, you should know the court dynamics," Beaton said. "Supper should be... interesting." He paused and Thomas sighed in impatience. He was anxious to complete this marriage for James and return to Scotland. Beaton continued, "The king's attention is being pulled in two directions: from Duchess Etampes, François's youngest son Charles, and Philippe de Chabot, the Admiral of France on one side, and the Dauphin Henri, his lover Duchess Brézé and Duke Montmorency, Grand Master of France on the other. They fight over everything."

"What about the Dauphiness?" Thomas asked about Henri's wife, Catherine de Medici, who had been thrust aside by Henri in his devotion to his mistress. The two were married when they were both fourteen.

"The Dauphiness says nothing," Beaton said, leaning in. "I believe she is biding her time until she produces an heir. Then she will exert her authority."

"But it's been over four years and no child. Perhaps she is barren," Thomas said. The French were worse than the Scots in their lack of respect for marriage. At least James wouldn't keep his mistress at court, not if Thomas had influence. If he finalized the marriage, James would be indebted to Thomas. Even if the king never reciprocated Thomas's feelings, at least he could get rid of the one person who had stolen his heart. And Thomas would get back at Maggie for the pain she caused him. He shook his head, unable to think about that now. He needed to focus on getting the contract signed.

Beaton released Thomas's arm, and he approached Jean, Cardinal de Lorraine. The Cardinal wore the red hat and robes of his station. His eyes were set deep, and his nose crooked, a bump on the bridge.

"Welcome, Sir Erskine," he greeted Thomas, who inclined his head in return. "Please, have a seat." Jean motioned to a velvet padded scissor chair between the Dauphin Henri and his brother Charles. Thomas sank into the tension between the two brothers. François made no secret of his feelings for his heir Henri—he thought Henri was moody and petulant and preferred his younger son.

Thomas turned to see Diana de Poitiers, the Duchess Brézé, the woman twenty years Henri's senior who had managed to steal his heart and keep him from his wife's bed. She wore the French-style, black, rounded hood, lined in white pearls, her strawberry blond hair curled at her temples, appearing almost golden, thanks to the liquid gold she reportedly drank to remain youthful. Thin, arching eyebrows framed her dark eyes, giving her a flirty expression. Her face was heart-shaped, small mouth. Thomas didn't understand her appeal, especially when he studied Henri, his down-turned eyes and long nose giving him a romantic aura. His black velvet barret with a white ostrich plume tilted and revealed his dark blond hair.

"I'm sorry for the loss of your sister," Thomas said to Henri.

"Thank you," Henri said, his voice tired and somber. "We all knew it would kill her, but she wanted to be the Queen of Scots. And now your king wants the hand of Duchess Longueville. He understands that her family is Catholic, yes?"

"I think religion is less important than her ability to produce an heir," Thomas laughed. There was a sense of discontent with the church and a reform movement in Scotland, but James hadn't prosecuted for religious reasons—at least he hadn't since the first year of his reign. His bishops were strong and he relied on revenues from the Catholic Church, so he would not accept dissolving the monasteries as his uncle had done.

"He should worry about Protestantism infecting Scotland, since it has been accepted south in England," Diane said, leaning forward to see around Henri. She wore her customary black velvet dress, lined with creamy pearls, a sign of mourning for her husband who died in 1531. With the mourning period long lapsed, the rumor was she wore black and white to symbolize the bright and dark sides of the moon, which she was named after—Diana, the Roman moon goddess. To Thomas, they represented the double-sided nature of her, and he felt repugnance towards her. Thomas nodded to be polite, but turned to his other side. He locked eyes with Beaton, who raised his shoulders in defeat.

"Is the peace treaty decided upon?" Thomas said to Chabot, the Admiral of France, who had just returned from Italy.

"Against my wishes, it is being negotiated," Chabot said. He was a large man, with large hands and a trimmed brown beard that covered the bottom of his face. "However, we want Milan, Flanders, and Artois returned to François's control, but the emperor is being stubborn."

Again, Thomas nodded, knowing that it was François who was being stubborn. Milan had been given to the emperor as part of the conditions for François's release from captivity after the Battle of Pavia. François entered the hall with Anne d'Heilly, Duchess E'tampes. Thomas stood with the rest of the party.

"Sir Erskine!" François clasped Thomas's forearm. His padded cloth of gold sleeves made him look wider than he was, a power move that Thomas recognized from Henry VIII. "I trust the trip from Scotland was good?"

"Yes, your Highness," Thomas bowed. "And I'm sorry for the loss of the Princesse Madeleine."

"Thank you, Thomas," he said. "But she is where she wanted to be. And we have another marriage to discuss, so this will be a joyous occasion!" He turned to his mistress. Thomas couldn't help but stare at this woman whom he had heard so much about. The duchess wore the French hood in gold and white, which highlighted her blond hair. Her eyes were wide and full of amusement, a smile curving her thin lips. She gripped Thomas's hand with a strength that surprised him. Her assertiveness aggravated him, knowing she was the real power behind the French throne. He wondered if Maggie had the same power over James. His fear was that she would become as powerful as this French mistress had.

The king sat and dinner was served. The servers, dressed in red and bleu de France livery, placed a roasted boar in garlic sauce. Thomas inhaled the mix of spices, which took him back to his days at university, after he escaped Scotland, trying to outrun his sexual desires.

"I received the Cardinal of Capri with articles for peace," the Cardinal of Lorraine said, stuffing the meat into his mouth.

François snorted, "Did the Emperor offer Milan? That is the only article that I desire to hear." Chabot and François's younger son, Charles, chuckled.

"The truce is coming to an end," Montmorency said, his face drawn from exhaustion. He had led the French forces into the Alps in autumn, but could push no further due to lack of supplies. François and the emperor had signed a three-month truce in November.

"Milan could have been taken had not my father been advised to take a defensive strategy," Charles interjected, making Henri turn waspish, not needing a reason to attack his brother, whom his father favored.

"The defensive strategy saved men from being killed and the emperor from overrunning our country." He loomed over Charles, who exchanged a glance with Francois. This increased Henri's anger, but Diane placed a hand on his arm and snuffed it out.

"It was the best decision," Montmorency said, "even the king agreed." François nodded, which enflamed Anne.

"You believe this because only peace can preserve your authority," she said, eyes flashing with venom. "You get fat off of France's inaction." Thomas choked on his quince butter cake at the audacity of this woman to insert herself into the king's business. A woman should never manipulate a king and voice her opinions over his.

Now it was François's turn to calm his lover's anger. Anne relaxed into her chair, gripping François's hand. Thomas imagined this was exactly how James and Maggie were, given his cousin's fiery disposition. He swallowed hard, disgusted at how women used their sex to gain power.

"Let's not fight, my love," he said, pulling her up from her chair. "Let's expend that energy in a more physical way. Dance with me."

She nodded and the king led her to the center of the room, but she narrowed her eyes at Montmorency. Thomas exhaled, releasing the tension in his shoulders. Court dynamics were certainly interesting in France, as Beaton had said.

Four men began singing in their tenor voices, accompanied by the violin, swarm, and tabor. François bowed to Anne, who curtsied to the floor. They moved in time with the slow rhythm of the music, step, step, shuffle, rounded each other step, step, shuffle. They held hands and François turned Anne around in a wide arch, a seductive smile pulling at her mouth. They repeated the sequence, both gliding across the floor, staring at each other, forgetting the rest of the audience. When the dance concluded, François bade everyone good-bye and left with his mistress.

The next dance was a brantle, couples linking arms and creating a foursome. Henri danced with his mistress Diane, and Montmorency danced with Henri's wife. The four of them faced off, side-stepping right and jumping left. The music was lively and the violinist danced while he played in the musician's loft. Thomas stood, leaning against a curving column, and observed the dancing, enjoying how the tension of the supper conversation created a frame to dance around.

"Quite a nice dinner, no?" a voice came from behind Thomas. He spun and found himself face to face with intense olive eyes. The stranger spoke French with a Germanic accent and wore the tilted barett with an ostrich feather. He stretched his hand towards Thomas and said, "Frances de Rohan, painter and artist to King François."

"Sir Thomas Erskine," Thomas clasped his arm and felt a surge of energy. "Secretary to the King of Scots."

"Ah, you are here for the marriage negotiations of your king and Madame Longueville?" he replied, smiling, his lips framed by a trim brown mustache and beard.

"Yes, my king trusts that I will be able to finalize the contract," Thomas said. He was tingling, a strange vibration surrounding him.

"It is good to be trusted, no?" he said, the sounds rolling out of his mouth. Thomas felt as if he were hearing French for the first time. "My king trusts me as well. I would love to paint you." His eyes traveled down Thomas's body.

"Me?" Thomas was shocked at how his voice squeaked, his heartbeat squeezing his throat.

"Have you ever sat for a portrait?" his eyes bore into Thomas. He flushed as he saw the same look in Frances's eye that he had felt for James. He shook his head.

"I will come by your chambers to do a preliminary sketch," he said and skipped onto the dance floor, breaking up a couple. His face shone as he laughed at the disruption. Thomas turned and headed to his chamber, embarrassed by his reaction to this Frenchman. He thought he only felt those animalistic desires with James, but here was a stranger who made him feel and also showed Thomas that he felt it too. It excited Thomas, but also scared him.

For the next few weeks, face time with King François was difficult to come by. Thomas and Beaton waited along with other courtiers for their chance to speak with François. De Rohan was waiting too, for another commission from the king. Thomas managed to be non-committal to sitting for a portrait, even though he longed to agree and see what happened.

One night, during those long weeks, as Thomas was retiring for the night, a knock sounded at his door. There was de Rohan, with an easel, canvas, and paints. Thomas allowed him to enter his chamber, inhaling his musk as he passed.

"So, I thought tonight we might do a sitting," de Rohan said after he set down all his supplies. Thomas nodded, unable to take his eyes off a triangle patch of chest hair showing from under his opened chemise. "Sit on the bed, don't worry about your clothes, I can add that later. Tonight I focus on your face," he said, guiding Thomas to the bed. His body collapsed on the edge of the bed, his legs losing all strength.

De Rohan stood behind the easel, using a thin charcoal to sketch. Thomas dropped his eyes and looked at his legs, covered in tawny hose, shapely and strong.

"Look up, please," de Rohan said. Thomas raised his eyes and felt a surge of desire. De Rohan's face was open, the desire naked. Thomas inhaled, throbbing all over his body. De Rohan switched his gaze from Thomas to the canvas, hand flying across the page, charcoal scratching. He bit his lip as he worked, beard pulled into his mouth. Thomas watched the hairs against the pink of de Rohan's lip, violent and defenseless. He closed his eyes to try to control his beating heart, thundering and causing him to shake. He breathed in deeply to steady himself when the charcoal quieted.

He opened his eyes and de Rohan was coming around his easel. A groan escaped Thomas as he realized his own desired had betrayed him.

"I feel the heat from you, no?" de Rohan smoothed his hands across Thomas's chest. Thomas nodded, his head jerking up and down. Rohan pressed his mouth on Thomas. He knew he could push de Rohan away and retain his morals, or he could kiss him back and realize what it felt like to act on his inherent desires. He chose to forgo his virtue and give in to his animalistic side.

***

The next morning, Thomas lay, frozen, wishing he could turn back time. Guilt ate at him, and he slid from the bed, de Rohan still sleeping, chemise rumpled. He dressed quietly and stole out of his own room. He ran into Beaton, who glanced into his chamber, noticing the easel and the outline of a body under the sheet cover. He raised his eyebrow and Thomas knew that he had seen. His body frozen, wishing he could disappear.

"Sir Erskine," Beaton said, lips curling into a snarl. "So were you the man or the woman last night?" Bile crept up Thomas's throat. Beaton had him. Beaton continued walking down the hall to the King's Counsel room, leaving Thomas to stand in his silence. He closed his eyes, and knew Beaton had ammunition to make him do anything he wanted. The punishment for sodomy was death.

François called for Beaton and Thomas a few days later. As they entered his chambers, the French king was doubled over in laughter.

"Oh, Bishop Beaton," François choked out between laughs, "you really made an enemy in England!" He handed the paper over and fell into new peals of laughter. Thomas read over Beaton's shoulder.

"Sir George Douglas, one of the King's gentlemen, has been accused by David Beaton, a Scotchman, of being disloyal to Henry, and offers to purge the scoundrel. For this he has asked leave of Henry to go to François, and the King has granted it that he may vindicate his honor, seeing that the man is in France," the letter read.

Beaton paled. He had been very loose in talking about the Douglases in front of the English ambassadors, but he never thought it would get back to George Douglas. Thomas smirked, knowing that Beaton was not a physical man. He would fight with words, but never with his fists.

"Are you granting him passage?" Beaton asked, fear unmasked.

"Of course not!" François laughed. "I have better things to worry about than a Scot's ego being bruised." François smacked Beaton on the back, who looked relieved. "We need to finalize the contract for Madame Longueville."

Thomas exhaled. *Finally!* He thought. *Then I can get out of here and forget what happened.* The Cardinal of Lorraine presented the papers. Thomas knew it was the terms of the marriage. He couldn't wait to dive in and solidify the details and go home.

"Your Highness," the cardinal bowed to François, "Bishop Beaton and Sir Erskine. First, my family wants it to be known that they feel this proposal is indecent, given the recent death of Duke Longueville and Queen Madeleine." Thomas nodded to recognize his family's wishes. He felt it was too soon as well, but he also understood the urgency of James to procure another French marriage—and French money.

"Jean, but we discussed the honor bestowed on Marie—and your family—by making her my daughter and endowing her with a princess's dowry," François said, irritation pulling at his mouth.

"Yes," the cardinal twirled a quill between his fingers, "the dowry does need to be considered."

Thomas knew that Madeleine's dowry consisted not only of one hundred thousand *livres*, but also included warhorses, armor, two war ships, and all the clothes and jewels that Madeleine had taken from François's wardrobe. Marie's family, while noble, could not generate that sort of dowry on their own. François had offered a dowry of one hundred and fifty thousand *livres*, most of which would come from revenue generated by the lands Marie had inherited from her husband upon his death.

"My sister-in-law, Madame de Guise, is very upset that the King of Scots wants to take money from her grandchild," the cardinal said. The land from Marie's late husband was in a trust until her son came of age. To take revenue from the Longueville lands was to take money from Marie's son. "The revenue from the Longueville lands is intended for Marie until her son comes of age. Antoinette doesn't feel it is right for her grandson's wealth to go to the King of Scots."

"And I'm sure she has a solution?" François said, well aware of Marie's mother and her tenacity to fight for her family.

"The de Guise family has raised eighty thousand *livres*," the cardinal said. "We are asking you, her royal father, to provide the remainder."

Thomas chuckled to himself. The Cardinal was playing on François's ego, make him seem like the savior. And it worked.

"Fine, I'll pay seventy thousand *livres*!" he exclaimed, slamming his hand on the table in excitement. "And I'll bestow Madeleine's jewels on Marie."

Wine was poured and the contract was finalized and signed, a copy sent by messenger to Scotland so the wedding could be planned. Thomas smiled, giddy from his success and knowing he would be leaving France soon. Beaton came up from behind him.

"So the contract is finalized and we will be returning home," Beaton said, his eyes narrowing in on Thomas. Thomas swallowed, but his mouth was dry. Beaton was naming his price for silence. "And stories will be coming back from our time here. The stories could make a man... or break him."

Beaton was fervent, his face contorted by ambition.

"What do you want?" Thomas asked, his voice flat.

"You will support Catholicism in Scotland," Beaton said. "Our new queen is Catholic, and you will encourage our king to remain Catholic." Thomas, who had no opinion on Protestants and Catholicism, now felt trapped that he had to push Catholicism. "And you will also," Beaton continued, "support the prosecution of heretics in Scotland." Thomas closed his eyes, knowing he had to agree with Beaton, but also knowing that it would make him many enemies. He nodded, even though he didn't want to.

The wedding took place on May 9 in the Sainte Chapelle at Marie's castle Châteaudun. James decided not to return to France, begging off because of a hunting accident during the summer and also to attend to domestic matters, sending instead Lord Maxwell, High Admiral of Scotland. Thomas knew the real reason James stayed in Scotland was that he felt his new bride inferior to Madeleine.

The chapel was narrow, wooden pews also narrow. Thomas adjusted the collar of his chemise, the French heat making him as uncomfortable as the thought of de Rohan visiting his chambers again. He just wanted to get the marriage over and return to Scotland.

Lord Maxwell was standing in front of the altar, dressed in a crimson and yellow doublet, red hose, and red flat hat with yellow feathers contrasted with his graying hair and beard. Beaton was standing next to Maxwell in his purple bishop's robes, and Thomas stood last. Marie's uncle, the Cardinal of Lorraine, stood in the center of the altar to officiate the wedding. Waiting for the bride on her side of the altar were Marie's mother, a woman with a sharp, long nose and beady eyes, and her sister, Louise, who was five years younger than the bride, a beautiful maiden dressed in the latest French fashion. Marie's small son stood in front of Antoinette, a miniature nobleman, dressed in a doublet, hose, complete with a flat hat tilted to one side.

The bride walked down the aisle, her arm linked through her father's. Thomas noticed she was very tall, and had a neck like a grey heron, highlighted by her white silk kirtle. Over the kirtle was a white and gold brocade gown, gold ribbon cutting across her chest and her puffy sleeves. Her hair shone in the light coming through the diamond windows, burnt red waving down her back. She was poised, feminine, graceful. Her face remained impassive during the ceremony, only an eyebrow raised as Maxwell slid the espousal ring on her finger, perhaps noticing how much smaller it was than the one James had given to Madeleine just over a year earlier.

Thomas remained in France for a few months while the new Queen of Scots prepared her son and his estate. He saw the tenderness as she explained to her son that he would be living at Joinville with his grandparents. The boy's eyes lit up with excitement, not understanding that the move meant he wouldn't see his mother again. Marie put on a brave front, but Thomas could see how affected she was and the tears that did not fall from her eyes.

In June, the Scottish delegation, including Beaton, Thomas, and Maxwell, made their way to Rouen with Marie, her father, and her sister, along with her entourage of servants and household members. Marie's family was sending her to Scotland with all of the comforts of France—ladies-in-waiting, embroiderers, cooks, bakers, gardeners. From Rouen, the retinue sailed up the River Seine to Le Havre.

The port town was bustling. Merchant carts were set up along the wharf, calling out to sell their wares. Three Scottish galleys were docked, the *Mary Willoughby, Salamander,* and the *Moriset.* Marie was flanked by her father and her sister, all dressed in their finery to impress the people. Part of the French royal family, they were now also part of the Scottish royalty. Scottish and French flags snapped in the wind from all three ships, and the brass shone under the French sun.

"Monsieur de Guise," Maxwell said, motioning toward the *Mary Willoughby.* "Please board the King's vessel which has been prepared for you." The duke nodded, and allowed Marie to go up the gangplank first, then Louise, them himself. Beaton followed behind the duke, but Maxwell stuck his arm out to prevent him from boarding.

"What is the meaning of this?" Beaton said, his upper lip twitching.

"Sir, you shall ride on the *Salamander,*" Maxwell blocked the gangway. Beaton puffed out his chest.

"You cannot dictate which ship I ride!" he shouted, taking off his cap. "I have worked for months on this marriage!"

"Yes, well, you couldn't close the deal," he jerked his thumb at Thomas. "Erskine had to be sent here for the contract to be finalized."

"I didn't need him to be sent to France!" Beaton said, his thin hair flying in the breeze. Maxwell grabbed Beaton's arm and twisted, Beaton's chest dipping. He kicked Maxwell, who had to let go of his arm, but grasped the back of his robe and pulled him away from the ship. Beaton swung to stop Maxwell and connected with the side of Maxwell's face. Maxwell swung back and the two men fell to the ground, wrestling. Thomas reddened, embarrassed by the cat-callers and crowd who had formed to watch the two Scots fight. The Scots already had a reputation for being barbaric and uncivilized. Beaton and Maxwell were perpetuating that notion. Thomas looked up and noticed that Marie stood at the railing of the ship, an amused smile covering her face. Thomas broke the two of them apart and pushed Beaton towards the other ship. He went without further fight.

Thomas sighed, glad to be leaving France after these two fools embarrassed their country. Yet another reason to return home! The voyage couldn't be over soon enough for Thomas. He wanted to be back in Scotland and in the service of the king.

Chapter 39

MAGGIE

JAMES ASKED MAGGIE TO meet him at Falkland, his hunting palace in County Fife, near Loch Leven. She rode her ambler from her home, across swelling meadows and plots of spring wheat, the shoots peeking from the black soil. After rounding Lomond Hill, she saw Falkland in the distance, across crisscross of orchards and wheat fields. The Clan MacDuff had built Falkland as a hunting lodge three centuries ago. There was a flurry of activity around the castle in the May sunshine, wooden scaffolding around the south and east walls of the palace. Maggie rode up to the entrance gate, flanked by round, pointed towers. The guards asked her to identify herself.

"Lady Douglas of Loch Leven," she said, pulling herself up to appear taller and more important. "The king requested my presence."

At the mention of her name, they sprang into action, helping her dismount, taking her horse. One guard led her into the courtyard, where James was monitoring the progress of the southern wall. James spotted her and waved the guard away.

"Maggie," he breathed into her ear, embracing her. She glanced around, the courtyard was full of workers, and pushed him away, embarrassed. The king didn't appear concerned.

"Look at the detail," he said, motioning to the façade of the building. Maggie noticed the symmetry of the building. It was made with purpose, unlike some of the other Scottish palaces, which seemed more haphazard. Corinthian columns separated five sections of cross-shaped diamond patterned leaded windows. Under the grand windows were a series of four green-glassed windows, each containing a gilded crest. Above the windows were stone-carved medallions. "This is the latest style in France. My adopted father built a palace like this called Château Chambord. He brought it to France from Italy—and I brought it here," he said, pride seeping from his voice. She smiled, proud of him too, bringing Scotland into the modern world just as he said he would.

"And who are those sculptures of?" she asked, allowing herself to fall into James's excitement.

"Those are Roman Emperors," he came up behind her, wrapping his arms around her so she couldn't fight him off. "That one," he held her wrist and pointed it towards the first medallion, "is Julius Caesar. Do you remember when Master Dunbar taught us about him?"

"I do, but I'm surprised you do," Maggie said, leaning back into him. "You and my brother only wanted to play joust."

"And you would never let us rescue you," James laughed.

"No, I wouldn't! I've never needed to be rescued," she turned to face him. "Unlike you this fall. I had to revive your health!" James crushed her mouth with his to keep her from voicing the memory—when he fell off his horse while hunting after Madeleine's death and Maggie stayed with him, bringing him back to consciousness by holding him, caressing his hair, making him feel safe.

"I want to show you my chambers," James said, walking with her in his arms, his eyes twinkling.

"Mmmmm.... Let's see the workmanship in there," Maggie said, feeling the heat climbing up from her abdomen. She didn't see the beautiful spiral staircase he built, nor the thistle covered fireplace with an unfinished coat of arms. The newly repainted and gilded ceiling could not catch her eye either. All she noticed were the soft linen sheets and the weight of James moving over her.

They laid in his bed until the sun had set and a servant crept into the chamber to light the fire.

"Thank you, laddie," James said, frightening the young page, who almost lit himself on fire. Maggie and James laughed, Maggie staring into James's eyes, wishing every day she could do this, but knowing they both had different destinies. Was it wrong of her to just want to be with him? Was she taking him away from Scotland?

"Let's go on progress together," James said, his voice heavy with sleep. It was his habit to move from castle to castle in Scotland to show himself before his subjects, showing his care and concern for his people.

"I can't go with you on progress," Maggie said. "I have my own household and children to take care of." She knew the comments would irritate James, but she still felt compelled to say them. "And your wife is coming."

"I know she is coming," James's eyes bulged in anger. "I *tried* to get you a divorce so I would marry you. *You* pushed me to marry French. Now, I have to remarry French to keep our alliance. Why do you make things so difficult? Why can't you just agree with me?"

She bristled at his demand of subjugation. He may demand that of other people, but she was closer to him than that. She wanted what was best for him even when he didn't. And now he was treating her like she was just another woman?

"I won't agree with you when you're wrong, even if you are the king!" Maggie said, louder than she intended. He was still so stubborn and seemed to be digging his heels into his convictions, regardless of what his advisors said. *Who were his advisors?* Maggie thought. James had alienated so many nobles with his steadfast prosecution of the Douglases. Finnart was out, Moray was still in France, Arran was still too young. Who was he listening to? Beaton? Maggie snorted. He was self-serving. Thomas, her cousin? Maggie thought he was a tuft hunter—just trying to get closer to the king for his own benefit. She always felt rabid jealousy from him, but she couldn't figure out exactly why. As the secretary of the country, Thomas had more power over the king than she ever could. Maybe he thought the king would listen to her in bed. Funny, that was the last place she tried to talk to him.

"You're just like everyone else!" he thundered back, raising onto his elbows. "You only think of yourself and what I can do for you. You have no loyalty! Just like a Douglas!"

The mention of her husband's name was fuel on the fire. She exploded. "I'm *not* a Douglas. I am an Erskine and we have always been loyal to you."

"Aye yes, your father has always been loyal," James said, his voice cold. "You think you are loyal, but then you say something like this and I have to wonder."

"I am only thinking of your good—for Scotland and for your

son," she said. "If that isn't enough, why do you keep coming back to me?" Her voice shook with desperation; she only wanted him to understand that she loved him and would always love him. He hung his head, letting the truth sink into him. Deep down, he knew that Maggie only wanted what was best for him. He may push her away to prevent himself from being vulnerable, but he would also pull her to him because he needed her loyalty and trust.

He laid his head on her bare breast, and she wound her hands into his hair. She knew he needed her, and as long as he needed her, she would continue to come to him.

When she woke in the morning, James was getting dressed, fastening his doublet. She ran her hand down his back. He turned and grabbed her hand, kissing it.

"We need to talk about Jamie's tutorage," she said, hoping he was in a good mood this morning.

"Yes, my lovit?" he smiled at her. She exhaled, he was in a good mood.

"It's about Master Buchanan," she said. Buchanan was educated in France and had been the regent for a college in Paris. He brought humanist thinking to Scotland, and James liked that about him. "I want him dismissed."

"Why?" James raised his eyebrows. He admired Buchanan's opinions about reforms within the church.

"I don't approve of his methods," she said, and James laughed. "He is violent. He uses a switch to hit Jamie when he didn't respond, which is no way to instruct a young pupil!" James continued laughing, so she punched his arm, frustrated that he wasn't taking her seriously.

"Ok, ok," he said, halting her violent onslaught. "I've been thinking, we have been granted the title of Prior of St. Andrews. I am going to appoint Jamie there and arrange for his move immediately," James said. "And it is closer to Loch Leven!"

Maggie sat up and threw her arms around his neck. "That would be wonderful," she said.

"He is a king's son. It's time he received a prince's education," James said.

Maggie's heart swelled with the love she felt for James for giving their son this opportunity.

"He will make his father proud," she said, kissing him.

Maggie oversaw Jamie's move to St. Andrew's. The castle was busy with preparations for the arrival of the new queen. Marie de Lorraine was expected to arrive at St. Andrew's any day, having left France on June 10. Maggie stayed in the castle with her son in the hopes of seeing the woman who would occupy James's bed. The castle lay on the sea, the air heavy with salt and surf. The rooms were comfortable and warm, which made Maggie happy. She didn't want her son to get sick.

After she had dressed for the day, she heard that James had ridden over to Crail, where his new queen had landed last night. Some of his retinue rode with him, but those who remained in the city gathered near the New Abbey Gate. Maggie pushed Jamie up to the front, through the woolen doublets of the commoners and velvet and silk of the nobility. She wanted her son to see the entrance of his father and his queen, but curious herself to see this new woman who would compete with her for James's affection.

The blasts from the trumpets cut through the music from the tabours and shawms to announce the royal couple. They rode side by side, and Maggie was struck by how good they looked together. The new queen, Marie, was wearing a crimson and gold brocade overgown with voluminous ermine lined sleeves turned back. Her kirtle was a deep mulberry velvet, lined with red satin. Her hair was covered with a golden rounded hood, and encrusted in amethyst and rubies, which contrasted with her bright red hair. Her neck was long, and so was her nose, but they were both proportionate to her tall stature. Her eyes were downturned, gray, and serious—the smile ending with her thin lips. James looked proud, relieved, excited. Maggie sighed, knowing this woman might capture his heart and push Maggie out.

They stopped before the gate and a wooden cloud descended by hidden pulleys to the ground. The cloud opened and revealed a young lass, dressed in all white, looking like an angel. She was beaming as she approached the queen and extended the queen a key.

"With this key of Scotland, we welcome you to your new

country. Please accept this as a token and know that the hearts of all Scots are open to receiving your Grace," the little girl spoke clear Scots, but the new queen looked confused. Lindsay translated for her into French, adding his own comments, "We welcome you and pray you serve God, obey your husband, and keep your body clean according to God's will and commandment."

Maggie rolled her eyes at the last statement. David was such a prude and disapproved of her relationship with James. He claimed that James was exhausting himself with pursuit of bodily satisfaction instead of pleasing God and marrying. Well, now he was married. She hoped David was happy, even though she knew James would still come to her.

After David's theatrics, they proceeded down the street, the people shouting salutations in Scots. The queen didn't understand, but she looked happy. And James did too. Doubt tugged at Maggie, told her that maybe this tall, elegant, French queen would take his attention away from her. She swallowed her qualms, pushing them down into her subconscious.

Chapter 40

THE QUEEN MOTHER

ON JUNE 18, THE WEDDING ceremony was held in St. Andrew's Cathedral. Her son had done it! He had a French bride. Margaret had looked her over and liked what she saw—a healthy woman who also looked mentally strong. *She will need it to survive here*, Margaret thought, remembering her own difficult transition to become a Scottish queen.

The church was packed—so many people wanted to witness the marriage of their king. Margaret swelled with pride. Her son was going to continue his father's legacy. Now he could focus on providing a legitimate heir. She had noticed Maggie with her son, Jamie. Margaret loved the boy, he had his father's good looks, even if he did have Maggie's personality. She chose to focus on the good today and looked over Marie's family—her handsome, tall father and her beautiful sister. They had an air of sophistication that made Margaret miss England.

She had dealt with the letters from her brother, first bullying, then pouting, that her son stole the wife God intended for him. Margaret was so annoyed with him. He still acted as if he were a twenty-year-old prince! He had his true queen, Catherine, who he put aside for the whore. He had an heir, even though his wife had died after childbirth. He needed to allow her son the wife he was due.

But, Margaret was happy that the birth of his son meant that Harry pardoned her daughter and moved her out of the tower and to Syon Abbey, not back at court, but not imprisoned. The young Margaret's lover had succumbed to ague in the tower, but her mother thought it was better for her daughter. She was upset, but Margaret knew she would get over her young love. Her brother was already in talks to contract her to a powerful alliance on the continent, even though she would prefer a Scottish union.

Her son looked so handsome—a perfect mix of Stewart and Tudor features. He wore white hose and a white overcoat with silver embroidery. His auburn hair was cut short to his head and he had a close beard, which reminded Margaret of her grandfather, Edward IV. He also looked like her brother had looked when she was last in London during her exile—broad shoulders, tapered waist, shapely legs. But he was not all Tudor, he had his father's sharp eyes, noticing all the details of his kingdom, and his father's thick hair, over which he wore a white flat hat trimmed in gold with a large ruby pinned to the front. His bride looked like a French princess—she wore a white overgown with gold embroidery, and a cloth of gold kirtle. The sleeves of her dress were full to her wrist, and slashed to show the cloth of gold undergown. Her hair was the same color as her son, flowing loosely over her shoulders. Her cheeks were ruddy, signifying her robust health. Margaret felt a weight lifted from her shoulders. Her son had a queen and would soon have an heir, who would unite the three kingdoms—Scotland, England, France. Then there would be peace, and Margaret could rest.

After Bishop Beaton performed the marriage ceremony and mass, the newlyweds retired to their chambers to prepare for the banquet. Margaret prepared alone. Her husband had not been invited. James would not grant her a divorce, but she refused to pretend that she was happily married!

The Old Guest House had been transformed into a French great hall for the event, cloth of gold hanging over the walls to highlight the Scots, French, and Lorraine banners. The new queen had changed from her wedding gown into a mulberry brocade gown with thistle leaves and pomegranates, entwining the symbol of Scotland and Lorraine together. Her enormous sleeves were lined in ermine, revealing slashed undersleeves and the most delicate black embroidery around the cuffs. Margaret glanced down at her own gown, a velvet that she recycled from an older gown and was angry that her own brother hadn't provided her with new material in the latest fashion. Even her English gable hood felt dated and heavy compared to Marie's rounded French hood, encrusted with garnets and pearls. Margaret, always conscious of her short stature, felt like a child next to her soaring new daughter-in-law.

"Queen Mother," Marie said in soft French. "It is an honor to meet you." She curtsied and Margaret found herself eye to eye with the new queen. Her gray eyes were sparkling with mirth, and Margaret was happy that she seemed content.

"The honor is mine," Margaret responded, holding her hand outstretched. Marie clutched her hand and kissed it, a sign of respect that the older queen appreciated. "I too was a foreign queen in this barbaric country."

"Oh no, Queen Mother! The country is lovely and the people are so pleasant. It is an honor to be their queen," she seemed sincere. Margaret smiled, refraining from warning her that Scotland was a harsh and fickle master. She would learn soon enough. Margaret hoped an heir would come before disillusion.

"I hear your adopted father, King François, and the emperor have signed a ten year peace," Margaret changed the subject. She knew the treaty was good for Scotland as France as her ally, but she also knew it would alienate her brother. And she could not predict how he would react.

"Yes," Marie said, a lightness projecting from her. "And that is good for both my country and yours."

"I am sure your mother is grateful to have your father out of battle," Margaret said, trying to gain information about the French family to confirm the rumors she had heard.

"Yes," Marie replied with a high laugh. "But my father is getting older and advises King François more than he fights."

"I love your hood," Margaret shifted direction again, frustrated at her tight-lipped daughter-in-law. "That was also the fashion of my brother's wife, Anne Boleyn."

Marie gulped, choking on her wine at the mention of the executed queen. Margaret reddened, realizing she had gone too far. She sipped her claret from her crystal goblet, glancing around the room, which was full of gaiety and laughter. Marie recovered and asked, "How goes things with your brother, the King of England?"

Margaret felt her flush deepen, knowing her brother had ignored her, but pride wouldn't allow her to admit that to her new daughter-in-law.

"He is very generous to his sister and nephew," she said, but Marie knew she was lying. Once again, she was embarrassed that her son and brother couldn't get along. She wished they would—it would relieve so much of Margaret's anxiety.

The next day was a royal joust. Claude de Guise's reputation as a master of the tiltyard created a flood of English nobles who were eager to try their hand at jousting such a master. Margaret enjoyed a seat of honor next to the new queen in the stands. Marie's father tied a favor from Marie to the end of his lance and lowered his visor. His horse charged full speed, crimson and gold livery flapping in the wind, Claude lowered his lance and connected with the chest of his opponent, unhorsing him. Margaret loved jousting, the power, the sounds of hooves thundering, the crack of lances connecting, splintering wood groaning. Her brother had also loved jousting, until he was unhorsed and unconscious on the ground. She could still feel the fear in the ambassador's letter as he described the horrific scene—Harry laying unconscious for over two hours as doctors attempted to revive him. The accident completely changed her brother's personality, the jovial boy turned into a capricious devil.

After the festivities of the new queen's arrival died down, Margaret returned to Methven Castle outside of Perth. Even though all the kings of Scotland were crowned in Perth at Scone Abbey, she still felt that her son was sending her away from court. She would much prefer to be at Stirling, in the middle of Scottish court, with her grandchildren, even if they weren't legitimate.

Methven castle rose from a slight hill in the middle of pasturelands and fields, between the woods. It peeked through the trees, four symmetrical domed towers in white limestone. She entered through the arched gate in the curtain wall, which surrounded the palace and looked up at the crow-stepped gables of the palace. Her husband was not at the castle—probably somewhere with his mistress, Janet Stewart, who was the sister of the Earl of Atholl. Margaret wondered if Muffin had kindled his love affair with the girl when they visited Atholl's lands and stayed in the green palace for the hunting trip in 1530. She scowled, remembering that was also when

Maggie betrayed her. Two betrayals from one trip was too much.

James hadn't approved of her third marriage, maybe poisoned by Ard to think ill of Muffin. Margaret sighed as she thought of the good times she had with Muffin, the birth of a daughter, Dorthea, here in the castle and the heartbreak of her death a few months later. She had been pregnant eight times and only her son James and her daughter Margaret survived. She chose to put all of her energy into James after his escape from Ard. Her guilt over his imprisonment made her attach to him and do what she could to make his reign successful. Is that what turned Muffin away?

She couldn't think about that now, she had to write her brother and assure him that things were good in Scotland, and that she could finally get her son to agree to a meeting between the two of them. Margaret's heart soared as she thought of the glorious future—a close alliance between her brother and her son. Now that Harry had a legitimate heir, and James would soon have a legitimate heir, it was time for a lasting peace between the two kingdoms that was supposed to have happened when she married James's father. She hoped that maybe the sons of the two kings could unite in a peaceful alliance.

She hurried to her chambers to write to her brother, in her own hand, "It is very long since I have heard from you. Your Grace shall understand that the King, my dearest son, is in good health, and the Queen, his wife, and great love between them. I trust she will prove a wise princess. I have been much in her company, and she has been very kind to me, and very entertaining."

Margaret paused, tapping her lip with the quill. She should stop there, but her son had not enforced her rents, which Muffin was still stealing. After seeing the trunks of rich dresses and jewels that the new queen brought from France, Margaret felt she should also be able to purchase new gowns so that she looked the part of a Queen Dowager, not a peasant! She wrote, "It has been long since I heard from you. I beg you, dearest brother, now that there is another princess here, please show what a gracious and loving brother you are to your only sister. Your silence looks as if you cared not how I am treated. A show of gifts would raise your esteem in your royal nephew's eyes." She hoped her brother would send money or material with his new ambassador who was expected to arrive in Scotland

251

later this year. The fortunes of Scotland were rising, and she hoped with them, she would prosper too.

Chapter 41

MARIE

FOR MARIE, SCOTLAND HAD been a pleasant surprise. After hearing of the harsh climate and the barbaric people, she found those rumors to be false. The king's herald, David Lindsay had prepared a wonderful welcome ceremony, which thoroughly delighted her. After walking around St. Andrew's, seeing the church and city, Marie knew she would dedicate the rest of her life to these people and this country.

Communication was awkward. Marie could not understand James's French, so they spoke through Bishop Beaton, whom Marie had gotten close to while he was in France, entertained by the scuffle between him and Lord Maxwell upon leaving France.

"I must confess," she said to Beaton to translate, "I never saw in France so many honest and good faces as I've seen in my new country. I was told that Scotland was a barbarian country, but I have seen the contrary."

Her new husband smiled, his auburn beard crinkling. "You have only seen a small part of your great country," he said, clearly proud of his realm. "You will see many good men and women throughout your land who will see to your contentment."

She had to admit, even though she was wary of him when he married Madeleine, he was brilliant and she realized that Madeleine could not help but fall for him. He exuded charismatic energy, and Marie was pulled into his enthusiasm. And she also was surprised by her new husband's passion for hunting. She had been raised on a horse, loved feeling the power of the horse galloping beneath her, the adrenaline of the hounds baying, having cornered their prey. While they remained in County Fife, she and James hunted together. He gifted her a fine hawk and Scottish hawker who was familiar with the Scottish landscape to enhance her hunting. She liked to keep the hawk on her arm as she rode, perched on a glove made of doeskin and decorated with the thistle blossoms and leaves made of inlaid metal threads. The hawk flew off to hunt smaller birds and prey as she rode below it. The bird came back to her, loyal already.

They rode from St. Andrew's to Falkland Palace, which James was renovating. The palace, which was part of her dowry from James, was surrounded in wooden scaffolding.

"I am turning it into a hunting château like François had in the Loire Valley!" he said, which Beaton translated. She observed familiar aspects of French architecture, but set in the rugged Scottish landscape, it took on a wild sophistication.

"I would like to oversee the construction," she said, hoping that she could oversee her kingdom and its administration much as her mother had done for her father's lands. While other queens might deem this work beneath their royal station, Marie felt it was her duty to help modernize Scotland, and inputting her views into the architecture was one way Marie could assist. She wanted to help realize the French architecture into her new country. When her comment was translated, James raised his eyebrows in surprise, but still happy that his wife wanted to do it.

"Come, look at the newest in court entertainment in Scotland!" James said, pulling her over to a large dirt rectangle, staked and dug out for construction. Marie smiled at James, confused by what she was seeing.

"It will be a grand tennis court," he said, motioning to one side. "This will be the spectator seats." He moved to the center of the plot, swinging an imaginary racket, "And here will be the court."

Marie was delighted, again another pastime that she enjoyed in France. Her husband was trying to make her feel at home. And with her French ladies-in-waiting, she had a part of France with her in her kingdom. If only she could have brought her son, she would be content. Her heart constricted as she remembered holding him in her arms before she left France. She had to trust that she would provide an heir for James, not to replace her son's memory in her heart, but to enlarge the love she had to give.

While she was enjoying her tour of Scotland, she was frustrated with the lack of communication with her new husband. She couldn't have an intimate conversation with him, and that prevented her from getting to know him. He would visit her room at night in order to produce an heir, but they could not talk to bond with each other, to learn about the intricacies of one's life that one only shared with one's spouse. Everything went through Beaton. Marie couldn't tell Beaton her innermost thoughts about her husband. That was indecent. So Marie tried to learn Scots, the harsh and unpolished language of her subjects and her husband.

"Now, I will take you to another of your dowager castles—Stirling!" James announced as they rode out from Falkland. Marie felt the morning chill, her toes tingling. She worried about how the winter would be if she felt chilled in the height of summer. The sun filtered through a low mist that clung to the green hills and her body. As the mist lifted, so did Marie's mood as the castle came into view. Perched above the green tree tops on a grey rocky crag loomed the castle. Marie followed James up the narrow paved road and through the twin towers of the gatehouse, Scottish flags flapping in the wind. They dismounted and entered the yellow-bricked Great Hall. The entire household was gathered, eager to meet their new queen. Marie nodded at each introduction, the names blurring under the Scots tongue.

James stopped in front of a slight woman, blond curls escaping from under her heavy English hood. Her eyed were narrowed and her arms looped around the neck of a young boy, a miniature of the king himself.

"This is my son, James," he said, beaming with pride. Marie's heart pounded. Was he really introducing her to his bastard children? She looked past to see three more children waiting to be introduced. Marie nodded at the woman, who spoke accented French.

"And I am his mother, Lady Douglas," she said, but her eyes never left the king's face. His mouth twitched under his beard in amusement, but he said nothing. Marie walked past without acknowledging her. Her first husband would never have paraded his infidelities in front of her, if he even had them! Marie wondered if Madeleine had also met the bastard children, and if she did, if she understood the look that had passed between her own husband and Lady Douglas. Marie had felt passion with her first husband and recognized the look in Lady Douglas. She gritted her teeth to remain smiling, not letting her irritation show on her face. She would ask him about it later—without Beaton translating!

After the introductions and supper, which Marie endured without betraying her anger, the king and she retired to his chamber. Her attendants disrobed her and urged her to let it drop, not mention the bastard children. Marie knew it wasn't the children's fault that their father had sinned outside of marriage. She would accept them and treat them as royal children, but she would not entertain their mothers.

After her husband had finished his marital duties with her, she decided to broach the subject.

"Your children," she said in Scots, "are welcome here and will be raised with our future children." James grunted, slipping into slumber. Marie continued, "But Lady Douglas will have to go."

"I am the King of Scots," he snapped. "You cannot tell me what to do in my own country."

Marie tried to compose her next statement in Scots, but her vocabulary was so limited that she lapsed into French. "I see the way you look at her, and she looks at you," as she spoke, her frustration spilled out. "If you want a successful marriage, you will send her away so that we can learn to please each other."

"I don't understand you," James said, turning away from her, signaling that he was finished with the conversation. *Fine*, Marie thought. *I will speak to the woman myself.*

On July 20, Marie got her first view of the capital of Scotland, Edinburgh. She followed behind the king's guard, dressed in scarlet and yellow livery, through the West Port gate. The Greyfriars monks, in their rough woolen robes, held up a piece of the true cross that Jesus was crucified on. Marie leaned over and kissed the rough wood, grateful that her new country was Catholic and not tearing the church apart like the King of England. A group of young girls appeared, dressed in white robes to mimic angels, and offered her a golden key to the city, which she accepted and tucked into her gown.

The procession passed St. Giles, where red wine spurted from the fountain, much to the delight of the citizens who held up full cups to toast her. The streets were clean, but Marie noticed the rough stones and timber of the buildings, reminding her that she was no longer in France. The frenetic architecture, with chimneys competing with gables and spires, was very different from what she was used to, but it wasn't unpleasant. She observed the tableaus created to greet her and support her marriage—of the Virgin Mary and Joseph, of the virtues trampling vice, of the judgement of Paris. The weaver captured the *ravissement*, enchantment, in Paris's face. Of course he was enchanted, Venus had just offered him Helena of Troy! Her smile stiffened, as she thought her husband needed this advice more than she.

At the end of the Royal Mile stood Holyrood Palace. They passed through the two-story gatehouse's wide arched doorway, with the red lion on a yellow banner painted above it. The palace had a pair of circular, crenelated towers topped with conical roofs and a curved roof on the west side. Stretching east was a long building with tall diamond pattern windows and four rounded towers. It looked like it was trying to be one of the Loire Valley château, but it lacked symmetry of the grand château that Marie grew up in. The windows were stained glass, displaying the Scots coat of arms, which were also carved above the heavy oak door. Marie admired the lion on a banner, flanked by unicorns.

James led Marie up a slate staircase, with carved balustrades. The stairway was bright, flanked by large leaden windows, which highlighted the tapestries lining the stairway. They entered a large hall with an oak honeycomb ceiling. Tapestries of biblical and mythological scenes lined the walls. They walked through a large outer chamber and into a smaller chamber, which was lined in tapestries and had a honeycomb oak ceiling. Sitting at a walnut carved desk was a man with light hair and green eyes. He had sparse facial hair that made him seem younger than he was.

"You remember my secretary, Thomas Erskine," James said. "You met him in France."

Marie nodded, remembering this effeminate man, who seemed skittish towards her and everyone.

"It is my pleasure to see you again, Your Grace," Thomas said in perfect French and bowed. Marie suppressed a giggle when she recalled Thomas's anguish when Maxwell and Beaton wrestled on the dock. He looked to be in more pain than either of the two men who fought. There was something dubious about him, but Marie couldn't quite figure out what it was exactly. Maybe it was that he always seemed to look through her.

After visiting the secretary, James took her to Madeleine's tomb in the chapel. Marie ran her hand over the limestone sarcophagus. The top of the tomb had the rearing lion, extending his tongue and braced by unicorns. She traced Madeleine's name, remembering the day of her wedding, helping Madeleine arrange and curl her soft hair.

"I'm going to be the Queen of Scots!" Madeleine clasped Marie's hands in her own. "Isn't he the most handsome prince you've ever seen?" Marie nodded, knowing that the king of Scots also thought he was the handsomest prince in Europe. But Madeleine's enthusiasm could not be extinguished. After she curled and arranged Madeleine's cascading brown hair, she placed a small round cap made of pearls on her head.

She met her husband, Louis, to watch her young friend get married, fearing it would be the last time she saw Madeleine. Marie's premonition proved correct. At her friend's grave, James was emotional, touching the name of his former wife gently. Marie wondered if he had gotten over her loss before he married Marie.

After Holyrood, James took her to Linlithgow, another part of her dowry. They passed under the forework, two octagonal towers framing a wide, pointed arched doorway, all in red sandstone. Above the entry were four crests carved into the rock.

"Those are the orders bestowed on me by the great kings of Europe," James said, pride encircling him. Marie was not impressed, but smiled so he thought she was.

"I never have seen a more princely palace," she said in French. When Beaton translated, she was rewarded with a wide smile, so she didn't regret the small lie she told. They passed into the palace grounds and dismounted. The palace was built as a square and opened onto a paved courtyard with an elaborate fountain spilling water over mermaids, unicorns, and all sorts of mythical creatures. Her chambers were nice, but not as luxurious as she had become accustomed to in France. Marie put on a smile though, since James would meet her disappointment with anger or depression. Once she had the tapestries and bed put up, it would feel more like home.

James left Marie alone at Stirling for most of the month of August. She sighed, knowing that she was not yet carrying a royal heir, which she was anxious to provide to Scotland. Her husband's absence made her lonely and feel distant from the man whom she should be intimate with. A letter from her mother increased her homesickness, even though she loved hearing news of her family and her son. The king of England had sent an envoy to Joinville to inquire about her younger sister, Louise, and get a portrait of her. Her mother said Louise was thoroughly entertained that she might become Marie's neighbor if the king proposed marriage. Marie wasn't sure how she felt about her younger sister being pursued by a man who had pursued her and was prone to fits of anger and indecision. She would believe it when her sister was in England.

She occupied her time by decorating her queen's chambers in the French style, with mulberry and green cloth of gold tapestries alternating on all four walls, but she kept the green stencils that the Queen Mother had done around the windows and the borders. Two golden eight-candle chandeliers hung from the ceiling, along with wrought iron candelabra. The four-posted bed was hung with rich green velvet that matched the stenciled border. She embroidered with her French ladies-in-waiting, Mahaut, Marie Pierres, Renée, and Joanna.

"I think I will take care of my husband's daughter, Lady Jean," she said, not looking up from her embroidery to see the disappointment on Mahaut's face. Mahaut was very pious and outspoken about James's illegitimate children.

"That would be a nice gesture, your Grace," Joanna said, always the diplomat.

"I will assign her a French nurse," Marie said, pulling at a stray string on her embroidery. She was nervous about saying the next part, but felt it was the right thing to do. "I'll also ask Elizabeth Beaton, her mother, to be a lady-in-waiting for me."

"Why?" Mahaut said, her voice as sharp as the embroidery needles. "She is a fornicator who had a child out of wedlock. I don't blame the child, but you shouldn't reward the mother."

Mahaut and Marie were both very devout, but Marie saw the position that the mother was in—unwed, needing a place in the royal household. Besides, Marie did not feel the heat between them that she saw between Lady Maggie Douglas and her husband. She needed a Scots ally in her household, someone who would be loyal to her and knew the politics of her new country.

"Everyone deserves a second chance," Marie said, patting Mahaut's hand. "Wasn't that Christ's message? I believe he said, 'forgive one another, as God in Christ forgave you.'" No one could argue with Marie when she quoted scripture.

Elizabeth Beaton accepted Marie's request to become her lady-in-waiting. She moved into Stirling, thrilled to be able to see her daughter every day. Jean, at five years old, was able to be molded, turned into a princess despite her illegitimate condition. She loved to dance as Marie played the lute and sang for her, and she was picking up French through eavesdropping on Marie and her French ladies-in-waiting. Elizabeth was not catching on as quickly, but she worked hard and was eager to please Marie. They made Scotland feel more like home.

———

After being in Scotland for over six months, Marie had still not conceived, which shocked her as she had conceived within months with her first husband. Clearly James could not be blamed, since he had fathered nine illegitimate children that were known. All of the blame for the lack of an heir would fall on her shoulders. And she knew that until she produced an heir, James would not accept her and crown her as the true Queen of Scots.

Chapter 42

THOMAS

UPON THOMAS'S RETURN FROM France, he went to visit his wife in Brechin. He forced himself on her, taking out his sexual frustrations. When he closed his eyes, de Rohan's face swam in front of him, desire in his eyes. He thought taking his wife would remove the image. Thomas returned to Holyrood alone when he realized that being intimate with his wife was just as disgusting as being with de Rohan. Maggie had always known his true nature, had been the first to call him out. He had been at Stirling for Easter, Lord Erskine inviting him to spend the holiday at the castle. Thomas was eighteen and preparing to begin his law studies at St. Andrew's University. His clothes felt plain compared to the luxurious fabrics that the king and Maggie wore. Maggie was raised with the king, she and her brother were the king's playmates. He felt awkward, an outsider. The king was ten, almost eleven and wanted to joust all the time.

"Will you joust with me, Thomas?" he asked, looking up from under thick lashes. Thomas felt the pulse in his abdomen, but he rationalized that this was the king and he should love the king.

Maggie chittered like a green woodpecker. "Thomas doesn't joust!" she doubled over in laughter. "He would rather be the princess!"

Thomas flushed, face on fire. James looked at him, cocking his head, perplexed that a man wouldn't want to joust. But since he had not reached manhood, he shrugged and ran off with Maggie's brother, Maggie trailing after them. Thomas stood, stock still, in shock. How had an eight-year-old recognized and vocalized what

261

he himself had struggled to keep hidden?

He told Lord Erskine that he wished to go to the continent to study instead of attending St. Andrew's in Scotland, explaining that he wanted to learn humanism from Erasmus and scholars in Italy and France. Lord Erskine did not suspect that he was running away from the truth his daughter had exposed. Maybe if he went away, the comment would be forgotten, his true nature kept hidden. It appeared to work—for everyone had forgotten, except Thomas. And if he remembered, then Maggie might too. He couldn't risk her exposing him.

Upon returning to Holyrood, he discovered that another flare up was happening on the English side of the borders. He read the letter from the king's uncle, "We perceive, by your letter dated Holyrood House, 26 March, that your zeal for the peace is concluded between our realms as your subjects have burst into acts of violence. We plead to learn our nephew's friendly inclination and how discreetly he behaves himself in the government of his realm. As to the damages in the East Marches, we have written to Sir Euers, his deputy warden there, to see to redress."

Thomas didn't want to disrupt James on his honeymoon progress, but he knew he needed to address it before Henry sent troops into Scotland. There was always trouble on the borders, but the letter was more aggressive than earlier episodes. Before he could jot off a letter to Henry's Secretary of State Cromwell, Beaton entered his office chamber.

"Sir Erskine," he began before even sitting down. "I'm sure you know that I have been recommended to become the first Cardinal of Scotland."

Thomas's mouth curled into a snarl that he hoped looked like a smile. Of course Thomas knew—he had written the letter which endorsed Beaton to the pope for James.

"Not everyone is satisfied with being on the bottom," he said, snickering. Thomas held his snarl, wishing he could tell Beaton exactly what he thought of him, that he was no holy man.

"The time has come to collect," Beaton said. "There is a heretic promoting dissention, a George Wisehart."

"And what sort of dissention is he promoting?" Thomas asked.

"He is preaching against the rules of the church," Beaton said, flicking a piece of lint from his robe in irritation that Thomas was questioning him.

"Which rules would that be? The same ones you ignore?" chuckled Thomas.

"The rules are made by people who can afford to break them," Beaton said, studying his fingers.

"I see. Just like you executed Patrick Hamilton for heresy because he married?" Thomas asked, knowing he should keep quiet, but unable to hold his tongue against the blatant duplicity.

"The difference is that I never married," Beaton said, his voice hard, warning Thomas to be careful. Thomas knew that Beaton had eight children with Marion Ogilvy and provided her a household, but he had never married her. The hypocrisy sickened him.

"The scholars at St. Andrew's have been discussing Luther's ideology and criticizing the pope," Beaton said, "in defiance of the 1525 Act of Parliament against heresy."

"But James laughs at the reformers and rewards poetic satires of them by Buchanan and Lindsay," Thomas said. "And he isn't going to prosecute heretics if his adopted father, François, does not."

"Well, François has begun prosecuting after the placard affair," Beaton said. In France, Protestants had hung broadsheets to attack the abuses within the Catholic Church. One of the protestors even broke into Château Amboise and hung one on François bedchamber, which shook the French king's sense of security.

"True, he has prohibited the printing of Luther and protestant literature, but he is not prosecuting," Thomas fired back, digging his heels even though it could anger Beaton.

"The king will be concerned that the Hamilton Clan is also creating trouble," Beaton said, ignoring Thomas's obstinacy. "Katherine Hamilton is also preaching heresy and calling her brother, Patrick Hamilton, a protestant martyr." At the mention of the Hamilton clan, Thomas saw an opportunity.

"Cardinal Beaton," Thomas said, a plan coalescing as he spoke. "If I assist in prosecuting this Hamilton heretic in spite of the king's indifference, then I need something from you."

"I'm listening," Beaton said, folding his arms across his chest.

"Hamilton of Finnart," Thomas heart pounded as he uttered his name. "He needs to be tried for treason."

"Finnart is favored by the king," Beaton said, eyes narrowing. "What reason would he be tried for treason?"

Thomas pressed his palms on the desk to keep them from shaking. "He opposed the French marriage, turning our ship around during the first voyage," he said, speaking slowly to keep the nervousness out of his voice. Beaton waved his hand, dismissing Thomas.

"But the king has already secured not one, but two French marriages," Beaton turned to leave. Thomas jumped up, his mind whirling.

"He has communicated with the Douglases," Thomas heard the desperation in his voice, but he was unable to rein himself in. "And he killed Lennox, the king's cousin and friend."

"None of that can be proven. Why do you bother me with these trivialities?" Beaton scowled.

"He has sympathized and supported the Reformers, just like his aunt, Katherine Hamilton," Thomas blurted the brazen lie. There was no proof that Finnart supported the Protestants, but Finnart was the nephew of the martyred Patrick Hamilton, so it was plausible that he would support the reform movement. Beaton wanted to prosecute Katherine for speaking against the Catholic Church, so why not add her nephew Finnart? It was a gamble, but Thomas had no other cards to play.

Beaton inhaled and looked up, weighing the consequences of prosecuting Finnart. "I will think about it. But you will issue warrants for the others immediately," he stood, signaling the end of the discussion for today.

Thomas planned how to plant evidence that Finnart was supporting the reform movement with other members of his family when another complication arose. James entered his office.

"Thomas," the king said, trying to control an undercurrent of anger. "When you sailed to France to finalize the marriage contract, did you stop in England?"

"You know that I did. You provided me papers to present to your uncle for safe passage through England," Thomas said, confused.

"And were the Douglases at court?" James asked, leaning in, anger making his eyes glow.

"Yes, of course. Your uncle favors them for some reason," Thomas said, attempting to diffuse the king's anger. Thomas wasn't sure why he was so angry, but then again, he did not act rationally where the Douglases were concerned. James stood tall, looking down his crooked nose at Thomas.

"As I thought," he said, the anger smoldering. "It has been brought to my attention that you communicated with George Douglas and Douglas of Kilspindie when you passed through England. You know what happened to people who communicated with the Douglases in the past?"

Thomas swallowed hard and nodded—they had been executed and Thomas had been on the jury.

"Your Highness," Thomas beseeched. "You know that your hatred is my hatred. I would not betray you as many others have done."

James paused, confusion narrowing his gaze. Thomas saw the internal struggle, James's need to prosecute those who showed the smallest favor to the Douglases against Thomas's loyalty. Thomas hoped his past service would win. But James had become increasingly paranoid, irrational when it came to the Douglases. Thomas held his breath, knowing he could be headed for the executioner's block.

"I don't know who I can trust," James grumbled, turning away from Thomas, shoulders slumped. "So many sided with Angus during my minority. And I cannot let that go unpunished."

Thomas wanted to comfort James, put his arms around him and assure him that Thomas could be trusted. If only the king knew Thomas's feelings—that Thomas would do anything for James, anything. He would do whatever the king wanted, James only had to ask, and it would be done. But Thomas couldn't say that without also voicing his inner desire.

"*Schir*," Thomas said, controlling his voice from cracking. "They will be persecuted. We have already begun to punish the traitors who helped your enemy. Lady Glamis and Master Forbes were only the beginning. At some point, Angus will slip up and we will capture him. He already grows too arrogant on the borders. He will be brought to justice."

"I just don't know, Thomas," James rubbed his brow. "My uncle seems determined to arm him and send him into Scotland against me. I am alone. Even my friend Finnart seems to have deserted me." Thomas recognized the melancholy that draped over James, blanketing him in misery. Thomas leapt at the opening.

"No, my lord," Thomas touched his shoulder, the only gesture he trusted himself to make. "Your people are with you. Scotland is with you. And to be betrayed by your stepfather and best friend…" he paused, not wanting to appear too eager to punish Finnart. "Well, their time will come. Just say the word and we will have Finnart warded." He held his breath, hoping for an affirmative from the king.

James patted Thomas's hand, sending waves up his arm. "You are a good secretary, Thomas," he said, moving away. Thomas let his arm drop at his side, coolness replacing the warmth, feeling his opportunity slip away. "I feel like an old man, in the winter of my life, and Death beckons me. Isn't that absurd?"

Thomas nodded, but he didn't understand. The king was only twenty-seven, not an old man like Angus and his uncle. He was in the prime of his life. James turned and left Thomas's office without another word. Thomas knew that when people felt the end of their life was near, they reconciled with their former friends. Would James reconcile with Finnart, try to understand if the betrayal had been real or imagined? Thomas had to make sure Beaton prosecuted Finnart before that could happen.

1540

Chapter 43

MAGGIE

MAGGIE TUGGED AT THE green velvet overgown, self-conscious of her enlarged belly. Even though she had let the gown out as much as possible, it still gaped over her pregnant stomach. But she had been determined to wear this gown to Queen Marie's coronation, to remind James that she had had a son for him first. Jamie, almost nine, stood next to her, allowed a position of prestige to see his stepmother crowned Queen of Scots. Instead of being draped in funerary velvets, Holyrood chapel was afire in white cloth of gold, over which hung the Scottish coat of Arms, the red lion on a yellow banner flanked by two unicorns, and the French coat of arms, three golden fleur-de-lies on a royal blue background, surrounded by flourishes and gold. The joined coat of arms of James and Marie hung behind Beaton, dressed in the scarlet robes of the cardinal's office, which he had been appointed to the year previous. Wooden tiered seating had been built to accommodate all of the nobles who wished to attend the first coronation of a queen since the Queen Mother was crowned in 1503.

The trumpets and hautboys sounded and the procession entered the church, Scots nobles dressed in crimson and yellow Stewart colors. Maggie spotted her father, looking regal in his crimson flat hat with a yellow ostrich feather. The Earls of Arran and Moray preceded the king. On the queen's side, Marie's French ladies-in-waiting marched arm in arm with the Scottish nobles. Near the end of the procession, Maggie spotted two Scots ladies—Elizabeth Beaton, the woman who had James's only illegitimate daughter Jean, and the

Earl of Lennox's sister, Elizabeth Ross, who had also been James's lover. Letters had been sent to all the noble families, asking that a lady from their family attend the queen. Maggie had not received a letter, which was no surprise to her after what happened at Linlithgow on Uphalieday, the Twelfth Night.

The Twelfth Night celebration, the last night of the Christmas season that commemorated the Epiphany when the three kings arrived in Bethlehem, was usually held at Holyrood, but James indulged his pregnant wife, and the venue was switched to Linlithgow, the queen's favorite palace. At the palace where he was born, James had put his former friend, Finnart, in charge of the renovations. Maggie wondered what happened to make Finnart lose favor. She knew James's temper, but Finnart seemed to be one of the only people James let get close to him, besides her.

Jamie was invited to attend the Twelfth Night celebrations along with Maggie. He wore a Venetian gray silk overcoat, a gift from his father, but Maggie had to repurpose a piece of velvet for the occasion to fit over her expanding stomach. It had been a gift from James, sent when he was in Paris. She made sure to hide it from her husband to circumvent his jealous wrath. As they approached the palace, Maggie marveled at its sleek look, created in part by Finnart. The outer gate consisted of two octagonal towers made of burnt sandstone blocks with an archway between. Adorning the crenellated parapet were the insignia of the four chivalric orders to which James belonged: the Garter, the Thistle, the Golden Fleece and St. Michael. Maggie swelled with pride looking at all of the honors bestowed on her lover. In the courtyard, a massive fountain shot water from the crown perched high in the air into a basin, which then spurted from the mouths of mermaids and human heads. She peered at one, which resembled James when he dressed as a commoner. Jamie ran to the fountain, fascinated by the water. "Look, Mam," he said, "Unicorns!"

"Yes, Jamie," she said, pulling him away. "That is a symbol of Scotland and your symbol as the son of the king!" Even as she said it, she knew the baby that the queen was carrying could change all of that.

They entered the Great Hall, paved with flagstones and a hammer beam ceiling, similar to Stirling Castle. An enormous, three flumed fireplace dominated the opposite wall, decorated for the season with twisting holly boughs. Above the main floor, in the minstrel gallery, which ran along the right wall, played the musicians—trumpets, fife, tabors, and a new instrument that James heard in France—the viola. The four violars blended three different pitches. Below them, the brick walls were covered in tapestries illustrating Greek mythology—the Trojan war, Jason and the Golden Fleece. *Also brought back from France*, Maggie assumed. In front of the fireplace was the raised dais where the royal family would dine. A place had been reserved for Jamie at the head table as the king's son, but Maggie would not sit with him. She would sit at one of the parallel wooden tables on a wide bench.

James and Marie entered the hall, and everyone stood at attention. Maggie saw Marie first, wearing a crimson kirtle of fine wool to keep her warm in the Scottish winter. Over her kirtle, she wore a cloth of gold brocade gown, which was open in the front to reveal her ever-growing belly. White miniver lined the sleeves and the cuffs of her chemise were pulled from under her kirtle to reveal intricate blackwork embroidery. She wore a rounded hood lined with pearls and covered with a brocade golden silk that sat back and showed her red hair. Her arm was linked through James's, who also wore crimson and gold. Maggie tried to catch his eye, but he looked straight ahead, smiling.

The king and queen sat and everyone followed. Marie took her linen napkin and placed it over her shoulder. The Scots looked at each other puzzled by this behavior, it seemed peculiar to place a linen on the shoulder. A few were about to titter when James threw his napkin over his shoulder, daring anyone to laugh. All in attendance put their napkin over their shoulders too. Maggie rolled her eyes. Scotland had been perfectly fine without this punctilious queen.

Dinner was served in deep rye bread bowls. Marie said in French, "Please enjoy portage al la partridge—it is a favorite dish of mine from my homeland. Also, we will enjoy poached pears from France and gingerbread!"

Maggie looked in her porcelain bowl at the thick, white portage. She smelled trout, her favorite fish, and partridge, a small game bird, mixed with spices, lemon, and a white wine. Even though she wanted to dislike it, the soup was delicious and she ate it all. Lining the head table were figures made of sugar plate, painted to look like James and his queen.

After dinner, James presented a bowl made of sugar, gilded with gold and silver. Marie lifted the delicate lid and gasped as she pulled out a golden ring with a garnet stone and golden chains. He also gave the Queen Mother crimson velvet and golden chains. She beamed under her son's attention, enjoying that she was going to be a legitimate grandmother. Marie also offered the Queen Mother an amethyst broach, which endeared her more to her mother-in-law. Maggie sighed as she remembered when the Queen Mother had favored her too. How different it would be if Maggie had been allowed to marry James. The Queen Mother certainly would never have accepted her as she accepted Marie.

After supper, the tables were removed for a performance of David Lindsay's newest play, *The Satire of Three Estates*. Lindsay, ever critical and pious, wrote the humorous play to make fun of the corruption within the church.

"*Schir*, this play is dedicated to you and those who would try to steer you from the true faith," David said with a flourish and bowed. Maggie rolled her eyes. His piety would have been absurd if he hadn't believed it himself.

A single actor entered the stage, strumming on a lute. He said, "This play is a general thing meaning nothing in special to displease a man, praying therefore no man to be angry with the play."

Maggie glanced at James, sitting in a red velvet chair. He smiled and pounded on the arm of the chair to get on with the play. Maggie had a sense of foreboding, an apprehension of something she had never seen. She pursed her lips and pushed the fear from her mind.

Next entered an actor dressed as the king, followed by courtiers who represented flattery, placating, and pickthank, who was someone who gained favor through underhanded means. The three were trying to outdo each other with their bragging of being the best looking, best hunter, best jouster.

"Where is Solace?" one of the courtiers asked. In came another actor, swaying as if he was drunk.

"Where have you been, Solace?" another asked.

"I ran away as soon as I could," he said, in a slurred brogue. "For our Lord's love, give me a drink! I have seen the loveliest creature ever created—red lips, white cheeks, and dressed in the latest fashion. Such a face! If I were king, I would send for her tonight!"

"No! We can't corrupt or mislead the king!" a courtier said with false revulsion.

"Well, if the priests can do it, that proves lechery is no sin!" Solace yelled into the crowd. James threw his head back, laughing.

"It's true!" James called over his shoulder. Maggie saw Beaton's beady eyes narrow in displeasure.

"Here she comes! Dame Sensuality!" Solace pointed to a male actor dressed as a woman with frizzy blond hair. His dress was tight and white linen mounds were pushed up to represent breasts.

"Lover, look at me, the daughter of Venus, lovely and full of joy," he said, undulating his hips as he approached the king. "My kiss is worth a million in gold and yet I readily give it to ye." The actor rubbed up and down on the king.

"Shall she come to you at once?" Solace asked, creeping behind the king and placing his hands on the king's shoulders. "Til you get a wife, take your pleasure."

"Bring her to me," the king responded. "I long for her to relieve my distress."

"I will not neglect you," Dame Sensuality said. "I will come immediately and do your bidding."

Suddenly, Maggie realized why her stomach flipped with apprehension. Dame Sensuality was supposed to be her, seducing the king! David had taken her innocent love of the king and turned it into something immoral and sinful. Rage wrapped around her, twisting her stomach. She stared at James, willing him to look at her and acknowledge David's disrespect. But James remained relaxed, arm slung over his chair, smile on his face.

The actors exited, leaving Dame Sensuality alone on stage. The actor clasped his hands at the fake bosom and said, "I have done it! I have taken the king, he delights in me, the bold youth!"

Tears welled up in Maggie's eyes, hot tears of embarrassment. Her love of the king was being mocked, scorned as wicked. Even though she knew David did not approve of her, she had no idea he was full of such hatred. And James did nothing—he just laughed at their love. She stood and stumbled out of the hall, blinded by the tears that fell. Once she was in the hallway, she wiped the tears away, rubbing the pain. All she wanted was what was best for James and Scotland. This was what she got in return—ridicule. And James just laughed. How could he not see that David deriding their relationship by making her Dame Sensuality? Maggie took a shaky breath. Maybe this was how she was to be treated now that he had a queen and soon a legitimate heir.

She removed her heavy gabled hood, ashamed of it after seeing Marie's sleek rounded hood. Maggie was Scottish, maybe James resented her for that, that she wasn't French. She clenched her fists around the hood, frustrated of her birth place, her station in life. If only…

Jamie—she worried about her son. Would he be thrown out of St. Andrew's now? He was still royal blood. Maggie had been confident that James's feelings toward their son would not change. Now she was not so sure.

Footsteps sounded on the flagstones behind her. She wiped both eyes and replaced her hood. As she turned, she saw the queen, tall, elegant, pregnant. Marie looked down her long nose at Maggie. Maggie lifted her chin in defiance. She was still a Scot, after all.

"Your son, Jamie," she said in broken Scots, "he is my husband's son, no?"

"*Oui*," Maggie answered, relieved that she had learned French with James. Her gazed burned with jealousy, masked with arrogance.

"And your relationship to the king?" Marie said, still in Scots. She placed a hand over her large belly to flaunt her pregnancy to Maggie.

"I love him," Maggie responded in French. "And I will do whatever he commands me to do." She smoothed the front of her dress over her own pregnant belly, trying to make this woman wonder if Maggie was carrying her husband's child. Maggie knew she was lying, she would never do something to hurt him or her son, even if the king did command it. But this woman wouldn't know that.

"Does he… come to you?" she asked, searching for the words in Scots to express herself.

"*Oui*," Maggie said, staring into her icy gray eyes. She would not reveal any more than she needed to. "But why don't you ask your *husband*?"

"I have," the queen's voice was as icy as her eyes. "He said it was not my concern."

Maggie smirked, at least she still had James's loyalty in that way. She was glad that he would not discuss their relationship with his new wife.

"But I am the queen now," Marie said. "And you don't want to make an enemy."

"I cannot control if he comes to me," Maggie said, even as she said it, she wondered if this woman could keep him away from her.

"Your son is welcome," she said, turning to return to the play. As she walked away, she said over her shoulder, "But you are not."

"I'll come if the king requests my presence!" she said to the queen's back as the oak door closed. Maggie didn't know if the queen heard her or not. She remained in the hallway, waiting for James to come to her. After what felt like an eternity, she realized that he would not come out of the hall. Maggie had been replaced.

She pulled her attention from the painful memory and to the chapel for the entrance of the queen, jealousy and desire tearing her in two directions. Even though James had pushed her out of his life, curiosity and duty required her to attend the coronation. She forced herself to look at the magnificence of the queen's clothing and carriage, knowing she had pushed James to this, but that didn't make it hurt any less. The crushing pain in her chest reminded her of the hopelessness of her love for him.

Marie wore a purple, velvet robe lined in ermine over a crimson kirtle, belted above her pregnant belly with thick gold band set with a huge sapphire. Maggie instinctively reached for her own enormous belly, rubbing the growing baby swishing in her stomach. She wished she was carrying another royal child, but since James had neglected her, she knew this baby was Robert's.

Atop Marie's head was an ornate golden crown, encrusted with gemstones and fresh water pearls. She held a silver-gilt scepter, topped with a polished opaque stone. Next to her, James was dressed equally magnificently, in purple velvet and crimson. He had his father's crown remodeled, ermine fur padding the bottom, a golden band inset with garnets and pearls with alternating golden fleur-de-lies and strawberry leaves. Four arms arched over the purple velvet cap and joined around a round orb, which represented the world, topped with a golden crown.

She knew she shouldn't, but Maggie tried to catch his eye as he walked past her. James was focused on the pageantry of the coronation, staring at the brilliance of the altar. Was he angry with her again for being pregnant by her husband? Was he thinking of her at all? She didn't know because she hadn't had communication with him, not after the Christmas play, nor when she heard that David had been punished for his portrayal of her in his satirical play. That has given her a glimmer of hope that James's feeling held, but then she had been left at Loch Leven. And now she was so big with child that she doubted he would ever come to her again. While the whole country was celebrating, Maggie never felt so alone.

Chapter 44

MARIE

MARIE WAS RELIEVED TO be due in a few short weeks. She prepared for her lying-in at St. Andrew's, her room overlooking the sea. Even though it was May, the sky was still gray and cloudy—so different from the sunny spring of France. Since her own mother was unable to travel for the birth, she asked the Queen Mother to be there for her, along with her French ladies-in-waiting and French midwife. They had all sewed pieces for the baby's trousseau, fingers sore from manipulating the gold and silver thread to embroider the sleeves and collar on the tiny layette of soft linen that he would be dressed in. The room was carpeted in velvet, tapestries covered the windows, blocking out all natural light. She lay on her bed, hung with yellow damask curtains, lined with gold—the only material regal enough for a first-born royal son.

When she failed to conceive in the first year of their marriage, James had taken her to the Isle of May to visit St. Adrian shrine, which he believed helped women who were struggling to conceive.

"My father had brought my own mother here when she didn't conceive, and she was blessed with a son," he explained as they sailed over the frigid waters. She wanted to tell him that her lack of pregnancy was due to his extramarital affairs, but she knew that would only turn him sullen.

The island lay off the east coast of Scotland, in the center of the Firth of Forth, battered by ocean waves and winds. Marie held onto her hood as she stood on the deck of the boat to watch the approach to the wild island. Steep cliffs dominated the shoreline, and

Marie wondered where they would anchor. But the ship turned into a deep canyon and revealed a rocky beach that sloped to the sea. James embarked before her, and her ladies-in-waiting helped her off the boat so she didn't fall into the cold sea. They hiked up the steep embankment and the stone abbey appeared. Apart from the abbey was a rounded stone mound.

"That is the shrine of St. Adrian," James said, taking her arm. Marie smiled at him, grateful that he practiced Catholicism—that was at least the same as her beloved home country. "He built a monastery here before he was killed by the Vikings. Here, I brought this from the beach," he said, placing an oblong cream pebble in her hand. He motioned for her to approach the mound.

"Place the pebble on the cairn and pray for a son," he said. Marie turned the pebble over in her hand, the smoothness instilling confidence that her prayer would be heard. She closed her eyes and asked God to give her a son—a healthy son.

As she placed the stone on the mound, her son's face swam before her, his full cheeks, deep-set gray eyes. She was grateful that her mother was taking good care of him, sending her two portraits of little François. He had been ill last autumn, but her mother assured her that his health had returned. Still, it pained her to be unable to comfort her own child. She prayed that God would give her another son, one that would bring her husband closer to her, that would create a family legacy and purpose for her in this distant country.

———————

In addition to her French ladies-in-waiting, Elizabeth Beaton, the mother of Jean, was a Scottish ally in her household. Elizabeth was humble and gracious, unlike Lady Douglas. Marie shuddered when she thought of that woman's jealous eyes drilling into her when she confronted the shrew at the Twelfth Night celebration. There was no shame in her situation, and James did nothing to assuage her fears. Marie wanted to know why that stout woman had a hold over the king. She called Elizabeth in.

Elizabeth was plump in the face, her light eyes wide and eager. She placed a pillow behind Marie's back.

"Elizabeth," Marie said in Scots, not wanting Mahaut to

understand what she was about to ask. "What do you know about Maggie Erskine, Lady Douglas?" Marie glanced at Elizabeth out of the corner of her eye as she embroidered. Elizabeth recoiled as if Marie had slapped her. Marie placed her hand on Elizabeth's arm to comfort her.

"What frightens you so about her?" Marie softened her voice. Elizabeth glanced at Mahaut, who was pretending not to listen.

"I've heard stories," she leaned towards Marie and whispered, her eyes darting to the other women embroidering.

"What sort of stories?" Marie said. Elizabeth swallowed hard, her throat bobbing.

"It is said…" Elizabeth wrung her fabric between her hands. Marie nodded to encourage her to continue. Elizabeth whispered while exhaling all of her breath, "that she is a *maleficas.*" Witch.

"Who is a witch?" Mahaut burst in, staring down her sharp nose. In Lorraine, Marie's homeland, persecution of witches and accusations of witchcraft was common, especially among those who were Reformers. Mahaut's sister had been accused of witchcraft after she spurred a marriage proposal, so Mahaut was wary of witchcraft accusations.

"No one, Mahaut," Marie said in French, sharper than she had intended. "You just keep embroidering the layette."

"I heard you say Lady Douglas," Mahuat was more persistent than James's hunting raches. "Is she a witch?" Marie sighed. She had hoped to keep this private. Now all of her ladies-in-waiting stopped sewing to join the conversation.

"I simply asked what Elizabeth knew of her," Marie said, picking up her own fabric and stabbing it with the needle.

"And Elizabeth said she's a *maleficas,*" Mahaut met Marie's eyes with an all-knowing look and said in French, "I told you that you cannot trust these Scot women!" Marrie shook her head, but Mahaut had already swung to Elizabeth. "Tell us everything you know." Elizabeth looked to Marie for permission. With her heart in her throat, Marie nodded for Elizabeth to speak.

Elizabeth swallowed again, her mouth dry. "There are rumors," she whispered, speaking in halting French, "that she keeps cats at Lochleven and that she put a love spell on the king after she had married."

Mahaut slammed her embroidery onto the floor. "I knew it," she pointed at Marie. "You said she was haughty. This explains where her confidence comes from." Elizabeth, captivating her audience, whose mouths gaped at the news, continued.

"They say that her husband is also in on the scheme. They say he *wanted* his wife to enchant the king and when he was the king's butcher, he served the king many meats, which were flavored with basil, cinnamon and rose hips," Elizabeth continued.

"All herbs which entice romance!" Mahaut said, frowning with an uneasy satisfaction.

"And mean nothing," Marie said, hoping her voice sounded calmer than she felt. "Have I had a love spell placed on me, since I eat basil, cinnamon, and rose hips as well?"

"You stay with your husband even though another woman warms his bed," Mahaut said under her breathe.

"Enough!" Marie said, jealousy and suspicion battling in her mind, cutting her heart to shreds. She folded her hands under her chin and closed her eyes to compose herself. She was the Queen of Scots. She was carrying the heir to the throne. A common Scots woman had no advantage over her. Once her son was born, he would quit his dalliances, Marie was sure of it.

"It is also said that she charmed him using lavender and honey in his ale," Elizabeth said. Lavender? James had told her that was his favorite flower. Marie imagined that shrew with her husband, using the power of lavender to make him fall in love with her. And James caressing her cheek, tenderness in his eyes, just as Louis did to her, which she hoped James would do, and he never did. Her stomach dropped, the baby sensing Marie's disappointment. She clutched her belly to keep the baby from falling out of her, doubling over in pain.

"Madam, all of this talk is vexing you and your babe," Johanna said. Sweet, peacemaker Johanna. Marie looked into her cherry brown eyes, face pinched with worry. Of course Marie was being foolish to believe these uncorroborated stories. Still... the baby kicked again, but Marie straightened up, pushing all of the unpleasantness aside.

"Bring your daughter in, Elizabeth, to dance and take my mind off these false contractions," Marie said. It was at least two weeks too early for the birth of her baby. She would distract herself and her ladies from clucking like old hens.

The little girl came in wearing the gift Marie had given her—a black velvet and taffeta gown with the upturned sable-lined sleeves. Mahaut handed Marie her lute, her brow drawn. She strummed an upbeat song, and the little girl twirled and jumped, chasseing left and right. Marie was singing, when pain overwhelmed her. She dropped the lute and grabbed the damask curtains to absorb the pain.

"Madame, perhaps the baby is early?" Renée said in French. All Marie could do was nod as another wave of pain crashed over her. She couldn't pretend that nothing was wrong, that this baby was going to wait. She breathed through her mouth to expel the agony building in her abdomen. The baby was coming early. Her sons she had carried for longer than this baby. She prayed for the Virgin Mother's protection—give her a healthy baby or take her to the next world. If the baby was too weak to survive, Marie would be blamed. A spasm rolled over her as a reminder of her precarious fate.

The Queen Mother hurried into the dark room. She was in a yellow kirtle, her hair hastily thrown into a low bun.

"Is there anything I can do for you?" she asked, taking Marie's hand. Marie shook her head no, but the Queen Mother placed a damp linen towel on her forehead. It helped calm Marie, and she smiled to express her gratitude.

The midwife called out instructions to her ladies, who scurried to execute the demands, fresh linens and water fetched. Once the contractions came at even intervals, it was as if Marie's body remembered her previous labors and took over. The pain became manageable, and the baby was born not even an hour later.

The baby, the long-sought son, was cleaned and dressed in the white layette embroidered in gold. Marie sent the royal messenger to alert the king, who was in Edinburgh planning a trip to the northern part of his kingdom, that his son had been born and then she prepared herself for his arrival. Her ladies washed her body and dressed her in an embroidered silk chemise and draped a flowered purple damask robe around her shoulders. They brushed her copper colored hair until it shone as if it were on fire. She then picked up her child and waited for her husband to arrive. She knew this would bring them closer, now that she had produced a legitimate heir. An heir was stronger than any love spell Lady Douglas could cast.

A knock at the chamber door announced that the king had arrived. Marie smoothed her long hair around her, then nodded to
allow her husband entry. James burst into the room, his auburn hair
waving uncovered. He wore a leather jerkin with slashes and silk
thread buttons. His wool hose rustled as he approached the bed.

"Is he hearty?" he asked, leaning over Marie. She breathed in his
musk, salty and earthy.

"Yes, your son is healthy," she said, tilting the sleeping baby in
her arms so that James could see his sweet face and his red hair.
To her surprise, James reached for the baby and took him from
Marie's arms.

"He will be called James," he announced to all of the women
present. He approached his mother, face shining with pride.

"I did it, Mother," he said, his voice full of emotion. "I have accomplished everything my father had accomplished."

"Yes, my son," the Queen Mother said, touching the baby's cheek.

"And I will tame the highlands next," he said. "My kingdom
will have peace, an heir, and a strong ally to protect against your
deceitful brother. My son will not have to endure a long minority
and chaos as I did!"

The Queen Mother flinched as her son's words slapped her in
the face. Marie's French ladies-in-waiting glanced at each other, but
were careful not to move their heads. Elizabeth Beaton, accustomed
to the rough words of the king towards his mother, had no reaction.
Marie would never dream of speaking to her own dear mother in
such a manner, nor would her brothers! Antoinette would eviscerate
them and put them back in their place. She had never heard her
adopted father, King François, speak that way to his mother, Louise
of Savoy.

"We will call him Jacques," Marie said, feeling the French name
in her mouth. She knew her husband would name him James—as
he had named two of his bastards, but she would still call her son
by his French name.

"Yes, and he will be invested as the Duke of Rothesay," her husband said, hunched over his son. Marie smiled at the overt display
of affection for their son. This would bring the two of them closer
and into a harmonious marriage. Yes, their son was the love spell
that Marie had at her disposal to win James over. She didn't need

to rely on darker magic as that harlot had. God had given her a son and He would lead James back to her. She prayed that he would pay more attention to her now and treat her as an equal partner as Louis had done.

Chapter 45

JAMES

BEFORE THE BIRTH OF his son, after Marie's coronation, James had a visit from the court of his uncle, an ambassador named Ralph Sadler. After he attended Catholic mass with Marie, he saw the Englishman in his chamber at Linlithgow, observing the man's velvet overcoat edged in black silk, open at the neck to highlight his pleaded white silk chemise. Even the ambassadors in England were wearing royal garments. James wanted Scotland to be that wealthy.

"Our Highness, your royal uncle, has sent a gift of six geldings for your pleasure," Sadler said, motioning out the window. James noticed their dull coats as they were led around in a circle. When his uncle had offered to send him horses, James thought he would send the beautiful Spanish horses that his first queen brought to England. These horses were mediocre and insulting. James smirked at the mention of gelding, a horse who cannot breed. The irony was not lost on him. Of course his uncle meant it to symbolize James's lack of virility. But his queen was pregnant, and Henry was having difficulties consummating his marriage to a German princess, if his ambassadors in England were believed.

"I thank my good uncle," James turned back to Sadler, knowing his smirk alerted the ambassador to his displeasure. "And if there is anything within my realm that will please your king, please make it known to me." He sat back in his velvet chair and waited for Sadler to get to the real reason for his visit. He knew his uncle well enough to know the gift was not free—his uncle wanted something from him.

"Sire, the king's majesty, your grace's uncle," he began with a flourish, "wishes to commend such a noble prince as you, so close to our majesty, for your continued peace and goodwill along the borders."

James stifled a chortle. He had to keep peace on the border because Angus kept trying to stir it up, but he had to be diplomatic and said, "Of course. And I will continue to do everything in my power to keep peace and amity between my beloved uncle's realm and mine."

Sadler began to speak, but James cut him off, "Of course it would be favorable if my loving uncle returned those within his realm that wish ill on Scotland."

But Sadler was a smooth statesman, and without a beat, said, "Sir, you know your uncle is a prince of honor and will punish those who intend on harming his true nephew."

James looked at Sadler out of the corner of his eye. They both knew Sadler was lying. Henry would support Angus as long as he was James's enemy and stirred discontent within the Scottish kingdom. Sadler cleared his throat and tried another approach.

"There is a matter which the king's majesty discovered which threatens your honor and kingdom," Sadler said, his azure eyes set in steely determination. "But your uncle begs that you must keep it secret."

James covered his mouth with his hand, unable to keep from sneering. Whatever his uncle had "discovered," James doubted that it was a secret, but he said, "Thank God that I can keep a secret."

"Your cardinal passed through England, having almost shipwrecked on our coast," he said.

"Yes," James interrupted. "And I have given thanks to my own uncle for providing him lodging and safe passage!" He felt his nostrils flare in anger, impatient that his uncle made him grovel every time one of his subjects wished to pass through England. All because James would not throw off the Catholic mantel and support the protestant religion.

"Yes sire," Sadler said, pulling a document out of his coat. "But secret letters were found after he left England."

"That is no matter to me," James said, Beaton already told him that his uncle's men roughed him up and stole letters written by him to his agent in Rome.

"But the letters contain treasonous intentions to take not only the spiritual jurisdiction of your realm, but also the temporal," Sadler said, leaning in to the desk. "The cardinal also mentions that in a few years, he will have more power in your kingdom than yourself. Your uncle, who loves and trusts you, doesn't want to see your power usurped."

James pushed his tongue against the top of his mouth, holding in the insults that he wished to say about his uncle. Henry wanted to usurp the power in Scotland and claim suzerainty over the country for himself. James needed to control his anger and exhaled before he answered.

"Spiritual jurisdiction is the business of the spiritual, and as far as temporal affairs are concerned, no King of Scots has ever been served more obediently than I," he said and crossed his arms to show he was not threatened by his uncle or his alleged found discovery.

Sadler held out the letters, "Please sire, just read what your subject has written."

James batted the papers out of Sadler's hand. They fluttered onto the desk.

"I don't care what they say," he thundered. "He wrote to Rome to procure authority to be the pope's representative in Scotland, which will benefit our subjects, and I also wrote to the Pope's Holiness asking the same."

"But what of suppressing religious houses to reduce the corruption and taking control of their income?" Sadler continued. James knew the ambassador wanted him to agree to break with the church as his uncle did, so he could alienate Scotland from her French allies. He felt his anger flare again.

"I think that it is against God's law to suppress these abbeys, which have served the people and God for many years and continue to do so," James said, twirling a quill between his fingers. "Besides, why do I need to confiscate their property to increase my income when they give me whatever I need?"

Sadler hung his head, defeated. James knew Henry would be upset, but he didn't care. He knew Henry's ultimate aim was to subjugate Scotland and subsume it into the English crown.

"But," Sadler played his final card, "unless your monks are holier than ours in England, nowhere is there more corruption, incompetency, greed, fornication, and other sordidness than in religious houses. But the King, your uncle, committed his trust to the protestant bishops and clergy, who fight against these sins and bring true holiness to his realm."

"Oh," James laughed. "God forbid that if a few are bad that all should be destroyed! I do realize that some are bad, but there are even more who are good. The bad must be reformed so the good can continue to work, and I will reform the church in Scotland, by God's grace, until I die."

Before he dismissed Sadler, James added, "And your king can hardly preach to me while he supports the scoundrel Douglases against their sovereign."

"Yes, that is disagreeable," Sadler conceded. "But all of this could be discussed if you agreed to a meeting with his highness your uncle."

"Of course, I would gladly meet with my uncle whom I have never met," James said. Sadler exhaled in relief, but James continued, "so long as my father, the French king, is also present."

Sadler, frustrated with the lack of progress from James, returned to England. James hoped his uncle saw how strong his position was now—he had a French bride and soon, a healthy heir to his throne. Next, he needed a show of his power to the lawless highlanders in the north.

His plans to sail to the northern reaches of his kingdom were postponed with the birth of his first legitimate son. He rushed to St. Andrew's as soon as the royal Messenger, Andrew Michelson, had told him that his wife had given birth to a fair and healthy son. His heart leapt into his throat—she said that the birth was still a few weeks away! *Well, my son is just as impatient as I am*, James chuckled to himself. He promised Andrew a new suit of clothing for his troubles and his groom readied his horse.

At St Andrew's castle, holding his son, he glanced around at all the women in Marie's birthing chamber. His mother, the midwife, three French ladies-in-waiting, two Scots women. He felt suffocated by the feminine energy, which he felt was accusatory—reproaching him for neglecting his wife. Guilt clawed up his spine because he knew they were right. Yet he had stayed away from Maggie, ignoring her at Marie's coronation to show that he did respect Marie as his Queen. But holding his baby son, the memory of Jamie's birth rushed back. It had only been the three of them, a cozy triumvirate. He could not curl up into Marie's bed with all of these women's eyes on him. He wanted to order them all out to recreate the intimacy he felt with Maggie and Jamie. But Marie was not a Scots woman. No, she was the adopted daughter of the French king and the queen of his country. So he had to remain composed and proper, even if that meant he never formed the same intimacy with his own wife. He handed the baby back to Marie and kissed her on the forehead, which was cool to his touch, just like his feelings for her.

He excused himself, with the pretext of seeing Cardinal Beaton to plan the baptism. Once away from the condemning stares of Marie's women, he felt like he could breathe again. He climbed the stairs to Jamie's chamber, surprising his nurse.

"Hello, my son," he announced as he strode into the inner chamber unannounced. The nurse leaped to her feet, apologizing for the disarray of the young boy. James held up a hand to stop her protests. He had not expected his son to be proper, and had actually wanted to see him in play. Jamie had tin soldiers sprawled across the Turkish carpet, which was a gift from his adopted father François. James got on the floor with his son.

"My son," he said, picking up one of the tiny soldiers. "You have a younger brother now, who will one day be king. What do you think of that?"

His son stared at him with the same mahogany eyes of his father and his mother's mouth, his brow furrowed in confusion.

"But Mam said I would be King of Scots," he said. James laughed, of course Maggie would tell her son that. He couldn't even be mad because he loved this boy as much as he did his legitimate son.

"You have just as important a position—you will be the protector of your younger brother," he said, smoothing the boy's waving hair. "He will need an advisor who has the best interests of Scotland in mind, and as his brother and my son, you must guide your brother away from those who would use him for selfish interests over the good of Scotland."

"Can I still joust?" he sprang to his feet, poking James with his arm, an imaginary lance. James laughed and poked him back in the ribs, causing the boy to double over in laughter. "And fight the borders reivers and Angus?"

James sighed, remembering how Angus destroyed his childhood. He hoped to kill Angus before that deceitful traitor could hurt his own children.

"Perhaps," he said, looking out over the sea, feeling himself sink into melancholy as he thought of the betrayal of Angus first and then his uncle by harboring Angus. The inclination towards despair had been worsening since his hunting accident the summer that Madeleine had died. He had been mourning her and had gone out in the fog, always unwise, but especially so since his mind was occupied by grief. His horse had spooked, rearing up and James grasped at the horse's mane too late to stay on. The last moment of consciousness had been blinding pain as his head connected with something hard—a tree root or rock and he blacked out. When he came to in his bed at Stirling, he had ordered John Tennant to fetch Maggie. She nursed him back to health, holding the cool linen on his head while his body spasmed in pain.

He wished Maggie was here to strengthen him mentally as she had physically done last summer, drag him out of the black hole he fell into when he remembered all of treachery he had endured. And his uncle was still goading him to break from the Catholic Church, the only institution that supported him throughout his minority and reign. He needed to see Jamie's mother before he left on his northern trip. He needed her strength.

Cardinal Beaton planned the baptism of the Scots heir. Four days later, the preparations were ready for a royal baptism. As was the custom, the baptism took place at night. Fifteen ells of white Genoese taffeta were wrapped around the candles, which lined the way from the castle to the altar of St. Andrew's cathedral, leading to Cardinal Beaton and the Queen Mother. They would be the godparents of the royal heir. Beaton conducted the ceremony in Latin, removing the baby's white linen cap and pouring the water over his head to remove the stain of original sin. The cardinal then dipped his finger into a golden bowl full of olive oil to make the sign of the cross on the baby's forehead, while the baby wailed under the cold shock of the water. But his soul was saved from Limbo. James embraced David Lindsay and his wife, Janet Douglas, thanked them for their service and participation in his heir's spiritual inauguration.

After the ceremony, James wrote to Maggie to meet him in Falkland, needing to see her before he left for the north, to calm his mind. Of course she came, even though she had had a baby boy of her own at Loch Leven and just completed her lying-in. He was waiting for her in his inner chamber. Before she even took off her riding cape, she struck at him.

"What do you need from me now?" she remained standing, hands on her hips. "You completely ignored me in front of your *queen.*" Venom seeped from her as she pronounced the final word. James chuckled, always amused by her fire.

"Sit," he said, patting a green and purple velvet scissor chair next to him. "Let me make it up to you."

She crossed her arms, but she sat in the chair. He placed his hand at the nape of her neck to feel her strength. She ducked her head to avoid his touch.

"I'm not one of your whores," she said, pulling her chair away from him. "You don't get to fuck me and discard me like your others. I *was* almost your queen."

He yanked her chair back to him, almost tossing her out of it. She grabbed onto the velvet-padded arms to steady herself, her eyes wide in surprise. It only made him want her more.

"Yes you were," he said into her ear, feeling the shiver of desire go through her body, "and as my almost queen, you should submit to my desires." A sigh escaped her open lips, and it took all of his strength not to kiss them.

"I am not like you. I can't just turn my feelings off like you can," she said. "My feelings are a wildfire—one spark and I am consumed in flames. I wish I could be cold like you."

Her brow furrowed in pain, her eyes naked and vulnerable. He wanted to respond that he had to turn his feelings off to the outside world, but she was wrapped so tightly around his heart that he could never disentangle himself from her. He fed off her strength, and it rejuvenated him. But all of that would require him being vulnerable.

"I have a new son," he said instead, deflecting the conversation that would expose him to further hurt. It was his reflex after the Angus hurt, and even though he knew Maggie would never hurt him intentionally, he still threw up his emotional wall.

"Yes, I was at the coronation of your pregnant wife," she said. "Don't you remember ignoring me and your son?"

Now it was James's turn to sigh. He was caught between his desire and his duty, a duty which she pushed him towards. After the Christmas play at Linlithgow, Marie had made it clear that she would not accept his infidelities paraded in front of her and the whole court. And James knew that she had the ear of François, the only person whose opinion mattered to him. If François withdrew his support, James was helpless against his stronger uncle's army. He had to acquiesce to protect his kingdom. He wished he could explain this to Maggie.

"I do," he said, bringing her hand to his mouth, his lips lingering. She did not pull her hand away. "And if I looked at you, I would have never made it to the altar, never have had Marie crowned queen."

He saw the tension melt from her shoulders. Her eyes bore into his and she wound her hand around his neck, but said nothing.

"And then I would have disobeyed your wishes to strengthen Scotland," he continued.

"I know," she said, dropping her gaze. "I know you are doing what I asked you to do—marry French and strengthen Scotland... but I don't have to like it."

James threw his head back and laughed. This is why he could never stay away from her, they were both the same, stubborn, fickle, self-seeking. She placed both of her hands on either side of his face, forcing him to look into her mossy eyes.

"As long as you always come back to me," she said, pressing her mouth against his. He returned the pressure, his arms flying around her body.

"Always," he whispered into her mouth, and laced one arm under her legs, picking up her slight body, warmth radiating to him. He carried her to his bedchamber and they satisfied each other as the sun set and night took over.

After the night at Falkland with Maggie, he headed back to Edinburgh to prepare twelve ships, fitted with heavy artillery, for his trip to the northern isles. His subjects were engaging in blood feuds related to their clans, which James needed to suppress them to show these highlanders that even there, his royal hand could reach them.

He invited the most loyal and important nobles with him—Cardinal Beaton, Arran, Huntly, and Oliver Sinclair of Pitcairn. Oliver had replaced Finnart as James's favorite companion, being promoted from cupbearer to Captain of Tantallon castle, part of Jamie's inheritance. Oliver was a jolly companion, eager to entertain, loved hunting with James, but more importantly, his ancestral lands were in the Orkneys, the farthest islands of the Scottish realm. He would rely on Oliver's knowledge of the terrain and people. According to legend, his ancestors came to England with William the Conqueror and settled north, supporting Scottish independence by fighting with Robert the Bruce. His father was the Baron of Roslin, a title that Oliver wouldn't inherit since his mother was a second wife, and his grandfather had been the Jarl of Orkney when it was still part of Norway. The party would stay with the Bishop of Orkney.

The fleet of five main galleys and seven smaller ships departed from Leith, sailing around County Fife, James noticing St. Andrew's abbey and castle where he had left his precious children. The seas were rough, even though the ships skirted the Scottish coast, and he suffered from seasickness. But he was determined to show himself to his northern-most subjects, a tradition begun by his great-great-grandfather, James I in a campaign he called "Daunting the Isles." The Orkney Island had been pledged to his grandfather, James III as part of Margaret of Denmark, his wife's, dowry.

The ships passed Aberdeen, rounded the Kinnaird Head peninsula, sailed passed the Earl of Moray's land holding and the Moray Firth before they traveled up the east coast to the last land on the Scotland mainland before the Orkneys. The entourage sailed around the main island and into the natural harbor of Kirkwall, the royal burgh in the Orkneys. It was difficult for James to tell what hour it was, as the sun never seemed to travel across the sky, reflecting off the water.

"Don't worry, *Schir*," Oliver came up behind the king. "The sun almost never sets this far north in the summer! We call it the Grimlins."

From the harbor, James and his party walked south along the packed dirt road to St. Magnus Cathedral. The church was built at the same time as the Bishop's palace, both using red and yellow sandstone to create patterns in the walls. The bells rang out into the cool air. James pulled his overcoat tighter and counted the peels.

"Sounds like it is supper time," he grinned to Oliver after counting seven peels. Oliver returned the grin and both men hurried, anxious to stretch their legs and have a good meal. James pulled up when he saw the condition of the palace. Bricks were crumbling, roof tiles missing, and the building was in general disrepair. The old bishop, Robert Maxwell, who had beseeched James for funds to make repairs, had become an old man in the four years since James had seen him. His black bishops hat pressed against the wrinkles on his forehead, causing deep creases which repeated on either side of his mouth, and his long forked beard had gone white, the pepper leeched from the hairs.

"Your highness," the old man bowed, his robe hanging off his wizened body. "I had hoped to be further along with the repairs. Most of the funds went into the church, which I felt more important to repair."

"Of course," James grasped the man's arm and held him upright. How old was the bishop? James guessed he was seventy at least. Robert had been a loyal bishop, but James felt it might be time to transfer the responsibility to a younger man who could oversee the repairs. These islands were part of Marie's jointure, and James wanted them to be profitable for his son. He would ensure that his son's country was wealthier and stronger than it had been when James escaped from Angus.

––––––––––––

The next day, they boarded the ships and took again to the seas. The highlanders were foreign to James, who had grown up under a Tudor-influenced court and now styled his own court in the modern French style of François. When the people rushed from their low mud-bricked houses, instead of the refined furs and velvet fabrics, the people donned sheepskin coats, with the wool inward to keep the sea breeze from chilling them, curving up around the back of their heads. The men kept their hair and their beards long and shaggy as further protection from the whipping winds. They seemed more Norse than Scots. The men wore yellow chemises with plaid, woolen capes tossed over their shoulders. Protecting their feet were leather boots that flared out at the calves. Above the boots, bare legs could be seen under a tartan wool cloth wrapped around their waist, secured with a fur pouch called a sporran. Oliver said the skirt was called a "breacon feile"—belted plaid. Many also carried unsheathed swords or bows slung over their shoulder with a quiver or arrows.

Being raised in a Tudor-influenced court and seeing the splendor and sophistication of the French court, the sturdy and rugged highlanders impressed James. "This," he motioned to the countryside, "is the true Scotland!" And he wanted to ensure the loyalty of his subjects for the future of his son.

Chapter 46

THOMAS

As soon as the king departed to circumnavigate the northern kingdom, Thomas sprang into action against Finnart. Beaton was still breathing down his neck, after the unsuccessful heresy trial against Sir John Borthwick. Two days after the baptism of the king's son, Beaton held a heresy trial against Borthwick, stating that he had written a letter to Cromwell, King Henry's secretary, after James received the title "Defender of the Faith" from the pope in 1537. Beaton alleged that in the letter, Borthwick told Cromwell that he would support the reform movement in Scotland, even if it went against the king's wishes. Thomas doubted that Borthwick would be that stupid to put that in a letter, but Borthwick fled to England rather than stand before a religious court stacked against him, and that sealed his guilt. In his absence, Beaton tried and found him guilty, and an effigy of Borthwick burned in the square in front of St. Andrew's cathedral, provided by Beaton.

While he was still trying to find a way to prosecute Finnart, Thomas got a break from Finnart's relative, James Hamilton of Kincavil, who requested an audience with Thomas. Thomas sat behind his desk and let Kincavil explain the grievance.

"Finnart has planned to assassinate the king for the king's reproach of him," Kincavil began. Thomas doubted this accusation as Finnart was overseeing the restoration of Linlithgow and was wealthier than ever, so had no motivation to assassinate James. *But,* Thomas thought, *it didn't have to be true.* He just needed to convince James that it was true.

"You know he is a cruel and terrible man who killed the Earl of Lennox," Kincavil continued. The mention of Lennox snapped Thomas to attention.

"It is known by all that Finnart executed the Earl of Lennox after the earl surrendered at the Battle of Linlithgow Bridge," Kincavil said. "Several of Lennox's fallen men had Finnart's mark on them."

Thomas rolled his eyes and said, "Yes, everyone knows this, but it cannot be proven."

"Ah," Kincavil grinned. "But there is proof. He has been paying six priests to pray for the soul of the deceased John, Earl of Lennox, for seven years."

Thomas raised his eyebrows. This was an interesting development indeed! The priests could testify that they received money to pray for Lennox to assuage Finnart's guilt over his execution. That was enough to ward Finnart.

He dismissed Kincavil and wrote a summons to have Finnart arrested and warded in the Tolbooth in Edinburgh. But the murder of a noble in battle was not a treasonous offense. He tapped the quill against his chin. A rumor had circulated that Finnart planned to assassinate the king. It was not certain, but he would call Finnart's servant, John Crombie, to the stand. To make sure the king was sufficiently angered to order the execution, Thomas would also prove that Finnart had been communicating with Angus and profiting from that communication. That charge would cause the king to act!

The royal guard and Sir William Kirkcaldy, the treasurer of Scotland rode out to Linlithgow with Thomas carrying the summons in his belted pouch. His heart thumped against the paper, beating faster as they nearer the palace. As the approached the crenellated gate, the watchmen recognized the royal guard and let them pass. Finnart was in the courtyard, holding architectural papers.

Thomas dismounted, unable to conceal his smile. "Sir James Hamilton of Finnart?" he asked.

"You know I am," Finnart replied, haughty as ever.

"You are under arrest for conspiring to assassinate our royal king," Thomas said, revealing the summons, unable to keep the glee from his voice. "And for communicating with the Douglases in exile."

"You can't be serious?" he said, mouth clenched, anger pouring from his eyes. The royal guard seized him, his papers fluttering to the ground. Thomas smiled, a sinister smirk that said it all.

"You will never make the king believe you!" Finnart shouted as the guard led him away.

"I don't have to," Thomas said. "You have done it all for me."

———————

In August, upon the king's return from the Orkneys, the trial began in Edinburg's parliament hall before the king could change his mind about Finnart. Timber stands were constructed to hold the jury, which consisted of twenty-one lords. All of the nobles who supported James were present, except his half-brother Moray, who was in France recovering from an illness. Archibald Campbell, the 4th Earl of Argyll, served at Justiciar. Argyll was a seasoned noble who had put down a rebellion in the Scottish Isles in 1529. There was no love lost between Finnart and Argyll—Argyll had been married to Finnart's half-sister and so he watched Finnart abuse the Arran estates to enrich himself. Finnart mocked him by calling him Ruadh—Scots Gaelic for red because of his hair, but also sounded like rude in Scots. Argyll was still grieving the death of his wife in the spring, so Thomas hoped that influenced Argyll to a stricter verdict—hopefully death.

Argyll first called John Crombie, groom to Finnart. Thomas swallowed the ball of anxiety threatening to choke him. He hoped Crombie stuck to the story he had confessed earlier and not change it out of loyalty to Finnart.

"Tell us the circumstances of September 1526," Argyll said, the scar between his eyes deepened, making him look menacing. Crombie swallowed hard before answering, avoiding Finnart's glare. Argyll might look intimidating, but Finnart was cruel. By testifying against him, Crombie was making himself a target. But Thomas had also reminded Crombie that the king could protect him—or have him killed.

"I was ordered to shoot into a band of Lennox supporters," he said.

"Did you not see the king's banner?"

"Yes," Crombie whispered.

"And still you shot after seeing the king's banner?" Argyll said, his voice rising.

"Yes," Crombie said.

"And who ordered you to shoot?" Argyll demanded. Thomas clenched his fists and willed Crombie to betray his master. Crombie twisted in his chair, eyes darting to Thomas, who nodded for him to continue.

"James Hamilton of Finnart," Crombie said, hanging his head. Thomas sneered with relief. Crombie had sealed Finnart's fate, admitted in court that Finnart ordered shots to be fired at the king's royal body.

"So my brother ordered you to shoot into a group holding the king's banner?" The Earl of Arran stood, Finnart's younger brother. He was tall and thin, being only nineteen years old, but Thomas could tell that he would grow stouter as he grew older, much like his father did. Arran's sense of loyalty to his half-brother surprised Thomas. Finnart was a bastard, and Thomas speculated he had misused Arran's funds to line his own pockets when Finnart ruled his estate during his minority. Apparently, Arran chose not to believe his brother's mismanagement of his estates, just as James had chosen to believe that Finnart hadn't murdered Lennox.

"Yes," Crombie said, not lifting his head. Arran spun to look at his brother, betrayal smoldering. Finnart refused to look at his half-brother, his ward whose interests he was supposed to be protecting. He remained upright but his broad shoulders slouched in defeat.

The men on the jury whispered among themselves. Thomas threw Finnart a smug grin. Finnart was pale, the gravity of his situation slamming down on him, anger bubbling. As Thomas predicted, Finnart's callousness would incriminate him.

"Thank you, Crombie, please be seated," Argyll said, and Crombie sat, throwing a panicked look at Finnart, who refused to meet his gaze.

"Am I not allowed to defend myself against this farce of a court?" Finnart pounded on the table in front of him, leaping to his feet. "This is brutishness! Of course Crombie would say I ordered him to save his own hide!"

Finnart glowered at Thomas, who tried not to shrink under the menacing stare. His forked beard, once thick and dark brown, was now marked with gray, evidence of his worries. As he said to Finnart, Thomas didn't need to build a false case against him. Through his own cruel character, Finnart had turned his own servants and the nobles against him.

"The jury will now hear evidence of a second charge, that of conspiring with the Earl of Angus and his brother," Argyll said as if Finnart hadn't spoken. Finnart returned to his seat, but still glared at Thomas.

"Now calling James Douglas of Parkhead," Argyll said into an echoing chamber. Parkhead had fled to England to avoid testifying and being executed himself. The charge alleged that during the siege of Tantallon in the fall of 1528, Finnart had met with George Douglas and Angus to discuss getting back into the king's graces. He proposed to convince the king to restore Angus's earldom and if that failed, he and James Douglas of Parkhead would enter Holyrood and kill the king while he slept in order to restore Angus. Parkhead was the only eyewitness who could confirm the plan. Argyll knew Parkhead was not in the hall, but wanted the drama.

"So there is no one to corroborate this mockery," Finnart sneered, pushing his hulking body back from the table. "I consider this matter moot." He began to leave the room, when Kincavil stepped forward.

"I stand behind the accusation," Kincavil stood, hand on the hilt of his sword.

"You besmirch my good name, Cuz," Finnart said in a menacing growl, anger seething from his stiff face.

"You have done that yourself," Kincavil said, stepping toward Finnart. Argyll motioned, and both men were restrained by royal guards.

"Gentlemen, quiet in the court," Argyll said over the din that erupted. "Do you wish to prove your accusation with your body, Sir Kincavil?" It was an archaic solution to an accusation that could not be proven with tradition evidence—trial by combat. The Germanic tribes had used trial by combat and when the Normans invaded the island, they expanded its use in England and Scotland.

"Yes, Justicar," Kincavel said.

"Then it will be a trial by combat!" Argyll said and the room burst into surprised conversation. "What is the wager?"

"I have my gauntlet to provide as wager," Kincavel held up an elaborately etched metal glove and threw it to the ground. All eyes swung to Finnart to see if he would accept the challenge. Finnart lumbered over and picked up the glove.

"The gauntlet has been thrown and accepted," Argyll said. "We will convene on the green at noon tomorrow."

Thomas could barely contain himself as he walked down High Street, past the Luckenbooths, merchants shouting out their deals to tempt passersby. The sun was high and the August air was humid. Thomas was already sweating from nerves and the heat was not helping. He stopped to fill his cup with wine that was flowing from the Market Cross fountain and then headed towards the kirkyard south of St. Giles church.

The yard had been fenced in with interlocking rough beams to form an oval. Pavilions were set up on either side of the green under which a wooden table and black velvet draped chair were provided. The timber stands had been dismantled from the Tolbooth and reassembled on the south side of the yard for Argyll, the nobles and other spectators to watch the battle. Thomas took a seat and adjusted the collar of his chemise, sweat rolling down his face. Thomas noted the wooden club placed on the table—the traditional weapon for trial by combat—along with a physician standing at the ready. Finnart walked out with his pledge, clothed in padded leather. Even though Thomas knew the character of Finnart, he still expected him to be a coward—tuck his tail and run. Kincavil approached with his pledge.

Argyll entered and took his place at the center of the stands. "Do you Kincavil swear an oath that your statement is true, that Finnart plotted the murder of the king, our sovereign lord?" Argyll asked, voice projecting across the list.

"Aye, my lord," Kincavil said, his short beard quivering. Even though he was eleven years younger than the aging Finnart, Kincavil knew better than to underestimate his opponent.

"And you, Sir Finnart," Argyll continued, "Do you swear that your accuser is lying?"

Finnart spit in the grass. "This is a sham of a trial," he growled.

"I accept that as your oath," Argyll said and raised his hand, "Let

299

them go and do their duty in God's name!"

Each man walked back to his pavilion and prepared for the battle. After putting on their protective leather jerkins, gloves, and helmets, the pledges smeared pig grease over the leather so the blows from their opponent's cudgel slipped off. Kincavil coated his hands in ash to grip his club and nodded. Finnart, similarly greased and ashed, also nodded that he was ready. The two men advanced towards each other on foot. Ritual called for light tapping of the swords, called king's blows, but Finnart scorned the chivalric ritual and raised his club over his head to strike Kincavel. Kincavel anticipated Finnart's duplicity and blocked his overhand slice. Finnart's bulky frame was knocked off balance and he staggered to the left, but he recovered and struck at Kincavil's side. He absorbed the blow as best he could from the brute, raising his own cudgel and bringing the pommel down on Finnart's head. Thomas held his breath as Finnart rolled over in the grass and leapt to his feet, lips curved into a wolfish snarl.

"Is that all ye got?" Finnart laughed. "You'll need more than that to take down the bull!" He charged at Kincavil, swinging the pointed end of his shield at his opponent's shoulders. Kincavil dodged the blow and Finnart's bulk once again was thrown off balance. Finnart may have been stronger, but Kincavil was younger and faster. He kicked Finnart in the back and Finnart sprawled on the ground again. A groan went up from the stands—kicking in the back was dishonorable. Thomas wiped the back of his hand across his forehead. *Damn those huddy Hamiltons!* he thought. *The entire branch cannot be trusted!*

After charging, slashing, knocking each other to the ground, the two sized each other up, catching their breath. Finnart coiled to strike at Kincavil, the wooden clubs cracking as they met. Kincavil swung around and hit Finnart in the side of the head. The beast fell hard, face planting into the grass. Kincavil placed his leather boot on Finnart's neck and held the club to his cheek. Finnart struggled to take a breath, but he still squirmed to get out from under Kincavil. Kincavil raised his club to give the deathblow to Finnart, smashing his skull. Finnart's faced was red, from exertion and embarrassment, to be bested in a duel. He croaked out, "Craven!" *I am vanquished.* Kincavil removed his foot from Finnart's neck and held his cudgel up in victory.

Argyll called the duel over, shouting, "Hora hora!"

———————

After Kincavil bested Finnart in the judicial duel, the jury retired to the castle to make a decision. After less than an hour, they returned and handed the verdict to Argyll. He read aloud, "Sir James Hamilton of Finnart, you are convicted of the treasonable ordering of the shooting of guns at the king and the treasonable planning of the assassination of the king with Archibald Douglas of Kilspindie and James Douglas of Parkhead during the siege of Tantallon Castle in consultation with Archibald Douglas, Earl of Angus and George Douglas of Pittendreich. Therefore, it is ruled that this James forfeit his life, lands, rents and possessions to the king as his escheat, to remain with him in perpetuity."

The royal guard seized Finnart and took him to the main jail in the Tolbooth, a formidable stone fortress off High Street, near St. Giles's Cathedral. Thomas rode down the crowded street, avoiding merchants with pushcarts and servants shopping. He wanted Finnart to know exactly why he was being executed. Thomas pulled up in front of the six story stone building, noticing the metal bars over the windows, and hoped Finnart was miserable. He walked past the jougs, iron collars used to chain offenders to the exterior of the jail so the public could harass them. He wished Finnart were displayed, but knew that he was too valuable to risk displaying and escaping. Thomas knocked on the heavy oak door to the Tolbooth, studded with metal spikes and heavy locks, and was admitted. The guard led him to the iron room where Finnart was kept, waiting his execution. The room was dark, no fire lit, walls bare, ceiling naked timbers. *Good*, thought Thomas, very different from the luxury Finnart had appropriated for himself. Finnart was slumped against the far wall, next to the barred window.

"What the devil d'ya want now?" Finnart said, looking at Thomas with rage and venom. "You've already falsified my execution because you think I fucked the king. And you know I didn't. So it must be fear that I will tell the king what you really are."

Thomas kicked his legs, lashing out in frustration.

"You condemned yourself when you sided with the Douglases,"

Thomas said. "Making an enemy of me just hurried your execution, but the king would have learned the truth about you. With or without my spurring. And now you will suffer the fate of all those who conspire against the king."

"You can distort the charges all you want, Erskine," Finnart snarled. "But we both know this is because of your prick."

"Well, maybe if you had used yours, you wouldn't be in this predicament," Thomas smirked, relieved that his secret was dying with Finnart. He wouldn't have to worry about Finnart using it to gain James's favor again.

The next day, Finnart was given a traitor's execution—he was beheaded, drawn and quartered. And now Thomas could focus his attention to the woman who held the king's heart.

Chapter 47
The Queen Mother

THE SUMMER SURRENDERED TO autumn early in Scotland, green hills turning vibrant burning colors. Margaret was enjoying her time at Linlithgow, where Queen Marie and her new grandson were residing. Marie had remodeled the rooms from when they were Margaret's room, when she had given birth to James. The fireplace had been replastered and the Scottish coat of arms refreshed. Marie was resting under the cloth of gold canopy, her son asleep in the ornately carved cradle made by the French craftsman Marie's family sent. Seeing that she was not needed, Margaret climbed the spiral stairs into the tower where she had waited for her husband all those years ago, knowing he would not return from Flodden. She found the room much as it had been twenty-seven years ago, salmon colored flagstones leading to a large square window, flanked by benches with velvet cushions. Margaret sat and looked out over Loch Lomond. The same feeling of dread crept over her again, foreboding of war. She shook the feeling from her head. Her son wasn't at war with her brother, like his father had been.

Although, Margaret knew that could change in a moment with her mercurial brother. Harry was becoming less and less stable with each year that passed. After vacillating on the young de Guise girl, her brother had finally chosen a new bride, the sister of Duke William of Jülich-Cleves-Berge, who was a leader of the Protestants of western Germany. He felt this marriage would strengthen his position against potential attacks from Catholic France and the Holy Roman Empire. Anne of Cleves arrived in England in December of last year and married Harry on January 6th. Her daughter Margaret had been appointed as the chief of six great ladies of the household. Her letter described the new queen as looking old with skin pitted with small pox scars. Margaret was relieved to read that her daughter had moved to the Princess Mary's lodgings and was given a double lodging, consisting of two rooms and a privy on the floor below the princess. She bragged about gambling against Princess Mary and winning a decorative band.

In July, Harry had Cromwell, his chief minister and advisor, executed—his crime was presenting Harry with an ugly bride. Her impetuous brother then married seventeen-year-old Katherine Howard. Margaret shook her head; what her brother was thinking! He was forty-nine and marrying a babe. But the new queen was good to her daughter, gifting her a pair of beads with pearl pendants. Margaret was aggravated, though, that Harry was too busy with his own dramatic love life to find an attractive betrothal for her daughter, who had just turned twenty-three, almost too old to be desirable. She was still within the prime age to contract into a powerful family, but they needed to hurry. Of course her letters asking after a betrothal for her daughter were met with silence.

She sighed, wishing her brother and son would meet. She knew that if they did, neither one would be able to resist the other's charms. But James was being obstinate, which was angering her brother even more. The apprehensive feeling clung to her, just as it had before her husband James had left for Flodden.

She had been in Scotland for ten years when the Perpetual Peace, which her marriage was supposed to ensure, was broken. Her brother Harry had declared war on France in 1513 under the pretext of supporting the pope and Spain, but his real reason was to expand his territories on the continent. The English army had won several battles and was moving to repossess the territory of Aquitaine, which had been lost almost a hundred years earlier.

The French queen, Anne of Brittany, had sent a letter beseeching her husband's support, full of chivalric rhetoric and painting herself as the damsel in distress. The enclosed white glove and golden ring holding a light blue stone from Turkey roused Margaret's jealousy. Here was a foreign woman who knew nothing of the Scots, appealing to her husband's weakness, his chivalry, to protect her country.

And Margaret knew her husband would enter into warfare to protect this damsel's honor. It was a code that had long faded away, but her husband didn't seem to realize this. She wanted to shake him and tell him that the French queen was just using him, luring him in through his sense of courtliness. Margaret begged James not to retaliate.

"Is the queen of France more powerful to you than the cries of your own little son?" she asked him, thinking maybe his sense of family was stronger than his sense of honor.

But James supported France and sent correspondence that said if Harry did not desist from attacking France, James would declare war on England. *Politics were far stronger than family*, Margaret thought. Maybe she could use that to work in her favor.

"Then take me with you," she grabbed his arms, forcing him to listen to her. "It is said that my sister, Queen Catherine, will be there. And if we could meet, who knows what peace we could agree to."

But he only pushed her away. She should have known he would not allow her to negotiate peace. She was the damsel that needed saving, according to her husband's archaic ideology, she and Catherine could not negotiate for peace; that was a man's duty.

Still, she didn't give up. In the middle of the night, she began wailing and crying, startling her husband out of sleep.

"What is the matter, my hen?" he rubbed her back to sooth her as she flung her arms around his neck.

"It was the most troubling dream," she said in between sobs. "I saw you falling from a great height, your body bloody and covered in arrows, and one of my eyes plucked out. Then, my jewels turned to tears of pearls."

James, fifteen years her senior, patronized her and said, "My lemman, these visions are not truth, but the products of lack of sleep."

"But why do you prefer to please the Queen of France, rather than me, your wife and the mother of your children?" she whined, looking up at him, hoping her large, doe eyes would sway him.

"Ah lass," he sighed. "You know I need to support my allies against your bellicose brother. Don't give too much weight to these dreams. They are only figments of your overactive imagination."

Margaret lost her Tudor temper and snapped back, "Well, it isn't a dream that you only have one son—and he is ailing!" The young James was not a healthy baby. "What a lamentable day that will be when you leave him behind under the government of a woman to inherit a miserable and bloody war!" Margaret's ears were ringing under her sleeping bonnet—rage cutting off her hearing. If her husband wanted to be stubborn, he would learn just how stubborn a Tudor could be!

James was a very pious king, attending mass every day. Margaret and he walked from their royal chambers to St. Michael's chapel for evening vespers, her feet skipping over the ground. They turned down St. Katherine's aisle and approached the altar. The organ music filled the nave. Margaret looked at the vaulted arched in the ceiling, tied together with a crown of thorns, smiling at her own craftiness.

As they reached the altar and knelt to pray, an old man appeared from a niche in the church, dressed in a blue gown with a white linen cloth belted over his shoulder, in the style of St. John the Apostle. On his feet were high boots, but his head was bare, dark blond hair hanging past his shoulders. He bent over the king as the king's guards rushed in. James stopped them with the raise of his hand.

"Sir King," the old man croaked. "My mother sent me to instruct you not to go where you are planning. If you do, you will not fare well on your journey, nor will those who travel with you."

Margaret noticed the blood drain from her husband's ruddy face, taking on a pallid sheen. She pressed her face into her folded hands to stifle a giggle.

"Furthermore," the old man continued, "she forbids you to follow the counsel of women. If you do, you will be confounded and brought to shame."

Margaret mouthed the last words of the old man, having created the message for him to relay to her husband. James turned toward her, mild amusement on his face. She raised her eyes to him in a way she hoped expressed her innocence.

There was a scuffle as David Lindsay and the king's marshal attempted to apprehend the old man, but he was too spry and vanished from the church apse.

Despite all of her machinations, her husband departed to Edinburgh to gather his nobles and raise an army. He must have sensed the seriousness of facing the English army because he wrote his will and named her regent of James, so long as she didn't remarry. And then he marched south, with members from every noble house in

Scotland. The English, led by the Duke of Norfolk, the same earl who escorted Margaret to Scotland ten years earlier, engaged the Scots army. Within three hours, it was over. The Scots had lost the battle, their king, and most of their noblemen. That was almost thirty years ago, but standing in that spot, the same feeling of dread overwhelmed her.

Feeling like a foolish old hen for her trepidation, she headed back down to Marie's chamber. Her grandson was awake, cooing in his cradle. Margaret picked him up, smelling his lovely head. She tucked him into the crook of her arm.

"He loves you so, Queen Mother," Marie said, awake from her nap and embroidering with her ladies. Margaret couldn't understand how she could accept Elizabeth Beaton as one of her ladies-in-waiting, but she was grateful that at least it wasn't Maggie. She knew that her son still met with Maggie, but at least since Christmas, she hadn't been at court. Margaret guessed she had her new daughter-in-law to thank for that.

"I am so pleased that you have decided not to divorce your husband, Lord Methven," Marie continued. Margaret smiled, knowing the queen approved because it was a sin to divorce in the Catholic Church. Margaret, never wholly religious, appeased Marie by going to Catholic mass with her. She didn't want to disappoint her daughter-in-law by explaining that her son would not grant the divorce. *Let her believe I'm pious*, Margaret thought, still seething over her husband stealing her rents. The infidelity Margaret could shrug off; it was the Scots way that she had come to expect. But he was taking money from her lands, making her live like a pauper at her own son's court.

She studied Marie, who never complained about James's treatment of her, even though Margaret knew it was not the loving relationship she had hoped for. James visited his queen, hunted with her, but his emotional wall remained unscalable. This woman accepted his treatment—and his illegitimate children—far better than Margaret had accepted his father's.

"Marie," she said in surprise, studying her daughter-in-law's face for a clue to her real feelings about the king's infidelities. "Your face is fuller. And your décolletage. Are you expecting again?"

Margaret was rewarded with a small smile and a nod.

"I am," she beamed. Her ladies tittered around her in excitement. She hushed them. "It is very early, I have not bled in two months."

Margaret knew the risk of miscarriage was ever present, but she believed Marie was strong and healthy. She would give her son another heir.

1541

Chapter 48

JAMES

JAMES RODE TO ST. ANDREW'S, where Jamie and Prince James were housed in the royal nursery. Marie was expected to give birth in the spring and remained at Falkland with her ladies. The female energy still suffocated him, so he came to St. Andrew's.

More troubling was that he was being haunted at Linlithgow. As he slept in his own chambers, velvet curtains drawn, the ghost of Finnart appeared at his pillow, brandishing a sword. Finnart's eyes were black out, like charcoal, menacing. James cried out, alerting his chamber man as he jerked himself upright.

"*Schir*, are you troubled?" John Denniston said, peering through a crack in the bed curtains.

"Ay," James said, opening the curtains. "That bastard Finnart was in my bed! He cut off my right arm and then my left with his sword. Then he told me he would come back and strike my head from me!"

"Crivvens, my Lord!" John said. "You need a medicinal drink." He retreated and brought a decanter with a malted barley drink called whisky. James's father had purchased the liquor from the Guild of Surgeon Barbers. He claimed it calmed frayed nerves. *My nerves are definitely frayed*, James thought. He threw back the liquid and waited for the effect to knock him out.

In the morning, he rode to St. Andrew's, despite a forceful wind driving sleet off the North Sea. He pulled his overcoat up around his ears and urged his horse faster. He surprised the guards at the crenellated keep, they scrambled to take his horse and hustle him inside. James felt like his face was frozen, ice stuck in his trimmed beard.

He crossed the courtyard and entered the palace, climbing the spiral staircase to the inner chambers. Warmth wafted over his face as he opened the oak door to the inner room. A fire was roaring in the white-washed fireplace.

"James!" Maggie jumped up from her seat on a walnut bench under the diamond-leaded window. Her embroidery fell to the Turkish carpet.

"Father!" Jamie said, standing next to his mother. Maggie placed her arm around Jamie's shoulders. James noticed that she wore a French rounded hood in green velvet, which made her honey hair glow.

"I came to see my sons," James said, feeling awkward. "I didn't know you would be here."

"I also came to see my son," Maggie said, mirth oozing from her. James missed her fieriness, suddenly feeling the pressure release that he had suppressed. "What a surreptitious surprise," Maggie continued, a half smile on her face.

"Jamie, go and tell the nurse that the king wishes to see the prince," James said, patting Jamie's head as he passed out of the room. Then James was alone with Maggie, her energy warming him as much as the fire.

"You trimmed your beard," she said, tilting her head. James reached up to his beard, close cut to his chin.

"It is the latest style," he said, trying to be glib. Self-consciousness overcame him. "Do you like it?"

"You know I do," she laughed. "But does it matter?"

He crossed the room and took her hands. "You already know the answer," he said, pulling her to him. She relented and fell into his arms.

"Oh Mags, Mags," he said, breathing into her hair, pushing the hood off her head. "I need your strength. I'm so glad you're here. I've stayed away out of respect to Marie, and she is carrying another heir... but no one understands me like you."

Maggie pulled back to study James. He shifted his eyes away from her, but she pulled his face back to hers. Her green eyes read everything—all his fears, frustrations, the black moods that he fell into.

"You're feeling guilty?" she asked, but it was more a statement than a question. He hung his head and nodded.

"He has been coming to me in my dreams, telling me he will cut off my arms and head," James said.

"What happened with Finnart?" she guessed the source of his melancholy. He pulled away from her, looking through the ice clinging to the metal frame of the windows, chilling him to the bone.

"You know I will punish all of those who sided with Angus during my minority," he began, fumbling to straighten his thoughts into a coherent stream. She nodded, understanding his vengeance as well as he did.

"Finnart... well, he... he distracted me, taking me out to carouse for women," he said, feeling her flinch, but needing to say the truth aloud. "And as much as I didn't want to believe it, he murdered my cousin, the Earl of Lennox, over *land*," he said, anguish leaching from him. "Lennox was the only one who was looking out for my interests and Finnart executed him so he could gain rights to land."

"I didn't know that," Maggie said. "I thought he was your friend, and he pushed you to me, so of course I appreciated that."

"I had to execute him," James said, his head pounding from the weight of killing the man who had been once his friend. "He had ordered arrows to be shot from the tower of Linlithgow when I was present! And all I could think of was my great-grandfather's accidental death by cannon fire." He shuddered, knowing that if he had been killed, his son would have the same long minority that James endured. He would do anything he could to avoid that happening.

"He also sided with Angus and said he knew how to get close to me and convince me to forgive my stepfather," James said, his face screwed into a grimace. "Finnart supported his father, who, on his deathbed, urged me to forgive Angus. I can't trust anyone who wants me to forgive Angus."

Maggie nodded, sitting down at the window bench again. James wondered if she understood, really understood what Angus had stolen from him—his childhood, his belief in humanity—which no amount of money or land could purchase back. But there was one more person who needed to be punished, and he needed Maggie's help.

"There is one more Angus supporter who needs to be punished," he said, hoping Maggie would agree. "James Douglas, the Earl of Morton. When Angus was apprehended in Dalkeith in July after I escaped his custody, Morton gave him shelter and allowed him to flee to England."

"Are you going to try him for treason as well?" Maggie asked.

"No," James shook his head, "I'm going to do worse. I'm going to confiscate his earldom. And I'm going to award it to your husband."

Maggie's head snapped up from her embroidery, eyes wide with fear.

"My husband?" she said with contempt. "Why would you give it to him? He hates you."

James chuckled, understanding Robert's hatred.

"Because then he is going to resign the earldom to me and I will hold it for Jamie," he said, encircling her in his arms.

"But James," Maggie pushed him back. "You can't trust him. He is still a Douglas."

"I know," James said grinning. "But I'll make him believe that he will get the earldom, then I'm going to make him beg me to take it back—punishment for how he has treated you."

Maggie shook her head, "He will do anything in his power to keep the earldom once you award it to him. I still don't trust him— and I've had four of his children!"

"Even more reason to humiliate him," James said, kissing her hand. "He will see what happens when he mistreats my Magpie."

Maggie rolled her eyes, pretending to be irritated, but she couldn't hold it and burst into laughter herself.

"I'm glad you love me," she said, leaning into him and biting his chin through his beard.

"Yes, I do," he pulled her into his embrace. He knew his plan would work, betting on Morton and Robert's covetousness for land and wealth. Then he would rip it away—first from Morton, then from Robert. And the last link to Angus would be destroyed in Scotland. He would have peace in his kingdom.

Chapter 49

MARIE

HER FOURTH PREGNANCY FLEW by with ease, her body acting on memory. She retired to Stirling to celebrate Easter and prepare for her lying-in. Her husband had renovated his chambers in the palace. She walked through the thick walls of the forework and to the royal palace to the left of the outer courtyard. The façade was symmetric and neared the perfection of the palaces Marie frequented in France. The second story had five rectangular windows, with twisted columns in between, which held statues of St. Michael trampling Satan, Jupiter, Venus, Orpheus holding a lute, and King Fergus from Scotland's ancient past. She climbed the stairs on the far side of the courtyard to the terrace and into the Royal Palace.

She entered the King's presence chamber to see the latest innovation. She opened the heavy door and stepped into the bright room, walls white-washed, surrounded in a thick, blue ornate border that continued into the recessed windows. The tapestries had not yet been hung, still in route from Linlithgow. But the stark white walls highlighted the colorful ceiling, consisting of forty-five carved medallions, painted in bright yellows, greens, reds, and blues. She spun around to take in every medallion. Some carvings were dressed in contemporary dress, and Marie saw one who looked like the Queen Mother, holding a greyhound. She found her own likeness, red hair waving under the French style hood, facing James, who faced Madeleine next to him. Marie's heart dropped. Yet again, she was reminded that she was not the first choice for his queen. She straightened her shoulders. *No matter*, she thought, *I am the mother of his heirs*. Her hand went around her rotund belly.

She passed through the king's chambers and into her own chambers, where her ladies-in-waiting were preparing her chambers.

"Has the gardener planted the pear and plum cuttings that my mother sent from Joinville?" she asked as she sat at her desk to go through her correspondence.

"Oui, I mean yes, my Grace," Mahaut said. Marie smiled, knowing her French ladies were more comfortable speaking in their native tongue, but she encouraged them to speak Scots.

"Lady Seton," Marie said, smiling at the use of her lady-in-waiting's married name. "How is your husband, Lord Seton?" Marie had encouraged the widowed Scots nobleman to pursue the hand of her friend Marie Pieris, and he was successful! The new Lady Seton was also pregnant and due in the summer.

"He is well, your Highness," she giggled. Marie leafed through her correspondence, happy that she could help tame the unruly Scots men. Her sister's handwriting caught her eye, and she ripped the seal, anxious to drink in news of her sister's wedding to the Duke of Aarschot.

"A la Royne d'Escosse," the letter read, Marie was enveloped in her native language, which always reminded her of home. "Since by the goodness of God, I have obtained a good husband, I have not had leisure to write. You may be assured that I count myself lucky in having such a splendid establishment and a father-in-law that treats me well, it would take three sheets of paper to tell it all!"

Marie sighed, wishing her sister would have written three pages to describe her wedding, since she could not attend, feeling more than a little homesick. She loved her new homeland, but it did not replace the closeness of her family, especially when James was so moody—mercurial and melancholy after the execution of James Hamilton of Finnart. Marie didn't understand why he was taking the execution so badly, and her husband had little patience to explain it to her. But she believed that with another healthy child, maybe they would grow closer.

Easter morning, she prepared for mass, excited that all of James's family was under one roof—his mother, his sons, his daughter. The household streamed to the chapel from all parts of the castle grounds. Marie held Jacques in her arms, the energetic baby squirming, enjoying the warmth of the spring sun on her back, even if it was under a thin layer of clouds. Marie sighed, wondering if she would ever get used to the grayness of Scotland. Jamie walked ahead with his grandmother and father, and Marie could not help but notice how much Jamie resembled his father. He was also serious and quiet like James could be. Little Jean and her mother Elizabeth trailed behind Marie with her other ladies-in-waiting. They took their position at the front of the nave, before the stone railing that separated them from the altar. Marie could not help smiling as she thanked God for all of her blessings and prayed that they would continue, especially asking that God relieve her husband's black spells and gloominess.

After the Easter celebration, Marie's rooms were prepared for the birth of her child. A week later, her labor began and she gave birth to another son a few short hours later. When the castle heard the news, canons fired from the ramparts, announcing another heir. The baby boy was perfect again in Marie's eyes, ruddy skin and hair, strong cries. He was baptized three days later in the chapel and given the name Robert and the title Duke of Albany. From her great bed, Marie watched the sky above the castle explode with fireworks. But her joy was short lived.

On April 21, a messenger arrived from St. Andrew's to inform the new parents that Jacques was gravely ill. Marie's heart constricted, the pain of losing her baby Louis afflicting her anew.

"Go, James," she said, her voice tight. "Make sure he lives."

James departed, but the fear kept Marie from sleeping. There were so many dangers to a baby, and she was afraid a disease would take her son away from her. She cradled Robert, inhaling the smell of his downy hair, praying that God would spare Jacques. Unable to sleep, she paced with Robert until the wet nurse came to feed him, and even then she was reluctant to give up her baby.

No news came from St. Andrews for three days. Marie noticed that Robert was becoming lethargic. She tried to give him her milk, urging her nipple to his rosy lips, but he turned his face away and cried.

"Nurse!" Marie screamed through her chambers. The wet nurse ran in and curtsied. "He is getting weaker. Has he been feeding?"

"Yes, my lady," the wet nurse said, shifting from foot to foot. Marie suspected she was not telling the entire truth.

"Why is he not thriving?" she said in French, reverting to her mother language in her anguish. Mahaut translated for the wet nurse.

"He eats only a little and then refuses," the wet nurse said, tears spilling from her eyes. Marie wished her mother was there. Antoinette would know what to do, having given birth to twelve children—ten surviving into adulthood. What would her mother do? Marie tapped her head to think. She took the tiny baby from the wet nurse, holding him up to her shoulder, bouncing the baby, hoping maybe gas had built up in his belly.

"You must get him to eat," Marie said, again in French and Mahaut translated. "And report to Mahaut how long he feeds each time." She dismissed the nurse, turning on her heel. After the wet nurse left, Mahaut led Marie to her bed.

"My queen, you must rest," she said. "Your children will need you."

"They won't need me if they die," Marie said. Mahaut crawled into bed next to her and rocked her to sleep. At least, she must have fallen asleep because when she opened her eyes, the sun had broken the horizon. Marie rushed to the nursery, to find the wet nurse trying to feed Robert. He was so weak, he couldn't keep his eyes open, nor did he have the energy to suck.

"Mahaut!" Marie ran back to her chambers. "Send a messenger to St. Andrews. Tell the king his son is dying!"

Mahaut darted from the room to send a messenger, and Marie took her son into her arms. His arms were like white sticks, no flesh sticking to them. She smoothed his red hair and felt his skull bones.

"No, no, no, no, no," she cried, rocking her baby. He was too weak to cry even, veins crisscrossing his translucent eyelids. His breath became shallower with each step she took, singing to him in French, songs she sung to Louis as he took his final breaths in her arms. Her tears fell on his face, and she brushed them away, feeling how cool his skin was becoming. As the sun slipped below the horizon, he ceased breathing, his small lungs failing to expand against her hand. The scream came from deep within her, primal pain erupting as she collapsed to the floor, careful not to drop her precious baby.

317

Mahaut took the dead baby from her arms. Marie couldn't focus on anything except her pain radiating over her. James burst into her chambers and took the dead baby himself, curling over his dead son, his body wracked with lament.

"We've lost them both," he said, kissing Robert's cold forehead. Marie closed her eyes, unwilling to comprehend his words. He repeated them in French, and she could not deny that they were once again heirless. Marie took the lifeless baby from her husband and gave him to Mahaut once again. She sent everyone out of the chamber. James collapsed on the floor.

"They were my right and left arm! Finnart was right. He will cut off my head next," he cried. His moans filled the chamber. Marie wanted to jam her fists into her ears so she could not hear his pain, which was deeper, more intense than her own. It frightened Marie. She rushed to him, kneeling on the floor, wrapping him in her arms. He turned and clung to her, his tears soaking her dress. His sobbing shook both of them in a frenetic dance.

"It has all been for nothing," he cried, his voice rising in frustration. "Everything I have done for Scotland—it has come to nothing."

Even though Marie was also in the grip of grief, she knew she needed to be brave for both of them. The death of their children could send him into a black tailspin from which he might never escape. She needed to be strong for him, for Scotland. She pulled him up and wiped the tears from his face.

"James," she said. "We are both young and virile. God will send us more children."

He nodded, swallowing his grief, even as he doubted her. Marie exhaled, and prayed that she would be right.

———

Marie used the black velvet overgown and hood as her suit of armor. James seemed to regain his composure, pushing his grief somewhere deep within him as they followed the small lead coffins into Holyrood Church. Cardinal Beaton said the Requiem mass for the two souls. Marie remained stoic as James did, even though she longed to release the grief building within her. After the mass, as the coffins were moved to the family crypt, the choir sang *In Paradisum* in their boyish soprano, sweet and haunting. Marie felt the notes in her chest, wavering, and she realized her babies would never be able to sing, never run, never hug her—and she broke. The grief spilled over the top of the dam she had built, tears falling. Marie did not try to wipe them away or hide her sorrow. It flowed from her as the boys' words rolled over her—*May the angels lead thee to paradise, may the martyrs receive thee at thy coming.* But Marie didn't want to let them go, she didn't want to give them to the angels. She wanted to be selfish, keep her boys with her.

James took her hand, squeezing, but did not look at her. With that gesture, she knew that he was still with her, and that they would have another heir. Her boys were laid in the tomb next to Madeleine. *Look after them my sweet friend,* Marie prayed, gripping James's hand harder. Her boys would run and play with Madeleine in heaven, and she would create another heir with James. It would happen, and that thought allowed her to place her grief in the tomb with her babies, sealed up forever. The tomb was closed, signaling the end of the halcyon period of her marriage. No emotion played on her husband's face. And she feared even if she produced another heir, his heart would remain cold and closed.

Chapter 50

THE QUEEN MOTHER

MARGARET WATCHED THE TWO lead coffins containing her grand-sons placed into the family crypt at Holyrood, next to her son's first queen Madeleine and his great-grandfather James II with his wife Mary of Guelders. It was a small ceremony, no procession through the streets, no purchasing new mourning clothes for the royal household. The couple were too grief-stricken to face the public. Her son was vacant in his lack of emotion. Margaret almost wished for Maggie to pull him out of his misery. Almost.

In the Queen's inner chamber at Holyrood, Margaret was worried about Marie. Her son had been influencing her state of mind.

"James thinks they were poisoned," she said.

"No, no one would want to hurt those sweet babes," Margaret said, although she remembered when she thought her youngest son had been poisoned. After she fled Scotland and gave birth to her daughter, news came that her younger son Alexander had died. Delirious from giving birth, she wailed that the Duke of Albany had poisoned her son so that he may be closer to the crown. Now she realized that it was hysteria.

"The Earl of Arran might," Marie said, her voice bitter and flat. "He would want them dead. That would make him next in line for the throne."

"I thought my baby had been poisoned too," Margaret said, trying to keep from breaking down, the tears rimming her eyes. "But once my grief lessened, I saw how foolish that was. Why would you think your sons were poisoned?"

"The king said there was a pallor on Lord Robert that suggested poisoning. He said he had seen it before," Marie said. Margaret rubbed her eyes, weary of Scotland for hurting her and her son, but she also knew her son's paranoia, which was similar to her brother's.

"Marie," she said as gently as she could, stuffing her rising impatience with her son's suspicion of everyone. "Trust your faith, as you have encouraged me to do. God has taken these children which he had given to you, but I have confidence that he will soon give you others."

Marie summoned her strength at Margaret's mention of religion. Margaret knew she would be comforted by God in ways that Margaret was not equipped to comfort her daughter-in-law.

"Go distract yourselves in the rugged beauty of your country," Margaret suggested. "Take James hunting and turn to each other in your grief and then make another baby."

Marie smiled weakly and patted Margaret's hand. She hoped that Marie would take her advice and pull her temperamental son along out of his melancholy.

She returned to Methven and wrote her brother,

To the King's Grace,

my dearest brother,

I thank you for writing. Here has been great displeasure for the death of the Prince and his brother, both with the King and Queen; and I have been ever with them to comfort them, so that I have no leisure to write of my own matters. Please do not write to the King, my son, without my advice. His mourning is so great. And please, dearest brother, keep this letter secret or it may do me great harm from the Scottish nobles.

She sent off the letter, hoping her brother could read her handwriting, which had never been good, but was worse because of her grief. Margaret remembered each of her children's deaths, grateful for her two living children. Her daughter was still at Harry's court, and Margaret still was concerned for her future, especially since Harry has executed their noble cousin, Margaret Pole, for being in succession for the English crown. Even though her brother had sired a son and heir, his paranoia that a usurper would rebel against his reign consumed him. The Countess of Salisbury, as Margaret had always known her, was the niece of Richard III, whom Margaret's father had defeated at Bosworth, making Henry Tudor king. She and Margaret's mother, Elizabeth of York, were first cousins, their fathers Plantagenet brothers. The Countess of Salisbury had a claim to the English throne as a York descendent.

Margaret remembered the Countess of Salisbury at her father's court, and especially at her brother Arthur's wedding to the Princess Catherine of Aragon. Margaret had walked with her mother down the Walk, as the main aisle of St. Paul's Cathedral was known, admiring the tapestries hung between the thick pillars, which held up the Norman-style upper level gallery with its rounded arches. Timber stands covered in a red wool felt had been built to accommodate all of the guests who wanted to see the young prince marry.

Trumpets blared, announcing the arrival of the bride. Her brother Harry walked Catherine down the aisle of St. Paul's Cathedral, dressed in a white satin tunic embroidered with golden Tudor roses over white hose, with a white satin flat hat tilted to the side. The choir serenaded from the upper gallery. As brilliant as her brother looked, Margaret could not take her eyes off the exotic Spanish princess. Catherine's dress was white satin, embroidered with pearls and gold thread along the narrow square neckline. Her skirt was held out stiff in a conical shape that Margaret had never seen before. She would learn later that this was because of the farthingale, which she would wear when she met her Scots king. Catherine's strawberry blond hair spilled down her back in gentle waves, a symbol of her virginity. On her head she wore a white silk veil that fell to her waist which had a border of gold and precious stones. She was delicate with pearl skin, bright blue eyes, and a small, upturned nose. The Countess of Salisbury held Catherine's train as she walked the long length of the cathedral on the red carpet. Arthur, waited on a platform built in front of the altar with the Archbishop of Canterbury, who wore the tall mitre of his station, and eighteen other papal dignitaries. Arthur, her favorite brother, with his reddish hair, small eyes, a high-bridged nose, also wore white cloth of silver doublet and coat embroidered with golden Tudor roses. Margaret could see the joy on her quiet brother's face.

Margaret watched the three-hour marriage ceremony with her parents from behind a lattice screen. Margaret stifled a yawn more than once. Finally, her parents stepped from behind the screen to bless the couple, and Catherine and Arthur turned to the crowd and joined hands as husband and wife. They walked down the platform where a mountain had been built out of jewels and gold. Atop the mountain was a fountain, from which wine flowed. Margaret filled a cup and gulped it, making her feel light-headed.

The royal family, along with guests headed toward Lambeth Castle, the archbishop's residence for a banquet and dancing. The front gatehouse, with its twin round towers and crenelated parapet constructed of deep red brick, was the model for her brother's great palace Hampton Court. After the entire party had eaten, Harry and Margaret took the dance floor to entertain the new princess. Margaret, wearing a crimson velvet gown, embroidered at the square collar in gold, curtsied to her brother, her trumpet sleeves brushing the ground. Her devious brother, after bowing, did not take her hand, but proceeded to strut around the dance floor, stripping off his tunic and dancing in his chemise, much to the delight of the audience. Margaret flushed with embarrassment and anger—how dare he embarrass her in front of the new princess? But her brother was staring at the young princess, awed by this exotic princess's beauty and grace. Margaret knew that was when his infatuation with her began, although no one at that time knew that Arthur would be dead within six months.

From the day of the wedding, the Countess of Salisbury was loyal to Catherine, falling in love with her just as much as Harry had. The Countess and Harry often did not see eye-to-eye regarding her family and lands, but she remained faithful to Catherine and Princess Mary, being appointed Mary's governess.

When Harry divorced Catherine and declared his own legitimate daughter a bastard, the Countess refused to give Harry back a gold plate and jewels when Catherine died, wanting them to go to Princess Mary. Her sons did not support the divorce and marriage to Anne Boleyn and backed the northern rebellion, the Pilgrimage of Grace, in 1538. The Countess was arrested in 1539 for supporting Catholicism and the rule of her son Reginald and the king's Catholic daughter Mary and put in the Tower, stripped of her title and lands. Margaret knew the Countess was well taken care of in the tower, received extensive clothing and fabrics. She assumed her brother would let the sixty-seven year old woman live the remainder of her life in captivity.

That's why it was such a shock that her brother had executed the Countess without stating her crime. Margaret was horrified when the Scots ambassador wrote to her about the bungled execution, the inexperienced executioner hacking at her head and shoulders because the elderly woman refused to place her head on the block. It sickened Margaret, who had also feared reprisal from the Scots for marrying Ard. But she was safe at Methven and out of the court's capricious eye. Still, she had seen too much death in her lifetime.

During the summer and into autumn, her son's behavior was becoming increasingly troubling. He was antagonizing Harry over church matters, refusing to hand over Catholics who fled to Scotland for protection. Harry was also antagonizing the French, preparing to invade, and he was upset over Scottish raiders at the borders, which James had done nothing to remedy. Now her brother wanted to meet James in York, and James was equivocating. Margaret hoped the two could meet and come to a lasting peace between the two kingdoms, as her father planned when sending her north to marry James IV all those years ago. Harry brought his entire court, which Margaret knew included his queen and her ladies-in-waiting, one of whom was her daughter. Margaret's whole body vibrated with joy when she thought of seeing her son and daughter together. But, even though her brother remained at York for the entire month of September, her son never intended on meeting him.

David Lindsay wrote to her from Falkland, where the king and queen were spending the summer hunting and enjoying the country, and Margaret hoped, each other. But when she read David's letter, she found that was not the case. David described jealous outbursts by her son. Marie, ever the courtier, was very friendly with the men at James's court. Too friendly, according to David, explaining that James argued with her in front of the court, embarrassing her and causing her to retire to her chambers. Margaret sighed, hoping this riff wouldn't prevent another child.

Her heart ached, and so she went to her bedchamber. Her head didn't feel right, thoughts slow to connect. She called in a messenger to ask her son to come to her, hoping she could talk some sense into him, but knowing that he probably wouldn't listen to her. She laid down in her bed, listening to the rain fall outside her window, and never woke up, finally retiring from the nasty Scottish politics.

Chapter 51

MAGGIE

MAGGIE COULD NOT BELIEVE the Queen Mother was dead. The woman who saved her from becoming a mother too early and banished her when Maggie fell in love with her son was no longer able to influence Maggie. She felt sorry for the once queen, set aside by her own husbands and son, harboring no ill will for the woman in the end.

She traveled to Perth for the funeral at James's request. The Charterhouse, where a royal Stewart mausoleum was, sat under the shadow of St. John's Kirk, an imposing medieval church, built more like a fortress than the lighter cathedrals further south. James I and his wife, Joan Beaufort, were buried in an elaborate stone sarcophaguses made out of blue marble adorned with the heraldic crown of Scotland with alternating crosses and fleur-de-lis from which hung a banner with the rearing lion, its tongue curling from its mouth.

A black velvet pall covered the Queen Mother's coffin, her initials embroidered in golden thread, laced with the Tudor rose and the Stewart thistle. James collapsed into Maggie's arms when he saw her. She glanced around, but Marie was absent. The king's groom John Tennent and his new familiar, Oliver Sinclair, were standing near him.

"Will you stay with me?" he asked her, and she could not say no.

He brought her to Scone Abbey, ancient site where the first King of the Scots conquered the Picts. James dismissed Oliver and John, and Maggie was alone with him for the first time since the death of both his princes.

"So much death," he said, burying his head in her lap. "How can

I create a modern Scotland if everyone keeps dying?"

"You have eight children still living," Maggie said, smoothing his hair.

"But none are legitimate," he cried. "And now even my own mother has betrayed me again. Before she died, she asked me to forgive Angus and allow him to come home."

"Then she didn't know you at all," Maggie said, indignant that the woman who drove James away from her was the same woman who broke his heart over and over.

"She also wants me to give my bastard sister her jewels," he said, bitterness hardening his heart. Maggie held her tongue at the mention of his sister. She was not a bastard; her only crime was having Angus as a father. James sat up, almost knocking Maggie in the chin. "I can't give her my mother's jewels. What if Angus intercepts them and uses them to make war with Scotland? I despise him."

"I know," Maggie said. "So keep the jewels! Use them to strengthen Scotland for your children as your mother should have done for you."

"Ah Mags, you know my heart better than I do, you ruthless knave!" he laughed, a sad, quiet sound. "I would hate to make an enemy of you."

"I told you long ago that you would never get rid of me," Maggie said, self-satisfied warmth spreading across her cheeks. "And I keep my promises."

He leaned into her, his lips lingering on hers. She responded to him as she always had, with uncontrolled animalism.

"It is time to call your husband to remit what I have given him," he said when he dragged himself away from her, heat lingering between them.

"So soon?" she murmured, her eyes closed to savor his kiss.

"Yes and in front of the entire court," he said, his voice a low growl of anger. "But first we will mourn my mother before getting back to ruling the kingdom."

Dinner was an intimate gathering of James and his men, Maggie allowed into their masculine circle. Oliver and John entertained James by telling stories from happier times.

"Remember the joke you played on the tinker?" John said. James nodded, smiling into his cup.

"What did you do?" Maggie placed her hand on his arm. He rubbed his beard against her hand.

"James asked the tinker for an ale, separating himself from the hunting party," John laughed. "The tinker said he'd never seen the king—not realizing who he was drinking with!"

James coughed and continued, "I told him that the king was near on a royal hunt and suggested we try to find them. He asked how we would recognize the king, and I said he will be the one wearing his hat. When we rode up to the party, everyone removed their hat," James looked at John. "Do you remember what that cheeky tinker said?"

"He looked at you and said, 'Then it must be either you or me, for all but us are bareheaded!'" John said and Maggie burst out laughing.

"It serves you right for tricking him," she nudged James and was rewarded with a true smile.

"And remember when we were hunting in the woods," Oliver laughed at John, "and you swore you had killed a wild boar."

"Ay," John picked up the story, "but I was too sottered to realize it was a poor wife's sow. And James grasped the nettle for killing her Christmas dinner!" The two of them pounded the table in laughter, doubling over. Maggie looked at James, who smiled, but his eyes were blank, shut down. He poured himself more whisky from a decanter.

"Don't," Maggie covered his chalice with her hand, which he pushed away. She set her lips, infuriated that he wasn't listening when all she wanted was what was best for him.

"It helps me handle my sorrows," he said after downing the brown liquid.

"It creates more sorrows!" she said, crossing her arms and glaring at him.

"You sound like my wife," he said, his mouth slurring the words.

"Your wife?" Maggie jumped up. "Fine. I'll go away from you, just like you do to your wife." Oliver and John looked at each other, saying nothing. Maggie stormed out of the room, locking the door to the bedchamber she shared with James. She laid on the bed and waited for him to try to get in, but no one came to the door.

She must have fallen asleep, and awoke to a jangling at her chamber door. The chamber was dark, the fire gone out. The door swung open, and James stood outlined by the torches held by John and Oliver.

"How did you get in?" Maggie said, still confused by sleep. James lumbered over to the bed, leaning into her.

"I'm the king," he said, eyes heavy with drink. "I always get what I want."

Maggie rolled her eyes and saw Oliver and John were still in the doorway.

"You can go now," Maggie said, her voice hard. "You have done enough by pouring him drinks."

James rolled over onto his back and laughed as the two men disappeared.

"Oh Mags, you know no one can make me do anything I don't already want to do," he said, grasping her arm and pulling her to him. "I don't want to fight with you, nor do I want to treat you like my wife. I want you to be my Magpie, my goldfinch, my whatever—as long as I can see the fire inside of you."

The fury in Maggie dampened, but the passion that James always kindled in her ignited.

"I only want what is best for you," she said, folding her arms to signal that she was still mad.

"I know, Mags, but I'm still stubborn and like to fight with you," he said, his hand winding around the back of her head, threading through her unbound hair. "It makes the sex better."

"You're so vulgar," she said, but the sting was gone from her words. She grinned as she studied his crooked nose, fleshy lips that yielded against hers.

"But you like it," he said and pressed those lips against hers. Of course she responded.

———————

James stayed at Perth, hunting during the day with his men and coming to her at night. He surprised her by coming into her chamber when the sun was struggling against the thick gray clouds. He slumped into a chair, holding a letter, still wearing his hunting clothes.

"My wife is angry," he said. Maggie raised her eyebrows, enjoying the distress caused to the woman who held the position that she

329

would have held, had she been a royal princess.

"She is suspicious of why I have remained in Perth so long," James smoothed her letter out on the desk.

"She has every right to be, you *swicker*!" Maggie laughed, using the Scots word for cheater. James snorted but made no comment since he knew she was right. "Let's write her a very nice love letter to ease her mind."

James picked up a quill to write. Maggie leaned over his shoulder, pressing herself against him.

"You know, I'm not going to be able to write with your breasts against my back," he said, inhaling her hair.

"Just write what I tell you," she giggled. "My dearest and most beloved queen…"

He snorted and said, "My royal queen and wife…. That's more my style."

"Fine," Maggie said. "Now write: I have received your letter…"

"Which it so pleased you to write to me," James added his own biting sarcasm. Maggie shook her head at his acerbity.

"Those who have told you that I mean to stay away have lied, for I have no other thoughts but of being with you on Sunday," Maggie dictated.

"Sunday?" James looked up at her in surprise.

"Yes, it is time to get back to ruling your country and producing another heir," Maggie said, sliding her arms around his neck even as she pushed him to return to his wife.

"You sound just like Diane de Poiters," he said, recalling Henri's lover who sent the future king of France to his wife Catherine de Medici so he could produce a legitimate heir.

"Who?" Maggie asked, not familiar with the intrigues of the French court, not needing to know all the machinations of that foreign court.

"Never mind," he said, his mouth on hers.

A few weeks later, Maggie's husband was summoned to Falkland. He insisted on her accompanying him, hoping her presence would soften the king's judgement. They rode amblers to the hunting palace near Loch Leven. Maggie had made the journey many times, her horse knowing the route by heart. Upon arriving at the castle, they were shown into the king's presence chamber, and saw the whole court assembled. The queen wrinkled her nose in distaste when she saw Maggie, but made no other indication of her displeasure. Maggie guessed she was to blame for James sending her favorite lady-in-waiting back to France. *Fine*, Maggie thought, *she can think what she wants*. It didn't matter to Maggie.

Thomas Erskine stood behind the king. Maggie observed him with narrowed eyes. Something about her cousin was perplexing, but Maggie couldn't put her finger on exactly what. She remembered him coming around Stirling, invited at holidays by her father. He was always awkward and discomfited around her.

"Sir Robert Douglas of Loch Leven," Thomas announced. "Do you know the reason for your presence before the king?"

Robert glanced at Maggie and she remembered their conversation before they came.

"He's taking back the earldom," he had told her, which she already knew. Her husband had become insufferable after being granted the earldom of Morton. He gloated that he was in the king's favor more than she, and Maggie had to bite her tongue. He met with a notary before he went to Falkland to record that he was resigning the earldom out of fear and dread for his life. Maggie rolled her eyes at his distress and paranoia.

"Ay," her husband responded to Thomas. He knelt on the slate floor, the carpets removed to make him as uncomfortable as possible. "I am resigning the earldom of Morton to his royal majesty."

Maggie enjoyed the humiliating submission of her husband, resigning the Earl of Morton title and lands that he so desired. His eyes locked with Maggie, full of malice and rage. She held herself erect so as to not flinch under his acerbic stare.

James raised his hand, the benevolent monarch, and Robert rose from the floor.

"It has been recorded and witnessed," Thomas said, his eyes lingering on James. What Maggie found odd was the look that flashed across his face. The look expressed everything that Maggie felt for James—desire, longing, lust. Suddenly, Maggie knew why Thomas was so awkward. It all clicked into place.

1542

Chapter 52

THOMAS

WHEN ROBERT DOUGLAS OF Loch Leven remitted the earldom of Morton, Thomas felt the weight of someone's stare. He looked up and saw Maggie's head tilted in curious surprise and knew that his mask had slipped. Maggie had seen his desire for James. Blood thundered in Thomas's head. She was more dangerous than Beaton—she had the king in his bed and Thomas knew she would expose him, just as she had when they were children. He would have to deal with that later, because there was another disruption on the boarders—antagonized by the king himself.

The situation between Scotland and England was precarious. Henry sent a letter with a Scots messenger to meet with him during the summer progress at York. Cardinal Beaton made Thomas promise he would dissuade James from meeting Henry in England—he feared that James might decide to break with the Catholic Church as his uncle had done. Thomas knew James would not benefit from breaking with the church, that he was dependent on their revenue due to his immense building projects to bring Scotland into the modern era. But Beaton used his leverage and Thomas had to comply and keep James in Scotland, which proved easy, especially when King François sent a letter thanking James for not going to England to meet his uncle and that he would supply troops and ammunition if his uncle invaded because of it.

James, never one to be told what he should do, replied in his dry Scots humor, "Tell my uncle that I am aggrieved that he is so far North, away from the places where he is accustomed to take his pleasure. And since he is so close to my kingdom, he should participate in all that this realm affords for the season; and therefore I send certain falcons by Adam Logan, the bearer, my servitor, so that he may hunt and be comforted."

"Sire," Thomas held his quill, trying to take a diplomatic view. "You should not agitate your uncle."

"My kingdom is as strong as his kingdom with the support of my French father," James had replied and stormed out of the office. "Let him attack Scotland and see what happens!"

The hairs on the back of Thomas's neck had risen, gooseflesh tingling with foreboding. And when the ambassador came back from London, Thomas felt even more unnerved. Henry told the Scottish diplomat that he had the same rod in store for James that he put to his father, a blatant reference to Flodden. Thomas knew that these two kings were far too stubborn for either to back down; their egos were too enormous.

While the King of England waited in York for James, the situation on the borders became even more unstable. Scots reivers had entered England and murdered four gentlemen before pillaging a border city. The English marsh warden ordered the burning of Scots crops and homes in the disputed territory.

Upon Henry's return from the humiliating trip to York, he discovered his young wife, Catherine Howard, had not only been betrothed to a man named Dereham and had sexual relations with him before her marriage to the king, but she also made a cuckold of him with his favorite courtier Thomas Culpepper. A letter written in the queen's hand was found in Culpepper's chamber, and one of her ladies-in-waiting saw Culpepper leaving the queen's chamber by a back stairway. Catherine was stripped of her title and warded in Syon Abbey, and both Dereham and Culpepper were found guilty of treason and executed. Catherine was beheaded in February.

As Thomas wrote a letter to update Beaton on the situation in Scotland, a man-in-arms announced he had a visitor. Who could be visiting him? He told his visitor to be shown in, and Maggie walked through the arched doorway.

"Hello, cousin," she said, her eyes twinkling with mischief. He stood so abruptly that his chair banged against the stone tiles. "I need to speak with you about a personal matter," she continued, eyeing the man-at-arms who remained in the chamber. Thomas froze, knowing what her visit was about, but dreading the discussion. Would she blackmail him as Beaton had done? What would her price be?

Despite his uneasiness, he dismissed the guard. Maggie sat on one of the hard wooden stools he had brought in after Finnart's confrontation to deter visitors. She wore a rounded hood in the style of Queen Marie. It was black, edged in gold braiding, and curved around her ears, revealed the front her golden hair. Thomas wondered if James had bought it for her.

"Cousin," he said, hoping she couldn't hear the anxiety in his voice, "what a pleasant surprise!"

She smirked, knowing he was lying. He wanted to blurt out an explanation of his feelings, issue a judgement of himself before she had a chance.

"I'm sure you know why I am here," she said. He did, but shook his head, not trusting himself to speak. "Thomas," she leaned forward and took his hand. He wanted to jerk away, her touch scalding him, but he forced himself to remain calm.

"I saw the way you looked at James," she said, and Thomas heard the pity in her voice.

"I have no idea what you mean," Thomas said, pulling his hand away from her. "I am the king's loyal servant and that is all."

"I'm not judging you, or calling you a poofter," she laughed, using the Scots slang for homosexual. "I understand that people are attracted to James. He has a force to draw people to him with no effort."

"I admire the king, and that is all," Thomas repeated, hoping he seemed indignant at her suggestion, when he was aggravated that she had seen his true feelings for the king. Maggie, who saw through him when she was a child, who shared the king's bed more than even his wife.

"I know how you feel because I feel the same way about him," she said, crossing her arms, signaling that this was not an argument.

"What is it that you need, Lady Douglas?" he said, staring into her green eyes, letting her know that he would not be intimidated by her as others were. He had gotten rid of the king's favorite minion. He could get rid of her if needed as well. It would be more difficult, but it could be done.

"Fine," she said, her eyes hardening. "I also need to discuss the king's son Lord James, the Prior of St. Andrew's."

So, Thomas thought, *she wants to get her bastard legitimized.* He remained silent, staring down at the slight woman. He knew that despite her stature, she was intimidating, her character as strong and harsh as any Scots man.

"Since the death of the two princes, would the king be open to legitimizing his sons?" Maggie asked. But Thomas knew this was no harmless request. She was asking because she knew the king was not sleeping with his wife. And Thomas would not advance her child, would not approach the king with the request.

"Of course," he smiled in her face. "I will ask the king upon his return to Edinburgh. He is hunting with his queen at Falkland right now."

Thomas hoped that Maggie would flinch at the mention of James being with his wife, but she was expressionless. He wondered if her blood was made of iron, cold and unmoving.

"I thank you, cousin, for all of your efforts to serve your king," she said, lingering on *serve,* accusing him of sodomy with her eyes. At least, that is what Thomas felt. It wasn't until she had been seen out that Thomas could clear his mind. Maggie was dangerous—to the king and also to Thomas. She needed to be stopped. He would call in a favor.

———————

Beaton returned from France in April and Thomas requested a meeting with him. He traveled to St. Andrew's, where Beaton had been holding his own ecclesiastic court. He was escorted into Beaton's chambers. The cardinal, too busy to properly greet Thomas, or maybe feeling he didn't need to, waved Thomas over without lifting his gaze from his paper.

"The king of England is angry," Beaton said, "over the refusal of our majesty to turn over Catholic fugitives."

"Yes," Thomas responded. "The English king has written that if our king would reject the true religion, he would be a much more reliable neighbor."

"I hope you dissuaded James of that," Beaton's beady eyes drilled into Thomas. He recoiled at the criticism of his diplomatic skills. Beaton didn't trust him, even after Thomas supported the prosecution of heretics, many of whom Thomas did not believe supported Protestant efforts in Scotland.

"Of course," Thomas said, hanging rancor on the small words. "I went to London at the end of February and had an audience with King Henry. I proposed a joint border commission for redress, but the king was angry over the men who fled religious persecution who are harbored in Liddesdale, whom he called rebels and demanded their return. But he did agree to a commission, so I will return later this year, when the king commands me." Beaton scoffed, anger flaring at Thomas's intimation that he would only obey the king. But Thomas needed Beaton's help.

"There is another matter we need to discuss which arose in your absence," Thomas said, savoring the surprise on Beaton's face. Beaton assumed he had known everything that happened in Scotland while he was abroad. "The king has not been spending his nights with the queen, he has taken up his relationship with Lady Douglas of Loch Leven."

"Why is that my concern?" Beaton asked, knowing the king's extramarital affairs.

"Because as long as he is spending his nights with his whore," his mouth twisted with acrimony, "she is threatening the monarchy, keeping him from producing a legitimate heir, while pushing her own son to be legitimized. And she is leading the king's soul to be damned to eternal condemnation."

Beaton smirked at the last point. Even though he was a cardinal in the Catholic Church, he did not believe all the rhetoric applied to himself and the king.

"I will put a stop to Lady Douglas and convince the king to return to his wife," he said, dismissing Thomas before adding, "Your concern for the king's soul is charming, given your own desires."

Thomas saw Beaton's menacing grin as the door to his office shut Thomas out. He hoped he could trust Beaton.

Chapter 53

MARIE

THE NEW YEAR FOUND Marie alone at Linlithgow, the constant dreariness of the country wearing on her cheery disposition. She has written her husband an exacting letter asking for the reason he was delayed in Perth. She received a sarcastic reply, but he came home shortly afterward. He was not home long, spending many nights away from her—and she could only guess with whom he spent them. It felt like she would remain alone in Scotland, maybe even put aside in the same manner his uncle had put aside Catherine of Aragon and Anne of Cleves. She shuddered at the thought, still believing her marriage to James could be a partnership, if only he would let her in.

She oversaw the beautification of Linlithgow, concentrating on the chapel. She had their combined royal arms cast in lead, painted, and gilded. Also, new stained glass windows were commissioned and mounted in the chapel, and the ribs of the vaulted arches were painted a bright azure. This kept her hands and mind busy those lonely days.

A letter arrived from her mother when she had gotten into a rhythm by herself. Just seeing her mother's elegant handwriting stirred her heart. She ripped the seal open.

A la Royne D'Escosse,

her mother began.

Our petit fils is well and growing big. He is beginning to

*understand and almost knows his paternoster. He is a pretty and
good child. Your son will soon be a man, if we can get a painter,
you will see how beautiful he is. He is the best of children, big
and healthy, and should live to be a joy to you."*

Marie was plunged into new grief, thinking about her three sons
she had already lost, knowing they would never reach six years of
age, nor would their portraits be painted. Three lost sons, and her
only living son so far away. It had been over three years since she
had seen her son François, and she counted on her mother's letters
to apprise her of François's growth and progress.

Enclosed was also a letter written by her son's nurse, Madame
Tetault, François's signature scrawled, almost illegible, at the end.

A la Royne Madame,

the letter read. Tears welled up in Marie's eyes, and she looked
up to keep them from falling, not ready to open the floodgates. She
continued reading,

*Grandfather has given me a horn for hunting. Will you send a
horse for me and Madame Tetault? You must come see me and
bring the king. Grandmere will send a painting of me to you and
you will see how big I am! She says I am so handsome with my
haircut like my uncles.*

She ran her fingers over his name, impressed into the paper by
his tiny hand. It probably wasn't so tiny anymore. She was indebted
to her mother for taking her son in, her father spoiling him with
presents and late night snacks, but she wanted to be the one raising
him. If only he weren't part of the royal family of France, then she
could bring him here to Scotland and be much comforted. The
Scots people were kind to her, but she had no one in whom to con-
fide, no one who would wrap her in their arms as she cried over her
dead boys. Her husband should have done it, but he didn't.

News from the court of England pronounced the execution of
the former queen Catherine Howard for infidelity. Marie wished
that men were held to the same standard. Women were executed for
adultery, but a king's infidelity was praised, lauded for his virility.

But as the frost melted across Scotland, so did her husband. He took her hunting with his men at Falkland. She wore a new riding gown, crimson velvet, a gift from her contrite husband. The dogs were released to corner the harts. Once the dogs had bayed the animals, she and James cantered towards them, Marie feeling the chilled air across her face. Her toes and fingers were tingling as she pulled her bow back and let the arrow fly. It connected with the red rump of the hart.

"Fine shooting!" James yelled and dismounted to deliver the ritual death cut across the neck. The forester collected the deer to bring back to Falkland.

After the dinner, James remained with her instead of retiring with his men. He led her to her bedchamber and undressed her without saying a word. Marie would prefer to speak with him and develop emotional intimacy, grieve their sons together, but if he wanted physical intimacy first, she would allow that. His hands were clumsy, the result of all the whisky he drank, fumbling with her laces to get her out of her kirtle. She helped him undo the stays and slipped the kirtle and chemise over her head. He ran his hands down her body, over her breasts, kissing her as he went. She removed his doublet, hose and chemise so that they were both naked. When he entered her, she almost wept, not from physical pain, but releasing the emotions that she hadn't been able to express—fear for their future, sorrow over their lost sons, frustration over his lack of intimacy with her.

He moaned and she moved her hips against his, feeling the tension build, the wave mounting in the base of her abdomen. She forgot about everything outside of the two of them. If she could produce another heir, he would come back to her. This moment was the only thing that mattered, this joining which was natural and uncomplicated by politics. She felt the rhythm they created together and was comforted. He tensed like a cat ready to pounce and she wanted to please him, make him happy.

As he released into her, he said, "Oh Mags!" and collapsed onto her. Marie went cold. She realized tonight hadn't been about Marie at all. *She* occupied his mind. He rolled off her and went to his bedchamber to sleep. Marie felt more alone than she ever had in her life.

The next morning, she did not mention what he said the night before. Marie realized that it would only push him further away, and he seemed to want to be with her. So she swallowed the hurt, insecurity, and self-doubt in order to remain the regal queen on the outside.

———————

When spring blew across the northern island, Marie knew that she was expecting again. But this pregnancy was different from her previous ones. She consulted with her doctor, who had come from France, about her sickness. He advised her to avoid rich meats, and only eat broth, gruel, and fruit. By summer, her pregnancy was known throughout the country and abroad. James had a change of attitude and remained devoted to Marie, taking her to a shrine at Peebles, south of Edinburgh. The bones of Saint Nicholas were housed at the shrine in a square, thick-walled monastery. Marie knelt at the shrine and prayed for a healthy baby. James knelt next to her, taking her hand and praying with her. While she was enjoying the attention from James, his uncle was causing trouble again to the south.

Chapter 54

JAMES

JAMES WAS ELATED, HIS forces had beaten his uncle's at Haggon Rig! When François declared war on the Emperor, James knew Henry would retaliate against Scotland, knowing France would be unable to provide military support to Scotland. On August 24, the English Warden of the Eastern Marshes, along with Angus and his brother George, entered Scotland with three thousand men. James's nephew, the Earl of Huntly, was in Kelso with two thousand men. Huntly and James had gotten close during his imprisonment by Angus. When Huntly's grandfather and guardian died in 1524, Angus assumed guardianship of Huntly, keeping him under guard with James. Huntly's mother, James's half-sister, worked with his mother to free her son, and was frustrated with the failed efforts. But when Angus fled to England after James escaped, Huntly freed himself and assumed responsibility for his earldom. James provided the support that Huntly needed to be successful. He appointed Huntly to be trained under Moray to be a commander.

Huntly rolled out of the fortified village of Kelso on foot with two thousand men as the sun broke the horizon. He ordered his men to charge, scattering the sheep and cattle that the English had attempted to steal. The English soldiers broke rank and fled. The Scots pursued and captured three hundred English men, including Robert Bowes, the Warden of the Eastern Marshes. Angus was almost captured, a lasso caught around his neck, but he sliced the rope with his dagger and escaped once again to England.

Even though James had been thrilled that his forces defeated his uncle, he had to be diplomatic in his letter.

"Right excellent brother and my royal uncle," James dictated, and Thomas furiously wrote. "We have just received the Master of Household a report of the displeasure and taking of prisoners at Haggon Rig, which is believed by my royal uncle to have been caused by an invasion by Huntly. My Master of Household has found a report by your servant, Sir Robert Bowes, showing the whole scheme was devised by the English warden. The prisoners were taken in defense of my country, not in aggression. Even though the English warden called for the invasion of my sovereign country, I very much am of the same mind for peace."

Thomas scattered sand to dry the ink and handed the paper to James to sign in his own hand. He trusted that Thomas would deliver the letter, and while he waited for a response, he rode with the royal guard to Falkland, with a very special prisoner—James Douglas of Parkhead, Angus's cousin. He rode up to Parkhead, hands bound behind his back, head bowed.

"You know there is a warrant out for your arrest for the treasonable planning to murder your sovereign," James said. Parkhead had been charged with Finnart for conspiracy to murder the king.

"*Schir*," he groveled. "I can tell you all of Angus's plans and who his spies are in Scotland if you spare my life."

"So you are eager to show fealty to your king, now that you have been captured?" James said, keeping his voice even, not wanting to show his excitement at finally capturing a Douglas traitor. He would have preferred to have Angus in custody, but Parkhead would do.

"But *Schir*," Parkhead leaned over the horse, holding up his bound hands. "You know as well as I how forceful Angus can be."

James tried to laugh, but it came out a harsh snort. "You willingly took the position in my household of Master of the Cellar while Angus kept me captive."

"I had no choice but to flee to Angus in England," Parkhead's voice rose with naked desperation. "My family has suffered, my lord, because of my last name."

"Your family has suffered because of your avarice and treachery. You have been put to the horn more than once, Parkhead," James said, fighting against his Tudor temper. "You were called to testify in the trial against Lady Glamis and you tucked tail and fled, just like Angus."

"Aye, my lord, and the Lady and her second husband are now dead!" Parkhead pleaded. "I feared for my life. Even Finnart was executed. Can you forgive me for fleeing?" A shiver went up James's spine as Finnart's burly face swam before him, thick eyebrows knitted together, daring him to execute another man because of his association with Angus. He shook the image from his head.

"All of those who sided with Angus will pay one way or another," James said, his head pounding, beating him down with all of the betrayals he suffered. He needed to see Maggie, to feel her strength. He spurred his horse forward, leaving Parkhead to wonder if James would be merciful or vengeful.

After warding Douglas in the keep of Falkland, he sent word for Maggie to meet him there. When she arrived in his chambers, she was already on fire.

"You engaged your uncle in battle?" she stood apart from him, hands on her hips. James laughed at how quickly word traveled in Scotland.

"Yes, lovit," he pulled her to him with one arm around her waist. "And we won." He pressed his lips on hers, but she broke away.

"You know he is going to retaliate," she said. James was irked that she couldn't be happy for a Scots victory.

"Ay, and we will be ready for him," James snapped back, turning away from her. He needed her advice on what to do with Parkhead, but she was just nagging at him, causing him to fortify the forework of his heart. Now it was her turn to caress him, reaching onto her toes to put her arms around him.

"That is what your father thought too," she said, barely audible. "Don't engage with your uncle! Send Thomas to negotiate; offer to marry Jamie to Princess Elizabeth!"

"It is beyond diplomacy now," James said, bristling at the upbraiding from her, resenting her for comparing him to his father. *He* was not his father, he had a French queen and Francois would support him against his uncle by sending the latest weaponry.

She narrowed her eyes, trying to read him, but James slammed the portcullis down on his feelings. "Why do you feel the need to prove that you are more powerful than your uncle?" she asked, stepping closer to examine him. He looked away, feeling like chided hound. "Why put your person in danger as you did at the borders?"

He scoffed, "why do you always remember the transgressions and never the victories? I won at the borders and settled peace between our kingdoms!"

"We see how long that lasted and how your uncle honored that promise," she said, disgust covering the fear in her voice. She dropped her arms and turned away from him.

"Exactly!" he said, wrapping his arms around her waist and pulling her back to him. Her warmth encouraged him that this fight was necessary. He had to defeat his uncle or he would fight him for the rest of his life—and the rest of his unborn heir's life. "He must be reminded yet again that Scotland keeps its promises and honors its alliances. We are not duplicitous like my uncle is."

She sighed and pressed her weight into his chest. "I'm scared, James. I… I have had a premonition. I was coming back from the market, and I saw your wraith." A wraith was a person's spirit who had separated from the physical body and foretold of the person's death.

"There are many who look like I do," James tried to chuckle to lighten the mood, but Maggie's body went rigid.

"It is not safe to mock evil omens," she whispered. James turned her to face him and cupped her chin.

"Mags," he said, his voice hoarse with passion. "Your love will keep me safe. You will see. I will defeat my uncle and secure the country for my heir and for Jamie."

"Your heir will have a long minority if you die, longer and more turbulent that yours," she said. "It wasn't just the wraith—I had a dream that you were shot with an arquebus."

"I promise you," he kissed her nose, "that I will not fight at the front." She was not comforted but said no more.

———————

That night he had a dream. He was riding full-speed towards the border, his troops advancing before him in a line and directly into a bog. James spurred his horse, yelling at his brother to stop the men before more were swallowed. The bog spread and he sank into the mud, his horse submerged. He held his head above the swampy water, decay and death filling his nostrils as he gulped for air.

He sat up in his bed, gasping for air. He looked over at Maggie, face relaxed in sleep and realized that she had been right. He needed to negotiate a truce and stop antagonizing his uncle, especially since François could not send reinforcements just yet. He kissed her forehead and slipped out of the bed, propelled by the desire for peace.

He rode to Edinburgh and called his council to discuss terms of a truce to present to his uncle. The earls and lords assembled with him in the Great Hall at Edinburgh Castle.

"I propose that we send a trusted man to negotiate a truce on the border," James proposed. "We should be conciliatory with my uncle, not bellicose."

His brother Moray shook his head, always distrustful of the English. "Brother, how many chances are you going to give him? He does not respect your sovereignty and would rather rule over Scotland."

"He is my uncle, and we cannot count on support from France right now. Let's sign a truce and build our army and weaponry," he said.

"He will never honor a treaty with the Scots. You are too easy on him, my royal brother," Moray hung his head in disappointment, but James couldn't act rashly, not as he had with Maggie, only to realize he was wrong later. Maggie always forgave him, but dead men forgave no one.

James sent Thomas, who he most trusted, James Learmonth, Master of his Household, and the Bishop of Orkney to York to negotiate with the Duke of Norfolk. While James gave his ambassadors power to conclude perpetual peace, his uncle had not. Norfolk demanded the Auld Alliance be broken, and that both kings should meet, with hostages provided by the Scots to ensure his attendance. Norfolk asked for Arran, Argyll, and Huntly as a pledge of commitment.

"I would hardly commit my best nobles into my uncle's custody,"

James scoffed when Thomas presented the report before the council sessions. "And I could not call myself a prince if I betrayed the Auld Alliance and my adopted father."

"Sire," said the Earl of Glencairn in protest, which did not surprise James. Glencairn had supported Angus in 1524 to remove James from his mother. James was wary of him because of this. His receding hairline accentuated the flatness of his face. "We should not ignore the repeated invitations to meet with your uncle."

"Yes, tell Norfolk that I will meet my uncle at either Newcastle or York," James said to Thomas. He knew there were many of his nobles who wanted to seek peace with his uncle. "But tell him hostages will not be exchanged until both armies disarm. I don't want the blood feuds on the borders to escalate until the weapons have been removed."

He sent Thomas back to York to relay the new set of conditions. His uncle was baiting him as if he were a chained bear by demanding things he knew James could not agree to, like breaking the Auld Alliance. James didn't have much faith that Thomas would be successful in York.

A week later, a blustering storm blew Thomas back to Edinburgh. His collar was upturned to keep the rain from soaking his clothing, head retracted and shoulders slumped. James knew Thomas had not been successful.

When Thomas had prepared himself, he delivered Henry's ultimatum: the English prisoners must be released and James needed to come to London before Christmas to meet with Henry. If not, then Henry would declare war on Scotland. James had no alternatives, and his nobles did not trust his uncle any more than he did. So he prepared his country for war with his uncle.

Chapter 55

THOMAS

THOMAS WAS TIRED, HAVING returned to Edinburgh from York, where he had been negotiating a treaty with Norfolk. Norfolk demanded Bowes's release, which Thomas could not agree to until both sides had disarmed. Knowing James's wife was due to give birth around Christmas, Thomas asked for the meeting between James and Henry to be postponed until January, but Norfolk thought he was stalling and refused to budge on the date. It leeched his vitality to have to tell James that he had failed. But the king set his jaw and moved ahead with mustering troops and weapons to use against his uncle. Thomas felt the weight of the disappointment, his failure to bring a diplomatic end. The disappointment settled into his bones like the Scottish haar, the sea fog that swept into Scotland off the North Sea, making him feel older than his forty-two years.

At the end of October, Norfolk ordered the burning of Kelso Abbey, as the English army marched into Scotland. But they hadn't gone too much further north before they turned back to Berwick, due to low food supplies and a rumor of Norfolk taking ill. Thomas knew James would act. James called all of his nobles, clergy, and commanders to Edinburgh Castle. He sent cartloads of food, axes, and spears from the arsenal at the castle south to Haddington. As the king dismissed the nobles from the courtyard, trumpets sounded the arrival of the queen and her entourage. Thomas removed his hat and knelt with the others, surprised that the queen rode to see them off.

Marie, heavy with child, dismounted with the help of her guard. She smoothed her riding gown, pulled herself up to her regal height, and said, "Please do not allow the king to fight with his actual person, but allow him to lead from the back of the battlefield." The men agreed.

James embraced his wife. "Yes, my Queen," he said, more to his men than to her, "My son James will be brought down from St. Andrews and kept safe with you at Linlithgow for his own protection." The queen did not flinch at the mention of her husband's bastard son, but her eyes hardened. The confrontation between Maggie and the queen had been grist for the rumor mill. But James wanted to protect his son; the English might sail up the coast and try to sack St. Andrew's. He wasn't taking any chances with his uncle, anticipating his treachery.

Thomas followed James to Lauder, twenty-seven miles southeast from Edinburgh, straight west from Berwick where Angus was entrenched. Moray also rode with them, angry over James's clemency towards his uncle. They met Huntly at the forework of Thirlestane Castle.

"Why didn't you attack Norfolk's rear?" Moray confronted Huntly. Thomas glanced at James to see his response at Moray's harsh words. Huntly had also been a ward of Angus while James was under his control. He and James conspired together to escape Angus—first James in 1528 and Huntly shortly after when Angus fled to England. Because of their mutual experience with Angus, James had made sure Huntly was raised by the best masters and that his estate remained intact. James lifted his chin but remained silent. He also was curious why Huntly hadn't chased the English when they were in Kelso, only eighteen miles away.

"I was outnumbered and low on weaponry!" said Huntly, arrogance brimming over. "How could I order an attack with no pikes?"

"You were not so outnumbered," Moray said, his voice ragged, frustration straining. "And you had the advantage of knowing the lanscape!"

Moray's veins swelled against the collar of his chemise, face red, beard shaking. Huntly had served under Moray in skirmishes along the border and in the highlands, so Moray was acutely aware of

Huntly's ability as a commander. It made Thomas wonder if all of this could have been avoided had Huntly pursued Norfolk. Now, the king was going into battle against his uncle and his life, all of their lives, would be put in danger.

"We did not have enough provisions," Huntly said. "Norfolk torched the land as he retreated. The men wouldn't pursue the English without vittles."

"My brother sent provisions from Edinburgh," Moray said. "You were too lily-livered to pursue Norfolk into England. You've always been a *poultron*." Moray showed his command of the French language, calling Huntly a coward.

"I am no coward! I defeated Bowes at Haddon Rig! And almost caught that knave Angus too!" Huntly puffed his chest up to match Moray's aggressive stance. Thomas feared they would come to blows, Huntly being young and brash and Moray always bellicose.

"But you didn't get Angus—he slipped out of the noose. Tell us," Moray leaned into Huntly, "that you want peace with England. You want Angus to return to Scotland? Surely you could have pursued to avoid Angus coming back." Huntly blanched at the mention of Angus's name, but took a deep breath to calm down.

"Are you questioning my fealty?" Huntly said, not backing down from Moray. "We needed food—Norfolk burned all of the crops that hadn't been ruined by the wet fall and rotted. It would have been folly to pursue foot soldiers."

Moray flexed his chest and arms. "Are you calling me a fool?" he had his hand on the hilt of his sword.

"Enough!" James said, not wanting to have one of his best men killed in a useless duel over insulted honor. But the point raised by his brother stayed with him.

The next morning, James summoned Thomas to the parapet of the tower house. He climbed the spiral staircase and found James peering over the crenellated wall, towards Berwick in the west. The fog had descended across the Boondreigh Water, but Thomas knew the English army—and Angus—were out there, and that was causing James to doubt his commanders.

"Do you think my brother is right?" he asked. "Could Huntly have given chase to Norfolk?"

"I cannot say for sure, but it seems that way, your highness," Thomas said. "I've heard grumblings among the men, calling him Captain Coward. Some say he could have pursued."

James walked back and forth across walkway, his boots clicking on the flagstones. He stroked his beard as he processed what Thomas had heard. Thomas felt a lurching within him towards to king. At least the women would not be in camp; Thomas wouldn't have to compete for attention with his own cousin or with the king's wife. He was James's secretary, and therefore, he would be at James's side, unless James ordered him back to Edinburgh. Thomas hoped he wouldn't. He had been too young to fight at Flodden, and the attempt to free James from Angus had failed. Thomas longed to prove his manhood to James, to prove his worth.

"I think I will put my brother in charge of the eastern army. Maxwell has control of the western troops and can meet him and block Norfolk from moving north. If he tries, he will be caught between my two armies," James said, not looking to Thomas for approval.

The next day, James appointed Moray in charge of this army, replacing Huntly, who stomped off.

"This is for the best," his brother embraced James. "I will lead the men into England and destroy Norfolk's army!"

Thomas wasn't so sure. He knew that Huntly was well liked among the nobles, and he feared there would be repercussions. On November 5, Henry sent a formal declaration of war with Scotland.

"Being now forced to war by our neighbor and nephew, the king of Scots, we assert our nephew's provocation, whom I maintained and protected in minority. Last year, when I received the message and promise of the king of Scots to convene at York, and, instead, England was invaded by the Scots," Thomas read, a groan escaping his throat. He knew the wording would upset James, antagonize him to retaliate, which is what Henry wanted.

"*Schir!*" Oliver Pitcairn burst into James's chamber before Thomas could present the letter to James. "The men are rioting for lack of food!"

"Let them loose to find whatever sheep they can to butcher and eat," James said, leaning his head into his hand. Thomas thought he looked a little pale. The Earl of Atholl had already fallen ill from drinking bad water. They needed more ale and food from Edinburgh. Thomas was about to present Henry's declaration to James when Beaton pulled him to the side.

"There is dissention among the nobles," he said. "Arran, Maxwell, and Huntly do not want to go into England to fight. They are swaying the king to meet with Henry in London. That can't happen. If James meets his uncle, he may be swayed to break from the Catholic Church. I need you to be persuasive and keep James in the fighting spirit!"

Beaton strode from the room before Thomas could ask how he was supposed to do that when the army had been scaled because there was not enough food. Huntly had been right about that—the armies had stripped the countryside bare as they raided across the border. With no food, the men were deserting and going home. A moment later, Beaton returned and pressed a rolled paper into his hand.

"Show him this black list of heretic traitors who are in league with England—either through the Douglases or by supporting the reform church. Many of his men are on this list," Beaton hissed into Thomas's ear. Thomas put the paper into his doublet, deciding to look at it later.

"Thomas," James said. "We have run out of food and must withdraw to Edinburgh to rebuild provisions."

James jumped on his horse, with John Tennent and Oliver Sinclair, to return to Edinburgh, leaving Thomas to tell Beaton and Moray the news.

Thomas escaped with only mild curses from Moray and evil looks from Beaton when he told them that the king had gone back to Edinburgh to resupply. Thomas rode back to Edinburgh alone as the rain turned icy and the roads were sludge. James and Beaton both wrote letters to the pope, beseeching him to help them against the heretic King Henry by sending munitions and troops. In a week, James had a new plan. He had walked, barefoot with his queen, to the shrine of Loretto at Musselburgh to pray for success against his uncle. Supplies were gathered—fish, meat, bread, ale, as well as grain stores—and shipped to Lauder. On November 20, Thomas went to Pebbles, summoned by James, along with Huntly, Argyll, Rothes, and others. Maxwell and the king would invade England in the West Marshes, and Beaton and Moray would invade from the East Marshes. The stage was set for the invasion of England.

Chapter 56

MARIE

MARIE OPENED THE DOOR to the nursery to fetch Jean, James's daughter, but she froze when she saw who was in the chamber. Seated at a table with Jamie playing with the king's jasper and crystal chess set was Maggie Douglas.

"What are you doing here?" Marie asked, her voice as cool as the November wind howling outside. The cold shot from her throat to her hands, freezing from the shock of seeing Maggie in the castle. She clenched her hands to bring feeling back into them. Her stomach roiled, acid bubbling up her throat. Marie would never have the audacity of this woman to flaunt an affair. But then again, she had seen it many times by King François and his son. Still, she expected more from her husband.

"I'm teaching my son to play chess, the game of kings," Maggie replied with a satisfied smirk. This woman thought she could go anywhere she pleased. Marie would have liked to drag her from the room by her hair, but she remained impassive. Maggie was trying to get a rise out of the queen, but Marie was above playing pedestrian games. She relaxed her hands and exhaled to remain in control. *She* was a queen. This woman was just the mother of a royal bastard.

"Jamie," she said, forcing a lightness into her voice, "can you please find Jean for me? I'd like her to help me embroider some coverlets for the baby." She placed her hand on the boy's head as he passed. He was serious and focused, loyal to the queen. In spite of his mother, Marie loved the boy, treating him as if he were her natural son. His presence helped keep her from falling into a chasm of grief. When the door had closed, she turned to Maggie, wanting to wipe the smug grin off her face.

"My husband is not here," she folded her arms over her enormous belly, another heir that would be born soon. This baby remained high, right under her ribs. The other babies had sat lower, on her bladder, making her constantly run to the commode.

"I didn't think he would be," Maggie retorted, her eyes flashing like a dragon's. This woman knew more about her husband than she did. She looked like she was coiling, preparing for a strike. Marie braced herself, spine erect, suppressing her fear of this woman. "I'm here to see you," Maggie continued.

"Me?" Marie could not keep the shock from her voice. She had tensed her muscles for an attack; the statement almost knocked her over.

"Yes," Maggie said, "I am not your enemy."

"No, you are not *my* enemy," Marie said, pulling herself up to her intimidating height. "You are Scotland's enemy."

Maggie snickered and picked up the scarlet queen, rubbing her finger across the crown.

"You sound like his mother," she said, knocking over a knight. "Even she couldn't keep him away from me."

"I don't try to keep him away from you," Marie said. Maggie stifled a laugh, knowing Marie was lying. Marie wondered what Maggie could possibly want with her. Before she could ask, Elizabeth came into the room.

"A letter from the king, Madame," she said, pausing when she saw Maggie. Elizabeth fingered the seal of the letter, eyes darting from Maggie to Marie. Even though Elizabeth feared this woman, Marie would not be intimidated by a Scottish Jezebel. She was a Lorraine, far more powerful than Maggie.

"I'll take it," Marie strode over and touched Elizabeth's arm to let her know that she was safe, and that Marie was in control. Maggie was up against Marie's back, peering around her to see the letter.

"What is he doing at Lochmaben?" Maggie asked. Maybe she didn't know everything. "That's on the western border."

Marie turned away from her, unwilling to share her husband's words with his lover. She broke the seal and read the letter, his writing almost illegible.

"My dear Queen," he wrote in French. "I have received the letter you were pleased to write me, for which I humbly thank you, assuming that your man will not be—"

The letter broke off, and continued in a scrawl, "I have been very ill these three days past, as I have never been in my life; but thanks be to God, I am well. François will tell you the news here, and praying our lord to grant you good life and long... Your humble husband, James."

Marie ran from the chambers, feeling Maggie follow her. She found her servant François in the king's chamber and asked him the meaning of this letter.

"Madame, he was very feverish and vomiting," he said, looking at Maggie, who was right behind Marie.

"Was the English army there?" Maggie asked. Again, Marie was annoyed because James was her husband, Maggie had no right to be here. But she held her tongue. Maggie grabbed both of her arms, assaulting Marie's royal body.

"Don't let him fight," she begged Marie, who shook off her hands.

"His nobles have promised not to let him fight in person," she said, walking away from Maggie. The woman ran in front of her, preventing her from walking.

"But he is too proud to lead from the back," she said, her eyes desperate. Marie swallowed the sour bile that crept up, reminding her that this woman knew her husband better than she did. She wanted to shake her head, deny that James would disobey a request from his wife, but indecision immobilized her. Maggie pleaded, "I know him, he will not listen. You need to go there and bring him back yourself. Remind him of the child you are carrying, his heir. It's the only way he will not fight, I know it."

"He is *my* husband. He knows I carry his heir, and what that means for Scotland if he fights. He knows my wishes and will honor them," Marie responded, her anger chilling her. Despite knowing that Maggie was right, she couldn't bring herself to admit that. Maggie hung her head.

"Then it will be over soon," she said and walked away from Marie. Her final remark was cryptic, causing Marie to pause. Snow began to fall outside the palace, coating the world in white, a symbol of peace. Marie hoped it was a good omen.

Chapter 57

JAMES

THE NEXT MORNING, JAMES regretted sending the letter to Marie in his delirium. His illness had compelled him to write, fearing that he might not survive the night, but writing to convince her—and himself—that he would. The uncontrollable vomiting frightened him, his stomach rolling after eating that questionable fish. His head spun as he concentrated on forming the words to placate his fears, sending the letter before he passed out.

In the sunlight, his head was clear and he felt foolish for even writing to his wife. His stomach was still unsettled, but he kept down some ale. The pounding inside his skull had lessened to a dull thumping, reminding him of his duty to Scotland. He knew Marie would worry when she read the letter, which could send her into premature labor, endangering the heir of Scotland. Perhaps he should write her this morning to justify his health. The ale came back up. He needed to know what was going on with the English army.

He sent for Oliver. His friend entered, shaking snow out of his hair, a ready grin for his lord. Yes, James needed to distract himself from his physical ailments, and watching his army discomfit his uncle's would cheer him.

"Oliver, I have promised my queen that I would not fight from the front," James said. "But that does not mean I will hide in a castle. I want to ride out to Burnswark Hill, so I can supervise the battle." Wharton, the leader of the English troops, had discovered their plan to invade the west and last night had been raiding into Scotland, trying to draw Maxwell out of Lochmaben. James was

358

shaken that the English were so close, but covered his fear with zeal.

"Of course, *Schir!*" Oliver said with enthusiasm, as James knew he would. "Your presence will provide great confidence, my Lord!"

James had his warhorse, a sturdy gray stallion, dressed in a Stewart yellow and crimson saddle blanket and a red velvet saddle. He mounted and galloped off with Oliver and several other guards, one carrying his banner. The snow had stopped falling, but white blanketed the ground, the horse's hooves punching holes in the cover.

Burnswark Hill rose from the Scottish plains, the site of an old Roman fort. James and Oliver reached the summit. From the vantage point, James could see the smoke from the south side of River Esk, where Maxwell had burnt the land before the attack. The Scots troops had burnt a two-mile swath and headed toward Carlisle, the major town on the English side. His men, numbering almost three thousand, carried axes, pole arms, and spears, wearing an assortment of jackets, made of padded leather or chain mail. James had held the same number in reserve to attack in a second wave.

"Look!" Oliver pointed southwest, past Maxwell's men. English prickers, carrying lances, moved off the slight rise of Oakshaw Hill and approached the Scots. The Scots moved east in a long chain, looking for a place to ford the river, before turning to face the English. Wharton's force of three hundred men marched at the Scots, arrows flying over their heads from the archers that remained on the hill. James could observe the entire field from the hilltop and saw the English swing towards the right flank of the Scot army, pushing them west into the marshy lands. He knew his men would be trapped in Solway Moss, the murky bog, if they didn't act fast.

"Oliver, I need you to tell Maxwell that he needs to cross the river to the northeast or he will be trapped! Ride under the king's banner. Go fast!" James said, handing the banner to him. Oliver flew down the hill towards Maxwell's men, yellow banner flashing as he galloped across the snowy plain. James clutched his saddle as he watched his men bunch together on the banks of the river, their formation collapsing on itself. Oliver crossed the river, but before he could reach Maxwell, the men lifted Oliver off his horse and onto their shoulders, mistaking him for James because he carried the royal banner.

The English, also assuming that Oliver was the king, chose to attack. Six standards were raised on Hopesike Hill and six regiments of cavalry descended the hill. Men tried to turn the Scots falconets, light cannons, but they were stuck in the bog, and the soldiers were unable to free them and shoot at the English. The Scots scattered in every direction, most running into the river, as the English overwhelmed them. The king's banner went down, and James lost sight of Oliver. He prayed that his friend had not been slain. Maxwell's banner was still flying, but soon that disappeared too as the British troops overran the Scots.

"*Schir*," his guard said as the English swarmed over the Scot troops. "We should depart for Lochmaben for your safety."

James nodded, Henry's prophesy lapping at him from the corner of his mind. His uncle's herald had delivered a letter when James was in Edinburgh resupplying. The herald said, "Our king will put such ruin to you as he put to your father, using the same sword that damned your father, the Duke of Norfolk who struck the field of Flodden."

His skin erupted into gooseflesh, his father's death kicking up foreboding. The Duke of Norfolk, whose son was commanding the attack by the English troops today, had been the commander at Flodden, and had been responsible for his father's death. History seemed to be repeating, war against his uncle, army commanded by another Norfolk. The specter of his father, who had driven James's actions, his illegitimate children, his French marriage, haunted him as he faced off against the English. And now his army was being defeated just as his father's had been. He leaned over in his saddle and vomited.

Chapter 58

MARIE

AT LINLITHGOW, MARIE HEARD of the defeat at Solway Moss and read the names of the nobles who were captured. But she had not heard from her husband. He had not come to see her, even though she knew he had been in Edinburgh for five days. Marie placed her hands on her lower back, straining to release the cramped muscles.

Finally, his herald announced he would visit the queen at Linlithgow.

"Elizabeth, Marie!" she called out to her ladies-in-waiting, who scurried to her. "The king is coming. We need to be as beautiful as possible." They went to her wardrobe to discuss which gown to wear. They chose a silver brocade overgown that Marie had planned to wear for Christmas, but she might not wear it if this baby came early. Her ladies placed a white linen chemise over her head and pulled it into place. They fastened the pleated collar at her neck with a braided gold tie. Next was a purple silk kirtle with no stays, as she could not cinch her waist. The overgown slid over her shoulders, open in front. The trumpet sleeves were pinned back to show the miniver fur. Her ladies tied the stays loosely over her expanded stomach. A partlet of matching silver brocade with a gold band studded with pearls and amethysts was pinned over the stays. They brushed her long, red hair, which hung below her waist. Elizabeth began braiding her hair to arrange under her coif.

"No, Elizabeth," Marie protested. "I want to leave it down, to remind my husband that I am still his bride."

"But your Highness," her last remaining French attendant,

Marie, said in French to avoid insulting Elizabeth, who still struggled to understand their language. "It is not proper for a queen to show her hair—even to her husband—in a public chamber."

"But these Scots care nothing for ritual and pageantry," the queen shot back, irritated that her lady-in-waiting was speaking French. Elizabeth placed her hand on Marie's shoulders.

"My lady," she said, pushing the French vowels through her nose in her Scots accent, "You should cover your hair. You are not Scots, you have a dignity that we do not possess. Do not lower your standards."

Marie relented, and so they braided her hair and secured it under a silk coif and then placed the round hood over it, edged with pearls and amethysts. A messenger announced that her husband had arrived at the castle.

James was slumped over in a chair facing the fireplace when she entered his inner chamber. Marie had to keep her face impassive as he turned to her. His normally close beard was disheveled, his face drawn, eyes red-rimmed.

"My uncle is my greatest enemy. Who can I trust if not my own family?" he asked, his voice hoarse. He curled into himself, shivering.

"My lord," Marie said in an even tone so as not to upset him. "You have had a trying time. Let me lead you to bed and guard you while you sleep."

She grabbed his arm, noticing how withered his hand looked.

"You said you were well," she said, trying not to chide.

"Ay, my stomach has been churning since supper in Pebbles. The trout seemed spongy, but I ate anyway. And my stomach has been upset with me since," he mumbled, words all running together. "They took Oliver. I sent him into the jaws of the English demons, and now he is gone!"

He leaned over and vomited on the floor. Marie recoiled, the smell making her nauseated, but she swallowed it down and helped him out of the chair, leading him to his bed.

"You must sleep, my husband," she said. "This child will need a father."

His response was to vomit on her overgown. Then he passed out. Marie called his chamber boy to clean up the mess, and she retired to her own chamber, where her ladies were waiting for her, anxious for news.

"He is delirious," Marie said, feeling the weight of the baby drop in her womb. She gasped and fell to the floor. Her ladies helped her up, removing the soiled overgown and kirtle.

"Madame," Elizabeth said. "You should be in your lying-in, you need to take care of yourself and this baby. It is not safe to expose yourself to such stress."

Marie knew she was right and allowed them to place her into bed. She wondered if Maggie had known her husband better after all, if she should have gone to Lochmaben herself. Her labor started in the night, violent cramps making her call out. Her ladies shut her in, the tapestries cocooning her from the outside world—including her husband.

Chapter 59

James

THE SKY WAS GRAY—was it morning or twilight? It didn't matter to James, his head pounding, eyes blurry. He needed to see Maggie, had to get to Maggie. She would give him her strength and then he could decide what action to take against his uncle, discover if Oliver was alive or dead. He ordered his horse ready so that he could travel to Loch Leven.

The snow was blowing, but it didn't touch James, the fever stoking his internal fire. He urged his horse on, across Stirling Bridge over the River Firth. He passed through the town of Dunfermline and attempted to turn his horse north to Loch Leven, but the wind was so strong, his horse would only side step.

"Ay Scotland!" he yelled, holding his fist in the air. "Even you thwart me!" He decided to go to Falkland and send for Maggie in the morning, or evening. He still wasn't sure what time it was. He entered a small woods and saw harts leaping on either side of the road. He grabbed for his sword, but realized he hadn't brought any weapons. Which was fine, because the harts disappeared. James rubbed his eyes, straining to see the fever vision. Out from the trees shot Oliver's face, covered in blood, swimming towards him, causing him to jerk his horse, almost being thrown off. He shook his head to chase the ghost's away. First Finnart, now Oliver. When would his dead sons come? When would they begin haunting him, just as his father's memory haunted him? Maybe he should stop at his treasurer's house, William Kirkcaldy, which was not far away. He shivered, the driving snow chilling him beneath his fur-lined cloak.

Hallyard Castle, Kirkcaldy's home, rose four stories out of the whiteness. The castle's gray limestone blended into the gray, snow-covered countryside. The building was square, with a round tower interrupting the straight line. He pounded on the heavy oak door, burning up inside, but shivering. A servant answered the door.

"Tell Kirkcaldy the king is here!" James said, lumbering into the vaulted entry. The servant, startled, took him up one flight of stairs to the hall. The room had white washed walls, an oak ceiling carved in an octagonal pattern, and flagstone floor. The fireplace had Kirkcaldy's arms painted over it, a banner with two stars above a white chevron and an upside down crescent on a red background, but James focused on the fire. He walked over like an old man, legs creaking from cold.

"Your Grace," Lady Janet Kirkcaldy came over with a chair, onto which James collapsed. "We were not expecting you, but we are pleased to have you here for supper."

"Supper?" James asked, his eyelids heavy. He pushed away from the fire, his head burning and pounding. "Is it that late?"

"Ay *Schir*," William came over and bowed before him. James patted his shoulder. "Can I get you something to drink? Ale? Whisky?" he asked James.

"That would be satisfactory," James said, "but you better bring a chamber pot as well. I can't keep anything down."

A servant brought a cup with ale. The drink did not quench James's thirst, his mouth arid, and his tongue swollen. He retched into the chamber pot.

"Kirkcaldy, I lost everyone," James lamented, head in his hands. "I lost all my nobles and friends. The English took them all."

A look passed between Kirkcaldy and his wife, and James knew they already heard about the humiliating loss. The invasion was his uncle's vengeance for not going to York in autumn.

"No, my lord," Janet said. "You must trust God's will and…"

James cut her off with a grunt. "My portion of this world is short. I will be gone in fifteen days."

Willy Kirkcaldy, the son, who was the same age as Maggie, came over to try to cheer him up. He looked in Willy's eyes, blue-green like Loch Leven and wished he had pushed his horse to continue to her home. He needed her arms around him, to make him feel whole and safe.

"Sir," Willy said. "Where will your Christmas festivities be this year? At Holyrood as usual? Or at Linlithgow if your child is born?"

"I cannot tell you," he said, baring his teeth in a snarl as he tried to smile. The pounding traveled from his head down his neck and into his chest. "But I can tell you that by Christmas, you will be masterless, and Scotland without a king."

They protested, unwilling to believe what James knew. Janet forced gruel down his throat, he struggled to lift the spoon to his lips. They put him in Kirkcaldy's bedchamber after dinner. As the curtains closed around him, he jolted up, crying out, "Is Oliver dead? Oh my friend!"

He sank back into the bed and fell into a fitful sleep, dreaming of his mother, his father's body riddled with stab wounds, his prince sons, all shriveled and dead. Finnart appeared, menacing smirk on his face as he lifted his sword. James screamed as the blade hacked off his head, and he jerked to a sitting position. Sweat drenched him as he opened the bed curtains and saw the faint light on the horizon, the sun not yet breaking over the rolling hills. His heart threatened to explode from his chest, blood pounding into his head, swelling his mind. He was afraid to fall back asleep, his dreams more terrifying than reality. Maggie—Maggie could help him process all that he had lost at Solway Moss. Maggie would help him plan his next move, give him the strength to face his uncle. He pulled on his clothes and woke William.

"We need to go to Loch Leven," James said, swaying, and grabbing the curtains to keep from falling. William blinked slowly, eyebrows raised.

"I do not advise that, *Schir*," William said after a long pause. The floor bowed and tossed James off balance.

"I'm the king!" James wanted to sound stern, but his voice warbled. William took his arm and led them into the hall.

"Yes, *Schir*," he said as he walked with James. "But we need to get you to a royal residence where you can be tended to and protected. Falkland is not too far away from here."

James swallowed the bile at the back of his throat. He needed Maggie, but he could send for her. She would come to Falkland; she had always come to Falkland when he asked her. He would draw from her strength and his health would return once he was in her arms.

"To Falkland then," he said and sank onto the bench beside the table. James slumped over, his energy drained even though he had just awoke.

"Yes *Schir*, we will leave after breakfast," he said, alarm in his eyes. A servant placed a bowl in front of James. The steam from the gruel warmed his face, coated his beard, making his shiver despite the heat. He spooned the beige mixture around the bowl, not trusting his stomach to keep it down. James felt he would fade away in Hallyard and not get to Maggie. He thrust himself up, propelled by desire.

"It is time to go," he said, walking out of the castle, William running after him. James felt stiff, death settling into his bones. As soon as his horse was saddled, he leapt on and spurred his horse. William rode up alongside him.

"*Schir*," William called, "Let me ride in front and lead the way." James nodded, grateful to follow, his mind boiling, unable to remember the route to Falkland. Maggie, he only wanted Maggie. All of his energy channeled into getting to Falkland and sending for Maggie. He could not comprehend his next moves without her.

It was not snowing, but the air was so brisk that his breath froze on his beard when he exhaled. The cold invaded his bones, removing their rigidity, and James collapsed over his horse and clung to the mane, blood thundering through his veins. His horse's footfalls lulled him into semi-consciousness. His head pounded out a cryptic message, which James could not decipher. The mane felt like Maggie's hair as it tumbled from under her coif when they were in Atholl. That was when he thought he could find a way to marry her, even after the disappointment he suffered at the hands of Angus, that he believed he could be happy. That was before reality thrust its sword into his heart. Did Maggie resent him? He needed to see her and explain all of the things he never voiced to her.

They arrived at Falkland and James tumbled off his horse, John Tennent catching him before he hit the ground.

"Thank you John," James said. "You are my last friend." Then he passed out.

————

Finnart came to him again, eyes blacked out, mouth gaping, flesh rotting off, cheekbones poking through his face. He lifted a heavy blade and sliced off James's right arm. James looked over at the blood spurting over the satin sheets. Finnart swung the sword again and James lost his left arm. James sat up to prevent Finnart from taking off his head, lunging out of bed. He woke up, caught in the velvet curtains surrounding his bed. His breathing was uneven, heart pounding against his ribs. Solomon judged him from the tapestry on the wall. His finger pointed, arm extended from his azure cloak, one dead baby on the floor. Just like his sons—dead. James collapsed back onto his bed, John coming over to him.

"Are you alright, *Schir*?" he asked. "Can I get you something to drink?" James nodded and John exited the room.

When the door opened, it was not John, but Beaton and Thomas who entered. James pulled the covers up to his chin, embarrassed to be seen in such a weak position.

"Your Grace," Beaton began. "Sir Erskine meant to give you something before the battle." He elbowed Thomas forward, whose face flushed. James didn't have the energy to address them, unwilling to address the urgent matters of state without first seeing Maggie.

"Your Grace," Thomas's voice shook as he spoke. "We found a list of men who support your uncle and the heretical religion." He unrolled a paper, hands shaking. Beaton ripped it out of Thomas's hands.

"The first person who is in league with your uncle is the Earl of Arran," Beaton read off the paper. James chuckled. His cousin would never support Henry! He opened his mouth to respond, but his lips were stuck together, so dry. John returned with a cup of ale, which James gulped.

"I want to see Maggie," he said when he could move his mouth. Beaton and Thomas exchanged a look that made James shudder. "Send for her to come here."

John bowed and turned to leave, but Thomas stopped him, shaking his head. Anger flared in James. How dare he disobey an order! Before he could scold Thomas, the ale came up and he vomited into the chamber pot. He fell back onto the pillows, sighing, weak, burning up, shivering, hallucinating ghosts. The men exited without a word and James slipped into sleep.

———————

When he woke, he was surrounded by the only men left who were loyal to him—Beaton, Thomas, William Kirkcaldy, John Tennent, Argyll, Rothes, and David Lindsay.

"David," James said, desolation coursing with his pounding blood. "I fear I am dying."

"No, my king," he said, touching James's arm, but pulled back from the heat radiating. "We have joyous news for you. Your wife has given birth to a girl."

He looked from face to face, wondering why they were smiling. The Stewart line had begun with a girl, when Walter Stewart married Marjorie Bruce, Robert the Bruce's daughter, and she birthed Robert Stewart, the first Stewart king. And now, the last Stewart, his only heir, was a girl.

"The Devil go with it. It will end as it began. It came in with a lass," James said, turning away from the men, "and it ends with a lass."

He felt the men fidgeting, unsure of what to do next.

"Why hasn't Maggie come?" he lamented against the wall.

Chapter 60

THOMAS

BEATON PULLED THOMAS AND William Kirkcaldy aside after the lackluster response from James about the birth of his daughter.

"He is dying," Beaton said. "We need to push for him to write a will that sets us up as regents for the young princess."

"The Earl of Arran will be regent, according to the succession. He is next in line after the baby princess," Thomas said, shocked at the depravity of Beaton, a man of God!

"I suppose you want us to honor his wishes," Beaton said, stepping towards Thomas. William looked between the two men in confusion. "Maybe we should send for Maggie and see what she says."

"No, no," Thomas waved his hands, more afraid of his cousin and the damage she could cause than Beaton. One person could be refuted, but not two. "We will present him with a last will." Thomas would agree with Beaton to save himself, but he would not benefit from his deception. Beaton grinned, looking like a demon in league with the devil.

———————

Beaton dictated the last will for James to Thomas.

"The king appoints as regents for Princess Mary, Queen of Scots four governors: the Earls of Moray, Huntly, and Argyll. Cardinal Beaton will be the governor of the princess and chief ruler of the council," Beaton said. Thomas stopped writing.

"You can't cut Arran out," Thomas said. "He is second in line for the throne after the baby princess. He should be regent."

"He is a Lutheran!" Beaton clapped back, eyes flashing. "You want to hand your catholic kingdom to a heretic? Perhaps you sympathize with them too."

"You know I would rather Scotland be Catholic and uphold the Auld Alliance," Thomas said, wishing he were in the sophistication of France. De Rohan's face floated before him, forcing him to physically recoil. He wrote Beaton's words, even though he did not agree, and knew that it would not be upheld.

"And," Beaton stared down his crooked nose at Thomas, "the king wishes to forgive the Douglases and welcome them back to Scotland."

"He will never agree to that!" Thomas exclaimed, dropping the quill, wondering why Beaton wanted to add it. Beaton just looked down his nose at Thomas, refusing to answer.

"The king is so ill, we don't have to have him sign it. We will have enough people witness that he agrees to it," Beaton said. "Just write."

Thomas shook his head, but finished the last statement and spread sand over the parchment to dry the ink. Beaton grabbed it out of his hands, throwing sand in Thomas's face. He called the men from the outer chamber and strode into the bedchamber to present the will to James. Thomas followed behind, knowing he had no influence, nor would he ever tell James how he felt about him. And now he was so ashamed of his actions and Beaton's blatant grab for power when the king is dying.

Gathered around James's bed were James Learmonth, the ambassador sent to England with Thomas to negotiate a peace that never happened, Michael Durham, the king's doctor, Kirkcaldy, John Tennent, Beaton, and two priests. Thomas hung back from the bed, unable to look at James.

"My lord," Beaton said, "we need to provide governance for your daughter, the princess."

James remained facing the wall, but groaned so the men knew he was conscious.

"Is Oliver dead," James said in a horse whisper. "Why hasn't Maggie come?"

Kirkcaldy glared at Beaton, "He isn't even lucid! How can we ask him to sign an order of governance?"

Beaton inhaled a long, deep breath before he spoke. "We need to provide the princess with proper and legitimate governance." Then, he leaned over James and said, "*Schir*, this will names myself, Huntly, and your dear brother Moray as the governors for the princess. Is that what you want?"

James rolled over, his face gaunt, eyes blood shot. "I want Maggie," he said. "Why is she not here?" His face was ashen, lips colorless. "I will agree to whatever you have written. I trust it is best, but I need Maggie!"

John stormed out of the room, slamming the door. Beaton ignored him and said, "We have his approval. It is witnessed and agreed upon."

The king gasped, and Beaton took him in his arms. "My lord!" Beaton shook him. James opened his eyes and looked around at the men that Thomas knew were betraying him. He summoned the energy to give them a faint smile, kissed his hand to them and exhaling, closed his eyes. Beaton attempted to rouse James. There was no response. The king was dead.

Chapter 61

MAGGIE

JOHN TENNENT WAS SHOWN into the chamber where Maggie was embroidering, trying to keep busy and wait for word from James. She heard that the queen had given birth to a daughter and wondered if James was taking it well, knowing how he wished for a son to be his heir.

"Lady Douglas," he said, breathing heavily. "The king is dead. He asked for you, but no messenger was sent."

Maggie jumped to her feet. Dead? She told Marie not to let him go to the borders, to convince him not to fight. And now he was dead!

"Why was a messenger not sent?" Maggie grabbed John's jerkin, fury taking over. "Where is he, John?"

"Falkland," he said as he uncurled her fingers from his chest and led her out to the loch. They climbed into a row boat to take them to the main land. "He asked Sir Erskine to send for you, but when you didn't arrive, I came myself. I know he loved you so."

Falkland? Maggie was alarmed. He was that close, she could have held him as he died. Rage burned inside her, but this was the last time she might ever feel James's flame. And her own cousin was to blame! Thomas had done this on purpose, to punish her for being compassionate towards his feelings for James. She saw his desire and tried to tell him that she understood, but he wasn't able to admit it to himself and so he punished her for being James's lover when he couldn't be. Worse, he deprived James of his dying wish to see her. She would never forgive him.

When she got to Falkland and strode past them in the king's inner chamber, Beaton stepped forward to stop her, but her father stopped him. Her father never encouraged her relationship with the king, but never stopped them either. In his bed, James looked so pallid, his cheeks sunken in, evidence of his illness. Maggie wanted to crawl into bed with him, warm his body, bring him back to life. But she couldn't, and so she collapsed at the side of his bed, clutching the vermeil curtains. Tears were hot in her eyes, full of rage and hurt. She heard the door to the chamber open and knew her time with James was finished.

Thomas cleared his throat, fiddling with his hands. He wore a white pleaded chemise, tied at the collar with blackwork embroidery and a velvet brown doublet with a high collar. Even though his clothes were pressed and neat, his hair waved in different directions, heavy bags underneath his blue eyes, deep lines etched around his mouth, making him look older than his forty-two years. All of Maggie's frustration riveted on Thomas.

"Why didn't you send for me?" she yelled. "He asked for *me*." Thomas shrugged and the lines on his face deepened. "Were you afraid I would tell James your feelings?" Maggie ran at him and punched in his chest, knocking backward. Thomas stumbled but remained on his feet.

"No," he said, refusing to look Maggie in her eyes. "You must leave now. The body will be taken to the chapel and prepared to lie in state."

Beaton and her father appeared in the doorway. Maggie ran to her father, burying her face in his beard. He wrapped his arms around her, leading her out of the chamber.

"I want to stay with him, Father," she sobbed. "I want Jamie to see him."

"That is not possible Maggie," her father said, his voice gentle, patting her on the back. "You will be given a place of honor at the funeral as Jamie's mother, but you cannot remain here."

"Why didn't you send for me earlier?" Maggie asked her father.

"I was not here, my lass. I just got here myself from Stirling early this morning," her father said. Maggie had no answers and no

James. How would she survive without his flame lighting her up? She would never look at thistles or goldfinch the same again.

The funeral was not held until January at Holyrood. His body was carried through Edinburgh along the Royal Mile, the tin coffin riding on a gun-carriage, pulled by four horses draped in black velvet, embroidered with the Scots arms, the red lion with a blue tongue on a yellow banner. John Tennent and Oliver Sinclair, who had recently returned from captivity in England, carried a black velvet canopy that arched over the coffin. All of the state officials, including Beaton, Thomas, her father, and others walked behind the bier, wearing black velvet cloaks and a hood over their heads. Over the cloak, they wore a tabard, a short, open-sided coat with a square collar and flared cap sleeves, embroidered with the Scots arms. Heraldic banners, signifying the four orders of the Garter from England, Thistle, Golden Fleece from the Emperor, and St. Michael from France, were carried behind the bier. David Lindsay carried the Order of the Garter banner. On top of the coffin, was a wax life-like effigy of James, wearing full royal regalia that he wore at Marie's coronation, lying on purple velvet.

As James's son, Jamie followed behind the bier, and Maggie was able to join him. Queen Marie was still in her lying-in, so she was not present. Maggie had a new dress made, a black velvet overgown with a high neck that opened in a V in front. Her kirtle was white satin with blackwork embroidery around the neck. She wore the pendant that James had sent her when he was in France on a short gold chain. Jamie wore a black velvet robe and hood. Maggie had threaded a sprig of white heather through his button hole, white heather being a symbol of sorrow.

The Royal Mile was lined with people, some sobbing, some dry eyed, all loyal subjects of James. Maggie stifled a sob as he remembered how much the Scots people loved James, how he looked out for their interests. She wiped her eyes with the back of her sleeve and smiled at Jamie, noting the grief in his face. James had always treated Jamie as his natural son, and was a good father.

The procession entered the Holyrood gate and passed into the church on the left side of the palace through the ornate pointed arch door, stained glass windows above, but no sun shone through them, the sky mourning with all of Scotland. Maggie looked up at the arched ribs painted blue. Her heart constricted when she realized that she would never be called to his sumptuous palaces to boast of his achievements.

The bier was placed in front of the great altar, with a wooden partition behind and a sculpture of Jesus on the cross, his mother on the left side and the apostle John on the right. Cardinal Beaton said the mass in Latin, but Maggie couldn't concentrate. She knew that he had been in league with Thomas to keep her away from James. David Lindsay had been there too, all these seemingly pious men not honoring James's last wishes because they didn't understand their love, thought it was wicked because James never married Maggie. If only they knew that it was Maggie who pushed for the French marriages…

After the mass, James's body was moved to the Royal Vault in the southeast of the chapel. He was placed next to Madeleine and his two sons. On top of the tomb was a gilded lion, rearing on its back feet. Maggie took Jamie over to pay a final respect to the man who had taken her heart into that grave with him.

"Father told me that I needed to protect my brother, the Duke of Rothesay before he died," Jamie said, his voice solemn. "Do you believe I will also need to protect my sister, the Queen of Scots?"

Maggie melted as she looked into the serious boy's eyes. At eleven, he had experienced so much death and abandonment. As much as Maggie tried, she had not protected her son from heartbreak as she promised herself she would.

"Yes, my son," she said, placing her hands on his shoulders, looking at James's crypt. "The baby queen will have lots of enemies who want to steer Scotland in the wrong direction. Stay close to your stepmother; help her when she needs you. Remind her of your father's intentions. And when the baby queen is grown, you must remind her and guide her to do the best for Scotland as well."

Her son lifted his chin, already accepting his role as the baby princess's guardian. Maggie's chest constricted, the pain squeezing her from the inside. She needed to avenge James's death—for Jamie, for the baby princess, for herself.

After the funeral, Maggie called on Kinneil House, the residence of the Earl of Arran, just north of Linlithgow Palace on the River Firth. The estate was a flurry of activity, a new wing being raised facing the river. Maggie was shown into the older tower house to a coffered room on the second floor. Leaping harts chased by hunting raches and creeping ivy were stenciled on the plaster walls. The ceiling was a complicated pattern of oak diamonds and squares, outlined in red paint. Painted above the fireplace were the Hamilton arms—two panels with a galley ship and two panels with cinquefoil flowers. The arms had been created for the first Earl of Arran after his naval victory before the Battle of Flodden.

She looked out the diamond paned lead window and watched ducks play in the pond below, trying to calm herself. Doubt gnawed at her. Would Arran believe her? He knew her relationship with James, the entire country did. She feared that he would not take action. He had a reputation for indecision, appeasing rather than standing up for his convictions. Maggie would have to be persuasive enough to overcome that hesitancy.

The Earl walked in, and Maggie was surprised how tired he looked, weariness tugging at the corners of his brown eyes, making him look older than Maggie. His hair and beard were clipped close to the skin, the same style that James had worn. He wore a burnt orange doublet with vertical slashes and silver buttons. He motioned for Maggie to sit in a blue velvet chair, which she lowered herself into, formulating her words.

"Lady Douglas," he began, taking a seat opposite her. "We are all grieving the loss of our king, but none more than you." Maggie exhaled, struggling to maintain her composure at the acknowledgement of her grief. Arran patted her hand in an awkward way, uncomfortable at her emotion.

"Thank you, Lord Arran," she said once she composed herself. "He was the love of my life, as you know. That is why I am here today."

He lifted his chin, intrigued, signaling for her to continue.

"Those who were with him in the end are deceiving Scotland," she said.

"I have suspected that Cardinal Beaton forged the last testament of our sovereign," he said, which Maggie had also heard. His admission prompted her to pour out her suspicions.

"It's not just Cardinal Beaton, my lord," she said. "Sir Erskine, the secretary, was there too. I think he and Beaton are working together."

"Erskine?" Arran's brow furrowed. "He lacks the gall to act against the king!" Maggie lifted her eyebrows, realizing that more people had seen through Thomas than she had thought.

"Look at the will," Maggie urged. "It was written in Sir Erskine's hand."

"Maybe so, but it was orchestrated by Beaton," he said, sitting back and crossing his arms. "Beaton is the true enemy of Scotland. He wants to usurp his ecclesiastic power and become temporal ruler."

"True, but Sir Erskine killed your brother to gain Beaton's favor," Maggie played her last card in an effort to get Arran on her side. At the mention of Finnart, his head snapped to attention. Maggie knew that Arran had been on the jury for his brother's trial and felt Finnart had been unjustly executed, but Arran could not voice his concerns while James lived. James, in his paranoia, might have misconstrued it as treason and siding with the Douglases, since Arran had married a Douglas, the Earl of Morton's daughter.

"What do you know?" he asked, a hard edge in his voice.

"I know James felt guilty about Finnart's execution. He confessed it to me," Maggie said. "He regretted having his friend killed." Arran narrowed his eyes, listening intently. Maggie continued, "And I know Sir Erskine ordered the arrest warrant while James was on progress to the Orkneys."

"Yes, I was on progress with him. He said nothing of arresting my brother," Arran said, pressing his finger to his lips. "It was only when we returned that we discovered Finnart's arrest. My brother may have been a vicious man, but he looked out for my interests in my minority after our father died."

Maggie nodded, feeling the same way about Finnart. She knew that against people he perceived to be his enemy, he was ruthless, but he also supported James coming to her and encouraged their marriage, even though Maggie knew it could not happen.

"I cannot arrest Erskine for arranging the execution of my

brother, but I can make it so he is banished to the highlands he came from," Arran said, showing his own malice. "But Beaton will be arrested for his part in the forging of James's last will."

The council and parliament convened in Edinburgh in late January. Maggie hurried along High Street and passed St. Giles Cathedral, with its wide, Gothic arches and open crown dome, but she couldn't slow down to admire the unique building, the biting wind pushing her toward the Tolbooth and warmth. Arran had invited her to observe the proceedings today, and her heart pounded in the same rhythm of her feet at the thought of seeing Beaton and Thomas punished for their actions against James.

She climbed the stairs in the Tolbooth and reached Parliament Hall. The room was bright, despite the painted red walls and dark oak hammer beam ceiling. Light streamed through the arched window on the opposite side of the hall. She stepped up the wooden stands and sat on the bench, breathing deeply to control her heart beat. The three estates were assembled—from the clerics, Archbishop Dunbar, who James trusted to be his chancellor, the Bishop of Aberdeen, the Bishop of Ross, and of course, Cardinal Beaton; from the nobles class, the earls of Argyll, Montrose, and Moray, among others. Also present were William Kirkcaldy, the king's treasurer, and Thomas, still in his position as secretary. *Hopefully not for long,* Maggie thought. Beaton stood, his red cardinal robes flashing in the sunlight. His red tricorn hat covered his thinning hair. Arran stood opposite him, dressed in a rich black velvet doublet to show his mourning of the king.

"The Cardinal has told this council many lies in the king's name, which I shall prove today as false," Arran began, puffing his chest in decisiveness. Maggie hoped he could hold up under scrutiny. Arran was easily swayed, but their plan should work as long as he followed Maggie's script—and he wasn't bettered verbally by Beaton.

"The Earl is of questionable birth," Beaton said, his mouth curled into a snarl, "as his father was not divorced from his first wife when he married the 2nd Earl of Arran's mother, which makes him a bastard!"

Arran placed his hand on his sword, "You false churl!" he yelled, and Moray held him back. Maggie held her breath, already Beaton was baiting Arran, and he snapped at it.

Beaton circled Arran, chuckling at his outburst while he strode over to a young cleric, who handed him a parchment.

"According to our late sovereign's own words," Beaton waved the paper under Arran's nose, who Moray still restrained. "He wanted a regency of Argyll, Moray, and Huntly, with myself as the chief ruler. He pardoned the Earl of Angus and his brother and stated he would like them to come back to Scotland."

Arran sneered at Beaton. "We all know that is a lie. Anyone who knew the king knows he would *never* forgive Angus!" Arran threw off Moray. Maggie willed him to stay calm to sway the council. If he were too excitable, the three estates might distrust him, and side with Beaton. Arran looked up and met Maggie's stare. She straightened herself up and rolled her neck, motioning for him to do the same. Curious to see who was coaching Arran, Thomas turned around. Maggie glowered at him, and enjoyed him shrinking into his seat.

"Aye," Moray said, eyeing Beaton with suspicion. "My brother hated Angus and his brother and never would ask their return."

"I have the document to prove it," Beaton brought the paper to Moray, who studied the writing.

"This is not my brothers writing," Moray said, shoving the paper back at Beaton.

"No, it was written by his trusted secretary, Sir. Erskine and witnessed in front of your brother, which is as good as his signature," Beaton said, delighting in what he felt to be an unassailable situation.

"Let's hear from the king's groom, John Tennent," Arran said, calling the one person Maggie suggested that she knew could be trusted. John stood, looking awkward in his yeoman's clothing among the clergy and nobles.

"John, you were present at the king's death?" Argyll asked.

"Aye, sir," John said, holding his hat in his hands.

"Did the king write this will and testament?" Argyll continued.

"No, sir," John shook his head, choking back his tears. "Our king was too weak to sign or agree to anything."

"So the will was not written nor agreed to by our sovereign?" Argyll snapped.

"No sir, it was created by Cardinal Beaton," he glared at Beaton, who remained expressionless, knowing John told the truth. Argyll and Arran exchanged looks and Maggie's heart leapt—Arran was convincing them!

"There is also the matter of the murdered English herald," Arran said, announcing the final nail in Beaton's coffin. "On November 25, Beaton ordered the Somerset Herald, Thomas Trahern, murdered to prevent him from taking an agreement to release Scots prisoners."

Beaton laughed, "An Englishman confessed to that crime! Why would I murder a herald? I was in Edinburgh with our king!"

"Ay," Arran said, turning around, knowing he had Beaton cornered now. "Your man ran the herald through with a sword and another stabbed him in the heart. Then, as commanded, they called out that they were English men."

"You still have not answered my question," Beaton's eyes flashed in rage. "Why would I order an English herald murdered?"

"To stop the message he was carrying from reaching the King of England," Arran smiled. "The message sought peace, and you could not allow peace with England, for fear of reformation within the church and your power taken away. You knew the king agreed to reform the church in that missive. That's why you *had* to the kill the herald!"

A hush fell over the hall, echoing off the towering walls. It was now Moray's turn to charge Beaton. Arran held him back.

"My brother wanted peace between our Scotland and his uncle's kingdom," he growled. "I didn't agree, I thought he was too soft on his uncle. But he was my king, I honored his wishes, even when they were opposite my own. You disgust me, you so-called man of God."

Beaton's face turned as red as his robes, flushing all the way to his cap. Maggie knew his fate was sealing if Moray, a staunch Catholic, was against him!

"I move that all of those who supported and aided war with England be warded immediately and removed from the council," Arran said, looking at Argyll, who nodded in agreement.

Beaton was seized and taken into the custody of Lord Seton.

The room erupted into loud discussion, some outraged, some vindicated. Maggie looked at Arran, fearing he would not bring up Thomas—the person who had caused Maggie and James the biggest betrayal of not sending for her at James's death. After all of James's betrayals, Maggie had to avenge James in the only way she could. She stood up, to be seen over the din of the room. Her eyes focused on Arran, who was being congratulated by Argyll. Her eyes bore into him, willing him to turn around, to look at her, to remember her vengeance. Arran smiled, smug in his victory and looked up, meeting Maggie's hard frown. She jerked her head towards Thomas, who stood to leave, men dispersing from the hall. Arran cleared his throat and waved his arms for quiet.

"There is one more matter," Arran said. Thomas packed his papers, clueless to what was coming next. "This false will was written in the hand of the king's trusted secretary, Sir Thomas Erskine."

Thomas stopped, swallowing, his Adam's apple wobbling against his neck. His eyes darted toward Maggie. She smiled, knowing that she was punishing the man who denied James his dying wish. Thomas was not going to remain in his position, not after betraying James. And he knew that Maggie was responsible for his downfall, that her loyalty to James surpassed his life. She would be loyal to him until her own death.

"Since he falsely wrote the document, I move to have him replaced by David Painter, Bishop of Ross," Arran continued. Thomas protested, begging for clemency.

"This motion is accepted and executed," Argyll said, ignoring the pleas of Thomas. Maggie remained standing, the sole woman in the hall. All of these men had to acknowledge her love for the king. Thomas hung his head, heading out of the hall. Maggie followed him, unable to let him off that easily.

"You should have listened to James," Maggie said when they were outside on High Street. Thomas turned, his eyes sunken under sleek eyebrows. He might look composed on the outside, but Maggie saw the depravity, the pride, the denial of himself to the end. "He wanted *me*. All you had to do was send a messenger to Loch Leven. That was all."

His mouth twisted into a grimace. "You always were his whore," he said, spitting out the last word. Maggie wanted to lunge at him and claw out his sunken eyes, gouge out his mouth, pull out his tongue so he could never utter that word against her again.

"You are pathetic," she said instead, her anger snuffed out as she had extinguished his power. "You can't even admit what I so clearly see. You are a coward, who hides behind a position of power."

She stepped toward him, enjoying his almost imperceptible cringe.

"You will never again use your power to punish someone because of jealousy," she continued. "You will be relegated to the highlands and forgotten. Your name will fade away and no one will know who you were. But the world will remember James because of me and my love for him."

Thomas pulled the collar of his coat around his ears and left her standing in the street, alone, but she was victorious. Through her son, she would see Scotland rise, see him become the man that James wanted to become himself if he weren't broken by Angus.

Maggie rode to Holyrood, entering the church. The sun was shining, but the air was still cold. Light angled through the diamond leaden windows, hitting the golden lion on the top of James's tomb, blinding her in death as she had been blinded by his brilliance all her life. The words of Christine de Pisan, whose poetry she used to teach him French, came to her now:

> Alone he has left me, in endless torment,
> In this empty world filled with sadness,
> My sweet friend, who with a true intent
> Held this my heart, in all joyousness.

"They may have denied you your dying wish," she said, touching his name in the granite, "But I have avenged you. For the rest of my life, I will teach Jamie to look after your interests and he will look after your daughter, Mary, and your wife, Marie. He will continue what you started, bringing Scotland into the modern era and making it the jewel of the north."

Maggie thought of all the hurt caused to James by his own mother, her disastrous choice in marriage, her power-mad brother, and the ghost of his dead father. Like his father, he supported the

French alliance, married to strengthen their country. And Maggie wanted to see his legacy remembered—the Gudeman of Ballenge-ich who loved his subjects, brought modern architecture to Scotland, fathered many sons. Even if she was seen as his whore, it didn't matter as long as the people always remembered James and his love for Scotland. Maggie would fight for Jamie to remember his father and help his sister so that Scotland could continue to prosper. And the world would know what James overcame through the strength of her love for him.

Post-script

Mary, James and Marie's daughter who was born a week before James died, grew up to become Mary Queen of Scots. After James's death, Queen Marie and her baby Mary went to Stirling and were guarded by John Erskine, Maggie's father, against an English attack. In July 1543, a condition of the Treaty of Greenwich stipulated that the baby Mary would be contracted to Henry VIII's son Edward when Mary turned ten years old. Marie agreed, even though she had no intention of fulfilling the contract. Henry launched the Rough Wooing—a series of battles between Scotland and England to force the marriage contract. Marie smuggled her daughter out of the country to France in 1548. Mary was protected by the Lorraine family and also Henri II, who became France's king in 1547 upon the death of François. In 1558, Mary married Henri's son, the Dauphin of France, who became King François II, although he died two years later, and then she returned to Scotland. In 1565, she married her half-cousin, Lord Darnley, who was the son of Margaret Douglas, the Queen Mother Margaret Tudor's daughter who grew up in England. Lord Darnley was murdered in 1567.

Jamie, James and Maggie's son, attended St. Andrew's University, although there is no evidence of his graduating, and he went with his half-sister to France in 1548. He was a Reform sympathizer and even signed a petition to allow John Knox, the Scottish Reformer, to return to Scotland in 1556. Two years later, he attended Mary's wedding to the Dauphin of France, Henri's son François II. He approached Mary about retiring from ecclesiastic life and in the following years, he argued with his stepmother Marie, who was the

Regent, over religion in Scotland. Mary returned to Scotland in 1560 after her mother's death. Initially, Jamie supported his sister as Queen of Scots. In 1562, he was made Earl of Moray and Mar, and he sought a Protestant husband from England for Mary, but when Queen Elizabeth failed to name Mary as her successor to the English throne, Moray was as upset as his sister. When Mary decided to wed Lord Darnley, Moray was against the marriage, even though Darnley had his own claim to the English throne, being the son of Margaret Douglas, the daughter of Margaret Tudor. Darnley was known to be cruel, egoic and spoiled—not a good match for the Scots Queen. How involved Jamie was in the assassination of Darnley has been speculated by historians. He left for France before the murder. After Darnley's murder, James Hepburn, the Earl of Bothwell, kidnapped Mary and forced her to marry him, which was not popular with the Scots as he was the prime suspect in Darnley's murder. After she and Bothwell lost the battle of Carbury Hill against the Confederate of Protestant Lords, Mary was imprisonment at Loch Leven by Moray's half-brother William Douglas, Maggie's oldest son with Robert. In July, Mary miscarried twins. A few days later, she was forced by Lord Patrick Lindsay to abdicate the throne and name her half-brother Jamie as regent. He returned to Scotland in August, visiting Mary at Loch Leven and advising her of the danger she was in. He initially declined to be regent for her son, James VI, but Mary begged him to accept. When Mary escaped to England from Loch Leven with help from George Douglas, Maggie's younger son, Jamie worked to strengthen Scotland against an English attack. Scotland descended into civil war, and Jamie was assassinated by a supporter of Mary in 1570, the first head of government to be assassinated with a firearm.

Robert Douglas, Maggie's husband, died in the Battle of Pinkie Cleugh, fought against the English in 1547 as part of the Rough Wooing. Ironically, Angus fought with the Scottish in this battle, which was another defeat for the Scottish. The Earl of Arran, commanding the Scottish troops against a vastly larger English force, took the offensive and charged in an attempt to gain the upper hand. But the superior modern weaponry of the English was too much for the medieval Scottish army. They retreated and were slaughtered when they were bogged down in the marshes. Maggie's younger brother Robert was also killed in this battle.

Maggie remained at Loch Leven, and she appeared to be close to Jamie's wife, Agnes Keith, and her son William's wife, Agnes Leslie. William inherited Loch Leven with the death of Robert Douglas, and Maggie continued to live there, where she was known at the Old Lady of Loch Leven or the chatelaine. When Mary Queen of Scots was imprisoned at Loch Leven by Maggie's son, Maggie was at Loch Leven; according to an English ambassador, she called Mary a bastard and said her son, Jamie, the Earl of Moray was the true heir. She claimed that she and James were married in Scotland, as the Spanish ambassador Eustice Chapuys wrote to Charles V and Bishop of Faenza, a papal diplomat at King Frances's court, reported in June 1536. She remained at Loch Leven until her death in 1572. Other than her marriage contract, there is no historical evidence about the relationship that she had with Robert.

Archibald Douglas, the 6th Earl of Angus, also known as Ard and the Earl of Anguish, returned to Scotland in 1543, sent by Henry VIII to secure marriage between his son Edward and the baby Queen Mary. Angus signed a bond with Arran, who was the regent for Mary, to support a French marriage, even though he maintained correspondence with Henry. Angus fought with the Scots during the Rough Wooing, although he later wrote that he had made excuses to Regent Arran and prevented his retainers from joining the siege of Broughty, which contributed to the Scottish loss. He died in January 1557 at Tantallon Castle.

Cardinal Beaton was removed as a regent by Arran, who believed the last will of James had been coerced. Beaton was arrested in January 1543, but was released within six months. When Arran signed the Treaty of Greenwich, which promised Mary Queen of Scots to Henry VIII's son, Edward, Beaton and many other Scottish nobles wanted the Auld Alliance upheld and backed Marie de Guise. This led to the War of the Rough Wooing by Henry. Beaton was opposed by Kirkcaldy, maybe seeing the ruthlessness of Beaton at James's deathbed, and Kirkcaldy broke into St. Andrews Castle in

1546 and murdered Beaton, hanging his mutilated corpse from a castle window.

Thomas lost his position as secretary when James died, removed in February 1543, but there is no historical evidence that he was removed for forging the will. He was listed as physically unable to serve on juries and battles in 1547. He also asked for permission to go to France and free his oldest son from captivity the same year. Thomas died at some point after 1550, when his name last appears in records. One source said he died Oct. 7, 1551. There is no historical evidence that he was sexually attracted to King James nor that he used his position to hide that.

Henry VIII died in 1547. Edward succeeded his father as King, but he died in 1553. Mary, the daughter of Henry and Catherine of Aragon, ruled until her death in 1558. Henry's last living child, Elizabeth I, became queen and during her reign, England went through a Golden Age of poetry, music, literature, expansion of territory and economy. She also worked to put an end to religious prosecutions. Upon Mary Queen of Scot's escape from Loch Leven, she went to England to seek the protection of Queen Elizabeth. Because Mary was Catholic, Catholic sympathizers plotted several times to assassinate Elizabeth and place Mary on the English throne. Mary was moved from castle to castle within England for the next eighteen years to keep her from Catholic conspirators. In 1586, the Babington Plot was discovered when an encrypted letter was intercepted, in which Mary ordered her rescuers to assassinate Elizabeth if it would secure her freedom and guarantee a Catholic-controlled England. She was arrested and put on trial for treason, a charge she vehemently denied since she was a foreign-born queen and not subject to English laws. A jury of thirty-six men found Mary guilty, only one voting not guilty. Elizabeth was wary to execute Mary, even with pressure from English Parliament. She worried that executing a queen set a horrible precedent, as they were God's appointed servants on Earth, but she did sign the order. The sentence was carried out at once, and Mary was beheaded on February 8, 1587.

On Elizabeth's deathbed in 1603, perhaps feeling guilty about executing Mary, she named James VI of Scotland, Mary's son, as king of England, joining the crowns of England and Scotland, one hundred years after the marriage of Margaret Tudor to James IV.

BIBLIOGRAPHY

I AM INCLUDING A bibliography of the primary and secondary sources I used for writing this novel in case the reader wants to learn more about the historical people in this novel:

Ashdown, Dulce. *Ladies-in-Waiting*. London, Arthur Barker Ltd., 1976.

Bain, Joseph ed. *The Hamilton Papers: Letters and Papers Illustrating the Political Relations of England & Scotland in the XVIth Century*, vol. 1, London (1890).

Bingham, Caroline. *James V King of Scots*. Glasgow, William Collins & Sons, 1971.

Cameron, James. *James V: The Personal Rule, 1528-1542*. Edinburgh, West Newington House, 1998.

Clegg, Melanie. *Scourge of Henry VIII: the Life of Marie de Guise*. South Yorkshire, England, Pen and Sword History, 2016.

Clifford, Arthur, ed. *The State Papers and Letters of Sir Ralph Sadler*. Edinburgh, Archibald Constable and Co., 1809.

Edington, Carol. *Court and Culture in Renaissance Scotland*. Amherst, The University of Massachusetts Press, 1994.

Ewan, Elizabeth, and Meikle, Maureen, eds. *Women in Scotland c. 1100-1750*. East Linton, England, Tuckwell Press, 1999.

Frieda, Leonie. *Francis I: The Maker of Modern France*. London, Weidenfeld & Nicolson, 2018.

Hannay, Robert Kerr, and Hay, Denys, eds. *Letters of James V.*

Edinburgh, Her Majesty's Stationery Office, 1954.

Henry VIII: August 1538 6-10, in *Letters and Papers, Foreign and Domestic, Henry VIII, Volume 13 Part 2, August-December 1538*, ed. James Gairdner (London, 1893), pp. 15-26. *British History Online* http://www.british-history.ac.uk/letters-papers-hen8/ Accessed 10 June 2020.

Hotle, C. Patrick. *Thorn and Thistle: Diplomacy between Henry VIII and James V 1528-1542.* Lantham, Maryland, University Press of America, 1996.

Knecht, R.J. *Francis I.* Cambridge, Cambridge University Press, 1982.

Lang, Andrew. "Letters of Cardinal Beaton 1537-1541." *The Scottish Historical Review*, vol. 6, no. 22, 1909, pp. 150–158. *JSTOR*, www.jstor.org/stable/25518064. Accessed 9 June 2020.

Lindsay, Robert. *The History of Scotland; From 1436 to 1565.* Glasgow, R. Urie, 1604.

McKean, Charles. "Sir James Hamilton of Finnart: A Renaissance Courtier-Architect." *Architectural History*, vol. 42, 1999, pp. 141–172. *JSTOR*, www.jstor.org/stable/1568708. Accessed 19 June 2020.

Rush, Sally. "French Fashion in Sixteenth-Century Scotland: The 1539 Inventory of James V's Wardrobe." *Furniture History*, vol. 42, 2006, pp. 1–25. *JSTOR*, www.jstor.org/stable/23410075. Accessed 9 June 2020.

Sanderson, Margaret. *Cardinal of Scotland, David Beaton 1494-1546.* Edinburgh, John Donald Publishers, 1986.

Strickland, Agnes. *Lives of the Queens of Scotland and English Princesses Connected with the Regal Succession of Great Britain.* vol. 1, Edinburgh and London (1851–1859).

Stuart, John ed. *The Miscellany of the Spalding Club,* 'Pittodrie Papers', vol. 2, Aberdeen (1842) pp. 75–208.

Tudor Times Ltd. *James, Earl of Moray: Regent of Scotland.* United

Kingdom, Tudor Times Ltd., 2016.

Watkins, Sarah-Beth. *Margaret Tudor, Queen of Scots: The Live of King Henry VIII's Sister.* Alresford, England, Chronos Books, 2017.

Weir, Alison. *The Lost Tudor Princess: The Life of Margaret Douglas.* London, Random House, 2015.

Wood, Marguerite. *Foreign Correspondence with Marie De Lorraine, Queen of Scotland: From the Originals in the Balcarres Papers, 1537-1548.*